An Oath of Vengeance

by
Harold M. Bergsma

Indie Excellence Multicultural Fiction 2007 Book Award
Best Book 2007 Award; <u>Finalist</u>, Multicultural Fiction

for
<u>One Way to Pakistan</u>

authorHOUSE®

AuthorHouse™
1663 Liberty Drive, Suite 200
Bloomington, IN 47403
www.authorhouse.com
Phone: 1-800-839-8640

First published by AuthorHouse 4/11/2008

ISBN: 978-1-4343-5825-7 (sc)
ISBN: 978-1-4343-5826-4 (hc)

Library of Congress Control Number: 2008900780

Printed in the United States of America
Bloomington, Indiana

This book is printed on acid-free paper.

Dedication

To *Khuki*, Sally Hazlett Woolever, Storyteller. She was a dear friend, fellow Woodstock classmate and a supportive literary critic. Sally died on July 10th. 2007.

Acknowledgements

Many people helped me during the writing of this book. I wish to thank those who read one version or another of the manuscript for their kind advice, comments and words of support and my wife Lily Chu for her encouragement and patience.

Thanks to Dr. Elaine Jarchow, Dean, College of Education and Human Services, Northern Kentucky University and Colleen Furber, Writers' Research Group, Brewster, MA for excellent reviews; to my son Mark S. Bergsma and Ruth Feierabend Gendzwill of Sault Ste. Marie, Michigan for proof reading and editing and to my son Harley Chu Bergsma of San Diego for his special technical and artistic contributions to the development and design of the cover.

Preface

This fictional work, <u>An Oath of Vengeance,</u> is the second novel of a trilogy. The first was <u>One Way to Pakistan,</u> an Indie Excellence 2007 Winner award as well as Finalist for the Best Book 2007 Multicultural Fiction category. It is a gripping story of corruption and crime in Pakistan in which three women were abducted and how their lives were shattered because of Sher Khan, The Senior Superintendent of Lahore Police. It is not a pleasant story, as all abductions of young women for sex slavery are tragic. But the tragedy continues on, even if the victims are somehow able to return to their families. Honor, shame to the family for having a daughter who was violated, turns the family against the survivor as does the *sharia* law of the land which frequently condemns such women and prosecutes them under the Hudood Ordinance, which in many cases seeks a death penalty for such a girl who has been raped. The victim is blamed. Freedom attained from the immediate sex slavery results in becoming a victim once again, this time with family, society and the religious laws of the land.

The characters in <u>An Oath of Vengeance</u> struggle with their seemingly hopeless conditions to survive and somehow gain their freedom against tremendous odds. It is a story of how three different women and their families deal with the tragedies of their rape and abductions in very different ways. It is also the story of men in their homes who live to defend their own honor and the honor of their families and their women, at all costs.

Among the Pathans there is a code of honor that is proffered in one proverb about *pushtunwali* which summarizes their zeal to preserve what is of highest importance; their code of honor. **Zar, Zan, Zamin.** There is a woman 'warlord' in Afghanistan who is called The Pigeon. Her name is Bibi Ayesha and her fame has spread among Pathans, particularly women, who admire Bibi's struggle for justice. She is a gun-toting force who has made an oath to fight those who violate her land and their way of life, yet, it is told that she never goes out to war and shoots unless she is accompanied by a man of the tribe, preferably a family member. So not only men are involved in preserving their code of honor, women also swear an oath of vengeance and in some rare cases, become the avengers.

Zar stands for wealth and gold which supports family enterprises, makes possible bride payments, purchases of gold for women. It is the first Z in the family formula of honor. In money affairs it is a matter of a man's word that seals a financial bargain, which transfers capital without receipt or formal contract. Vast sums move around internationally on such words of honor. The Pathans are people of honor. Pathans defend their guests and friends with zeal.

The second Z is **Zan**. The zennanah is a place for the secure living of women of a household that is guarded with zeal. It is has been well documented in numerous stories and novels about life in harems of the mighty ones, The Arabian Nights, or in stories of the <u>zennanah </u>of Akbar the Great. (See <u>Lalla and Lavina</u>, Stories of Indian Women, by Harold Bergsma). Islam has officially allowed a Muslim man to have four wives, at once, that is, as legally sanctioned marriages. Muslim men have throughout Islamic history taken slaves and had slave women in their homes. The Prophet, peace be unto Him, spoke of showing honor and mercy to such women and not to call them slaves, but the women of your hand, and to treat them with respect and serve their needs, including their sexual needs by attending regularly and fairly to their *tilths*. And there are other 'marriage' contracts that are either not revealed or hidden so that the four sanctioned marriages can remain a matter of religious devotion and law. Women are a matter of honor within the family. Money can be borrowed, spent, traded and invested (without interest) but women of the *zennanah* are the private and exclusive wealth domain of the landlord, the master of the house who speaks on their behalf, controls their very existence, their travel, their daily life. The second Z stands for the honor of family.

The third Z, **Zamin**, the good earth, the possession of fields and land, the ownership of a household, is a matter of honor that underlies all the rest. My country! My land! My tribal area! My very identity! The thought of having an intruder to this third Z is enough to make a man, or a woman like Bibi, rise up and take arms to protect the land. The tribal areas of Pakistan, the Northwest Frontier Province and all that vast territory which borders on Afghanistan has been the traditional home of many tribes including the Pashto speaking group who are "a law unto themselves", that is, unto their code of honor. It is unthinkable that infidels, enemy persons who threaten their very way of life should tread this ground, this *zamin*. To die, for the honor of preserving the land is in itself an eternal blessing. To die as a martyr in such an endeavor opens eternal glory for the staunch believer. In the western world we may understand this zeal a bit when we think of our great land being threatened, violated, such as during Pearl Harbor or in the 911 attack in New York. Our President's resultant zeal moved vast military campaigns against such terrorist attacks. Zamin, the land, the heritage of the fathers is the greatest Z of all.

In <u>Oaths of Vengeance,</u> both men and women are part of this great social force to maintain honor and if violated, to seek a life for a life, an eye for an eye. The avengers are seldom women, simply because of their socialization and lifelong training of being subservient and under the name, honor and care of a man. But women are indeed people of honor and are letting their voices be heard. One of the women in this story, Chamuck, departs from the norm and upholds family honor in her own way, aggressively. Another, Gulab, violated by her husband's interest in a school girl seeks honor in her own way. Ankh, an infidel from the Muslim perspective, develops a personal sense of honor which is highly unusual, particularly for one who was a slave girl.

Stories of girls being raped, abducted, taken behind *char divari*, the four walls of some fortress-like compound in tribal areas, such stories, are all too common in Pakistan. As this fictional work is being published, Muchtar Mai, a young woman from the Gujar tribe in Pakistan who was gang-raped, is telling the world about her ordeal in her memoir, <u>In the Name of Honour.</u> Pakistani women authors are writing about their own experiences and their stories are now being told, stories that were once unthinkable to tell, as a matter of honor.

The fiction writer puts in words, what he or she has lived. The writer can only speak from having been spoken to and having understood and listened; can envision from having looked at and witnessed; can interpret from having been culturally befriended and imbedded; and then can communicate in the languages that he or she dreams in, which I refer to as the mothers' tongues. Cross cultural linkages can be enriching, but they can also be confusing and obfuscate the voice if it is a non-harmonic duet.

The voices I have heard are Islam and Christianity, which have been the major religious forces that have formed me. I lived as a child and worked as an adult in Muslim communities, territories and countries for almost thirty years of my life; Pakistan, India, Yemen Arab Republic and Northern Nigeria. I value this socialization. It is a part of my own personal heritage. But there is also the strong reality of my other heritage. I was raised in a strict Calvinistic home and a Christian Reformed Church society with its own religious zeal and customs, its belief in the infallibility of the Scriptures and its faith in predestination. Thus, living with people from two religious systems which assert the absolute veracity of their Scriptures, the Bible and the Holy Koran (in Arabic) were part of my early socialization. My father was a zealous believer. My Yemeni, Nigeria and Pakistani friends also were zealots and spoke to me frequently about Islam.

I have been spoken to in Urdu, Punjabi, Hindustani, Hausa, Arabic and English and I have listened. I listened to the voices from Pakistan and Afghanistan, calling out their prayers to the Almighty, based on their faith and submission, Islam, in His absolute control. I have heard the word *inshallah (God willing)* so often it has become part of my thinking. I heard their cry, Allah Akbar! But I also heard the voices of young Americans singing in churches, A Mighty Fortress is our God, a bulwark never failing. I have sung with them in numerous choirs and have reveled in the music of the Messiah and many other oratorios.

Half a century later has my thinking become relativistic? I think not. To use Diana L. Eck's words, I hope I have developed more than a tolerance for such diversity, rather have developed an "... energetic engagement with diversity." Or as she says, "...the active seeking of understanding across lines of difference." (The Pluralism Project: What is Pluralism. 3/27/2007. //pluralism.org/pluralism/what_is_pluralism.php) What amazing lines of difference there have been for me to consider and live with over the span of many decades! What amazing differences there are between the cultures, in which these religious expressions are made, many cultures, each with its own history, its own sense of pride and sure knowledge that their way is the way, their truth is the truth.

I have incorporated such lines of difference, at the beginning of each chapter. A saying or proverb in Urdu or Hindustani is introduced which becomes part of the linguistic dialogue of the story. Thus, to my *desi* readers, those from Pakistan and India, such introductions are a means of acknowledging the tugs of home to mother India. To the rest of my readers, these proverbs are used as a means of inserting tiny swatches of local color into the fabric of the story. A few key words and phrases in Urdu have been used within the text for the same reason because these were what came first to my mind as I wrote and dreamed the story line.

* *

In the **Prologue,** a summary of the plot from the first book in this series is presented for those readers who have begun with this second book, An <u>Oath of Vengeance</u>. The brief Prologue introduces the protagonist and other major characters in the plot of <u>One Way to</u> <u>Pakistan.</u>

* * *

A section, **References,** is appended at the end of this book. This is a select annotated bibliography of materials I found to be informative and helpful. Research into the legal systems, the politics, the cultural practices, the flora and fauna was important to me because it provides evidence for the warp and woof in the development of the fabric of the story line. The political occurrences in Pakistan and Afghanistan which occurred during the period of this novel were amazing to say the least.

It has often been said that truth is stranger than fiction. When I talked with laborers, cooks, guards, shop keepers, carpet salesmen, musicians, and even female entertainers, strange stories were told to me about their families and lives. I wish to emphasize one point about this; the characters about whom I write are <u>not</u> people from the rich, elite, landed aristocracy, the sophisticated group of Pakistanis who live in grand mansions in Model Town, Lahore or Islamabad, whose dwellings put houses in La Jolla and Del Mar to shame. Nor are they about well-to-do urban families such as those portrayed by Uzma Aslam Khan in her book <u>Trespassing,</u> written from the point of view of educated, wealthy Pakistanis. Rather these are the stories of common people who may have a total annual income of less than five hundred dollars. Their stories are often newsworthy. Daily local and regional news reports provide accounts of the amazing occurrences in the lives of common people. A few of these reported news incidents have been included in the **References.** I have woven their strange stories into this work of multicultural fiction.

PROLOGUE

The story-book one of the trilogy:
<u>One Way to Pakistan</u>.

Dohst and his father Sheikh Mohammed trade in carpets, avoid customs on the Iranian border whenever they can. In Lahore they set up their business, selling and packaging Persian carpets to ship to New York. Dohst, a young and good looking man is not nearly as serious about his father's business as he is in keeping an eye out for contacts with women.

"She looked interested; she turned around and looked at me, she wanted me, that is what I think."

Sher Khan, the Senior Superintendent of Lahore Police has an eye for capitalizing on the problems and weaknesses of others. He maintains excellent records of persons who break the law and are arrested. The wealthy among these soon face him in his office with offers or deals to keep them out of the courts. His extortion scheme catches dozens of citizens who were able to continue on with their lives in politics or business, because of Sher Khan's secret interventions. Now they are legally free but tied to him. A few common people are also caught by him, especially if they have money, or stacks of oriental carpets and no custom's receipts. With his profits, he invests in arms and rockets which he stores in his tribal home and sells to the Taliban.

"Our big pay off will happen, when we sell our own two sweet little kanta, the Stingers!"

Dr. James Bernard retired when he finished his contract with US-AID in Manila; however, his young and beautiful wife, recently his secretary in Cebu, has other ideas. Restless and spoiled, she seeks more than the simple life of her elderly husband's retirement home in La Jolla, California. She pushes him to apply once more for one last overseas challenge: Lahore, Pakistan. This becomes his new posting. He settles into his new contract project with US-HELP. Maria gets around. She makes friends with two other single women AID workers and they begin to explore Lahore. Dohst, the young carpet merchant, notices the single American women: one black and athletic, one white and pretty and Maria, a voluptuous Filipina. He makes moves to contact them. He writes love letters. Maria is abducted and disappears. Her husband James searches for her to no avail and dies.

"You are beautiful. I am a strong, young Pakistani and I want to make dating with you."

Ankh is a strikingly beautiful slave girl who Sheikh Mohammed, the wealthy carpet merchant acquired during a raw opium trade in the northern territories. She is kept in his ancestral island home on the Indus. She is a non-Muslim, from the people called Black Infidels. Sheikh Mohammed is very busy trying to work out arrangements with the Police Superintendent to avoid conviction for carpet smuggling. Meanwhile his son Dohst attends to business for him in their island home in Sukkur. Here, Ankh, his father's sex slave, becomes Dohst's willing lover. Dohst is apprehended on the island by the police and taken to Lahore to face Sher Khan. He is imprisoned with his own father. In the prison cell they almost kill each other in a fight about Ankh. He threatens his father.

"If you ever touch Ankh, I will kill you. You will not be buried but become vulture shit."

Sher Khan the policeman has been busy. He targets Maria and sets up his abduction scheme which will put the blame on Dohst. Maria is kidnapped and taken to his compound on the Afghanistan border where she becomes his sex slave. Ankh, in the meanwhile, fears that Sheikh Mohammed will either kill her or cut off her nose because of her affair with his son Dohst and escapes in disguise under a *burkah*. She is caught by Sher Khan's men and taken to his border village.

"...he lit the kerosene lantern and awakened the girl Ankh, who sat up and rubbed her face, confused, then surprised. She jumped out of the bed, shivering."

Maria and Ankh meet in captivity. Maria escapes into Afghanistan in the night disguised as an old woman under a *burkah*. Ankh, drawing water in a deep step well, survives a bombing of the village by American forces. Both women now strive to find some way to put their lives together.

Maria struggles into Afghanistan and Ankh is returned by the Pakistani Red Crescent to Sheikh Mohammed's island home where she hopes to meet Dohst, having heard of his father's suicide when captured by Sher Khan the Superintendent.

"If I am taken back there, my family will not accept me. I have had children with a Muslim man and now they think I am unsuitable for marriage. If I say I was his slave, they will treat me even worse....It is hopeless! She wept...."

Chamuck, an athletic and talented high school student, daughter of an arms merchant is promised as surety for a loan to her father. Her father's death, at the site of the arms cache, means she is to become the unwilling concubine of the fat merchant, Sahib-Ji, who put up the money.

"I want a document that agrees for you to let me have your eldest daughter, to marry me. If you die, I will get your daughter."

☪

"Maria struggled up the steep incline, panting. She smelled wood smoke. Then she saw a small shack-like dwelling and the light of fire, shrining like a votive candle, through a tiny window." Page 404

CHAPTER ONE

Be-rahmi shaitan ki pahli sifat hai. (Urdu saying)
Cruelty is the primary attribute of the devil.

"Don't take the charcoal heater down into the *tah-khanna*! Do you want to die?" Mahtari stood at the top of the wood staircase and shouted down to Chamuck who had just brought the heater down the stairs to the ancient cellar of their Peshawar home, hoping to put it next to her cot as she slept.

"You may not believe me, Chamuck, but your youngest uncle died when he slept next to a charcoal heater when you were a baby." Mahtari, her mother, was a fat middle-aged woman of thirty-six who seemed to be in every part of the household at once.

"Mahtari ji, it is cold down here. I want to use the heater for only an hour, and then I will bring it back upstairs. Please." Chamuck, a fair-skinned sixteen-year-old girl was already taller than her mother, slender at the hip but with full breasts. She stood at the foot of the staircase and looked up at her mother and pouted.

"One hour. I will check on you." Mahtari turned on her heels, her loose garment swirling around her ample hips.

Chamuck set the *ungithi* (metal heater box) on the hard-packed dirt floor; stooped over and blew the grey charcoals with a metal pipe until the coals turned bright red. She sat on her cot and put out her hands, feeling the warmth against her palms and shins. She looked around the huge cellar room where she had decided to place her own cot for privacy. The zennanah upstairs was a busy place with her father's co-wives arguing, children crying, servants calling out from the kitchen. Here, in the deep cellar, built fifty years ago, thirty feet under the ground, it was quiet and cool. She looked at the walls, carefully bricked up by craftsmen more than half a century before. She looked at the benches along the wall where, during the blazing hot summer time, the entire family came to sit to escape from the heat.

Along the walls a variety of foodstuffs were stored, oranges in big boxes of sand, *kadu* and *mitha ghiya*, large yellow pumpkins and the sweet rose pumpkins, potatoes and garlic spread on large cloths on the floor and fat sacks of basmati rice and lentils stacked against the wall. The room had the smell of the richness of the earth with a slight odor of mold and mushroom. Now, in winter, the room was too cool for most of the family, and they huddled in the rooms upstairs around heaters. This room was now hers.

The kerosene lantern behind her cast her shadow on the far wall of the cellar. She lifted her arms and looked at the shadow of her arms, two dark pillar-like images. She got up and began to dance, slowly, swaying her hips, moving her arms, dancing with the ghostly image of herself against the far wall. She could faintly hear voices upstairs; the hollow sound of bare feet on the heavy wood floor above her was comforting, as if they were now part of her privacy. Someone dropped a heavy metal object and she started at the sharpness of the sound.

On her cot was a book she had taken home from school. It was a strange book, printed in the English language. It had an unusual picture on the cover of a donkey-like man and young women sitting around with garlands in their hair. She formed the words, A Midsummer Night's Dream, trying to remember her teacher's pronunciation. She opened the book and moved her eyes to the pencil mark she had made on the page. It was her assignment to read the ten lines aloud the next day.

Thou hast by moonlight at her window sung,

With feigning voice verses of feigning love,

And stolen the impression of her fantasy

With bracelets of thy hair, rings, gawds, conceits,

Knacks, trifles, nosegays, sweetmeats, messengers

Of strong prevailment in unharden'd youth:

With cunning hast thou filch'd my daughter's heart,

Turn'd her obedience, which is due to me,

To stubborn harshness: and, my gracious duke,

Be it so she; will not here before your grace

Consent to marry with Demetrius,

I beg the ancient privilege of Athens,

As she is mine, I may dispose of her:

Which shall be either to this gentleman

Or to her death, according to our law

Immediately provided in that case.

Chamuck read the words silently, not understanding many of them. The English teacher had encouraged each girl to memorize a short passage, then to work on the pronunciation. She had told the girls that the books, though very old, had once been used in a school run by the British before the partition, and had been donated to their school. Because other books were expensive and unavailable, these small books would be their project for the year. Chamuck was the teacher's pet because of her excellent grades.

She read now, "*As she is mine, I may dispose of her: Which shall be either to this gentleman, Or to her death, according to our law.*"

She stood facing the wall and talked to her shadow, memorizing the strange words, not understanding their meaning, and wanting to ask her teacher about this oath. '*Or to her death, according to our law*'. She tossed the small book to her bed and turned toward the light and took off her outer clothing and stood naked, except for her cotton under shorts which was tied with a string around her waist. She looked at her rounded breasts with their dark nipples and areoles, reached up and held them, shaking her head. She sighed, sat on the edge of her cot and pulled a face, feeling herself to be gross and earthy.

Only two days earlier a suitor's parents had come to see her father with a request for her marriage. The man, she was told, was a merchant, one who dealt with gold and silver, not arms and ammunition like her father. She was told that he had another wife and four children, but that he was willing to make a substantial financial arrangement with her father. But her father was on a business trip and the suitor's go-between had left, hoping to meet within a week after her father Abdul Haifa returned.

Chamuck looked down her body at her long legs, her bare feet, and her knees and the back of her heels which had a darker color than the other skin of her legs. She shook her head again, upset with her body, its new big bulges and its coloration in the wrong places. She could not imagine any man, particularly an older man who had four children looking at her body. Her face took on a look of distaste.

She thought about her schooling, that she wanted to complete high school, perhaps try for a scholarship and go to the university in Lahore. But her father Abdul had acted strangely around her during the last school year. He seemed not to be able to look at her except for a moment, and then he would look away. He no longer showed physical affection toward her. He talked to her mother Mahtari about the need for Chamuck to marry, that she was already too old, that her body was too quickly ripe and that marriage was the only way to preserve the family honor. He regretted that she was not already married. Times had changed, he had said, and young unmarried women in Pakistan were a constant target for men seeking sexual favors. The honor of the family must be preserved and no blight of sexual scandal could be tolerated. Chamuck now covered her head when she came into her father's presence, became shy and unhappy with what she heard. She had begged her father to let her finish her senior year and take entrance examinations to the university. That had been the last straw. He had become hard-eyed and distant.

She lay back on her bed, pulled the quilt over her, forgetting the charcoal heater next to her and looked up at the heavy beams and boards high above her, listened to feet shuffle to a fro. "*As she is mine, I may dispose of her.*" She formed the strange words and wondered what they meant. Did the English also receive money for their daughters? Did the fathers have the right to give them to others without the girl's consent?

"I told you not to bring the heater down here! If I had not remembered you could be dead by morning. Get up! Help me to take stones out of the rice. I hope your father will be back tomorrow. We have much to get ready."

Chamuck held the heavy quilt against her chest and looked up at her mother. Her head ached.

"What? Are you sleeping without any clothes on your body? Shameful! I think your father is right. Get up!" Mahtari turned and began the climb up the long staircase, puffing at the effort to get her heavy body to move.

Chamuck was startled by the screams from the rooms above her. There was the sound of footsteps running on the *shisham* boards, doors slamming and the high keening of women who have been told of a death in the family. She hurriedly put on her school uniform and climbed the stairs, terrified at the noises. As she stepped into the sitting room Mahtari, her mother, threw herself on the floor and screamed. The children began to cry. Two men were there, one of whom was her father's older brother Mohammed Rafiq. They stood in the room, their backs against the wall, as if in need of support.

"What? What is it?" Chamuck called out to the men, ignoring *purdah*, looking at her mother crouching on the floor.

"Abdul Haifa is dead. He was killed in a gunfight in a place called Bahadur." Her uncle had to yell the information to be heard above the keening of the women and the wailing of the children. "His body was discovered by local Taliban riders two days ago. The vultures had already begun to desecrate the body." He put his hands against his cheeks and looked up and began to recite from the Holy Koran.

Chamuck sagged to the floor, stunned. No sound came from her. She stared at the boards under her feet, smooth and oiled from thousands of passing feet. An ant crawled across her toes. She stared at it, not seeing it. Abdul dead. Abdul dead. Then she reached up and covered her head with her shawl. She could feel the eyes of the two men on her. Their stares gave her goose pimples. *"As she is mine, I may dispose of her..."* She crawled over to her mother and put her hands on her shoulders. Her mother screamed again and looked at her daughter with wild eyes.

"A widow! I am a widow. Allah have mercy. A widow." She cried bitterly staring at her daughter. Chamuck did not comprehend at first, and then as the meaning of what her mother had said became clear to her she began to shudder violently. Tears streamed down her cheeks. The man standing against the wall, her older uncle, a mullah, was now the person in charge of the family, the four wives, the children. Her father Abdul Haifa had fought this man, her uncle, when he had sent her to school. Her uncle, who was older, long bearded, supported the Taliban and had been against girls being schooled. Her father had insisted, saying that this was not Afghanistan, but the new Pakistan; this was a new era and that she should go to the UNICEF Primary School. When she had done well she had been allowed to continue on into the Independent Yusaf School for Boys and Girls. She now turned her back to her uncle as she held her mother. Their tears puddled on the floor between them.

The two men waited, standing by the door. Then her uncle, Mohammed, strode to the large table and sat on a stool facing Mahtari. He cleared his throat but his brother's wife continued to weep, knocking her head on the floor. "Listen to me! His body will be brought here in two hours. I will arrange to have it buried. It is wrapped in heavy canvas. Terrible! The vultures and jackals were at it for two days. It is badly decayed. May Allah be merciful to him in the judgment day when the bodies of all the slaves of Allah will be raised among those who have been buried with honor as the holy prophet commanded, praise be unto him." He waited again for the women to quiet down. Finally Mahtari looked up at him.

"Abdul's truck had papers in it which we do not understand well. He had made agreements with the arms dealer, Sahib-ji, before he went on his trip. The truck is no longer ours. He signed it off to the arms dealer before he left. He did more, which is a matter of family *izzat* honor, which I am going to oppose with all the *taqat* I have in my life. He signed away the right of marriage of Chamuck to the Sahib-ji, the arms dealer. He must have been insane. Our family will get nothing! No gold *Shabka*, no cash." He was now screaming toward Chamuck who looked up at the mention of her name. "Nothing! My brother was a fool. No gold, no marriage payments. Never. I will never agree to it." He pointed at Chamuck. "Sixteen years of being reared, school uniforms, books, shoes, even your badminton rackets and now nothing!" His hand pounded on the table.

Chamuck stood and faced her uncle, covering the lower part of her face. "Uncle, my father would never sell me off to some ancient arms dealer who we have never seen, who has never darkened our door."

"Sit down! Be quiet and do not speak. Schooling has given you no right to speak at a time like this. You are wrong in everything you say. The man has been in our home. I was here when he was fed. He has shared our salt. You, Chamuck, have served him tea with your miserable, shameless head uncovered and he saw your face a year ago. He has no name. He is simply called Sahib-ji. Those who oppose him die strange deaths, falling off bridges, throats cut. He is a *Shaitan*."

Chamuck sagged to the floor, her face exposed as the scarf slipped from her head. She remembered now. Both her hands had been busy carrying food and tea and for a moment her face had been displayed. She remembered the man now; a huge, fat man with a grey beard and grey eyes. His hands were fat, so fat that his fingers looked like claws as they picked up the sweets she served. She shuddered.

Her mother had stopped crying and she moved to her daughter and held her in her arms from behind, swaying from left to right. The two women swayed left and right, left and right as they stared at Mohammed who now unfolded a paper and placed it onto the surface of the table.

"Here is the copy of the agreement. The truck now belongs to Sahib-ji. I expect that within the day he will appear. He is not to be let into the interior of this house. He may stand in the outer courtyard and wait until I am ready to meet him. You are to remain in your room until all this is solved. I will not be cheated of the bride payments by any man. We are an ancient Pathan family, people of honor." He read the document in front of him, looked carefully at the changes that had been made in the original. He looked at his brother's signature and the thumbprint, the signatures of witnesses and their prints.

"Shaitan! The man is the devil. He is cruel and should be dead. There are three things we Pathans hold in great honor. It is *Pukhtunwali*, the way of our people. *Zar! Zen* and *Zamin*. (Gold, Women and Land) This devil Punjabi is trying to undo the honor of generations of our fathers. Never!" He got up and stormed out of the room, the paper contract copy was left on the table.

Chamuck got up and moved unsteadily to the table and bent over to read the contract. Yes, there was her father's signature which gave over all rights of marriage and ownership to Sahib-ji in the event that the arms transaction failed and he died. Tears dripped onto the document as she read it, blurring the first part which gave ownership of their Toyota truck to Sahib-ji.

Passersby on the old Peshawar Sethi Street paused by the heavy carved wood door and looked up at the small wood balcony when they heard a loud prolonged shriek coming from behind the latticework. That was followed by another and another piercing cry of women wailing for a deceased family member.

C⋆

They never called him farter to his face, but even his wives and servants called him *Pad* behind his back. Sahib-ji lived for three things, food, young girls and money. But it was really food that came first. Twenty years earlier, during the years of his chubby adolescence he had come to the conclusion that anything that contained milk gave him gas, but milk products were his addiction; *panir* or cheese, *gulab jamins, barfi, ludoo, rus-milai*, all were sweets made from milk. He was never without them.

On the table in front of him now was a paper box with freshly made sweets of five varieties that his cook had bought that morning. He slurped his steaming hot tea noisily, made with boiled milk laced with sugar and spiced with cardamom seeds. He blew the hot tea, then took bites from the confections and smiled as he read the document on the table, already knowing each word of it, but feeling again the sweetness of a good bargain. A great business deal. He mouthed the words as he read silently, the words that Abdul Haifa had signed and had marked with his fingerprint. "... if I die, then my daughter Chamuck will become your wife." Abdul Haifa had been killed, his body desecrated, turned into carrion, eaten by vultures and jackals before he had been found in the bombed town of Bahadur.

Chamuck. He said the word out loud now, remembering, more than a year before, remembering her fair-skinned face and sparkling eyes as she bent to serve him. Her head scarf had slipped from her face and she had replaced it hurriedly, her eyes had flashed as she looked away, upset. *Jis ki ankhen chamukti hon*, he whispered. The girl with the blazing, sparkling eyes. She was his! Not only that, her dead father's truck was his as well, now being cleaned and detailed as he sat having his tea.

Chamuck. (Sparkle) I must give her a better name that does not draw *Shaitan*, the very devil himself to look at her. And though she is well rounded she is so young; could she now be fifteen? Yes, she is like ripe like a pomegranate which splits open to reveal the dark red juicy seeds. I will her call her Anar. My Pomegranate.

His cell phone buzzed. He hated ringers. He kept the phone in the pocket of his *chamiz* and he could feel the vibration next to his hip. He took it out, looked to see who was calling and then flipped it open.

"Hasan. Listen, don't talk now. The rockets were <u>not</u> destroyed in Bahadur. You know, the ones I purchased last year, before I, in turn sold them to Sher Khan," he paused to listen, "yes, the very ones. He has taken them into Afghanistan. He will be calling me back I am sure, to try to resell them to me. When he calls, put him off. Tell him I have a new girl to deal with and don't want to do his dirty business now. Give him my FAX number and tell him to draw up a written offer, a detailed offer and send it to me next week before he calls again." Again he paused and listened. "Hasan, keep your gun oiled. We have new deals to make." He laughed.

He heaved his huge bulk from the low bed made especially for him so his feet could touch the floor when he sat up. He rose and passed gas noisily. Sahib-ji waddled to the far wall on which there was a photograph of thousands of the faithful who were making the pilgrimage, all circling the *Kaaba*. He carefully removed the picture and set it on the table. A wall safe with a double security system was at eye level in front of him. He first punched in the combinations and pressed the handle which released a metal bar in front of a slot made for the key. He put in the key which was shaped like a carrot and looked as if it had a number of small holes or indentations in it. There was a click and he pulled open the safe. He put the marriage contract into the safe on a pile of carefully stacked documents. Next to these was a metal box with a lid. He slid the box forward and lifted the heavy object and eased it onto the table. He lifted the lid and sighed. Sweet, he thought. Very sweet! The bars of gold gleamed dully in the light from the table lamp. He removed one and brought it to his cheek. It sparkled where it had been marked and numbered. His Chamuck! His short, fat fingers stroked the cool lustrous metal.

☪

It kicked and bellowed. The two of them struggled with the buffalo bull. Dohst had placed the rope around its neck, but it resisted being pulled toward the covered stall, shaking its head and then lowering its horns. Ankh stood behind the beast with a hoe handle and hit it a smart blow on its rump. It was startled by the pain and moved forward. Dohst wrapped the rope around a small tree swearing at the animal.

"Let's leave it here until we bring the other two animals into the shed and tie them. Then it will be more willing to be brought inside." He slapped the rump of the buffalo with his palm. "We are going to return you to your owner. Your job is done and you are nothing but trouble!" The young bull shook its head and rocked its head showing the whites of its eyes.

"When is Jhika coming back to take these animals and look at trade items?" Dohst turned toward Ankh now who stood in the path in front of him, her abdomen extended with her pregnancy.

"Jhika comes and goes when he wants to. He said he would be here two days ago but he never keeps his word. Why don't you take some of the blue and white dishes to the bazaar yourself when you leave and see what you can sell them for. Jhika will cheat us for sure" Ankh walked up the path and talked over her shoulder.

"Yes. They will come to get me tomorrow. It is the fourth day and the current is not as strong as it was when I came. Yes. I will take two of the white and blue plates and see what I can get in the bazaar. I can catch the afternoon bus to the north toward Lahore later in the day." Dohst, a young man in his early twenties was thin, almost gaunt, and his hair was growing out like a brush from his head which had been shaved a month previously. His clothing was loose and ill-fitting. He looked like a common laborer, a rickshaw *wallah*.

"Your father has clothing packed in boxes in the back of the armoire. See if you can use any of them. Even if they are too large for you, at least you will look better than in those clothes." She began to laugh. "When I saw you two days ago at the gate I thought you were a dacoit. How did you become so dark?"

Dohst frowned, upset that Ankh had spoken unfavorably about his appearance, but then he looked down at his soiled pajamas and nodded. "Yes. Perhaps there will be clothing he had when he was younger. Sheikh Mohammed, my father was a miserly man, never threw anything away. Yes. Perhaps we will find something."

They walked single file up the path toward the huge island compound, Dohst walked behind, looking at Ankh's hips sway, at her black curly hair bobbing on her neck. He still could not get used to the idea that he owned a woman, that she was carrying his child, that he was the new landowner of Khawaja Khizr Island. The last three days had been strange, confusing.

He had arrived at the ancestral home in the evening as the last rays of the sun shone against the walls of the old compound. Ankh had met him at the gate, amazed at how thin he was and how dark his skin had become in the sun. The first evening they had sat in his father's bedroom, Ankh squatting on the bed, her legs drawn up under her, he sitting on a *mura*, a cheap bamboo stool facing her. He told her of his escape from the police, his hiding in his uncle's home in Sialkot, his old aunt and the death of her husband, his close call with Sher Khan the Senior Superintendent of Police who had come looking for him. He did not mention his mentally retarded cousin, Pagali, who had crawled into his bed. He talked for hours.

The old servant brought in a kerosene lantern and set it on the table and then brought them tea and left, looking over his shoulder at the strange sight of the pregnant slave girl sitting in the master's bed, the young master sitting on a stool facing her like a school boy.

"I have told you all. Tell me about how you escaped and how you got back here." Dohst sipped his tea.

"It is a strange tale. I only know a part of it. I left this place and took money from the caretaker's box. I got the fishermen to bring me to Sukkur. There I got a lorry and traveled many, many hours to the north. Then I changed to another truck heading toward Swat. It took me far to the north and when the truck stopped at a deserted place the driver and myself went to the bush to relieve ourselves. He drove off without me and left me stranded. I was in the old woman's burkah. I had nothing. The place I was left was a kind of shrine to travelers on the Korakoram road. An old man, a beggar, caretaker was there. He took care of me. I stayed there many weeks and begged. Then a truck which was heading back toward Swat stopped and I paid for a ride, except the man kidnapped me and took me to a place called Bahadur, a walled compound right on the border of Afghanistan." Ankh moved her legs in front of her and bent to rub them. Then she got up and shuffled out of the room to the latrine and was gone for while.

"Where did you stay?" asked Dohst when she returned.

"In the huge walled compound, the zennanah of Sher Khan, in a small room with just a cot. I became a prisoner in Sher Khan's compound." She lied.

"Did Sher Khan, did he then take you to his rooms?"

"No. I never saw him. He had gone to Lahore to do his work there. I just heard the women, his wives talk about him. But I met an American woman there who was his sex slave and we became friends. Her name was Suraj." Now Ankh smiled broadly, remembering her friend.

"That is not an American name. What was her American name?" Dohst was confused.

"It was the same as the mother of Jesu. Maria. But that is not what we called her. Sher Khan had given her the name Suraj." She now reached into the folds of her clothing and took out a paper on which there was a drawing of an eye and the words, ANKH and EYE. She passed it to Dohst who looked at it with interest.

"Maria! Maria Bernard. I knew it. I knew that Sher Khan had abducted her. This is amazing. Where is she now?" He leaned forward and handed the paper back to Ankh.

Ankh said nothing. She turned her head and tears streamed, filled her eyes.

"What happened?" Dohst got up and moved to the bed and sat on the edge near Ankh.

"She was killed during the explosion that killed Sher Khan. Killed and made into dust by the bombs that fell." She wiped the tears on her cheeks.

"Then how did you survive?" Dohst looked at Ankh's beautiful face, her cheeks wet with tears and he breathed in deeply, feeling again a strange, strong urge to hold her.

Ankh looked up at Dohst's face into his eyes and her memory was stirred, how they had both looked at each other's eyes when they sat on the sandy beach of the river after their embraces. She was quiet for a moment and looked into his eyes so intently that he dropped his own. She reached over and touched the tips of his fingers with her own.

"I had gone into the well to draw water just before dawn. The air ships came and bombed the village. The blasts were so loud that I lost my hearing for a long time. When I was in the well the fire shot down the shaft for a moment and sucked all the air away so that I could not breathe." Ankh's voice was rising in emotion.

"How did you get into a well? I don't understand. On a rope? Did you fall in?" He shook his head.

"It was a *baoli*, you know, a stepwell that has a staircase leading down into the ground more than forty feet to the level of the water. I walked down the steps to draw water when the village was bombed. Suraj, Maria, had a small room near to the big house and that was destroyed. There is a big hole in the ground in that place. It is so strange that a person can go up into the air like the steam from a kettle." She shook her head, obviously disturbed at her own story.

"So, you are now here in Sukkur. How did you get back to the island?" Dohst now held her fingers and she glanced at him with her large light-colored eyes, then at his hand on hers. She turned her hand over and held his fingers.

"There were helicopters and buses. There were people from Peshawar who wrote the newspapers. Lots of people came and talked to me and took my picture coming out of the step well. Then I was taken to the Red Crescent station in Peshawar and they drove me here to Sukkur and I came to the island. They gave me a bag of lentils and a bag of rice. But the rice was old and part of it was moldy. It must have got wet. We fed the moldy parts to the chickens." She looked upset.

"The boatman told me that a policeman had come to the island a few days ago. What did he do?" Dohst was staring at Ankh's long, slender, pale fingers, being held in his own shorter dark and hairy fingers.

"His name is Feroz Hakim. He is the Deputy Superintendent of Police in Lahore. He came here, all the way to Sukkur to talk to me about Maria. He took the comb that she gave me." She touched the dark hairs on the back of his index finger as she spoke.

"What? A comb? That is strange. Why did he do that?"

"No one knew what had become of Maria and when I told him that we had been friends he seemed satisfied that she had actually been in Bahadur. But he wanted something real from her to prove that she had been there. I did not like him. He really did not take my word but always doubted everything I said. So, he has Maria's comb. He gave me a small paper and told me I should give it to my son." She smiled as he reached over with his other hand and began to stroke her arm.

"This is a very strange story. You seem to have forgotten almost everything except the well and Maria and now a paper that the policeman gave you." He glanced up into her eyes.

"The bomb blast did it. It sucked all my memories from my head. I only knew I went into the well. What happened just before that is... is, I don't remember now." The baby moved in her womb and she placed her free hand on her stomach. "There. Do you want to feel it?"

He nodded and reached over and placed his hand on her belly. He felt it move under his hand. Then it gave a small kick. Dohst smiled. "It is a boy. It is already playing football." He let his hand remain on her abdomen.

"Yes. If it is a boy, it will be born a slave."

"What do you mean?" He drew his hand away from her abdomen and stood up.

"Have you forgotten that I am a slave? Remember what we talked about when we lay on the sand together? When you gave me this small silver bell?" Her large eyes stared at him, standing next to the bed. He stood with his feet apart, as if ready to confront an enemy. He shook his head.

"Remember what you told me about your holy book and that Allah is pleased when slaves of the household are liberated and made into free men?" She held a small paper in her hand under the folds of her clothing, a paper that she would one day give to her son which made him owner of Khawaja Khizr Island.

☪

The traveler in this part of Afghanistan looks out from the top of a rise at a series of jagged brown ridges running off into the distance. Valleys are nothing but dark shadows. In the winter when snow falls the tops of the hills are white and the areas facing the sun's warmth quickly turn to a dusty brown color as the snow melts away. Wind whistles across the hills, saw-toothed and rough and the traveler pulls the loose wool scarf about his neck to keep in the warmth. Nothing seems to be alive. Everything is brown and white, deserted.

Maria struggled up the incline, panting. She smelled wood smoke. She saw a small, wood, shack-like dwelling, and the light of a fire, like a single votive candle shrining through a tiny window. Snow flakes hit against the mesh of her burkah. Her feet ached, her toes were numb. She hugged herself under her burkah and sobbed for breath as she staggered forward. She smelled wood smoke more strongly now and stared ahead looking for the source of the smoke. A path branched toward a flat area from the one on which she walked. She saw fruit trees, now without leaves, their branches held like skeletal fingers up to the sky. She left the main path and walked toward the small light. Nestled against an outcrop of rock was a dwelling which appeared to be built out of the face of the outcrop. A dog saw her and ran forward barking wildly. She stopped and the dog circled her, barking and showing its teeth, its ears cut off close to its head giving it a devilish appearance. She stood her ground, talking softly to the animal which turned away, then again returned to give a series of loud barks before it ran back toward the small dwelling. Maria walked forward, her every sinew wanting to be near the fire that gave off the smoke. The door opened and a woman peered out, her hair matted.

"Who is it?" The woman cried out with a high unpleasant voice that cracked as she spoke.

"Suraj. Suraj." She said no more, her voice almost in tears.

"Come closer. Where are you from?"

Maria guessed that she was asking where she came from. "Bahadur. Bahadur." She called out, and then moved her hands from the protection of her covering and held them up to pray. "Allah. Allah."

The old woman waved for her to approach. Maria staggered forward, almost unable to remain upright. She came to the doorway and the woman helped her to move into the small house which was no more than a tiny cluttered room. In the corner there was a mud-brick stove with a pot of water on it which was steaming. Maria moved to the stove and sank to her knees and held out her hands to the warmth. She began to sob.

The old woman put tea leaves in a pot and poured water in it and spooned three large helpings of sugar into it and stirred.

"*Shedee.*" She shook her head and held her breasts. "*Shedee..tshaai.*" (There is no milk) She handed the cup to Maria who held it between her two hands worshipfully, soaking up its warmth. She removed the burkah from the front of her body, and leaned forward to sip the warm gold liquid. The old woman looked at her in amazement and began to talk wildly, agitated and cautious. She came closer to Maria and looked at her face and her clothing and asked her questions which she did not understand.

"*Farangay?*" Maria did not understand that she was calling her English. Now she came closer and looked at Maria's abdomen and again talked animatedly. She smiled and took a brass wide-mouthed pot from a shelf and put it near Maria. In it were raisins, apricots and almonds. Maria nodded and put her hands together in thanks. She reached for a raisin. The old woman muttered, "*Angur, angur.*" She sipped the tea and ate for many minutes hardly pausing to breathe. She had never tasted anything so wonderful in all her life. The flavors of almonds mixed with raisins and apricots brought fleeting memories of fruit cake she had eaten in their house in La Jolla at Christmas time. She sighed. Finally satisfied, she looked at the old woman and smiled and again put her hands together in thanks, then held them palms up and said words she had heard hundreds of times when she had been a captive in Bahadur, "*Allah bismillah.*" The old woman clapped her hands and the two of them said *Allah bismallah* together, over and over again.

☪

Two ragged beggars sat with their backs against a filthy beetle-nut stained concrete block wall. Passersby hardly heard their pathetic high pitched whine as they called out for alms A deserted skeleton of a vehicle, rusted and stripped, leaned into a ditch with dirty standing-water nearby, the front wheel slightly submerged. Trash was burning next to the small ditch and the smoke smelled of burned hair and chicken feathers. Passersby on their bicycles dismounted and walked around the hulk of the deserted car bringing them close to beggars who stretched out the stumps of their arms calling for a penny or two. "*Paisa deh. Paisa deh.*" Their voices were pitched in a pathetic nasal falsetto to elicit mercy. The masonry wall ran for twenty feet until it ended against a low cement brick building with an exit and entry door and no window facing the street. Cyclists turned their head as they passed, listening to the sound of a woman's voice singing.

Meher Jamal was not aware that she was singing as she worked, her voice rising and falling with the *ghazal,* a sad ballad of unrequited love. She paused in her singing. It was awkward to hang the bed sheets with only one hand. Meher called to Pagali to come and help her stretch the soft cotton sheet across the rope hanging from the walls at the back of the small house which abutted a cement block wall. Pagali held the sheet and played with it, moving the material up and down.

"Lift it up over the rope. Like this." Meher demonstrated and Pagali, a mentally retarded woman smiled and lifted the cloth. "Yes. You know how to do it. You can help me whenever I wash the clothes to hang them out. Come. Now you can have a sweet *jalaybee*."

Pagali clapped her hands. She waddled toward the house, her abdomen swelling in pregnancy. In the small kitchen was a box with screen mesh on four sides, hanging from a wire. This was the food safe, a place to keep away ants, flies, mice and even the curious cat. Here was where Meher placed treats such as sweets and bread. Pagali stood in front of the safe and watched as it was unlocked by Meher with a small key. She was given two orange, sticky, deep-fried confections that had been soaked in boiling syrup. Pagali held the sweets in her hands and began to eat her treat, making small sounds of pleasure all the while.

"Aziz Shabash your cousin should be returning any day. He said he would only be gone for two weeks at the most. Tomorrow is the fourteenth day. Perhaps he will return. Then we will go to the bazaar in a *tonga* to the vegetable market and buy beets, carrots and onions. We will go to the sellers of clothing and have the *darzi* measure you for new clothing. Nothing fits you anymore. We will buy sweet smelling soap and perfumed coconut oil for our hair. He will take us to the old fort on the hill and we will see where the British soldiers were buried over a hundred years ago. Imagine! Their bones are still there, unvisited by their relatives all these years. Then we will go to Mian Abdul Hakim's tomb, our great Sialkot scholar and finally to the mosque of our saint Hazrat Imam Ali-ul-Haq who converted our people to Islam." She glanced over at the smiling face of her mute companion. "But today I will make curry from the small pumpkin that grew in the yard. Tomorrow we shall welcome the master home. He will be sad about his aunt." Meher talked all day long and Pagali listened to her and smiled constantly, following her about as if connected with a string.

"What is Aziz going to think about your belly getting big? He is going to be surprised." She waved her index finger in front of the sticky face of the young woman. "When you crawl into the bed of a man, Pagali, your belly will get big for sure. Do you remember Aziz?" She turned toward her ward who just then was licking her fingers. Pagali nodded happily. "Allah will be merciful. He will protect the weak and helpless one."

There was a noise at the front of the house as a horse-drawn carriage stopped to unload its passenger. Then someone pounded on the front door.

"He is here! Pagali, run and open the front door. Hurry."

Dohst Mohammed stepped inside the house and waited for a moment for his eyes to adjust to the dim light. He saw the two women standing, waiting in the hallway. His cousin Pagali ran to him and held his hand, making sounds of pleasure. She looked plump; she had gained weight. Meher Jamal stood shyly and backed toward the kitchen.

"Where is Auntie?" Dohst set his small box down on the floor and walked toward his aunt's tiny bedroom. It was empty. He quickly made his way through the other three small rooms and stopped at the kitchen. "She is not here."

"Aziz, she died on the day after you left while we were reading from the Holy Book." Meher looked apologetic as if the death had been her fault.

Dohst stood quietly for a moment biting his lip in thought. "Did you go to get the retirement allowance from the Railway Station while I was gone?"

"Yes, Aziz ji; the mullah took us. The money is now finished." She cut the hard yellow skin from the small pumpkin as she talked. "She was very quiet at the end and did not talk. The yellow Balium tablets did not seem to help her. She took many of them but she just slept and could hardly walk to the latrine."

"My name is not really Aziz Shabash. It is Dohst Mohammed. I used the name Aziz because my enemy was trying to find me to kill me. He is now dead. I am Dohst Mohammed, the friend of the Prophet, peace be unto Him."

"Aziz ji, it is strange to change one's name. Forgive me if I forget. Aziz is a good name and suits you well. Dhost. I will try to remember. Forgive me, we have nothing to eat but pumpkin and a little rice. Will you be able to take us to the market to buy food, tomorrow? We have no cooking oil, no onions, and no wheat flour. I am so sorry." Meher was having a difficult time with the pumpkin using her only good arm. Her flipper arm was short and of little help to her in holding things in place.

"Yes. Tomorrow we will go to the market and buy many things. I have sold some of my possessions from our ancestral home and now we can eat. I have decided to become a merchant and set up a small store and sell to-bacco." He walked to the room where he had previously slept and pulled a small tin box from under the bed, unlocked it and opened it. Meher and Pagali stood and watched, curious about what the box contained. They had both held it in their hands many times before and had shaken it, but could not guess its contents. There were two books, ledgers with red cardboard covers. There was an Indian Bollywood magazine with a beautiful woman on the cover. He quickly turned this over on the bed, but Pagali moved past him and picked it up and looked at the picture and laughed. On the bottom of the box there was a leather purse. Dohst looked behind him at the two women.

"Leave me alone. I want privacy. Tomorrow we will go to the market. I must think. Go!"

The women backed away from the room, Pagali still carrying the colorful movie magazine. Dohst took money out of his pocket and counted it, placing it in piles of one thousand rupees. He opened the ledger and took a pencil and entered a figure on the last line. Then he glanced at the rupees in the leather purse.

"A merchant. I will become a tobacco merchant and use the remaining money from the sale of your car, Sheikh Mohammed. He repacked the small tin trunk, locked it and hid the key under the mattress.

He sat alone and ate spiced pumpkin and a little rice. Meher watched from the doorway of the kitchen. Pagali sat across from him watching him eat every mouthful, her own mouth opening each time he opened his.

"She is pregnant, Aziz ji. I thought I should tell you now so that you would not be surprised later." Meher spoke softly from the kitchen.

"What do you mean, pregnant? She has not..." He turned and looked at his cousin as if he had never seen her before. He glanced at her abdomen. "Has anyone come...?" He looked at Meher.

"No one but you has ever come into this house. You have been the only male here. She is pregnant. Allah be merciful, Aziz ji. I have told no one, not even my uncle, the mullah. I am fearful of what he would say, or do to her. No one." She turned away from him, unable to look at his face. The pumpkin curry lay neglected on his plate. Pagali reached over and took the plate and ate the food and set the plate on the floor and looked first at her cousin, then at Meher, smiling at them both.

"Then I will write a temporary marriage contract for her. You can witness it. It is the only way. Yes, I will write the contract, a *nikah urfi* contract, or the *nikah mut'ah* allowed by Islamic juridical law. My father told me of it. He had two women under *nikah urfi* which he called the unregistered or hidden marriage, and this allowed him to still have his quota of four legal wives for whom he paid *mahr*, the dowry. I will write the secret marriage paper and you can witness it. I will place my mark on it and sign it. If anyone ever asks then you say that she is my cousin, my temporary wife by contract."

"Yes, yes that will suffice. It is good that she will be your wife of a hidden marriage. You are feeding her, providing her clothing and care and that is her *mahr*. You are a generous man to care for your helpless relative." Meher looked at Pagali and smiled, yet as she looked at him and then at Pagali she had a hard time to imagine that they had been locked together physically. Since she had never had a man, the images were confused having only seen mating animals.

"I will write up the paper now and let us be done with it this very hour." He got up and went to his room, opened the box, removed a ledger and tore out a page. It did not rip cleanly, so he bent the torn edge and ripped it in a straight line. He wrote the words of the hidden contract, the unregistered marriage to his cousin. It was only two lines in length.

I Aziz Shabash agree this day to marry my orphan cousin called Pagali. This is an unregistered hidden marriage contract and I will pay no dowry since I will care for all her needs. Aziz Shabash._____ Witness_____ Date_____

Dohst stood at the small table in the kitchen. Meher stood across from him. Pagali stood next to him and stroked the dark hairs on his arms. He read the contract aloud and signed the paper. Meher Jamal took the pen and signed the paper and the date.

"Wait here, both of you. I will take a rickshaw to the sweet maker and buy a big box of assorted sweets. Make us strong tea. I will bring back two cans of condensed milk and we will have a celebration. The women clapped their hands.

"Tomorrow I will go to see your uncle the mullah and pay two thousand rupees *mahr* for you, Meher, in spite of your deformity. It is not right that I live with you here without my aunt present. You have done much to keep this house going. I hope you will continue to work well as you did before. I can not offer you a regular marriage, but a *nikah mutah* marriage, but I will pay a token dowry and request a marriage contract for you as well. Then we can all live in harmony."

They drank strong sweet tea and gorged on the heavy sweet candies. Pagali became sleepy and crawled onto her mother's bed and was asleep in minutes. Dohst looked over at the woman sitting across from him and she became uncomfortable at his intense stare. She turned her head to the side and looked down.

"I am going to bathe. It has been a long day." Dohst got up and went to the bath room and washed the grime of travel from his body. The water was cold but he rubbed himself down with a small towel. He returned to the front room but Meher had already left. He could hear her moving about in her room. He walked to the door of her room and opened it. Meher stood in a pull-over slip. She held her hand to her neck in surprise. Dohst walked in and sat on the bed and looked at Meher, his eyes roving over her body, from her bare feet all the way to her face.

"I will sleep with you tonight. It is a chilly night." He continued to look openly at the woman in front of him. She now did not turn away. She said nothing. She stood in front of him and pulled off the slip that she was wearing. She crawled naked into the bed, her heart pounding furiously as she watched him undress.

☪

Screaming hooters sounded! Ambulances and police cars came with their blue lights flashing when the rioting began. The Mohurram parade had ended in fights; there were clashes between supporters of the Shiites and a gang of young men who called out slurs against them. Not only were the self inflicted wounds of celebrants bloody, but now at least a dozen young men sat glumly at the edge of the road waiting for the ambulances, blood streaming down their faces. Feroz Hakim, the Deputy Superintendent of Police had called out almost a hundred of his foot patrolmen to shadow the religious celebrants as they marched down the Mall. When the fighting began, these men had used their clubs and *lathis*, the heavy cudgels carried by most police to subdue the men. Heads were cracked. A hot tempered man became a despondent injured patient in seconds. These were carted off in ambulances. Others who had been trouble makers now stood silently and looked at the dozen or so of their group sitting or lying bleeding at the side of the road.

Feroz Hakim drove his sedan up the street behind the stragglers of the crowd and parked in the middle of the street. He sauntered over to where the injured men sat and took out a camera, a new digital camera that he had purchased. He walked to the first man and told him to look up. When he did so, he snapped his picture. All thirteen men had their photographs taken. He returned to the beginning of the line again and asked the first man his name. He wrote the names of all the men in the same order that he had taken the photographs. He turned and was about to take pictures of the crowd that circled this action but immediately the men turned their backs and began to walk away. Feroz smiled. His predecessor, Sher Khan had never thought of using a camera for crowd control.

Back in his office he waited for the usual newspaper reporters to show up for an interview. He was surprised when only three appeared.

"Gentlemen. How may the Lahore Police assist you?" He smiled with his mouth, but his eyes showed disdain.

"Why did your report say that the case of the missing American woman had been solved?" Ikbal from the Dawning usually opened the questioning.

"Mr. Ikbal I thought we were dealing with the matter of the Mohurram celebration. What is your question again?" He was fishing for time.

"I have interviewed two American women who work for US-HELP and it is their opinion that the abduction of Mrs. Bernard remains a mystery. I asked why you issued a statement last week stating that the case had been solved." Ikbal's voice was high and squeaky and irritated the Deputy Superintendent.

"It was stated quite clearly that physical evidence was in the hands of the police which proves that Maria Bernard was at the site where the bombs fell and was destroyed by the explosions."

"Excuse me sir. What was the physical evidence and how was it obtained if the woman was destroyed by the bombs?"

"It was a folding pocket comb. It was given to me by a woman who made friends with her in the Bahadur compound. It had two dark hairs sticking in the teeth of the comb." He pointed to another reporter but Ikbal persisted.

"So, are we to assume that forensic testing of the hair was done to match it to the DNA of the deceased? Where was such sophisticated analysis done? How was the hair DNA matched to that of Mrs. Bernard?

How long had the comb been in the possession of the woman who gave it to you and had she used it?" Ikbal turned his head to one side and peered at the Deputy Superintendent out of the side of his bi-focal lenses.

"I am not prepared to answer that question at this time for security reasons. Rest assured that Mrs. Bernard was at the site. One witness, who was her friend there, provided a statement and evidence. That is all I wish to say at the moment."

"Are we to assume then that some DNA samples of the allegedly deceased woman were made available to the police? What were these?"

"That is being sought at the present time. We also have fingerprints. Analysis is being made presently to match finger prints of the deceased against objects owned by Mrs. Bernard."

"Apparently the statement made last week was premature. From what you now say the case does not seem to be solved. What has been the reaction of your superiors to this matter?"

"Thank you gentlemen. That is all for today." Feroz Hakim turned on his heel and walked off stiffly and got into his car and drove away.

Iqbal wrote a note on his pad. Tomorrow, headline. "Police Deputy Jumps the Gun."

☪

His stomach rumbled loudly and pained him. He had chronic gas problems which resulted in frequent loud farts. Those around him had secretly given him a nickname, *pad*, and had learned not to stand down-wind of him. Now Sahib-ji, as he was called by his followers, dropped two Eno Fruit Salt Tablets in a glass of water and gulped this effervescent solution down and waited momentarily for the satisfying belch that was soon to follow. He belched happily, settled back against the round cushions and called for his eldest son.

"Beta, what is the news about the expedition to retrieve the Katyushas?"

"Sahib-ji, the news is the same. All were shot to death. The truck is presently in the hands of the Peshawar police, however, we have shown them the sign-off for its title and they have agreed to release it. You will have it tomorrow. I already have a buyer for it. All the rockets had been taken away."

"Beta, have you contacted the family of Chamuck and given them a letter with a copy of the contract for the girl to become my youngest wife?" He belched again.

"Sahib-ji, the letter was given to the eldest son of the family, Mohammed, however he is a hot tempered Pathan. It is a wonder that the messenger was not killed. We are going to have trouble with that one."

"Beta, our advocate will handle this one. Let him get shot. Have him see me tomorrow. He will earn his legal fees on this one. Personally, I do not even wish to see the uncle of the girl. Let the lawyer handle it and report to me. We have every legal right and we will win this one for sure. Give the lawyer a photo copy of the contract. Tell him to phone me tomorrow; wait, I have changed my mind. I do not wish to see him personally, his perfume irritates me. Where have they taken the body of Abdul Haifa to?"

"It was buried in a plot outside the regular cemetery."

Sahib-ji got to his feet with a groan, opened his brief case and took out a pistol and a shoulder holster. He put this on, pulled out the firearm, inspected it and smiled. He called for his driver to bring his car around.

CHAPTER TWO

Hath pair lagao, Khuda barkat dega. (Urdu saying)

Use your hands and feet (means) and God will add the blessing.

"Smash it . Smash it! Kill it!" The girls yelled from the sides of the badminton court as Chamuck waited for the shuttlecock to descend. She snapped her wrist and sent it speeding across the top of the net. A senior girl team member on the other side of the court lunged and scooped the shuttlecock and hit it back but it clipped the top of the net and fell short. The crowd of girls yelled and screamed.

Chamuck was the heroine of the day. Her classmates crowded around her and patted her on the back. The players made their way to the shower room where each girl took a turn bathing in the single shower stall, carefully closing the door for privacy. She emerged with wet hair wearing her street clothing, a loose fitting pajama bottom and a long-sleeved shirt. The teacher walked over to her and held her elbow.

"That was a brave thing to do. I am so sorry about your father's death. So unexpected. I was worried you would not be able to play this final match game." She looked into Chamuck 's eyes which welled with tears.

"My uncle has not yet heard what I did today. He was too busy cleaning his guns. I played today without informing him. He opposed my going to high school and now that he is our senior male family member, I am afraid of what is going to happen." Now tears streamed down her cheeks.

"Allah is merciful." She tried to comfort the girl about her father's death.

Chamuck nodded. "Forgive me but I am afraid that Allah will be on the side of my uncle who is a mullah. He will arrange a marriage for me as soon as a suitable suitor is found, one with plenty of money to sweeten the bargaining for me." She bent over and sobbed. "My own father sold me to an old man, an arms dealer. He made a formal contract before his death. An old, fat man, a chronic farter with four children. What am I going to do?"

"What? I had not heard. Are you sure?" The teacher was appalled.

"I read the copy of the contract, signed and with his fingerprints and those of the witnesses." Chamuck was hitting the badminton racket against her fist over and over.

"Perhaps you had better get home quickly before your uncle returns and notices you are not there." The teacher put her hand on Chamuck's arm to encourage her, worried about having to deal with the irate relative.

"He told me I could not leave my room. I am in trouble already. I may not be able to return to the school." She bent over and ran from the room as the other girls watched, wondering what had happened.

Chamuck's return went unnoticed. She climbed down the long wood staircase to her cellar room and lit the kerosene lamp. She picked up the book with the strange picture of the man with donkey ears on its cover and tried to memorize the passage, knowing full well that she would not be able to leave the house in the morning if her uncle returned. The walls looked dark and gloomy, dark shadows from the lantern played like ghosts on the wall. Above her there were no sounds of scurrying feet and laughter. The house was quiet. Her mother was in her room where she had been since the notice of the death of her husband. The other women were depressed as well and kept the children quiet. The once busy house was now grey and gloomy, waiting, waiting for the return of Mohammed the mullah who would soon decree what would happen to each of them.

Two of the younger women had been taken under *nikah mutah* marriage arrangements. Their status was most insecure, as well as that of their children. The newest young woman, seventeen years of age, had been brought under a hidden contract, the *nikah urfi* arrangement and was pregnant. Her name was Thirta, a name given to her when she was a baby because she was such a tranquil and quiet child, one that seemed to be peaceful.

Chamuck heard the door open and glanced up at the top of the staircase to see the youngest girl Thirta enter and begin walking down the stairs. She sat up on her bed and motioned for the pregnant girl to come down.

She came to the side of the bed, weeping, filled with her own foreboding and fear of what was going to happen to her. Chamuck reached out and put her hand on Thirta's leg.

"Nothing, Chamuck. Nothing for me. Your father took me secretly in a hidden contract and now what will happen to me? To my unborn child? My own father has died six months ago with whom the contract was made. My eldest brother has to be cared for at home because he can't speak so he doesn't work. I will receive no inheritance as a widow. Nothing. Who will take me? How will I live?" She turned and looked at Chamuck. "At least, you, a daughter, should receive some *mehr*, some inheritance from your father's estate. I will have nothing and may end up sold as a ..." She could not continue, placing her hands on her swelling abdomen.

"It is bad for all of us. My father co-owned this house with his elder brother, the mullah. He spent all that he earned from his sales of rockets and bombs. He bought a new truck this year. That he signed away. What estate? I have never heard of a bank account. He seldom gave money to us and we had to beg for school uniforms, books, sports supplies. You may not have heard, Thirta, I was signed off by my father to marry the arms dealer who financed his last trip. Allah!" She sat quietly, tired from crying, tired from thinking of the hopelessness of her situation; tired of waiting for her uncle to return to tell them more of what was going to happen. "Inheritance is the last thing you should worry about. You are young and pretty. After your baby is born, do you think that a young and pretty woman like you is going to remain without a man in her bed? It does not happen in Pakistan. What about me? I am sure that it will be a matter of days before Sahib-ji will make his move for me."

There was a loud banging sound on the outer compound gate. The sweeper hurried to the gate and was met by three men, all bearing arms.

"Where is Mullah Mohammed?"

"He was here yesterday. We do not know where he is now." The sweeper stood in the doorway blocking entry.

"Who is home now?" A lean, very tall man with a scar on his face leaned toward the servant.

"Only the zennanah. Women and children living in the house. The wives of the master." The sweeper moved backward as the tall armed man moved closer to him. "You may not enter. You would be violating the women's rights to privacy." He stepped back another pace. All three men stepped through the door set in the gate into the outer courtyard and stood menacingly.

A car pulled up in the street behind them. A bearded man, Mohammed the mullah, the co-owner of the house, stepped out of his car. His face was screwed up in fury. In his hand he held a rifle which he was aiming at the back of the nearest man."

"Back out now or you will all die. How dare you force entry into my privacy? Are you insane? Back out! Put your weapons on the ground before you move." The tall leader spun on his heels and faced Mohammed and began to raise his weapon. "We are here for the girl." A shot rang out, the sound echoing down the street. The tall man slumped forward, his weapon falling from his hands. The others lay their weapons on the ground.

"Blood on my doorstep; you have violated my property. Carry him away. You brought the fight to me. It is my right before Allah to maintain my honor. Tell your Sahib-ji to take great care how he next meets me. He sent you as *dushman*, enemy! I am now going to call on my clan brothers to join me. Take care lest the war be taken to your gates, just as you took it to mine. I know who you all are. Obviously you do not know who I am. You have come to abduct a *beeplaara*, a defenseless, fatherless child, from my household. Mad! You are all mad. The death of my brother will be avenged."

The two men helped the wounded man to the car. He remained bent over, holding his stomach, having been shot in the lower abdomen through the bladder. He was placed in the back seat. The mullah kicked their guns out of the compound into the street. The car sped away heading to the hospital.

☪

"Two thousand Rupees, no less. We lose a faithful helper in the house, one who cooks and cares for other children. No, one thousand for Meher is not acceptable." Mullah Ahmed stood in his small room in the mosque located in the business district of Sialkot. His bushy brows were raised; his eyes held wide open as he looked at the slender man in front of him.

"Will you give me a contract? A paper that will place her in my care and under my authority and release her from any obligation in your household? Once she is accepted by me as a hidden, secret contract wife she will become part of my household with all that implies." Dohst knew he had lost the argument already. He had taken the extra thousand rupees in his pocket in the event that he had to bargain.

The mullah had one thousand rupees in his hand and was trying to hand it back to Dohst who was now fishing in his pocket for additional money. "Draw up the contract now. Today, while I am waiting. The old auntie has died and it is only proper that Meher Jamal now stay in my household legitimately. Because of her impairment and the fact that she lacks one arm, I do not want it known widely that I have taken her. Few men would ever consider such a thing. It is like an act of charity. You will no longer have to feed her. "

Mullah Ahmed went to his desk and took out a sheet of paper and began to write.

He turned to Dohst. "Has she consented to such a marriage contract? Should I come to your house to verify it?"

"She has agreed. She is happy to stay in my home now and become a part of my family there. There is no need to..." He took out the remaining One Thousand Rupees and held it in his hand. Mullah Ahmed glanced up at the money and continued to write. He finished and signed the paper and handed it to Dohst who read it quickly. "There should be at least two witnesses to this. Are there men here who could make their mark as well?"

"That is just a formality. Just give me the money and we will be done with it." He got up and moved toward Dohst.

"One witness, then. Get another man from your family to witness that that is your signature and you agree to the *nikah* contract."

The mullah went to the door and called out. "Bashir"! A young clerk ran up. "Here, sign your name here, under my signature."

"What is it Sahib?" he asked.

"It is a contract. A private matter between this man and myself. It does not concern you. Sign; acknowledging my signature."

The young man tried to read the information on the contract, however, the top half of the page had been turned over so all he could read was that the contract was final and that both parties agreed. He signed it.

"Give the man sixty rupees."

Dohst was able to come up with sixty rupees change from his pocket. The man was dismissed. Dohst gave Ahmed the additional one thousand rupees and took the contract and put it into his pocket. He nodded his head toward the elder respectfully. "Thank you. She will be well taken care of. She will never lack food or clothing. She will bring more of the knowledge of Allah to my household. She is always reading the Holy Book."

Dohst returned to his small house and went to his room, took out the small tin box, unlocked it and was about to put the contract in it. Once more he decided to read it. He read it carefully and was surprised that the amount Ahmed had written was One Thousand Five Hundred Rupees, not Two Thousand Rupees. He stood up, ready to return to the mosque, then sighed, folded up the paper and locked it with his other valuables.

He met Meher Jamal in the small kitchen sorting stones from the rice. "I have seen your uncle, the Mullah. The contract for an *urfi* marriage has been agreed upon. I paid two thousand rupees for you to your uncle for your family. You are now part of this family and my woman. I will arrange to give you a small dowry of gold soon." He moved to the table across from her but she avoided his eyes, shy, remembering the initial flash of pain, then the sounds, the sensations and the odors of the night before. He lifted her chin so she had to look at his eyes. "You are now mine in all ways enjoined by the Holy Prophet, blessings be unto him. I will move my things to the larger bedroom where you are sleeping. You can help me carry my things."

Pagali walked up silently behind Dohst and made him jump when she put her hands on his neck and began to massage him. He turned, feeling irritated and held her hands away and shook his head. "I have no time for massage now. I have to go to the market to look for a small place where I can sell tobacco." Pagali smiled at him and quickly moved to where Meher was working. She watched as Meher cleaned the rice, putting tiny stones and sticks to one side. Pagali stirred the small pebbles with her finger, then arranged the tiny pieces of debris in a line, carefully putting all the dark stones together, all the light ones together and the pieces of stick and leaves in a little pile.

☪

The Deputy Superintendent of Lahore, Feroz Hakim had forgotten that the picture and application form for Mistiri's daughter Jasmin was in his dark suit pocket. He had put his hand into the inner pocket and wondered what the papers were. Now he looked at the picture of the girl of about fourteen or fifteen years of age. She was wearing a school uniform that appeared to be too small for her. He looked more closely at the picture and saw the swell of her breasts under the uniform. The application form was carefully filled. He saw that she had excellent grades in most of her subjects, except English Language. Her marks in Mathematics were excellent. He again picked up the picture and took out a rectangular magnifying glass and inspected the picture of the girl again. She was staring straight at the camera and smiling at him.

All the way to the office he kept thinking about the girl. Perhaps, he thought, she was now sixteen and of high school age, marriageable age. He told his peon to call Mistiri to his office. Half an hour later the carpenter appeared, biting his inner cheek in nervousness.

"Mistiri, come in. Have you had tea? You always say no. This time I insist. We shall have tea and order some salty nuts as well." He called out to the peon who was listening at the door of the office. Feroz gave him some money and he turned to Mistiri.

"When does the new school term begin for your eldest daughter?" asked Feroz.

"We have not considered it, Hazoor, lacking fees for books, tuition and uniforms. But I believe it is not yet for six weeks." Mistiri had an irritating habit of playing with the edges of his shirt, rolling one area up, then another, then unrolling them, staring at them as if he was creating a masterpiece.

"Look at me. Leave your shirt alone. When you speak with your superiors, you should sit straight, and look down at your feet until you are spoken to directly. Then you should look briefly up into your superior's face and reply. Don't play. It is a dreadful habit." Feroz lectured the hapless man who was now more nervous than before, wondering what the occasion could be that brought him into the Deputy Superintendent's office. He was surprised that the policeman had mentioned his daughter's schooling.

"We have not considered her schooling, Hazoor. My cousin has been enquiring about my daughter asking about the possibility of obtaining her for marriage. He is small *zamindar*, a land-holder near Changa Manga and he even has canal irrigation water to his plot, though his is at the end of the service ditch." He glanced up at Feroz Hakim and was surprised that he was frowning and looked unhappy.

"I had not forgotten about your daughter. It would be a disgrace for her to marry now. She is very young, a mere child. I see that she has good grades in Mathematics. You should definitely send her to high school. I have set the money aside. Bring me the bills from the school's bursar tomorrow, tuition, boarding expenses, uniform, books, everything. I have been saving money for her education and strongly oppose your considering her for marriage to a small landholder who has an end of service irrigation ditch. Being at the end means he will always fight for water and get into arguments with all the men along the ditch. A bad omen. I cannot image her working in the mud of a farm."

The peon entered carrying the tray with tea and salty snacks and set it on the desk of his boss, backed up and then left the office. Outside the door he reached in his pocket and extracted a handful of salty roasted *channa* and began to eat. He had just stuffed his mouth full when Feroz called out. "Bring me the change."

Feroz sat behind his desk in the large stuffed chair of his predecessor Sher Khan and sipped his tea, looking over the edge of his cup at Mistiri who had poured half his tea in the saucer to cool and was now slurping it noisily.

"I am curious. Has your cousin already started with the bargaining, *mangni*? Has engagement already taken place?" He sounded irritable. "How much did your cousin offer to bring for bride engagement presents to you? Surely she would get two sets of 22 carat wedding gold necklace and head sets. Surely. What gifts did he say he would provide? Did he offer the gold bracelets and a necklace?" Feroz looked down at the picture of the pretty girl on the desk in front of him and imagined her decked out in wedding dress, gold jewelry hanging from her forehead.

"Hazoor, no. They are poor land holders and offered one set of gold-plate necklace and a pure gold ring with a red jewel in it as well as wedding dresses."

"Has the *mangni* already begun then? Are you already that far along in the negotiations? "

"No, *hazoor*, it was to be considered this next week. I have not yet spoken to my daughter about it, however, she knows about her cousin. His first wife died in childbirth leaving small children. He sorely needs a wife to help him now." He began to roll his shirt again and neglected to drink the rest of his tea.

"This matter should have been brought to my attention earlier. I forgot, has your cousin arranged for the *nikka* as well as an *imam* to officiate the signing of marriage papers?"

"No Hazoor. We have just begun to discuss this matter. No. Nothing formal yet. Our people seldom contact a ..." He caught himself. He was about to admit that the cousin was not Muslim and they would not have an Imam sign wedding papers.

"Mistiri, I am willing to pay for all the girl's expenses. Support her through school but only if I can be assured that both you and the girl say the words of conversion to Islam before a mullah in the mosque. I remind you of our previous conversation and how you must avoid blasphemy at the cost of your soul. Do you understand? I am willing to request a pay raise for you as well, as a matter of good will. A two hundred rupee pay raise, however..." He leaned forward and stared at the man's dirty hands rolling the edge of his shirt.

"It will be done. I will take my daughter to the mosque on Friday and we shall both say the words and convert to Islam. How many gold jewelry sets did you provide for your own wife?"

"Three, heavy 22 carat gold sets, three wedding outfits and many, many gifts to her family. We had a *valima* feast that my wife's sisters still talk about. Such food!" He stood, signaling that the matter was concluded. "Bring me all the costs for her schooling tomorrow. You can go to the school during the morning hours. I will not expect you to be here for work until ten. Everything will be provided. Such a good student must be encouraged to finish her secondary schooling. I can hardly imagine your child becoming the mother of a family and tending to the irrigation ditches, standing barefooted in the mud with a hoe in her hand. I can not imagine it."

The carpenter scuttled from the room, bending over before he got halfway through the door anticipating picking up his flip-flops quickly and moving off. Only when he was at the far edge of the compound did he turn and glance back at the door of the Deputy Superintendent. His bicycle was chained to a post near the room where he kept his tools. He undid the lock and pedaled away in haste down the crowded road, looking down at the unguarded chain of the bicycle which had just left a black streak on his pantaloons.

It was not a hot day, yet he was sweating. How could he tell his cousin? How was he going to arrange for his own conversion? He mouthed the sentence necessary for becoming a Muslim and decided that it was not so very difficult to say the sentence. "There is only one God and that his Prophet is Mohammed." Mistiri said it to himself softly as he pedaled his bike and felt no difference. His thought about a two hundred rupee raise made him sweat more. Why so little? That would hardly pay for a bag of vegetables? Ever since he had helped Feroz Hakim cement a safe in his house his life had become very complicated. He used to talk to all his friends as he sat in a circle and smoked a *hookah*. Now every time he sat with them he wondered if he was telling something that would bring him trouble. And his daughter. He had been pleased at the prospect of getting her married off to his needy cousin. It would be a good thing to keep his daughter close within the family circle of relatives. Many cousins married each other. Now it was apparent the policeman was going to provide complete support for his daughter and allow for the impossible, that one of their family members, most of whom were illiterate, would finish the high school and thus lift herself, and perhaps her brothers and sisters to a different level of life. But why?

He was not paying attention to his bicycle and his trousers got caught in the chain, practically pulling him from the seat. He moved to the side of the road and worked on extricating the material from the sprocket. By the time he was finished his pants were ruined, his hands were black with grease and he was shaking. He did not understand why he was shaking. He pushed his bike the rest of the way home. His daughter opened the gate and let him in and cried out in surprise at how terrible he looked.

"Did you have an accident?" she asked looking at his hands and black pants.

"No. The Deputy Superintendent wants to pay your school fees and all expenses to go to high school instead of you marrying your cousin Ranjit," he blurted out.

"What are you saying about marrying my cousin Ranjit? I would never marry him. His wife who died in childbirth always complained that he beat her whenever she was late with food or put in too much salt. He has three children. What do you mean?" She was shrieking.

"No, that is not the plan now. You will have a complete scholarship to go to high school paid for by the Deputy Superintendent. Everything. I will get a raise." He stood by the faucet and rubbed ashes on his hands and arms and then worked to get rid of the grease.

"Why? I don't know the man? Why would a stranger want to pay for everything? How did he know about me? What is happening?" She was becoming emotional and was almost in tears.

"Because I gave him application forms to the girls' school and attached the picture of you that was taken at the end of the year by your mathematics teacher when we were together at the school. You remember the picture that she took of you."

"You never told me that you gave someone an application for me. Why did you put my picture on it? So he knows what I look like? That picture was not good. It was for women's eyes only."

"I will not talk more now. I need tea and a bath. Heat water for my bath. I will talk later. You ask too many questions." He walked into the house and took off his clothes. There was a small shriek from his wife as he entered the bedroom naked.

☪

The rain came down steadily. Puddles formed in the courtyard. Bedraggled chickens stood under whatever shelter they could find waiting for the rain to stop. Two dogs huddled on a dry spot under the overhang near the entrance door. The buffaloes were tied under a lean-to shelter that provided little shelter because it leaked everywhere. Water dripped onto their backs. They were restless and shook their heads and made small bellowing noises. A cobra that had a resting place in a hole in the foundation of the wall slithered out as water began to flow into its lair. It snaked its way across the deserted courtyard and slithered into a stack of firewood for shelter. The skies rumbled and lightning struck a tall poplar tree on the far bank of the river.

Ankh lay in the big bed with the heavy cotton quilt pulled over her. A small ceramic dish filled with oil in which a crude wick was placed was lit and provided the only light in the room. Ankh looked at the little flame which seemed to pulsate, gaining strength, then smoking and shrinking low again. She could hear the rain pounding on the flat roof of the building. The splashing sound of water spouting from the drains outside predominated. She closed her eyes and listened to the sounds of running water, feeling that she was floating in a boat moving on a river.

Two weeks had passed since Dohst had visited her. The time had passed slowly. Each day seemed to drag by as she did a variety of chores. There was only the old man and woman to talk to, but they no longer spoke to her unless she first spoke to them. Since Dohst's coming and his staying with her in the master's bedroom, they had become distant. Her transition from slave to Dohst's free woman had evolved strangely.

Dohst had slept in her bed the first night he had returned. They had lain quietly next to each other not speaking until they both fell asleep. In the middle of the night Ankh got up to go and relieve herself and Dohst had awakened. When she crawled back into the bed her leg had rubbed against his. He had reached over with his hand and put it on her leg. They spoke no words. He had reached over in the dark and drew her hand toward him. He rolled over toward her. She was confused. He was only interested in her hand.

In the morning they ate cold food from the night before and drank hot tea. Again, they did not talk. It seemed as if each was waiting for the other to speak, but not wanting to open communication about something they did not understand. It happened when Dohst turned to reach for a cigarette and his elbow bumped the brass glass in which his tea was served. It fell to the floor with a clang. Ankh jumping back to avoid the splash, laughed. Dohst looked at her and laughed as well.

"That is what comes when a man and a woman eat together. Things get knocked over. This is the first time I have eaten with a woman." He laughed again. "Perhaps tomorrow I will eat alone and then I will not spill my tea."

"Perhaps tomorrow I will sleep alone and then the man will not spill his tea." Now she laughed.

"You are making a joke of me. Are you making a joke of me?" He frowned.

She smiled. "I think we are making jokes with each other. I have never made a joke with a man before. Is it so strange that a man and woman can laugh together while they drink their tea?"

She got up and picked up the brass goblet and walked with it to the kitchen area to refill it. She returned and Dohst was standing looking at the shiny brass table with the collapsible folding legs. "I don't remember this table being here. Where did it come from?"

She replied, "It has always been here but it was covered with dirt, old tea stains and dust. I cleaned it. Perhaps when you leave you can take it with you and try to sell it. It could provide some money for your trip."

"Yes. It is so interesting to see the things that my father collected over the years. Very strange things. Look at that copper tea kettle. Why would anyone buy a teakettle that is decorated with engravings? It makes it rather useless. No one would put this on the fire because it would turn black." He walked around the room touching objects that he did not remember seeing before.

Ankh watched him. She finished her tea and sat back and looked at the man who had shared her bed the night before. She could not imagine her awkward physical contact with her hand on his genitals. She could not imagine that she had once, months ago, embraced the thin dark man that stood in front of her. It had been pitch-dark in the room. All she could remember were sensations, the strange sounds he made and the smell of sandalwood in his hair. Her groping of him had had no face, no form in her memory, just sensations and sounds. Never before had she touched a man intimately.

"I will leave tomorrow. The boat is coming for me. I will make arrangements for Jhika to come when the water subsides and bring you tea, sugar, some fresh milk and vegetables from the market. I don't know when I will return. I have to go to Sialkot to do business. But I will return within three months before your baby is born. Can the old woman watch over you?" He looked at her now with new eyes. "You are thin. Have you eaten enough?"

"I have eaten food when it was available. It was never enough." She looked at him now. "You are thin as well. Why are you so thin and so dark?"

"I had a job delivering parcels and letters. I had to ride my bike all day long in the hot sun. It was a terrible job. I thought I would die from thirst and could never get enough to eat. Now I am going to become a tobacco merchant. That is why I am going back to Sialkot." He looked at his dark arms and frowned. He took money from his bill fold.

"While you are gone it is important that the old man and woman know your wishes about me or we will have trouble. They just sit and do nothing. They still think of me as a slave." She looked at his eyes and held his gaze until he dropped his eyes. "Am I a slave? Is that how you think of me? That I have to do anything you ask me to?"

He was silent for a moment or two. He drank more tea, lit a cigarette and walked to the window and looked out. He turned on his heels. "You are no longer a slave. Before Allah you are free. I give you your freedom that my father took from you. You are like the servants now, free to come and go. You are not a slave. I do not wish my child to be born from a slave." He sounded impatient, almost angry. "I wish my children to be Muslim. You can convert to Islam. It would satisfy me."

"I am a *Kala Kafir*, not a Muslim. It is not possible to convert simply because another says convert, change, become something else." Her voice was strained and close to tears. "I don't believe that there is just one deity."

"It is easy. Just say the words. My children must be Muslim." He shook his head impatiently.

"Though I am a person not wanted by my family, not valued by your father more than a brick of opium, little wanted by you except your concern for your child to be; I can not change, convert my heart." Her lips were pursed.

"Why not? It would make it better for me. Islam is the only true way. All other beliefs lead one to *gehennah*."

"*Kala pe rung nahin charta.*" (Black will take no other hue). I am a black infidel. Islam does not mix with my belief." She said nothing more, just stared at him. Tears streamed down her cheeks and fell on her bare feet leaving darker spots. Is this how it would come about, she thought.

"I will write it down. I will write it down and the old man and woman can make their finger marks on it and I will give your freedom to you." He walked to the bedroom to get his case. "What is your full infidel name?" he asked unhappily.

"My name is Ankh. Nothing else."

"What is your father's name?"

"His name is Terha."

He wrote on the paper and let her see it. She could not read what was written.

He now called the old caretakers to come into the room. They stood uncomfortably. He said, "This paper gives Ankh her freedom. She is no longer a slave. Before Allah I free her. Put your mark here and here. Bring black pot grease to leave a mark for your fingers."

The document was completed. Dohst handed it to Ankh. She smiled wanly now. "I have a paper for you as well." She reached into the pocket under her outer dress and took out a folded yellow paper. She handed it to Dohst. He unfolded it and read it.

"This is the paper for the ownership of this property! It was in my father's possessions. How did you get it?" He read it again, mouthing the words aloud and smiled broadly. "You kept this and never told me about it."

"Yes. Feroz Hakim the policeman gave it to me as a gift to give to my son when he was born, or to the father of my child if I so desired. I exchanged this paper for a comb from Maria." She folded her new paper of freedom and put it into the inner pocket where the other paper rested that Maria had drawn, a large picture of an eye with the words EYE and ANKH carefully printed on it.

Dohst read the document, looked at the ancient signatures, amazed. "Were you going to keep this and not show it to me?"

"Were you going to give me my freedom from slavery when you first came here? No. I was going to hold it until I became free for the sake of the child."

"So, what other secrets are you keeping from me?" He stared at her face.

She stared back at him so strongly that he dropped his eyes. "I will tell you other secrets if you tell me all of yours. What secrets are you hiding from me about your aunt's house? Who else is there?"

"I have changed my mind. Give me back the paper." He stepped toward her.

"Dohst, I will tell you now that I will protect my freedom from slavery with my life. It is gold to me. It is shiny bright gold, like the gold of a wedding necklace I never had." In the corner of the room was an old ornamental cane with an elephant carved on the handle. She backed toward it as she spoke, her hand behind her back reaching for it.

"Freedom does not suit you, Ankh. You do not look beautiful now." He turned and went to the bedroom to pack his things and looked at the book of poems. There was a paper stuck in the book which he removed and read. "Beauty Mark". He read the poem and just then the bent old woman came into the room carrying a short broom. He glanced at her and could not imagine that this old hag was the subject of the poem he had just read.

"Tell me old woman, do you have *til* mark on... on your breast?"

The old woman did not reply but her hand flew to her sagging left breast as if to cover it. She scuttled out of the room muttering to herself.

CHAPTER THREE

*Jo khana bachche ko palta hai woh bare admi
ko kafi nahin hota.* (Urdu Proverb)

Food which nourishes babies doesn't satisfy adults.

The half-blind mare came on heat. Tur-ali sat astride her back and
snapped the reins each time she whinnied, answering a stallion at the back
of the line of animals which were moving up the steep mountain path. Next
to him, his captor, a bearded fierce man rode on a huge gelding and kept
his steed next to Tur-Ali's protectively.

"She wants the stallion. They will not stop calling to each other for two
days. When we make camp tonight I will have him brought over so they can
jor lagana mate. It will calm everything down for a while." He looked at
Tur-Ali's animal more critically. "She looks old. Has she had any foals?"

Tur-ali looked over at the man and shook his head. "It is always the
same problem. She comes on heat regularly which becomes a problem for
local stallions, but she never foals. Something is wrong with her."

"Why did you keep her?" The leader of the mountain fighters, Sardar,
looked over at the lad next to him, admiring his beautiful face and curly
black hair. He was about to reach a hand over to stroke the curly hair, but
held his hand back knowing he had time.

Tur-ali spoke, ignored his admiring eyes. "She is a good pack animal
and a good riding animal. She became irritable when she was blinded in
one eye by a chip of stone made by a flying bullet. We kept her because she
works well in spite of her problems."

"It is true. A barren female is good for work and working over." He
laughed at his play of words. "Horse or woman it is all the same. But dry

graying old women do not come on heat like this old mare. That is the difference."

"She kicks. It is not a good idea to bring the stallion over. It always looks like they are fighting. She once injured a stallion's front leg." He shook his head at the memory.

"That makes it even more interesting. How will the stallion eventually overcome her shyness? Now you have convinced me. It will be our entertainment for this evening when we prepare our food. But perhaps this is eye food only for adults, not a boy." He laughed.

"I told you that I am no longer a boy. In my household, I am now the oldest male. My father has left me property. He has two houses and twenty one apricot trees. They are all mine now." Tur-ali turned toward Sardar and challenged him.

"We shall see if our entertainment suits you. I know that it will be 'eaten' happily by all the real men present." The stallion whinnied shrilly again and the old mare whipped her tail from left to right.

More than twenty animals and their riders moved up a steep slope, rocks slipping under the hooves of the animals. Riders dismounted and pulled their mounts behind them, all struggling to maintain their footing. The band made it to a flat rocky outcrop and now both men and animals rested. The horses and mules were foaming wet with sweat, the men mopped their brows. Sardar with Tur-ali next to him took the lead for the last leg of their journey for that day. On a large ledge above them was an opening to a huge cave in the hillside. It was formed naturally when softer dirt was eroded from under a slab of granite. This shelter had been augmented by men who had undermined more of the area. Twenty men and horses could bivouac here concealed from spying American eyes from above.

At last the leaders made it to the mammoth cave and dismounted and waited for the rest of the caravan to make it to the cave. They tied their animals to a bush and walked to the edge of the large rock to watch as the animals and men struggled upward. As they watched, a horse loaded down with two rockets struggled and then panicked. It chose a sandy area and lost its footing there and sagged to its knees, the *sais* yelling at it in frustration was pulling on its reins for dear life. The animal made one more leap upward, slipped and fell backward screaming. It bounced on the rocks below it and the men could hear the crack of its bones as it landed. It slid down about one hundred feet and then stopped against a small scrub tree.

"Don't stop now. Bring the rest of the animals up before they panic. Keep coming!" Sadar shouted down at the small band below him. They struggled upward. Finally all reached the platform, the pack animals panting, their heads hanging low in exhaustion.

"You four go down the hill and untie the wood boxes from the horse. I will send six others to help them carry the boxes up one at a time. Cut the throat of the horse with a knife and let its blood flow and give thanks to Allah for the meat. Did not Asama'bint Abu Bakr say that he had slaughtered a horse by Nahr during the lifetime of the Prophet and that they ate the flesh?" Sardar gave orders as he undid the saddle of his mount. Their tribe considered horse flesh suitable only in situations of dire need and hunger when other food was not available as long as it was *hallal*. All had eaten horse flesh and camel flesh. If a camel started to run away it was killed and held to be a wild animal and thus could be eaten.

The men slid down the hillside toward the dying animal, hanging on to bushes as they approached the animal. One man pulled out a knife and in one motion slit the horse's throat. It kicked feebly, made a groaning hissing sound and then lay quietly, its blood running down the hill. The men mumbled an incantation.

In the distance two F16s appeared, screaming toward the men. They lay prone on the ground, blending in with the earth. The fighter jets thundered past the hill where the men and horses were hidden in the huge cave. The jets moved toward Bahadur where the bombing had occurred, turned and screeched back toward them. The exposed men on the hill lay on their backs looking up as the jets raced above them and returned from where they had come.

A number of men slid down to help the others. The boxes containing the Katyushas were cut loose from the dead horse, ropes were tied to the boxes and they were dragged back up the hill toward the cave. Others worked on the horse, cutting huge hunks of meat from the body. One man slit the stomach, reached in and located the liver and cut it loose. He carried this tied in part of his turban cloth and made his way back up the hill.

"Light a fire at the back of the cave behind the two large rocks. Smoke will not be a problem. Night is coming" A five gallon plastic container was taken from one of the mules as well as two large metal tea pots. These were filled and set on stones to heat. The men settled down preparing for the long night ahead.

Tur-ali put his saddle against the wall and sat on it. He poured water in a small tin and brought it to his mare which drank eagerly. There was no grass or hay for the animal, but he had kept two large flat breads. He broke these and fed them to the animal and then tied her to a sharp rock. He checked her hooves one at a time to see if she had injured herself during the climb. After tending to her needs he then looked to his own. He stepped out beyond the overhanging rock and looked for a place of privacy for his own toilet. He had to walk more than fifty paces before he came to a place where bushes grew tall.

Before he got back he could hear the whinny of his mare. He hurried back in the gathering darkness and as he entered the cave he saw the circle of men around the mare. One man held the bridle of a stallion which approached the old mare. It reared up and kicked at the aroused male approaching her. It jumped back but as soon as the feet of the mare touched the ground it moved forward and pushed against her rump. Again she kicked back. The crowd of men shouted encouragement. On the fifth attempt the stallion was able to mount the mare and mate. The men became quiet, aroused as they watched the coupling, the shuddering of the male. The stallion was returned to the far side of the cave and men now took out their aluminum cups for tea, strong, sweet and black. They avoided each other's eyes, thinking their own thoughts. There was the smell of meat roasting and cigarette smoke.

The new moon came up shyly, revealing itself as a tiny sliver. It was a sliver crescent that hung in the black sky. It seemed to welcome the planet that nestled next to it for companionship. The men looked up at the new moon and its companion and felt contentment and hope. It was the month of Jumaad Awal, the fifth month and the beginning of the first freeze as defined by the Prophet, peace be unto Him.

One man had a small portable short wave radio and tuned to an Indian station. A high-pitched woman's voice, almost childlike in its timbre sang "Chup Chup". (Quiet Quiet) The men settled back and moved to the rhythm, their memories of women at home flooding their consciousness. They smoked and drank tea, waiting for the meat to become hot so they could slice a still red hunk off with their knives and sprinkle it with salt and powdered red pepper, holding the meat in their teeth, their knives cutting through the flesh near their noses.

Tur-ali lay on a cloth and leaned against the saddle thinking of his home and what his mother and sisters would be doing. He thought of the food she would cook and how he and his father used to sit in the small meeting room with cushions around the perimeter and eat from a large tray that his mother would bring to them. There would be rice with almonds and raisins and thick goat stew. They would eat with their hands, not talking, glancing up at each other and smiling at the richness of the oily food. Father, he thought, now buried under a pile of rocks a day's journey from his home. Father. The memory of seeing his father shot in the head now brought tears to his eyes. He swallowed to control crying, not wanting the men to see his grief.

Sardar squatted near him and handed him a metal plate on which there was a slab of almost rare salted liver, seared brown on the edges, still dripping blood. On the plate was a mug of hot tea. "It has been a hard day. Eat now and sleep. Use the horse blanket under you or the cold from the stone will make you ill. Eat now." He placed the meal on the stone in front of Tur-ali. He sat up and nodded saying thanks softly, confused by this act from the leader whose word was law, confused by his own thanks to this enemy. Sardar left him to get his own food. Tur-ali took out his knife and holding the meat with his right hand, sliced a piece holding it in his teeth. He ate steadily, amazed at his appetite. He drank his tea and settled down, more tired than he had ever been in his life. He spread the horse blanket by the saddle, wrapped himself in his heavy blanket and lay down to sleep. The smell of horse urine was now strong near the mare. Then to his surprise he smelled tea. It was dawn.

He looked at the other men in the cave. All except he were bowing now, engaged in their first *namaz*, giving thanks to Allah for sparing them from the fighter planes, for sparing their lives. All of them bowed in unison and their first morning worship was like a sigh after a meal, a satisfaction that they rested in the hands of the Almighty and submitted themselves as slaves to Him, the All Knowing, the Almighty, and the Merciful.

The prayers were interrupted by his mare. She was calling and being answered by the stallion again from the other side of the cave. The sun rose above the horizon and the men prepared for another march, one that could well be their last, but they were calm, resigned to Allah's will, that *inshallah*, they would reach their destination, that they would prepare to drive the infidel from their land; confident that their *jihad* was sanctioned by heaven. Some moved about preparing tea, saddling the horses and putting loads on their pack animals. Tur-ali sat up yawning and saw to his surprise that the bedding of Sardar had been laid next to his own, though he was now busy preparing for the day's march. A cup of steaming hot tea was set next to Tur-ali's mat. He picked it up and sipped it, grateful for the hot bitter-sweet drink. Sardar glanced back at him momentarily and Tur-ali lowered his head just a little in thanks, unaware that he had done so. He was disturbed by the intense look of admiration in Sardar's eyes, almost burning.

☪

Jhika and the old caretaker pushed and prodded the larger of the bull buffalo up a board resting on the sand. The animal was wary of the water and it took considerable pushing and pulling to get it onto the boat. It was tied securely to the small mast with less than a foot of spare rope which was tied in turn to the ring in its nose.

Ankh stood on the shore and watched the men loading the two animals, pleased that they would be taken off the island. The grasses and even edible weeds were short and hardly had time to grow back before the animals had grazed them off again. The cow buffalo seemed less bony than before and stood chewing its cud as her mates were loaded on to the boat. It let out a low pitched lowing noise. The males pulled against their ropes but the pain of the metal ring in their noses kept them from moving.

"When will you return again?" Ankh shouted to the men on the boat.

Jhika turned and waved. "When will you offer sweet tea and tamarind fish curry for us to eat?" He laughed.

"When you bring me the fish and tamarind you shall eat all you wish. When?"

"Friday. On *juma*, after the second call to prayer." The stern of the boat was caught by the current and it swung away.

"Bring a tin of milk. Tea without milk makes me think of Peshawar, the refugee camp." She shouted in a voice that was unnaturally pitched high to carry.

"If I sell enough fish I will bring a tin of milk powder instead, Klim."

Ankh walked back toward the high mud walls of the compound followed by the dogs close at her heels. She looked up at the clouds forming for a downpour and smiled to herself, thinking how grass and weeds would grow now that the monsoon had arrived.

Dohst's short visit had changed everything. She walked now taking large steps, thinking of Maria and how she had walked with energy. Her change of pace affected the dogs which gamboled near her, their faces smiling, whining in pleasure that Ankh was moving for the joy of moving.

The caretaker followed behind with slow steps, watching Ankh move toward their compound. He could not fathom what had happened in the last few weeks. The slave girl was now as free as he, and bearing the child of the owner. He mumbled to himself, "If the caliph says you are a cat, then you are a cat." He carried a real cigarette in his right hand between his third and fourth finger. Thus, he could close his fist and put his mouth to the top of his fist and inhale the smoke without touching the cigarette to his mouth. He carried a small clay pipe. When the cigarette burned down to a small butt he placed that in the pipe and was able to enjoy it in its entirety. Each time he inhaled he let out a little groan as the smoke burned his throat, but when the burning ceased he felt almost like Ankh, like moving with big sure steps, but his old bones and thin legs did not get the message.

Ankh entered the sitting room, dark with its shutters drawn, and went to the wall where an ornate calligraphy hung in a frame behind a smoky glass. She could not read the Arabic, but knew that the words said that there was only one Allah, and that his Prophet was Mohammed. She took the picture frame down from the wall and a sleeping gecko awakened, and scurried away. The wall was lighter where the picture had been hung for decades. She placed the frame upside down on the table. The glass was held in place with a cardboard and tiny nails. Ankh went to the kitchen area and retrieved the knife for cutting vegetables, thin and curved from years of sharpening. She pried the nails loose and removed the cardboard. Two silverfish scuttled away and hid in a crack of the frame.

She took a paper from her pocket and smoothed it flat on the table. She took the calligraphy and reversed it putting it behind her paper; then placed these against the glass, but was not pleased that it was smoky and dirty. She removed the glass and washed it in the kitchen and dried it on her blouse. Finally she inserted the paper and its backing, pushed two nails in the tiny holes and hung her prize on the wall. She could not read it but she knew every word. This was the paper, crudely written and smeared with the prints of the servants as witnesses that she, Ankh was, before Allah a free person, no longer a slave.

The old caretaker's woman entered the room looking for the kitchen knife. She looked up at the wall. "So, there is no slave in this house. Only three hopeless servants, just *naukar* who rely on the whim of the young master to keep them working and perhaps drinking spiced cardamom tea until the money runs out." She picked up the knife and shuffled off to her work laughing softly.

The words of the old crone irritated Ankh, ruined her small victory celebration. Three servants! The woman was right. *Naukar*. Dohst had given her freedom from slavery but she had nothing more now than before he came except the paper with words on it. He, however, had left with everything, a yellowed paper that made him master of the island; that carried forward the family wealth to him. Now she regretted the exchange. She had been hasty because of her feeling of the physical man that he was, her feeling of trust. Servant! He had not even said what she would be paid if she worked to maintain the island home. He had not spoken once of the child she carried when he left. She had not spoken of marriage to him, it had not occurred to her to do so. She looked up at the framed paper, sighed, turned it to face the wall and left the room.

She went to the bedroom where only days before she had spent the strange night with Dohst. She lay back on the sagging bed and closed her eyes, remembering the unfamiliar intimacy of her hand on his aroused body while she lay confused at his quick climax after which he slept, snoring.

The evening sun crept down the outer wall and a single shaft of sunlight shone through the high ventilation window onto the bed, onto her face. With her eyes tightly closed, but seeing the redness of the blood through her eyelids, she could see the face of Gunga, the man who had abducted her and raped her in the pine forest of Shinkiari and how he had stood naked in front of her, offering her a cigarette. Still a slave she thought, slave of this female body that men desire, which is now heavy with that memory of that one embrace on the small sandy beach.

G*

Feroz Hakim returned to his office in the police headquarters after dark. He switched on the light and was surprised at how dim the single bulb glowed above his desk. On his desk was a pile of newspapers that had been brought to him the evening before. He opened The Dawning and leafed through the headlines. Then his own name caught his eyes. He looked at the headlines. "Lahore Police Deputy Jumps the Gun." He read the brief article with the byline by Ikbal. He had been made to look like a fool, a bumbling idiot whose statements not only were premature but inaccurate and naïve. He read the article again and his anger seethed. Squeaky voiced Ikbal. How he hated the man. His hatred was so intense that he found himself biting his cheek and tasting blood. Ikbal had thrown down the gauntlet. He would pick it up, with vengeance.

Other newspapers neglected to mention the same story. Mr. Ikbal, he thought, how can I rein in your journalistic enthusiasm? He smoked one cigarette after another, lighting the second from the first. A mosquito buzzed near his head and irritated him. He swatted at it but was unable to kill it. Then one bit his ankle. He got up, picked up his briefcase, strapped on his service pistol and left the room.

That night he was restless. His wife had rolled next to him and had placed her leg across his, her signal. He did not respond; just lay looking at the ceiling, watching a moth crawl slowly across it. It flew and landed on the newspapers he had brought home. It made a rustling sound with its wings. He sat up, surprising his wife.

"What is it? Are you well? Do you need to take Fruit Salts? What?" She sat up as well and reached over in the semi-darkness for his arm. He got out of bed and went to the closet in which the safe had been cemented. He got the keys for it from a pocket in his wedding suit which hung in a plastic sack. He switched on the light in the closet and squatted, fitting the keys in their respective holes. Finally, after a couple of tries he managed to open the safe. He pulled out a cardboard file in which there were thirty folders hanging from file separators. One after another he looked through these and was about to close up the safe. Two more folders remained. The second to the last read, Ikbal Sufi.

His heart beat faster. He removed the folder and walked to the sitting room and switched on a small lamp near the heavily upholstered chair. He began to read and as he read a smile began to cross his face. He read the folder twice. The contents were dated, almost ten years old. In the folder was information about Ikbal Sufi, an Ikbal Sufi who had hair on his head, who smiled from the pictures at the camera as a younger fairly attractive man except for ears that stuck out and the gap between his two front teeth. There was a complaint letter from a woman and her daughter to the Superintendent of Police, Sher Khan, in which the mother requested that Ikbal Sufi be arrested for rape.

The story was similar to many which Feroz read. The young reporter was known to the family because of business arrangements between their fathers. The young school girl, Piari, had been walking with her friends, returning to their homes. The girls left Piari half a block from her home, her gate in sight. She had walked on alone. The white car with the logo of the newspaper on the door was parked along the side of the street. As she came by it, Ikbal had rolled down the window and called out the girl's name. She bent over and looked in the car and recognized Ikbal and greeted him respectfully. He in turn greeted her. Then he said, "Our fathers are meeting in my home on a business matter. Your father asked that I drive you there and he will drive you home after the meeting." The reporter went on to say that the girl had hesitated, however, the back door swung open on the driver's side and she got in behind Ikbal. He clicked the lock shut from the driver's locking mechanism and drove off in the general direction of her father's home.

"The girl, Piari, reported that Ikbal had driven to a deserted area near the Bari Doab Canal, parked the car and got in the back seat with her. He then began to fondle and kiss her. She had shouted and resisted, however, he was very strong. He removed her lower clothing and raped her. Then while she was crying and trying to dress herself again, he smoked a cigarette and told her to take off her blouse and bra. She refused. He told her that she had no choice, and that he did not want to harm her. Weeping, she obeyed. She stated that soon after that she was raped again. Then, strangely, he told her to get out of the car and arrange her clothing properly. He told her that he had wanted her from the first time he had seen her in her father's home. He said that he could not sleep at night thinking about her. Then he apologized for forcing himself on her, saying that he had been driven by *Ishkh*. He drove her back to the spot where she had got into the car, a stone's throw from the gate of her own house."

The other documents consisted of a signed statement from Ikbal Sufi that he had in fact had sex with the girl; however, she had been the one to greet him as he sat parked in his car and had asked if he could take her for a ride. She had made advances to him in the car when they parked and had taken an active part in the sexual encounter. He denied that rape had occurred and said that he had been seduced by the young woman's charms, in fact that she had exposed her breasts to him in the car which resulted in the sexual act and he had acted as any man would. He said that no one had witnessed the act of sex.

Another document was signed by Sher Khan himself. It was a copy of a statement from his office to the parents of Piari that the evidence was strong that the girl had been a willing partner in the sexual act, and that if the matter was pursued farther that the girl herself would be charged with violating a number of civil and *Sharia* laws placing her in jeopardy of being tried with possible dire consequences to her, perhaps even death.

The last document was one with Ikbal Sufi's signature agreeing to transfer a car to Sher Khan. It was an older Humber Sedan, but in mint condition with low mileage.

☪

A million dollar view, thought Maria; as good as in front of our house in La Jolla. She stood in front of the tiny shack-like mountain home and looked out across the hills of southwest Afghanistan. On higher peaks there was snow. As far as she could see, the brown, dirt-colored hills undulated. Deep shadows in the valleys looked black against the light colored slopes now illuminated by the morning sun. A vulture circled high above, a small speck like a fly, circling without flapping its wings. In the nearby hills, black partridge called to each other with a strange grating sound, but Maria did not know what the sound was. The dog in their compound barked. Its voice was high-pitched and intense. She listened carefully and to her surprise in the far distance she heard the barking of another dog, a sound she had not paid attention to before. Then she heard the flute on a distant hill. The player only used three or four notes, repeated the tune again and again. She wondered who could be playing a flute and imagined a small boy watching his flock of goats, sitting on a rock and playing to amuse himself and to let the animals know that he was nearby. In the far distance she saw the fighter jets before she heard them. They were tiny dots, smaller than the vulture and were heading directly toward her. Her heart beat faster. American fighter jets, perhaps on a mission to bomb another village, to bomb the Taliban. She watched in fascination as they came toward her, high in the clear, cloudless blue sky. They hurtled by and then the screaming ripping sound she knew so well followed by the thundering of their jets enveloped her and she covered her ears with her hands without knowing she did. Arrows of death, she thought, huge, screaming arrows of death that had killed Ankh; that had bombed Bahadur.

When she looked up for the vulture again it had disappeared. She searched the sky and was amazed she could not locate it. The black partridges had stopped their calling. In fact it was now deathly quiet as if the earth held its breath, waiting. Then in the far distance she heard the rumble like thunder, but the skies were clear of clouds.

"Those are your brothers. They are here to kill us." The old woman stood in the doorway of the shack and shouted at Maria, who turned when she called out, but did not understand a word she said, however, her hand pointing at the sky gave her a clue that she spoke of fighter jets. The look on her face said the rest. Hatred was written there and she was shaking her head. The old woman yelled again and waved her arm for Maria to come to her.

She nodded her head and moved down the slope toward the woman. Each morning she walked up the slope to a rocky outcrop which she had chosen as a place for her toilet. She did not know where the old woman went, but she hobbled around all day and Maria had not followed her. As she approached the old woman she saw that she held a pot in her hand and was pointing down a tiny trail that led behind the hill. She jabbered away and gave the pot to Maria and turned and went back into the small house.

Maria took the pot, carrying it in her right hand, surprised at how heavy the earthenware was. She strolled down the path, hardly more than packed dirt between the stones. She walked for more than five minutes and the path descended toward the base of the hill. She headed downhill for another five minutes and saw green bushes and a single green area of grass. At first she did not see the spring, and when she did she was amazed at how small it was. The water was not more than two feet across, half of which was protected by a large flat overhanging stone. In the dirt near the water there were footprints of some kind of hoofed animal, and two cat-like prints. On the rock there was a tin can that had once contained corned beef. She bent down and began to scoop the water into her pot, but noticed that the scooping action roiled up the sediment on the bottom. Now she submerged the can carefully, letting it fill slowly. Then she poured the water into the pot. It took her almost half an hour to fill the pot and then she wondered how she was going to carry the heavy object home, up the slope, a half hour hike.

She stripped off all her clothing and laid them on the warm rocks nearby and stood naked near the small seep-spring. She stood below the edge of the tiny water tank and dipped a tin of water and poured it onto her head and gasped. It was icy cold and goose pimples rose on her arms and breasts. She poured another and then scrubbed at her face. She poured another into her face and mouth and rinsed her mouth. By the time she had finished her toilet there was not more than an inch of water in the small stone tank. She dried herself in the sun, enjoying the feeling of cleaner skin, the warmth of the sun and the quietness of the place. A black bird with a yellow head that wagged its tail up and down approached the watering hole. She stood still and the creature hopped onto the stone near the water hole and bent to sip water. It sipped three times, each time lifting its head. Maria had not realized that birds used gravity to move the water into their stomachs. She smiled and the small bird made a sound like a tiny hinge squeaking, and then flew off downhill in undulating flight.

She dressed and then tried to solve the problem of how to carry the water pot. She could not hug it and walk or the water spilled out. She had to carry it on her head. She could hardly lift the pot up so high but when she did the rounded surface of the pot hurt her scalp. She undressed again and took off the blouse she was wearing, dressed again and then made a pad out of the blouse. After a few attempts she solved the problem and had a padded roll which she put on her head. Onto this she set the pot and began her climb up the hill, back toward her new home. As she did so she could see in her mind's eye the figure of Liela and her mother walking down the staircase of the stepwell in the Bahadur compound. She could see Liela climbing the steps to the top of the huge house where she had first stayed before she had fought against Sher Khan, had tried to escape by using his cell phone. Liela had walked straight as a stick, balancing the pot on her head. Her neck muscles rippled and the muscles on her legs moved under the skin like snakes.

She had never carried a pot before and in order to do so she had to put both hands up against its belly to hold it in place as she walked. In a few minutes her arms ached and she stopped to rest. It took her more than thirty minutes to walk up the little trail, stopping to rest. She was drenching wet when she arrived. The water splashed out of the top of the pot when she overbalanced or moved too quickly. The pot was three quarters full by the time she reached the house. The old woman looked at her and began to laugh, her toothless gums startlingly pink. She walked to a small bush, plucked a few leaves and threw them onto the surface of the water, stooped and picked up the pot, balanced it on her head and walked into the hut, still laughing.

Tea, hot sweet tea was waiting. Maria had seldom drunk anything so wonderfully satisfying. She sipped the liquid and realized that it had been carried all the way from the small seep-well. The old woman pointed to a pan covered with a wet rag. Maria shook her head, not knowing what to do. The woman shook her head, mumbling, made a small ball of the dough, put it on a rock and with a small rolling pin made of a single piece of smooth wood, rolled rounded bread which she scooped up and plopped onto a hot griddle on the fire. She pointed again. Maria's first bread was strangely shaped and too thick. After it was cooked, the old woman handed it to her, talking all the while. Maria made ten round flat breads and each one was an improvement over the last. The old woman chatted and stirred some kind of stew as the breads were made. The smell of the unleavened bread and the stew was inviting. Maria salivated in anticipation.

A new smell came to Maria now, one she had largely ignored, thinking it was the odor of the room, but as she came close to the old woman to receive her plate of stew, the smell was strong. It was an animal smell, somewhat ammoniac, a heavy odor of soiled clothing, unwashed skin and wet hair. She took her food and backed off to sit at the edge of the room, wondering when the old woman had last bathed, if in fact she ever did. She looked at the hands of the old crone, at the long, cracked, dirty fingernails. She saw for the first time that on her left hand the woman had only three fingers. One was a stump from which a dark bone-like protrusion stuck out. Maria ate all five of the round breads and all of the stew on her plate and looked around for the pot in which apricots and raisins were stored. The old woman followed her gaze and pointed to a shelf. Maria got up and took a handful of dried fruit and offered it to the woman who shook her head. She got up and beaconed for Maria to follow her.

She hobbled up the hill to a small bush. Under the bush was a cleverly made trap made of saplings and flexible bark. The trap door was weighted with a stone. The trigger was a simple device with a rope tied to a stick tied to the bait. The bait was an apricot. In the trap a small animal, almost mouse-like moved around when she approached. Maria peered at the little animal and at first though it was a hamster, but then noted its little tail. It was an active little creature that jumped around in the trap. The woman had her knife with her and reached through the slats and pinned the animal down, pushing hard. Unable to breathe the animal died.

She took the animal in her hand and stroked its soft fur and smiled. She pointed to her mouth and laughed. Back at the house, the mouse was impaled on a small stick, its little body put into the fire where all the hair was burned off. Then it was gutted with a single motion, and cut up into small pieces. These were thrown into the pot with a handful of green leaves and put on the stove to cook. When the mixture began to sizzle, she sprinkled salt onto it, talking all the while, pointing as a teacher does when demonstrating a chemistry lesson. Finally the old woman handed an apricot to Maria and pointed up the hill toward the trap. Maria took the apricot and walked up the hill slowly. She thought of the thanksgiving dinner she had hosted in Lahore, the huge turkey and the ham, the cranberry sauce and pies. She thought of the vodka and tonic drink that she had carried in her hand as a constant companion during the evening's social events. She thought of Celia and her beautiful evening dress, and strangely she thought of Commander Pervez Shah sitting next to her on the steps, flirting, inviting her to make a trip to Murree. James. Dear James. Where are you now? Do you think of me too sometimes? Sorry James. Stupid. I was so damn stupid James. Pakistan. We bought a one way ticket to Pakistan and shipped all our furniture including the Lazy Boy and seventy four bottles of California wine. Stupid!

Maria bated the trap, hoping she had done it correctly. She placed the stone on the door as a weight and stepped back. Then she looked around the area and noticed that there were many holes in the ground. She circled the area and was surprised to see holes in the ground near most of the scrubby bushes. This was a colony of rodents of some kind that lived off of grass seeds and the small dried fruits on the numerous bushes. It did not appear that there was water for them to drink, and she could not imagine that they all traipsed down to the water hole for a drink.

As she approached the shack she could smell the stew cooking and strangely, she salivated. The old woman was waiting for her and motioned for her to follow. She struggled along a path leading to an area where a few scrub trees grew amidst bushes which looked to Maria like sage she had seen in America. She followed behind, amazed that the partially crippled old woman had been able to fend for herself without assistance. On reaching the area where small trees grew, the woman stretched a rope on the ground, and then went from bush to bush breaking off only the small branches that were dry. These she placed across the rope. She pointed at Maria to do the same, talking all the while and chewing on something with her gums.

Maria worked to gather material for their fire. The old woman sat and watched her, nodding her head with encouragement. One of the trees had a dry branch that was eight feet above the ground, too high to reach. Maria was able to climb up on another branch and put the weight of her feet on the dry branch and it came crashing down. The old woman clapped her hands. They tied their huge bundle of faggots together and the woman handed Maria a grass head pad and helped her hoist the load to her head. Maria walked down the path carrying her load, her belly sticking out in front of her.

Later she sat in the sun in front of the shack made from sticks plastered over with mud. She leaned back against a huge rock and considered her situation. She mused, I am alive; I have survived. I am now the servant of some type of ancient woman who may even be a hermit or even mentally deranged. I don't know where I am, where I am going. There are Americans in Afghanistan, soldiers and others who help the people. I am going to find a way to contact them so I can get out of here and go home. Home. La Jolla! James and I own a magnificent home with an ocean view now leased out to a couple of lawyers. Home. I will go home. The baby moved in her womb and she sighed. A baby, Sher Khan's baby. God. I have to get home so this child has a chance. I have to get to civilization of some sort so that the baby is born with medical assistance. The old woman could be no help to me. The old woman. How does she get her flour for her bread and the cooking oil in the bottle that is now almost finished? How does she get the salt she uses in her food? She can't travel. Someone must know about her and bring things to her. Yes. I will make contact with the outer world through those who come to help her.

She returned to the shack and looked at her small pile of possessions. The Pashmina shawl that had been wrapped around her waist was carefully folded. It lay on a thin mat on the floor. Her slipper-shoes, now almost worn out were next to the shawl. She looked down at her bare feet, then at her hands, scratched with thorns from the bushes. She looked at her dress, dirty, smelling of smoke and sweat. She had no comb. She had given that to Ankh as a gift. She lifted her hands to feel her hair and used her fingers to untangle the snarls. She looked into the pot of water and could see a blurry reflection of herself. She was shocked at what looked back at her, a poor, dirty, wild-looking Afghan peasant woman with grass and small sticks in her snarled hair.

☪

His office was lavishly decorated. Persian carpets covered the floor. Heavily upholstered locally made furniture with red and orange colored cushions surrounded the perimeter of the room. Low Kashmiri tables made of chinar wood were set in front of each couch. A desk, the only modern object in the room was Swedish made, stark in its simplicity. On it a goose-necked lamp with a green glass shade completed the scene. Sahib-ji sat on one of the couches and smoked a hookah. The sweet smell of dark cured tobacco mixed with *afyun* filled the room. It was his habit to mix a tiny amount of raw opium with his heavy dark tobacco.

"Did you take him to the hospital?"

"Yes. He was operated on. The doctor said that he was lucky. The bullet went through the front part of the lower stomach into the bladder and out his lower back just missing his left kidney. One inch to the right an artery would have been severed and he would be dead." His driver, a short and stocky man with dark beard stood in front of his boss, fidgeting with his car keys.

"Stop playing with your keys! Where were the three of you when Mohammed shot him?" asked Sahib-ji.

"We had stepped inside the door in the gate and were talking with the sweeper who had come to enquire about who was at the gate." For such a stocky man, his voice was high, almost womanlike.

"So I am sure the sweeper informed the home owner where Chamuck resided, that you three had entered the premises without permission, forcibly." He took a long drag on the pipe and the noise of bubbles was hollow in the pipe. "Why was Akela shot? Did he threaten the homeowner?" Sahib-ji reached for an almond.

"When Akela turned to face Mohammed he may have raised his weapon." His keys fell to the floor and he stooped to retrieve them.

"So, it has moved from threats to a blood war. The entire clan of that damned Pashto mullah will now get behind him. This is going to be messy if we approach the matter frontally with our lawyer and demand that the girl be turned over. Look, the girl can't stay in the house forever. She goes to school, to the market with other women in *purdah* and if we know her schedule then the simplest way will be for her to simply disappear one day. They will come howling here, perhaps with the police and all will be quiet and calm. She will never be heard from again. Arrange it. Have the new peon assigned to watching the house. He should be dressed with shabby clothing and appear to be like a beggar on the street. Report to me in five days." He blew smoke at his toes. "Sahib ji, it will be done. Akela asks for money for the doctor and the hospital. I will return there later."

Sahib-ji took out his fat billfold and counted off one thousand rupees and handed them to the driver. "Tell him not to spend it all in one place."

His cell phone rang and he looked at the number of the person trying to reach him. He replied. "Yes. Perhaps this is a wrong number. Hello. Sixty six. Yes."

He listened to the person talking and wrote notes on a pad of paper. "How many did you say? Of the Russian type? How many *kantas?* (Stingers) Where are they now? I see. Yes I am interested but I will find another dealer. Your prices are crazy. If you want ready cash you know how it will work. The materials will be brought to the warehouse in Peshawar at midnight. You will receive a receipt at the warehouse with my signature. The payment will be made in cash, American dollars, during a take-out luncheon in my store front across the street from Salatin's Restaurant the next day. The entire operation will be arranged as previously. The materials will be unpacked and carefully inspected by me to ensure that no damage occurred to them in the explosion." He paused while the other man spoke.

"I am no fool. I even know the registration number on each of the items. I was involved in the sale of these same items. My last offer is exactly half of what you have offered. American dollars, in cash, twenties and one hundred dollar bills." He drew smoke again and listened to the voice, smiling broadly at what he heard.

"I suggest you try to sell them yourself. My price holds. Not one rupee more. I am sure you have heard the old saying, "It is easy to buy if you have cash, but it is very difficult to sell if you need cash." He laughed. "Look I am tired, it has been a difficult day. Bargaining wearies me. Listen! I am going to disconnect in thirty seconds. Decide now."

He smoked again looking at his watch. "Good. I have your word, you have mine. To go against our promises makes us *dushman*. I will arrange the financing, you arrange the rest. Yes, sixty six again." He disconnected.

He tapped in a number and waited for a connection. "Kohlu? Yes, this is sixty six. Let me speak to Amin. I will wait." He settled back into his cushions expecting a long wait. "Yes. Amin I have the materials. I will fax the information to you in code. It should be available within two weeks. Top quality bathroom sinks, mostly made in Russia, two of high quality made in America. Yes, we will communicate in code as you requested. I have the letter you mailed me here." He disconnected.

The newspaper he was reading quoted American sources. "High value target, Zawahiri of the al Qaeda terrorist network along the border... Osama bin Laden. The Secretary of State was quoted as saying, 'The middle east is going to be a much safer place.' 25 million Iraqis are now *free* and there are no more rape rooms and torture chambers in Iraq." High value target! How he loved the words Americans made up for their enemies. It sounded like they were playing poker. He smiled as he thought of those designated as 'high value targets' in Iraq, the Ace of Spades, and the Jack of Diamonds. He laughed out loud and his peon glanced into the room to see if his master was all right.

He enjoyed reading about American opinions of the Middle East, and of Pakistan. He had read that in the CIA there was not one staff person who had a native fluency in Arabic. Those Level 5 proficient speakers of Pashto and Urdu in the Foreign Service staff could be counted on the fingers of one hand. Everywhere the Americans went they needed 'faithful' translators to make sure that their messages were understood and accurate. He had also read that among interpreters used by the Americans for Urdu,

Farsi, Arabic and Pashto, all were mother tongue native speakers who had degrees in America and the UK in English and Linguistics, in Anthropology, computer science and in Communications and were thoroughly bi-lingual and bi-cultural and all were faithful Muslims. These interpreters worked with their American counterparts in various parts of the world, even helping to translate sensitive information for the highest American officials. They were the ears that listened in on Arabic transmissions and interpreted these to their bosses. They were the mouths that whispered back.

☪

The Deputy Superintendent of Police phoned the Dawning newspaper office and requested to speak with reporter Ikbal. Ikbal came on the line, his high squeaky voice loud and strident.

"Ikbal speaking."

"Mr. Ikbal, this is Feroz Hakim. There is a matter that I think you would have interest in that I would like to report to you. Could you meet me in my office at 2:00 this afternoon?" He tried to keep his voice even and authoritative.

"Is this in regard to the article recently written about Mrs. Marie Bernard, Mr. Hakim?"

"Oh, no, no. Not at all: it has to do with your good self, sir. I think you will find it most interesting."

"So mysterious. Well, I will bring along a tape recorder. Is that suitable?"

"Tape recorder? Yes. That would be a most excellent idea and may be helpful to us both. So. Two o'clock is it?" He sounded cheerful.

"Yes. I will be there, all ears so to speak." He laughed, because his own were large and protruding.

Feroz Hakim took out his personal check book and wrote a check for the full amount of school fees, uniforms and books for the Girls High School. On the bottom of the check he wrote 'Mistiri: Jasmin scholarship.' He put it in an envelope with a covering note to the effect that a scholarship fund had been established for the girl and that he requested a receipt for his own records. The return address was his parent's home in Gulberg II. Once again he looked at the girl's picture and was struck by the slight look of apprehension or fear in her eyes though she was smiling. Her mouth was smiling but she looked like she was ready to flee. He set the envelope on his desk and sat thinking.

"Call Mistiri." He shouted to the peon outside his door.

"Ji, Sahib." The lad ran off to find the carpenter.

Twenty minutes later the carpenter came, dripping sweat. He parked his bicycle against a tree and knocked at Feroz Hakim's office door.

"Come in, Mistiri. It looks like you were running a race. What happened?"

He stood uneasily, getting his breath. "I went to the bazaar to purchase hinges for the windows in the store room, sir. Your peon found me in the bazaar."

"I have been thinking about your daughter Jasmin's education again. I have written out a check for her schooling, here." He pointed to the envelope. "Since I am going to make a significant investment in your daughter's education, I think it is best that I interview her personally before I send the money. It would be a wise thing for me to do to know that she is a worthy candidate for the scholarship money. I would like you to bring her to my home in two days, suitably and decently dressed. My wife will be present to ensure propriety. Ask her to bring one of her English books. I would like to hear her read aloud. I will ask her a few simple questions to see how she responds. Does this sound like a suitable plan?" He did not smile.

"Yes sir. Very suitable. She will be very frightened, sir. I hope she will be able to answer your questions." He wiped a drop of sweat from his nose.

"I understand that you have converted to Islam. Am I correct?" He stared at the carpenter intently.

"We are meeting with the local mullah tomorrow at our local mosque and he will hear our words and give us instructions about what more we should do." He looked at his feet as if they were new to him.

"He will probably write your name down and that of your daughter. Good, I will see you both in two days directly after the last call to prayer." Now he smiled.

Mistiri pedaled his cycle away toward his home. His lips were forming words that only he could hear as he made his way through the busy, crowded bazaar toward his home.

A car pulled up in the lot outside the office of Feroz Hakim. Feroz strolled to the door and greeted the newspaper reporter at the door and extended his hand to shake that of the reporter. He looked at the hand, raised his eyebrows, and shook the extended hand briefly.

"Have a seat. Have a seat." He strolled casually to the door and closed it and stood in front of the man and looked at his face, studied his large protruding ears and wondered if he always looked so ugly. "I have asked you to come here privately. If you wish you may use your tape recorder for the questions I am going to ask you. It may be helpful to us both later on." He smiled.

Ikbal took out the small pocket recorder, placed it on the desk in front of him and pushed a button. "Yes?"

"Have you ever known a girl by the name of Piari?"

Ikbal recoiled as if he had confronted a cobra. "What a strange question to ask me. I have known many girls by the name of Piari, in fact there are two in my daughter's school." His half bald head began to perspire.

"Did your family ever own an old Humber Sedan in mint condition?"

"I do not understand the meaning of the question. How can I remember what cars my family owned? Humber?" He looked worried and was becoming defensive.

"Are you aware that there are records that show ownership of vehicles, all the owners of them since the time they were new and that a vehicle that was destroyed in the bomb blast in Bahadur was a vehicle that was once owned by your family many years ago?"

Ikbal stood up, his feet wide apart. "Whatever you are getting at say it!"

"I have simply asked a few questions and these have been recorded by your little machine. As a policeman it is my duty to solve mysteries and a few mysteries are now emerging about you and your life. One final question. How much did Sher Khan pay for the Humber sedan that he used for nine or ten years before his death?"

Ikbal reached over and shut off the machine and put it in his pocket. "What do you want? What are you hoping to achieve?"

"Justice before the law. Justice is patient, it is not hurried. The truth will out, Mr. Ikbal Sufi. You print what you call the truth in your newspaper and feel you have the great power of the press right at your fingers tips as you hold the pen which is more powerful than the sword. People quake when they see their names in the paper. People are also ruined by innuendo, half truths, snide questions that open cans of worms."

"How much?"

☾⋆

Mistiri parked his bike inside the front room of his house so it would not be stolen. This room served as a meeting place, storage place, eating place and an entrance way. There were two small rooms leading from this entry room, two bedrooms about the width of two beds. Out in back there was a kitchen area covered with a corrugated tin roof and the latrine. His wife was in back preparing food when he arrived. Jasmin, still in her old school uniform from the year before carefully peeled long white radishes. They both looked up as Mistiri joined them.

"The policeman is going to pay all your expenses, everything including clothing, books and tuition, even a small weekly spending allowance for sweets or pencils. He has requested that Jasmin and I meet at his house in two days. He is going to interview her, listen to her read English and ask her a few questions. He wants you to choose a passage from your English book to read to him. You are to dress suitably with a head scarf, like the woman newscaster on Pakistan television. His wife will be present. Tomorrow you and I, Jasmin, will go to the mosque and say the words to become Muslim." He talked quickly without stopping. Now he looked at the two women who looked at him as if the news he had brought was of some great earthquake or some terrible disaster. Jasmin glanced up at her father, her face in panic. She dropped the peeling knife and hurried from the room.

"You will become a Muslim? Why? How can a Hindu become a Muslim? I don't understand."

"It is just words. Like words of *puja* that the priest says in the temple. Words. The words are in Arabic. I do not understand them but it is like magic. If I say them then I will be as one of them. If I do not, I may lose my job, perhaps more. I lied to the Superintendent that I had already become a Muslim through the conversion of my father. You would not understand. It is complicated. I have to say the words. Listen I can say them now and nothing happens. He began the chant that stated that there was only one God and that Mohammed was his Prophet. He completed the words in Arabic and his wife looked at him curiously.

"So, have I changed? Has anything happened?" He turned around so she could see the back of his head.

She shook her head. "What else must you do?"

"I must learn to pray in the mosque and even at home, five times a day. I have watched them do this. I know how to kneel and hold my hands up to the sky and make my lips move. Yes, I must do it. Jasmin will go to high school. I will get a raise of three hundred rupees a month and keep my job."

"What about me? Jasmin? She will have to say the words. Will you teach them to her tonight?"

"I think that if the man in the house is Muslim, then he makes all his household Muslim as well. If you say the words and I hear you say them with another Muslim present then you will be like me, a Muslim convert. All the persons living in the home of a Muslim must convert to Islam."

"You will have to have it cut off! Sliced off like cutting the tail of a chicken." She looked appalled.

"No, I will not do that. I think that is only for children, for small boys. I will not do it. I will not have it cut off. I have heard that when some adult men get it cut off that they..." He looked uncertain.

His wife began to chuckle. "Ramadan. What about Ramadan and fasting? We have never fasted. Will we all have to fast, not drink water during the day, not eat, not make....?" She spoke quickly as if the speed of her words would erase her questions.

"Yes. Our neighbors will see. Yes we will fast." Now he looked very uncertain.

"So, you will be saving your money and going on the Hajj to Mecca too?" She smiled at the thought of walking around a large stone.

"I must try to do it in my life-time, but remember I am just saying the words, not ...."

"We are poor. You will be asked to perform *zakat* and give money to the poor. We are poor."

"That is no problem. There are poor all around us. Most of our neighbors are not Muslims, they are just poor farmers and laborers and carriers of dung and those who deal with smelly animal skins. We will give something to them."

He walked into the house to find Jasmin. She sat in the front room on a pile of jute sacks, hunched over with her head in her hands. She looked up at her father and shook her head. "I heard what you said. I am afraid of going to the mosque. I am afraid of standing in front of the Superintendent of Police and talking, reading English. It is my worst subject. I am afraid of going to secondary school and living away from home with strangers."

"Would you be afraid of becoming the wife of a man who already has had other women, of living in a home where you will be like a slave? Are you afraid of my finding a complete stranger for you to marry, perhaps a young farmer you have never seen? Are you afraid of bearing a child each year, every year for your husband, serving him in the house, the field and in his bed, day after day? Look at me. If you can truly go to secondary school and do well, you could become a teacher, a nurse, even a secretary in some institution. You will not be married for another three years at least and you will know more about the world." He did not plead; he simply set out what he knew to be the truth. "I have to say the words of *shahadah* to become a Muslim. I have no choice. If I don't I may not have a job, you will not get supported to go to school. Our family will starve."

Jasmin looked at her father. "They will make me take a new name, a Muslim name. What name should I take?"

"I think you should be called Jamilah and I will be called ..." he thought for a moment. "I will be called Ahmed the Mistiri. Ahmed. Ahmed."

"Tell me again the words of the *shahadah* that I will speak." Her lips were pinched together in concentration.

"I will tell you later. You already know the words. Bring your English book and read to me from it."

She went to one of the bedrooms and pulled a small box from under the table. She took out a small book and brought it to her father and handed it to him. "What does the book say?"

"English Reader Number Three. She opened the book to the second page and began to read. "Jack Sprat could eat no fat, his wife could eat no lean..."

"Translate for me. What is Jack Sprat?"

"I think it is the name of a man, like Mohammed Ali. I do not know the meaning." She read the poem again.

"Then?" he asked.

"It says that his man, like Mohamed Ali could not eat fat, *churbi*. I do not know why he couldn't eat fat, perhaps he had bad teeth, and perhaps he was forbidden to eat it because of his religion, like a Hindu." She shrugged.

"His wife, we do not know her name. She had a different problem. It says she could eat no lean. I have looked in the dictionary for the word, lean. It says that it means tipping, like a leaning wall. So how could his wife eat no lean? That is a great mystery. My grades in English are not good. I do not understand what is written. I try, but it is not a clear language."

"Then what does this man and his wife do, the one with no fat in his mouth, the other with a leaning wall?"

"They lick the platter clean. That is a real mystery. It does not say the platter was dirty, yet they both used their tongues to lick it, to clean away the dirt with their tongues like dogs lick a dirty tin can. It is a very strange saying and it does not make sense to me." She was going to close the book.

"No. It is a very good saying. Say it out loud fast and I will listen to it again."

She repeated the poem.

"Yes. It is not the meaning of the words; it is the way it sounds like a *bhajan,* a song that repeats the sounds. Read this Jack Sprat to the Deputy Superintendent. I think that this is something he will understand."

☪

Chamuck had been told to stay in her room ever since the shooting in the front courtyard. When her uncle was not around she moved about the house and helped in the kitchen. When he returned in the evening he sat at the table and was glum, agitated and did not talk. He ordered tea and drank two cups before he spoke.

"I shot the man in the stomach. Sahib-ji will take revenge. I am going to carry my rifle with me now. They came to take you away, by force. If I had not come when I did you would now be his sex slave. I wish it was Sahib-ji that came to the gate. He would be dead now. He is Shaitan."

Chamuck and her mother moved about the room, putting things in their place, bringing tea and stopping from time to time to listen to the old uncle. When her name was mentioned she looked up, and then sat down on a chair facing her uncle.

"Uncle may I speak?" She had waited until he was sipping tea.

"Good. You are learning. Yes. What do you have to say?" He looked at her over the rim of his tea cup.

"I am going to say something that may not please you, but I beg you to listen. I have been the one who has brought the attention of the arms dealer Sahib-ji to our home. My father who is dead thought he would not die, he had done many arms deals, so he did not dream that by signing the paper that he would die and that I would become Sahib-ji's woman. I know this because of what he said to me many times. He said if you do well in school, if you are at the top of your class then our family can get a good man for you to marry, one from a good family with wealth, one who has an education. He was a brave man and feared nothing. He was sure he would live and do business as usual. No one thinks they will die. His contract was a way for him to make money." She paused and cleared her throat.

"You are saying many words. So far you have said nothing new. Your father and I disagree about the need for a woman to be schooled. When they do, they talk too much, they create trouble in the home with too many ideas and they attract the attention of men. In the long history of our tribe our custom has been to have women who remain behind the walls of a man's house, secure and away from the eyes of other men. Our system has worked for us, for my father, for his father. Why? Because Allah has placed women in our care. Men must watch out for them because of their instincts to..." He took out a cigarette.

"May I speak again?" She stood quietly and watched him smoke. He nodded impatiently.

"I have heard you speak of gold, three sets of gold necklaces, bracelets and rings for the bride. I have heard you speak of receiving cash from a prospective husband. Poor men from poor families, ones who have no influence do not have gold coins or heavy gold necklaces. I have seen pictures of weddings of educated rich people and they drape the bride with gold. Please, uncle. Let me finish my schooling. If I do very well, a very rich man may seek me out and drape me with heavy gold and pay heavily for me. It is not long to wait three years. I am now your ward. I respect your care for me. Please let me go to a school where all the girls are behind walls, carefully cared for while they get an education. Please, I beg you." She got on her knees and crawled toward her uncle.

He got up and began to walk around the room. "Get up. All right. Finish your exams and then I will consider what you say. Finish your exams and I will see the marks you receive and then make my decision. I will have my driver take you in my car every day to the school. You will not walk with

the other girls in groups on the streets. You will not go out shopping with
the other women of the house. Do you understand why?" He glared at her.
"It is not my intention to honor the marriage paper your father signed. It
could well have been written under threat. Already Sahib-ji has tried to take
you away, abduct you when I was not present. He has violated this home.
Our honor dictates that I protect the women of this household. He expects
to have you without paying one paisa, no gold, no dowry for you, nothing.
Never! The man is a demon and he should die. He brings nothing but
misery to everyone. He will now stalk you. Do you know why I am telling
you to never go out alone, never to be without a family member guarding
you? Do you know why? Our family and his are now in a feud. I shot his
representative. Blood for blood we say, life for life."

"Yes, uncle. I know why. It is not my wish to become the plaything for
the fat-toad farting arms dealer Sahib-ji. I would die before I let that devil
touch me." Again she sank to the ground to place her head at his feet.
"Thank you. Thank you."

He stepped back, picked up his gun and before he left the house he
turned in the doorway and said, "Why would you want to die if he tries to
touch you? Why? Think the other way. Why let him live? Men think differently. Women are weak. 'I would die before...'", now he spoke derisively,
mocking her. "Why not kill to protect your own honor instead of groveling
and wishing for your own death. Weak! Women are weak!"

After he left Chamuck sat on the floor, shaking, breathing as if she had
run a race. Her mother looked at her and shook her head. "If I had spoken
such words to your father he would have beaten me. You have a chance
now. Try hard. I do not read. You read. Perhaps your children will teach
others to read. What will happen to me? "

Chamuck climbed down the long staircase to her room, turned up the
kerosene lamp, picked up her book and worked at memorizing the passage,
repeating over and over the strange English words;

As she is mine, I may dispose of her:
Which shall be either to this gentleman
Or to her death, according to our law

"Weak. Women are weak." Her uncle's words rang in her head. She now changed the words of the poem, muttering to herself;

As I am mine, I may dispose of him:
Which means I shall not be for this gentleman
Or to my death, but his, according to our law.

CHAPTER FOUR

Jo hona ho so ho! (Urdu saying)

What ever is to happen let it happen.

The two donkeys were related. The smaller was the daughter of the older bony one. Both were loaded with side packs and as they walked down the mountain paths, their loads swayed from side to side. As they moved, their tails swung like small pendulums. Behind them were two men and they too were related. The taller, Atiqullah, was crippled in his left club foot, but in spite of his disability he could walk at a good pace. He carried an ancient 303 rifle over his shoulder. His companion and brother, Jalaluddin, was stockier. His face was deeply pockmarked and scarred by boils. His hair was grey and sparse, his eyes bloodshot from using too much opium and hashish.

"Spogmay may be dead. We delayed our coming for two weeks because of the Americans coming nearby to bomb the Pakistani village. She is such a stubborn old one. When my elder brother married her she was beautiful and pleasant. Her eyes flashed white when she laughed, so my brother called her moon, Spogmay. I don't think she has laughed for ten years. Since Habibullah died five years ago she refused to move. That place was never meant to be a year-round house. He only stayed there to care for his goats during the rains." Atiqullah turned and looked at his elder brother to see if he was listening.

"We can't force her to return. She would die of loneliness for the place. I don't know why she doesn't die of loneliness without anyone around for months at a time. I will sleep outside. I can sleep in the horse stall, but not with her. I wonder if she bathed this year?" Jalaluddin spat on the road. He reached over and held to the tail of the donkey in front of him, letting her help him make the upward grade of the path easier for him. The little donkey strained upward with her load and the additional burden of her tail being held.

"Well, we can drop off the food tonight and leave in the morning. There is nothing to do there. At least my woman has provided me with four fat oven breads."

They moved along the trail at a regular pace, commenting on the life of Moon, the senile old wife of their dead brother. They stopped for a short meal but did not remove the loads from the donkeys. The sun was warm and they sat with their backs to large warm rocks and smoked, looking out across miles of terrain, one range of hills after another that appeared to have no life. High above them a jet plane left a white contrail and they looked up at it hardly seeing the speck that was the plane.

"There are three hundred people up there in that tiny shiny spot. That is the PIA plane to London. It goes so high that the plane shrinks smaller than a grain of sand. I think if it went higher it would shrink away completely." Atiqullah had never been able to understand how a plane could fly, much less how it shrunk when it went far up in the sky.

"I heard that on the PIA airplanes there are beautiful women that serve tea and sweet breads and they walk with their faces exposed. Their uniforms reveal the shape of their bodies and their voices are sweet like honey. These women come from across the ocean from Pililpeens and Jakarta. They sometimes stop the plane in Kabul and the women get off and stay in a hotel near the airport. I have heard that they are the harem of the captains that fly the airplane and stay with them in the hotels. Thus, they can all travel constantly and never lack for companionship." Jalaluddin was smiling, pretending he was a captain.

"I have heard that the infidel women are all whores, like all the women in the American military. There are some of them right here in Afghanistan. They wear army uniforms during the day and drive jeeps and even carry weapons but at night sleep in special tents so that the soldiers can go in and plow their tilths. It is true. A friend of mine saw American women in uniforms and two of them had nice faces and one was round and very..."

"You have been away from your wives for two days and all you can talk about is women. The Taliban are right. Cover them up from head to

toe, keep them busy and pregnant at home. Don't let them go to school
so they get ideas like flying in airplanes and becoming soldiers and serving the needs of all the men who stare at them. They are weak. If given a
small chance they will quickly sneak off with any man. The Taliban way
would purify our country." The elder had a faraway look in his eyes as he
imagined the airline stewardesses sleeping with the captains.

"The American infidels have no honor. If they let their women sleep
with many men how can they know who the father of the children is? They
are like cats. Six kittens, six fathers. Animals." Atiqullah was smiling
broadly. He liked to talk of women. Because of his club foot deformity, his
uncle had forbidden his marriage with his cousin. Other women heard of
it and they too refused his advances, fearful that their children would be
born deformed, touched with impurity.

In the distance they saw the white haze of smoke, though the crude
dwelling was still hidden behind a small hill. They increased their pace,
making clucking noises at the donkeys which did not increase their pace
but moved their ears backward and listened to the men who encouraged
them to greater effort.

It was Maria's custom to climb on to a portion of the flat roof and
spread her Pashmina robe and lay in the sun, taking off most of her clothes
as she sunbathed and napped for an hour in the late afternoon winter sun.
She spread her clothing in the sunlight, hoping for it to provide some degree
of freshness. She fell asleep.

The men came around the edge of the hill and moved into the courtyard
in front of the small shack. The donkeys brayed. Maria sat up stunned by
the noise. The two men looked in amazement at the sitting figure of a half
naked woman on the flat roof of the shack. They stood transfixed their
mouths open. Maria ducked down and drew on her clothing and wrapped
her shawl around her head and stood up looking away from the two men
as she climbed down from the roof.

They did not move. They stood and waited for her to get down and
pass by them, staring at her as if she was unreal. She kept her face averted
and moved into the shack. Now the men heard the voice of the old woman,
Spogmay, talking loudly, telling Maria that donkeys were bringing her
tea, spices, rice and flour. That she would have cooking oil and sugar and
could make sweets. She stood in the doorway and did not bother to cover

her head or shoulders, but hobbled outside yelling at the two men, smiling broadly, her toothless gums pink and smooth.

"Who is the angel that is visiting you? The one who sits naked on the roof?" Atiqullah talked over the back of the donkey that he was unloading.

"She is not an angel. She appeared out of nowhere. She does not speak our Pashto language, but I have taught her to do my work. She eats too much because she is making a baby. Perhaps she is an infidel from Pakistan." She reached for a package being taken from the donkey.

"I have seldom seen such breasts..." He paused and inflated his cheeks. "She looked like an angel on the roof. I want to look at her again to see if my eyes were playing tricks on me." Atiqullah lifted a sack of ground wheat from the back of the donkey, threw it over his shoulder and moved toward the door of the shack. He kicked it open with his foot and stooped to enter, waited until his eyes adjusted to the near darkness and then set the sack down near the stove and turned to look at Maria standing with her back to him.

"Turn around," he ordered.

She continued to stand, facing away from him. Maria was excited to see other people, men, but she was also afraid, not knowing what such men would do or what would happen to her.

Atiqullah strode across the small room and turned Maria around with his hands on her shoulders. She stared up at him, at his sharp eyes set next to a large hawk-like nose. His skin was deep bronze and he smelled of tobacco, donkey urine and campfire smoke.

"Where are you from?" he asked She shook her head. He pointed at her. "Ameerika?"

Maria nodded yes and said, "American from Pakistan."

He turned and shouted to his elder brother. "She is an American from Pakistan!" He laughed now, as if the idea of an American woman from Pakistan who sat naked on a roof like an angel was a huge joke. He walked outside for another load of goods, laughing all the while.

Maria listened to the three of them talking animatedly, laughing and seeming to make jokes. Then the second, older, shorter man entered and only glanced in her direction, put down his load and left the room without a backward look. She decided that the sack of flour was the best place to sit and wait to see what would happen. She sat and watched as the men came in and stacked the goods. When they were finished they stood outside and smoked, uncomfortable with the presence of a woman in the shack.

Moon said, "She is my guest and has the protection of my house. She works for me and helps me. Both of you will have to sleep outside this night. I will bring food for you later. Did you bring dried onions? Did you bring me a dozen of boiled eggs? I long for an egg. Did you bring me dried slabs of my goat meat? I have not eaten anything but the rodents from the hills for months. My apricots are almost finished."

"I told you to raise chickens here. Where do you think the money comes from to buy you all this food? The next thing you will want is for the delivery of fresh milk." Atiqullah laughed.

"Chickens eat as much grain as I do. How would they survive here on a few bugs a day. The Jackals and mongooses would take them. You know where the money comes from. My husband had over one hundred goats before he died. Where are they all now? In your compounds. Have they had babies? Have you sold any of them? How many have you eaten this year that you did not pay for? You know where the money comes from. Before Allah, the Just, the Merciful, the All Knowing, I hope you brought me a dozen boiled eggs."

"I brought the eggs. Look, you should come back with us. You can ride on the donkey all the way. You are old and may soon die. How would we know if you died? We would have to make a useless trip bringing goods here and you would be dead." Atiqullah shook his head and then spat on the ground as he got a whiff of the old woman.

She laughed loudly and replied, "You brought it up. You were the one to speak of death. You know the old saying; he who warns of the death of another speaks of his own death, drawing his own eternity closer to himself. I will outlive you. I may be old and toothless but still catching rats to eat when your body is nothing but bones. You brought it up."

Maria left the shelter of the shack and walked up the small path to her toilet area behind huge rocks. The men looked at her walk and knew where she was going, having used the same rocky area in the past. They glanced at each other.

"An American Pakistani woman is going to pass water. That is amazing. An angel that passes water behind rocks like other women. I wonder where she is going to and why she chose this deserted place? Perhaps she walked here from Pakistan." Now he looked at his elder brother with an idea written on his face. "Perhaps she was one who escaped the bombing at the Pakistani border. Yes! That must be it. Perhaps if we let the Americans know we have one of their women we will get much money." He smiled at the thought.

"Perhaps you are not thinking. Why would Americans with all the guns and rockets and airplanes need to pay two helpless men anything? Perhaps they will question her and we would be considered guilty of something, and then we would look at the ends of their guns. Perhaps it would be better to take this woman from here, take her back to the village and confer with the elders about what to do."

Jalaluddin looked at his brother and shook his head. "Allah. The Taliban are right. Cover them up. They are too much temptation for a mortal man to resist. I can see your thoughts now, brother. Before Allah, she is the guest of the wife of my elder brother and guest she will remain in our protection until she is brought before the elders of the village. Two senior Taliban are there and they will tell us the best solution for this American Pakistani woman who sits on the roof with clothes off in the sunlight with breasts like melons." Now he could see the vision in his own head and knew he would never forget it. Allah. Shaitan was pulling at him. There is only one way to... Cover them up.

Maria returned and both men watched her every move as if she was totally unaware of their stares. They were surprised when she tired of their staring and made a face at them, raising her eyebrows like a monkey. They looked at each other and laughed but continued to stare, undressing her with their eyes.

C*

Meher Jamal glanced over at the naked man lying in her bed. Aziz was still asleep, his mouth open, his right arm flung over the place she had just left. The sheet was thrown back revealing his lean body. She looked at it now as he slept unawares, studied the pattern of his body hairs, the matt of black on his chest, a river of black sliding down his abdomen into a dark bush. She had never looked at a naked man before. She sighed, a strange warm feeling suffused her, and a feeling she had never had in her life. In the darkness they had embraced and she had reveled in the feelings that his body gave her. Even now as she looked at him she shuddered. In the nearby minaret someone tested the loud speaker, blowing on it. Her primary duty came to mind.

The first call to prayer was being broadcast in the nearby mosque. Meher rose from the bed, went to the bathing area and washed herself ritually. She took her prayer mat and placed it to face toward Mecca and knelt and gave thanks, she submitted herself before Allah, placing herself in his will. She completed her prayers and shuffled across to Pagali's room but decided to let her sleep. She lay on her back, her pregnant abdomen rounded up under a single sheet, her lips in the eternal smile that played on them whether awake or asleep. She stared at Dohst's pregnant cousin Pagali and wondered if she would now also conceive, whether she would have a child to care for to call her own.

Meher made heavy flat breads, heavy with *ghee*, she set out mango pickle that she had made the week before and next to this two boiled eggs. A hot cup of spiced tea was steaming next to the food as Aziz walked into the sitting area, yawning and scratching himself. He glanced at the food, then at Meher Jamal and a tiny smile came to his lips which she understood all too well. She responded by being busy in the kitchen, cleaning the griddle, but she could feel his eyes looking at her, aware of what he was also thinking, what he had felt and heard her say in the darkness. She brought the tea pot over, an excuse to approach him as he sat eating his food.

"Will you go to the bazaar today?" she asked.

He nodded; his mouth full. He sipped tea and replied, "I am looking for a small storefront, not large, just big enough to spread different kinds of cigarettes and *bidis*. I thought it would be good to become a shopkeeper, to buy and sell. Many people smoke and if I can find a spot that is cheap in an area away from the main market then perhaps I will get the business of people passing by. When I was at my father's property, no, now my own property in Sukkur, I sold a few things from the old house, just a small table and some plates and got enough money to pay for my bus fare home and with enough left over for a month's rent." He stood up and smoothed his shirt, smiling. "Look at the new *dukandar*."

She smiled at him standing, pushing his belly out and tried to imagine him as a fat shopkeeper with silver rings on his fingers and a tin full of money. "I will have to feed you more. Shop keepers are fat. They sit all day and eat constantly." She was amazed to be speaking to a man like she would speak to her sister; talking about things that would happen, making jokes. She poured more tea in his cup, smiling at her thoughts.

Pagali stepped into the room and walked straight for Dohst, a smile on her face. He held out his hand to stop her approach. "You must help Meher Jamal today. There is much laundry. All my clothes from the trip need washing. Will you help her?"

Pagali smiled and held the outstretched arm with her two hands and nodded. He pulled away, now turned off by her easy and innocent intimacy in Meher's presence. "I will take my bike and may not be back until later in the day. Keep the door locked. Do not let any man inside, Meher, including your uncle if he shows up. Tell him any thing you want to, but put him off; tell him that you are bleeding, unclean or...anything."

The sun was shining but it hardly penetrated the smog. The city skies over Sialkot were grey with haze and the smoke of ten thousand fires, the smoke of motorcycles and a thousand garbage piles smoldering in the gutters. Thin dogs wandered the streets checking out the piles of garbage for anything edible. Crows hopped about competing with myna birds for scraps, beetles and maggots in decaying matter. The street on which Dohst cycled was crowded with pedestrians, lorries and hundreds of bicycles jostling for position. The noise level was high, horns beeping, people shouting, loudspeakers blaring, but he hardly noticed. Shop keepers had opened the metal shutters of their stores and were arranging their goods for sale, putting old merchandise on top, turning the bruises on mangoes to the back, stacking oranges in pyramids that defied gravity, hanging posters from Bollywood movies which revealed large breasted beauties lying on a lawn in front of roses the color of their lips; each shop setting up business for the day just like it had been the day before. The people moved about busily, but it seemed just moving about doing nothing, pushing, shoving, and yelling at each other. Few women were to be seen except for a group of four, draped from head to toe who were standing in a chemist shop purchasing Valium and other non-prescription drugs.

Dohst did not notice the garbage, he avoided hitting a bitch with huge pendulant dugs, he steered around piles of horse dung left by the *tonga wallah's* horses and yelled at pedestrians to make way, his bell ringing constantly. He did see unopened store fronts and he pulled over in front of one of these that looked like a possible site for a new business. Next to it on one side was a sweet seller whose glass boxes held sugared goods which were already buzzing with eager bees seeking a stolen treat, seeming to lick the sugar on the glass with tiny black tongues. On the other side was a merchant selling motor oil with three different colored tins for the various grades, 10W, 20W and 30W motor oil. The green and white cans had the label Kwakor's Motor Oil. The others were labeled Superior T2 Motor Oil. To his surprise, while he stood looking at the store with closed shutters, three buses pulled over and shouted out asking what the price of the oil was. Their drivers bought many tins of the T2 oil which was marked for special sale. Only today. Buy Now!

He strolled to the front of the oil sellers shop. "*Salaam Aliakum jenab.* Do you know who owns this closed store?"

"No, it has been closed for at least two months. I think the owner has died. I thought I heard a cat in there for a week but then it was quiet. Now it smells bad. I think it has also died." He stacked the cans neatly and adjusted the sales sign which was tilting to one side. It was a picture of a film star standing next to her car, a tin of oil in her hand.

"I was thinking of starting up a tobacco business and I am looking for a cheap place to rent. I thought this would be a good location." He offered the proprietor a cigarette.

"So, you must have some money if you think of renting and starting up a new business all on your own. Did your father leave you a lot of money?" He blew a neat smoke ring. His feather duster stroked the tops of the stacked cans that did not look dusty.

"Not really. But yes, some. I have inherited property in Sukkur but really want to do some kind of business in Sialkot or Lahore."

"You are looking at it! Oil. Motor oil is the hot thing now and the market is just opening up for those who have a little to invest in stock." He picked up a quart tin of T2 and showed it to Dohst. "See this? Well, I am selling it for one third less than the one in the green can. Look, here is an opened can. See the color, just the same, feel it between your fingers, even slicker. One third less and they are buying it as if it was soon to be discontinued. T2 is where you should put your money." He swatted flies with a fly swatter made from the tail of a buffalo with his left hand, deftly flicking a fly that landed on his big toe.

"Why is it cheaper?" Dohst asked.

"Because it is made secretly in Iran and now even in this country. It is big business, friend. I was told that fifty tons of the oil has been imported from Iran and that they are looking for men like me, retailers, to promote the oil. The manufacturer is kept absolutely secret. I make cell phone calls to a certain number in Lahore, and after dark an unmarked truck pulls up and unloads a dozen boxes of oil cans of T2 and I pay the driver in cash. I do not know his name. Each day when I call the cell phone number I hear a recording, a woman with a silken voice who tells me that the number I am calling is in error. Then she says to leave a message after the beep as well as my own number. Then I get a call, order my oil, pay them cash or by a check I mail them. Then I mark up the price of the oil by ten percent on what I pay. Oil! It is gold."

"But why is it cheaper than the other regular oil we have used?" Dohst frowned.

"There is a secret ingredient. I can not say for sure, but do you know that car tires are made from petroleum, oil? Well, they can unmake them as well, extract the oil from them, from the tons and tons of discarded thrown away tires and make this beautiful oil at a fraction of the cost. I am not sure of this but that is the story that is going around. We Pakistanis are a clever people at making a profit. You look like a clever man." He laughed and sold a box of oil to a bus driver, then watched as the vehicle drove away emitting clouds of dark smelly smoke.

"So you are encouraging me to rent this shop here that has a dead cat in it and call a secret number and start selling T2 Oil right next door to you?"

"Are yarh, no, I am saying that I need a partner. A partner who can share my costs equally so the business can be expanded and who can then share half of the profits, that is if my partner comes up with half the money I have put into this business. Not only that, I will not have to sit here twelve hours a day. I will be able to go home at noon and not return until four in the afternoon. I will cool off in my house and eat spicy food and let my wife serve me sweets in bed." He laughed and slapped his knee. "Now when I return I am so tired that she complains of being lonely and that I no longer desire her and that she sits around waiting for me to come home and all I do is eat and then sleep." He looked up at Dohst who was waiting for the next sentence. "Then I wish I had a partner."

"What about the room next door?" asked Dohst.

"What about a huge stock-pile of oil. What about finding out who it is that is selling it to Pakistan from Iran and buying direct and cutting out the middle man. What about getting rich?" He leaned toward Dohst conspiratorially and lowered his voice. "I can see a business man immediately. You are one. I saw it when you got off your bike, the way you coolly looked at the empty storefront. But you will have to get better clothes, look rich, prosperous, and you will have to get a cell phone."

"Look, this is very foreign to me. I am not sure about this. I will enquire about who owns this vacant shop and then I will return to you, perhaps the day after tomorrow."

Dohst was uneasy because the oil shop keeper smiled too much and he remembered the mullah's words; that smiles were put on the sinners faces by *Shaitan*.

"My friend, I have not told the whole story. Listen, a few government officials who control the production and sale of motor oil support T2 oil sales. Every month I have to make a special money order payment for permission to continue my business, by the very government agency that controls oil imports and sales. They take one percent of my profits. That is a small price to pay. Not pleasant, but it buys my success. Look, think it over and come back tomorrow. I have someone I would like you to meet. Eleven o'clock, here. You will be happy if you come, *yarh*."

Dohst talked to the sweet seller and found the name of the owner of the vacant store. He looked it up in the telephone directory and was surprised to find the name. He made the call at a pay phone at the post office. A woman answered and he asked for the man of the house. She said that he had died, but his brother was there and would talk. He found out that the small shop had sold Peacock window air conditioners, made in China, and yes the brother was willing to meet him at ten the next day and show the shop with a view to renting it out.

Dohst stopped at a tailor's shop where there were a number of ready-made suits of various sizes hanging on hangers. He tried on three before he found one that fit him. He looked at himself in the mirror, at his strange head, wild hair sticking out above the business suit and decided that he would also see a barber on the way home. He bought the suit after three cups of tea and two *samosas* and endless bargaining and got it for half the original price quoted. He stood with the new suit of clothes on and decided not to take them off and had his old clothing wrapped up.

When he stepped into the house, having been shaved and with a hair-cut, Meher Jamal did not recognize him for a moment. She stood with her head extended on her neck like a turtle as if to get a closer look.

"What happened? You look so different that I hardly recognized you." She smiled broadly revealing her pleasure.

"It is because of business. I may not sell tobacco but am thinking of going into the oil business, selling T2 oil. I have to meet a man about renting a storefront tomorrow in the morning and then another man an hour later about going into business with him." Dohst was pleased at Meher's reaction to his appearance. He was unconsciously pleased that he could tell her about his work and that even though she was a woman they could talk together, almost like he used to talk with his friend Ali in Lahore.

"What does going into business mean? I don't understand." She was already preparing tea and set a small plate of carrot *halva* on the table that she had made that morning.

"It is simple. I take all of rest of the money I got from the sale of my father's car and pay the man who sells oil. He then says that I am his partner and gives me a share of the profit from all the sales." He ate a mouthful of the sweet oily carrot confection.

"So you get nothing when you give him the money? He doesn't give you half of the oil that is to be sold? Nothing?"

He sipped his tea and thought for a moment. "No. I do not get oil but he will write on a paper how much I gave him and give that to me."

"Is he a blood relative of yours? Can you trust him? What if he takes your money and tomorrow says he doesn't know you?" She poured more tea.

"I have the paper with his signature on it." He sounded assured and sophisticated.

"I am sorry, but what if he wrote a false name on the paper and signed it in a way which was not really how he wrote. Then he could say that you made up the paper and that he doesn't even know you and keep all your money."

He got up, getting impatient, but also looked worried. He walked around the room and then sat down again and looked at Meher Jamal. "You are right. He seems like a very nice man. He seems to sell a lot of oil. He is friendly and nice looking but he smiles a lot. He is not a relative. Let me think."

He got up and went to the back room where he kept his metal box and opened the lid and took out the folder that contained all his money. He removed the money and counted it onto the cot, putting it into piles of one thousand rupees. He made fifteen piles and set the rest of the money aside for possible rental of a storefront. He looked at the money, more cash than he had ever had before and in his mind it represented a fortune of savings, clean cash savings. He wrapped piles of one thousand with a string and replaced these in the tin box. He returned to the sitting room. Meher was waiting.

"Yes, he could do that. Lie and keep all my money, but then I would kill him. He must know that I would kill him if he betrays me." He stood with his legs apart, thinking on his feet.

"If he fears you he may not go into business with you. Is there no other way?" Meher had gesticulated with her arms and the flipper arm under her scarf moved up strangely, like a hidden ghost. Dohst had forgotten for the moment that she had a deformed arm and he frowned. Meher picked up the expression and sat down and turned partly away from him, moving her deformity out of his sight.

"I am trying to think of another way. Can you think of another way?" He stared at her.

"Does he have a car? Does he have a driver's license? Do you have a driver's license? My uncle's license has his picture on it. That may be a way." Meher was upset with herself for having reminded him of her deformity. It has sidetracked their conversation terribly.

"I see. Yes. I could see if the name and the signature on the paper are the same on the license which has his picture. That is a good idea." He nodded, pleased at his insight.

"How many tins of oil did the merchant have in his shop?"

Aziz was taken by surprise. "Of course I did not count them." He looked at the ceiling mentally counting and calculating. "Perhaps two hundred tins. Yes. Two hundred. Why?"

"If you go into business with him will your money buy half of the tins so you own half of them?" Now she was mentally trying to calculate the value, wondering about their worth.

"Tomorrow I will talk with him again. I will ask him many questions. I will count the tins and he will not know that I am doing it. I will know how much it costs to rent a similar storefront. Tomorrow I will not give him any money but I will find out about his driver's license and his family." He looked relieved.

"Why did you buy the suit today?" Meher smiled, looking at how nice Dohst looked.

"I bought it because he said that a business partner had to look nice and more prosperous. He said my clothing was not suitable to be a store keeper." He looked down at his new clothing and noted that there was already a tiny spot of grease from the bicycle chain guard on his lower trouser pants. He resolved to buy a metal trousers clip immediately. "I was thinking already that I was a shop owner so I bought the suit."

"You said that you paid my uncle two thousand rupees when you obtained a hidden marriage contract for me. Did he give you a paper with his signature on it?"

Dohst could see the contract and that it had only fifteen hundred rupees written on it and that he had not checked it carefully, but that he had believed the mullah. He sighed. "Yes, I have a paper with his name written on it and the signature of another man as well." He walked off into the back room stiffly.

Meher cleared the tea dishes and she too sighed, thinking of their conversation. The only other non-family person she had talked to in her life had been the Arabic teacher who had held classes in the mosque for male children and for a few young girls as well in a separate small class. She had attended the class to learn to read the Holy Koran for six years. She had also learned numbers. Because of her disability, he treated her differently, as if she were a person touched by the Almighty. She had memorized the entire Holy Quran and her family held her in awe. He was like a brother. He often stood behind her as she recited the holy words, leaning close across her back as she swayed backward and forward during the recitation. She could feel his body against her back, his maleness. He was like a brother. They talked about his life, his trips to Arabia, his own teachers, about a trip he had made to Egypt where he met another Arabian scholar who was like a brother to him. He was the only other man, aside from intimate family blood relatives that talked with her. He had said to her, the last time she saw him before he had been killed, "Meher Jamal, Allah has given you a gift, the gift of memory. You are one of the only women I have met who has memorized the entire Holy Koran. You have been touched by an angel." He had pointed to her deformed arm. "Do you know the story of Jacob who wrestled with an angel who was touched on his thigh and crippled for life? She shook her head. He told her the strange story of Jacob wrestling with the angel and not letting it go unless it blessed him. How he and the beautiful fair angel had been locked in an intimate embrace and Jacob refused to let the angel part from him, so it had touched the sinew of his thigh, and he limped from that day forward, and in spite of his grasping an angel, that he was righteous. *And we bestowed upon him Isaac, and Jacob as a grandson. Each of them We made righteous. Surah XXI v 72.* "You have been touched by an angel, Meher, and you will be made righteous if you submit to the will of Allah in all things."

Later her teacher had been struck down by a lorry while riding his bicycle on the Mall. It had been at night. The driver of the truck said he did not see him; he had no light on his bike. He was struck by a lorry. Meher had grieved his death. She had missed his teaching. She no longer sat for long periods of time reciting, moving backward and forward.

C☪

The gates were made of heavy planks reinforced with metal straps. Tur-ali had never seen such heavy gates before. In the gate was a door cut-out through which only one person could pass at a time. This door was made of the same material as the main gate. He sat on his half-blind mare and waited while their leader, Sardar called out. There was the sound of excitement behind the gate. Men called to each other and the voices of children and women could be heard. The small door opened and another bearded man who looked like Sardar emerged. He and Sardar embraced each other and kissed, exchanging greeting, then in emotion, embracing again and kissing each other's cheeks again and again. The caravan of mules and horses milled about and dust rose from their hooves. Sardar entered through the door in the gate. Tur-ali sat on his restless mare and held the reins of the huge gelding that was Sardar's.

The gate, he saw, was set into mud brick walls that were about four feet thick. The walls were three times as high as a person and appeared to be ancient. Now, as he looked, children appeared on top of the walls, shouting down at the men on the horses. They ran along the top of the wall which extended some fifty yards away from the gate on both sides, then curved away as they encircled the small village within. The gates were pushed open by two men and the riders and their animals moved inside the huge open *maidan,* a place large enough to hold many hundreds of people, animals, carts and he saw numerous trucks. Tur-ali looked to his left and saw smaller compounds within the larger walled area, homes of men and their families. On the right were open rooms which resembled those in the inns near to his own home, he remembered.

The men dismounted. Sardar and his brother supervised the storage of the arms which were carried off to a fortified warehouse room on the left wall perimeter. Servants came to the travelers and passed each of them a cool tin of Coke. Tur-ali had never had such a drink presented to him before. Yes, his father has bought him Coke in the market before, but the welcoming drink had always been hot, sweet tea. He snapped back the opener on the lid and drank down half of the fizzy cool liquid, panting to catch his breath when he stopped. The servant offered him another tin and he took it but did not open it, holding it in his hand and enjoying the feel of the cold sweating metal of the can.

Sardar gave orders to the other men and then walked to Tur-ali and smiled as he watched him drink. "Yes, we have a refrigerator here in my home. Operated by kerosene. This is my home. Welcome to my Laghman home. It is only fifteen minutes by truck to our nearest city called Mehtar-lam. Some day we will go there, but it is a dangerous place. People are restless and one never knows whose side a stranger may be on. Come."

They walked across the large courtyard, avoiding tethered animals and running children. A corner section of the wall, triangular in shape was the back wall of Sardar's personal compound. Tur-ali was brought to an entrance room for guests and told to sit and wait. A servant came and told him to follow. He was taken to an area for bathing. A large earthen pot containing water and a calabash scoop floating on top of it welcomed him. He removed his clothing and poured water over himself, enjoying the fragrant smelling soap and a wood comb to pull through his curly hair. To his surprise there was a large towel folded over a clothes rack. He dried himself, wrapped the towel about his loins and looked around. On a low wood bench there was a clean and new set of clothing. He tried on the *qamis* and it fit well as did the light cotton pajama. The material had been embroidered. He had never owned such a soft and decorated set of casual clothing.

The servant re-appeared and motioned for him to follow. He was taken to a sitting room with a Baluchi carpet on the floor and big round sausage-like pillows set around the walls. He squatted and leaned back. Across from him was a wood plaque some six feet in length on which the *shahdah* was written in beautiful Arabic calligraphy, highlighted in shiny gold. He mouthed the words, speaking softly, *There is only one God and Mohammed is his Prophet.*

"My home is your sanctuary. My home is your resting place. Be at peace in my home." Sardar stood in a beautiful tribal robe, his beard trimmed and face shining with mustard oil. He held out both hands toward Tur-ali.

Tur-ali stood, embarrassed at the generous welcome of his host, his captor, his *dushman*. But somehow, the man who stood in front of him did not appear to be an enemy, rather, a wealthy tribal leader who provided succor and protection to him.

"Thank you. You are most generous. Thank you, *Hazoor*. May the blessings of Allah be on your home and all in it." He replied in habit with well learned polite responses as a guest should.

"In a half an hour we will eat together. Then I must go. I have business in Mehtarlam. I will show you a small room where you can rest and catch up on your sleep. I must tend to the work of supporting this entire village through the sales of our cargo."

"I am not tired. Thank you. If you have room for me in the truck I would like to see the city of Mehtarlam with you. Everything here in Afghanistan is new to me."

"I must think about that. I hesitate because of the danger, because it is not a place where one displays one's wealth, one's wives, or one's valued friend who would be an immediate attraction. Tur-ali, I may not have said it before, but you are exceedingly beautiful, you have a face so rare that men will stop and turn to behold it again. Stay, and rest this day. Perhaps another day in different circumstances." He turned and left the room and spoke to a servant to show the visitor to his room.

The drive to Mehtarlam was over rutted dirt roads. Sardar was at the wheel and in the back three of his men stood with semi-automatic rifles held high, looking out with fierce faces at all whom they passed. People glanced up, then away, not holding the gaze of the wild faces and sharp eyes which seemed to beg confrontation.

The town was like many others in the Laghman Province. Few buildings were over two stories high. There was evidence of bombs, bullet holes in walls and buildings, broken glass in some stores that had not been replaced. People milled about, men in drab clothing, Taliban with their dark beards walking in twos and threes with critical eyes. Not a woman was to be seen. A store which advertised cell phones, radios and electronic devices was their destination. He stopped the truck in the street near the store. The three men stayed in the back and smoked.

The proprietor greeted him effusively, kissing his hands, calling down the blessings of Allah on him. He was given tea and after polite exchanges his host fell silent which was wont of him.

"Has the cell phone signal been installed? Can we now call out from here?" Sardar took out his own phone and handed it to the man.

"Good news. Yes. For two weeks now we have signals. Look. Your phone shows two bars. A signal. We can now do business with Kabul, with Peshawar, with Iran." He smiled broadly and handed the phone back.

"I have a number in Peshawar I wish to call. Please give me privacy for ten minutes." Sardar looked at the face of his phone.

"This is as your own home. You are my guest. Please." The man backed out of the room and shut the door. Sardar could hear his footsteps moving away.

He tapped in the number but it did not go through. After the third try he heard the ring. A man answered. "Sahib-ji this is Sardar. I have a shipment of new beautiful sinks ready for you if you are interested in buying them." He listened to the voice on the other end and replied.

"There are two sinks that are made in America." He nodded and wrote information on a paper. "Sahib-ji, you are asking that the sinks be delivered. That may create problems of crossing at the Khyber Pass. Usually I sell sinks and they are picked up by the buyer." Again he listened. He sighed and again wrote on the paper.

"Dollars. Only dollars. I will call again in two days before I leave to verify our arrangements."

Outside there was the sound of gun fire; people were yelling and running to hide and take cover.

☪

Ikbal sat at his Lahore newspaper office desk. It was not a private place, just a desk among ten others in a large room. People moved about, clerks delivered letters, phones rang and cigarette smoke filled the air. His desk was not neat. It was piled high with a number of files, newspaper clippings and an ashtray filled up with crushed cigarette butts. His chair was the exception. It was a modern bright red desk swivel chair, cushioned and with arms. When he was thinking he could tilt it back and put his feet up on his desk after all the rest had left for the day. He called a number on his phone.

"Have you found anything yet? Yes. Yes. I want you to go through the archives, back ten years and search for any items that have Superintendent Sher Khan's name in them. No man! Use the computer. No. Of course you can't read all that material. It has been scanned electronically. You can pull up names, information under "Find" on each document. Just type in the name and find it. Mark and print each item. At three I will expect you here again. Bring what you have found." He hung up.

On his own computer screen he had brought up the most recent article that he had written about Feroz Hakim. He read it again. He was glad it had not been written about himself. Now he typed in 'Maria Bernard' and was surprised at how many entries there were. So many national newspapers had covered her case during the time of her disappearance and had fed on the news item with a peculiar frenzy, most of the articles reinforcing what others had written. Many, filled with statements like, "abducted and perhaps never to be found again" and "disappeared behind *char divari*, four mud walls, in some tribal compound" or "a case of an infidel beauty captivated by some tribal beast".

His last search of the day was motivated by a curiosity, about a woman who had survived in a *baoli*. He entered the word for stepwell and was amazed to see pictures of many ancient structures in India, some in and around Lahore, all built in the era before electricity and submersible pumps. His search brought up the name of the woman, Ankh who survived the American bombing. The last entry was interesting. The woman, apparently a slave of the man accused of Maria Bernard's abduction, Sher Khan, was reported to have been returned to an island in Sukkur. This was the place that the current Deputy Superintendent, Feroz Hakim, had said he had gone for an interview during which he had found evidence that Maria had in fact been abducted by the dead policeman, physical evidence. He wrote a note on a pad of paper and leaned back to think.

"Here are the entries sir. So many! The man at the archives was upset with all the paper I wasted copying material." He placed a small pile of printouts on Ikbal's desk. Ikbal nodded a brief thank you and immediately began to look at the material.

"Sir. Anything more, sir?" The young man was rewarded.

"No. No. You are excused. Take off the rest of the afternoon. Good work."

His search was an interesting one on the career of the late police superintendent. A pattern seemed to emerge. Often there were initial inquiries made about complaints, such as family feuds, inheritance squabbles, possible fraud, violence, all routine police matters, however, the rich and the famous entries frequently were singularly untouched. The cases were dropped, there was not sufficient evidence, the matter would be looked into, the witnesses appeared to be biased or motivated by greed, many reasons, but for many a person of wealth, rank and high social standing, the work of the late Sher Khan appeared to be most interesting. Few cases were brought to justice. He sorted the papers into categories and wrote the names of people and was surprised that he knew many of them. The small clipping about his own case had simply mentioned that a young and hysterical school girl had given a report to a policeman who had filed an FIR, a first information report about her being sexually assaulted.

"The case is being looked into, however, the lieutenant reported in his initial investigation that during his interview of the girl and her parents that she was beautiful and disturbingly aggressive. The matter was referred to higher authority for further investigation. In Pakistan there are hundreds of reports daily by young women of assaults by men, not by some aggressive stranger, but close relatives, acquaintances and even family friends are accused. Few of these have resulted in arrests. The girls in most cases do not wish their names to be known for obvious reasons of family honour. It must be remembered that there were recent cases when such matters were pursued by the girl and she was found to be guilty of adultery and indecency and paid a terrible penalty herself, being sentenced to death."

Ikbal sat back in his chair remembering. Yes, she had been very beautiful indeed, he thought. He had not again in all his life, not once, held such beauty. Her breasts were perfection. His own wife, arranged by his family was plain and plump. Their wedding pictures showed him to be thin, hawk nosed with large protruding ears and his wife's plain, unhappy face was partially obscured with gold jewelry hanging from her forehead.

He picked up his notes thinking murderous thoughts. Feroz Hakim could not have known the girl's name Piari, nor pulled it out of the hat without information from Sher Khan himself who had investigated the case. He knew about the deceased Sher Khan, that he was a tight-lipped man, one who held things to himself. He also knew that he disdained his deputy and would never divulge any private information to him. So how did the stupid Deputy know about the matter? Yes, the car was a possibility, but not Piari. He wanted justice. By Allah he would get it. Again he wrote on paper, this time on a ToDo note pad. "Who are all the people that Feroz has as friends? Who are those who work for him? Who did he marry? Who are his servants?" He put this in his pocket with his reporter's pad and left the office mumbling "pen is mightier than the sword".

C☾

Ankh was getting better at being in charge of her island home at Sukkur. Jhika would come and sit in the outer courtyard and wait until she came out. Sometimes she made him wait for half an hour before appearing, being concerned that his interest had shifted from being a salesman for her, to her. She came with an object in each hand and stood in front of the young man and said nothing. He took the object, this time a small piece of ivory carved in the shape of an elephant, a perfect, tiny elephant with a howdah. The other was a coin she had found with strange writing on it. The coin was crude and misshaped, thick as her finger. He looked at each item not really knowing what each was but eager to try to sell them in the local market.

He looked up into her face and smiled. All the other women, other than intimate family members, always covered their faces. Ankh had never covered hers and he continued to be intrigued with this, since her face was beautiful and her hair was dark and curly. "Yes, I can get a few rupees for each of these. What are they?" He was putting the objects in his pocket.

"No. I am going to have you draw each of these on a paper as best as you can. Then you will go to the dealers, many dealers and see what they say. Then you will come back and tell me what they all said and what their reactions were. You will look in each of the shops first and ask for similar items before you talk about these items. Perhaps you will find a coin like this one and see how much they sell it for. I want the name of the man who sells it, the name of his shop. When Dohst sahib returns he and I will visit these shops together and I am going to check up on you. No more expensive Navy Cut Cigarettes for you, even if you are young and handsome." Her eyes flashed.

"Begum, you sound like you do not trust me." He gave her his best smile.

"Jhika, did you notice that I did not invite you into the house today?" She did not smile.

"Never, Begum ji, that is not what I do." Now he looked at her rather openly, at her pretty face, her swelling breasts and thought, no that is not what I have done, yet.

He drew each object. Then, inspired, he put the coin under the paper and rubbed it with the pencil and a facsimile appeared. She watched, fascinated, her mouth slightly open, her teeth held on her lower lip. Jhika looked at her teeth. They were white, almost translucent. He had not noticed her teeth before, they were the color of the little ivory elephant.

"First look through the entire bazaar and ask for such items before you show them the paper." She spoke with him as if he were her brother. His smile was not brotherly as he looked at the young woman in front of him. He now noticed gold flecks in her eyes.

The old woman brought a cup of tea and set it on a table in the courtyard and left, obviously not pleased with Ankh talking to the man without supervision. She had glanced at Jhika's expression and knew that look well. If only Dohst knew, what would he do? She mumbled to herself as she moved away, remembering another boatman many years ago who made frequent trips to the island when the master, Sheikh Mohammed was away on business. He had even written a poem about her. She knew the look a man gives a woman who he desires.

☪

Peshawar was pleasant in the winter months. Many people moved about which gave beggars an audience to seek alms. A beggar sat across the street from Chamuck's home, whining at passersby to be merciful. His left arm was wrapped in a filthy bandage on which there appeared to be dried blood. His head was shaved and a crude bandage was stuck to the back part of it, also with dried blood. His clothes were rags, his ugly feet bare. Passersby glanced at him; some tossing him a coin, others stepping around, avoiding having to pass too closely. He had chosen a good place. It was in the shade all day and he could see the gate of the household clearly as well as the second floor windows. He brought his own food with him, two flat oven breads and a half white radish dipped in salt and red pepper. Around noon the first day he had fallen asleep but was awakened by the sound of a car door slamming. He looked up and saw Mohammed the mullah park his car and walk into the house. He was alone. About an hour later he left. When it became dark the beggar got up and walked home.

On the second day he saw the car pull up again early in the morning. He did not recognize the driver, but it was the same car. Chamuck, in school uniform, her head covered, walked out of the house and got into the car and was driven away. Later, at two in the afternoon, the car returned and she got out and went into the house. For two days the activities were the same. When it was dark the beggar used his cell phone.

"Sahib-ji she does not walk to school. The mullah's car comes in the morning to pick her up and it brings her back in the evening. No one else comes and goes into the house, not even the women in burkahs walking to the nearby stalls to buy food." He nodded. "Yes. I will find out what school she attends and call you tomorrow."

The next morning he sat next to the gate of Chamuck's house. The sweeper opened the gate and dumped garbage into the street, glanced at him and was about to go back into the compound when the beggar spoke.

"How can the girl afford to go to the university when I can not afford a pair of shoes. Allah!" He whined.

"Move to the other side where you were before. She does not go to the university; idiot, she is too young; she only goes to the Yusaf School for boys and girls. Move away from here." He took out a rupee and gave it to the beggar who grudgingly picked up his things and moved back across the street. He called on his cell phone again. "Sahib-ji it is the Yusaf School."

Two days later Chamuck left school, climbed into the back seat of the car. She took a book out of her backpack and read her assignment. The school was at the edge of the town in a less populated area. Near it a bridge, not more than a lane and a half wide spanned a huge culvert. The car slowed down to let a truck pass. The truck stopped on the bridge. Her driver got out and shouted to the truck to move aside and let the car pass. The driver did not feel the cudgel that hit him in the side of the neck. Two men jumped into his car, one in the back seat next to Chamuck, the other drove. She screamed and lunged for the door near her but was hit on her arm with the fist of the man sitting next to her. He grabbed her arm and she thrashed around struggling against him. His grip was like iron and his arm bulged with firm muscle.

Frustrated, and knowing that she had to escape, Chamuck leaned forward and bit the exposed skin of his wrist and she tasted his blood. Her teeth met through his flesh. He yelled and clouted her on the side of her head and he cried out *kuti*, bitch. She slumped against the door stunned almost unconscious from the blow. He looked at his arm which was bleeding. A flap of skin had been lifted up. He struck her again, hard, this time on her shoulder, worried that he would bruise her face. He reached over and began to choke her.

It all happened in seconds. Chamuck's injured driver lay on the side of the road, the truck moved across the bridge and the car sped away into the heart of Peshawar city.

Chamuck struggled to sit up, gasping for breath. Her head and arm ached, and her throat was sore. She was terrified. She looked at the man sitting next to her, trying to identify him. He had wrapped his wrist in a handkerchief. His head was wrapped up and only his eyes were exposed. He looked at her in fury but said nothing more, only put his finger to where his mouth would be if he were not covered.

Then he whispered in English, "If you try to escape again, I will let you get through the door and as you run I will shoot you. I swear an oath to Allah, I will shoot you. If you scream, I will choke you. If you move about I will hit you in the face. Please, at the next place we stop, try running!" He reached over and grabbed her wrists and drew a plastic tie band around them and pulled it tight so that the pressure against her skin was painful.

"If I had a gun you would be dead too." She panted. "I have read that the bite from a human is worse than that of a *kuti*. I hope you die from my bite." She spat the words at him.

The driver pressed the door lock button that was used so children could not open the back door. After almost half an hour the car stopped in a courtyard next to a parked car. The man told her to get out. She did so and he and the driver walked next to her, opened the car door of the parked car and pushed her in and drove off.

"Who are you? Where are you taking me?" She looked at the man next to her in fear, backing away as far as she could. Her hands began to swell.

"Keep quiet. If you want a name, my name is George Bush. I am taking you for a long trip." He laughed. "Does that help, *kuti*?"

"George Bush, please take me home." Now for the first time she wept as she pleaded. "My hands are going numb. Please. Remove the plastic. I will sit still."

He looked at her swelling hands and remembered Sahib-ji's words. "Bring her to me without damaging her. Do you know what I mean?"

He wore a short dagger on his belt. He pulled it out and Chamuck backed away. "Sit still bitch, I am going to loosen your restraint." The point of the knife was inserted between her wrists and with a single motion he cut the strap away.

"*Kuti*, I am taking you to your new home." He had a paper sack at his feet. From it he extracted an old *burkah*. "Put it on." He handed it to her.

Chamuck looked at the garment. It smelled slightly of sweat and urine. She held it in distaste, hesitating to wear it.

"Put it on now, quickly!" He leaned toward her threateningly, poking her with the gun.

She pulled the garment over her head, remembering when she was a child playing with her older sister. They had each worn their mother's *burkah* and a pair of high heels, pretending to be women, tripping around peering through the mesh in front of their eyes.

"Put out your hands."

She extended her hands. He reached over and snapped a pair of metal handcuffs on her. The car pulled over at the side of the road. He jumped out and went around to the front seat and climbed in, his injured arm held up to lesson the throb. He looked over the seat at her.

"Good. That is how you will be from now on. The bride's new clothes."

Chamuck sat alone in the back seat, slumped down, depressed and terrified. The car passed through a number of crowded villages. Pedestrians glanced in the back of the car and saw the covered huddled figure and looked away quickly. She had not been told where she was going, but she knew without being told. She had been abducted by Sahib-ji. The car traveled for more than three hours. Strangely, she slept part of the time. She had an urgent need to urinate but hated to ask her captor. Finally she could not stand it any more, not wanting to wet herself.

"Find a place to stop where I can relieve myself. Hurry!"

The driver pulled off the road next to an abandoned village site. The mud brick walls were partially destroyed and only a donkey was grazing.

"Get out." He pointed to the wall.

She hurried to the wall and glanced back and saw that both her captor and the driver were staring at her. She squatted and tried to cover herself as best she could from their gaze. The bottom of her garment was wet and soiled with dirt as she walked back to the vehicle, humiliated.

"Next time don't wait so long. Next time when we take a break, you take one as well. Understand?"

She had heard of walled villages, but had never seen one until it appeared in the windshield in front of her as she peered through the screen mesh of her garment. Her feelings of terror now moved to despair and sorrow. She wept, loud wailing cries of despair as the car drove through the gates. Her father had talked at length about what happened to women behind *char divari*, that once they were taken behind the four high walls of a traditional tribal village, they would never again have the freedom to leave, go to school, and seldom if ever visit the family of their birth. They became the chattel of the home owner.

The man turned in his seat and laughed. He still spoke English, though with a strong accent, much like her gym teacher in school who was a Gujarati. "Welcome home. You have now graduated from school. You have entered the real life made for women."

"Look, since you speak English you have gone to school and understand what that means. I am a school girl and I have a scholarship to go to college. Please. I beg you, I ask as if I was your daughter, take me home. Let me have my life back." She reached over toward his injured arm and he recoiled as if it was a snake.

"Don't! The more schooling I have had, the more I believe that the evils of the *gora* world must be driven from Pakistan. Never again bitch, reach out to touch a man! There is only one man who will touch you and who you will touch; Sahib-ji! You could be killed if you do that again. You are now the possession of a new master who will have you stoned to death if you as much as look at another man or even talk to another man as he passes. It is a matter of honor." He reached out toward her with a small key. "Put out your hands. I will remove your handcuffs. I am done with you. *Jo hona ho so ho.*" (What ever is to happen, let it happen.) He leaned forward toward her peering at her eyes behind the mesh. "And, *kuti*, you know exactly what I mean. And it will happen to you very soon."

CHAPTER FIVE

Koele-vala aur uska rupaya dono kale. (Urdu Proverb)

The coal (collier) man is black and so is his money.

Black Partridge begin to call before dawn. They sit on high rocks or on the top of a scrub tree and call out to establish their territory. One cries out and is answered by the next. By the time of the first call to prayer, when light is just enough to see a hair held against the sky, the birds are off and running, seeking grass seeds and the odd insect, running from one patch of cover to the next, their heads always cocked to the sky watching out for Goshawk which flies from high promontories and swoops low near to the ground to snatch its unwary prey. Their enemy is a stealth hunter, not announcing itself with territorial calls, except in the mating season when their high cries can be heard on the slopes in Afghanistan when the male pursues the female in the air and they carry out wild acrobatics in their courtship flights. The partridge's other enemy the jackal, has four legs. Its high voice carries over the valleys at dawn and the partridge hide. It is answered by a pack more than a mile away across a deep ravine.

Maria had hardly slept. The sounds of animal life around the shack were strange and new to her. She could not imagine what the creatures were already moving about in the deserted area around the shack. She shivered. The shawl and thin mat beneath her did not protect her bones from the hard floor or cockroaches which scurried whenever she moved. Her words to her husband James, when they lived in La Jolla came to her. "James, the mattress on the king size bed is too firm. They have a new kind of mattress where I can dial in my preference for softness. Let's get one James." He had ordered one the same day to please her.

She turned her body frequently and finally lay prone on her back and stared at the crude ceiling of the shack. Twice she got up and added fuel to the fire in the adobe stove and the old woman did not awaken. She stepped outside and was threatened by the darkness of the place. She looked around and did not see anyone. She relieved herself near the wall. The partridge called its grating cry, from the roof of her dwelling. She got up and put a pot of water on the fire for tea. There was a tin of sweetened condensed milk that the men had brought and quietly she punched two holes in the lid and sucked a mouthful of its thick sugary contents, relishing the heavy sweetness, closing her eyes. She knew the old woman would be furious, but it would be too late. She sucked again, wondering why she had never bought this treat before when she lived in California. She had seen the tins of sweetened condensed milk piled high in the oriental store where she shopped in Ranch 99 on Claremont Mesa Blvd. but she had always walked by. By the time the water was boiling, she had finished half the tin and now hid it away behind her shawl on the floor hoping the old woman would not notice as she unpacked the rest of the goods brought by the two men.

She had watched how the old woman had made tea many times. She measured a large handful of tea leaves and threw these in the pot to boil with a half cup of sugar. She had an idea. She blew on one hole of the milk tin and the thick creamy liquid poured out into the pot from the other. She emptied it, then took the knife and cut the lid off and licked her fingers as she scooped the last remnant from the tin. She set the tin next to the tea pot so the woman would think that she had poured all of it into the mixture.

Outside she could hear the men milling about, preparing the donkeys for the return trip. One shouted out for the old woman to get up and serve them tea before they left. The old woman struggled to rise, groaning from aching, stiff arthritic joints. Maria covered her head and most of her face, filled two brass glasses with tea and pushed the door open. She walked to the men and handed them each a glass of steaming tea. They were surprised to see it was she but they sipped the tea talking to each other. Maria left them and walked the small trail up the hillside to her area of toilet, they eyes of the men on her back.

"I am going to take her away from here. The old woman lived without her before and she can live without her again. I am going to take her back to our village and get a hearing from the two Taliban in the council. I will claim rights to her and request she be given to me." Atiqullah drank too large a gulp of tea, almost burning his throat.

"How can we take her back? She can't walk the entire way in her condition. Her feet look soft like a small child's. The stones would tear her feet up." Jalaludin was not pleased at his younger brother's ideas of trying to bring this foreign female infidel to their home.

"I will tie her feet up with strips of cloth. She will be able to walk. We have a long journey. Tell the old woman to boil wheat flour in water with sugar and make gruel. We won't cook on the way."

Moon prepared the gruel, grumbling that most of the food they brought was already going to be eaten up by them. The thick sweet mixture was poured into their cups and they drank three cups each. Atiqullah finished his meal and poured another cupful and to Maria's surprise brought it over to her. She looked at the thick brown cereal and shook her head. He stood in front of her and told her to eat it, making gestures she could not fail to understand. She drank it down and was surprised at how good it tasted. When she was finished he pointed at her shawl spread on the floor. She did not understand so he walked over and picked it up and handed it to her and pointed to the door. She walked outside. The early morning air was chilly when she stood in the shade of the shack. She draped the shawl around her shoulders and head. Atiqullah emerged out of the shack with yet another bundle, her old *burkah* that she had worn when she escaped from Bahadur which hung on a peg against the wall. He gave it to Maria and motioned for her to put it on over the shawl.

The old woman shouted at him, yelling and carrying on. He ignored her. After Maria had put on the *burkah* he motioned for her to sit on a rock. Again he went into the hut and emerged carrying a piece of canvas-like cloth. He cut it with his knife and tore it into long strips. Then he removed the slippers that Maria wore and proceeded to carefully wrap her feet like a mummy. He was not pleased with his work the first time, undid the bindings and rewrapped them, this time starting with a strip running the length of her foot as a sole, then wrapping again. Satisfied he got up and motioned to the largest donkey. Maria knew his intent. She had known it when he forced her to eat the gruel. He was going to take her away. She was being abducted once again, this time by a man who had wrapped her feet tenderly. His hands had remained on her ankles for a few seconds as his fingers felt the smoothness of her skin, felt the soft dark down-like hair that grew on her unshaved legs now. She had known his intention from his eyes when she came down from the roof. She could feel his intention in the tips of his fingers which stroked her ankle softly.

The donkey stood patiently while she straddled it. Her long legs hung down almost to the ground. He took the reins and walked in front of the animal, hobbling along at a good pace, glancing back from time to time at Maria who leaned forward to hold on to the mane for balance. In spite of her situation of being abducted, covered with a *burkah* and riding on an ass, she smiled. She smiled at the irony of it. Mary, pregnant Mary riding a donkey with Joseph pulling the reins walking into the small town of Bethlehem must have looked like this. Except that she, Maria, carried the child of a devil in her own womb and walked toward an unknown town in Afghanistan.

Strangely, leaving the hut of the old woman was a relief. She had carried water up the hill on her head for seven days, had gathered fuel for hours on the hillside, caught rodents and lay miserably on the hard floor like an animal. She had no idea where they were headed, what fate held for her, but she was still alive. She knew that if she once again was taken behind a large walled compound, her chances of leaving were much slimmer than had been the case when she was in Pakistan in Bahadur. This was tribal Afghanistan. Then she thought of the child she was carrying as she bumped along on the bony back of the donkey. Sher Khan's child, a child of forced, unprotected sex. She felt it move insider her now like some strange, foreign thing apart from her.

Moving up the gradual incline to a new destination was a relief from being stuck in a situation of pure animal survival. Strangely, when Atiqullah had bound her feet with the strips of cloth she had felt his tenderness, his caring of another person, for her. For a moment she had felt the ministering hands of one who not only did a job in a rough way for her survival, but who had done it twice to get it right, to make the bindings comfortable on her already bruised feet. When he had stroked the dark hair on her legs she had not been surprised, but said nothing, simply moving her legs away.

After an hour of riding, her bottom was sore. She called out the only word she could think of at the moment. "Bismillah."

The small caravan stopped and she got off the animal and motioned for them to continue up the trail. She walked along behind the donkey, trying out her booties, walking the last in line holding to a rope that he had tied to the saddle. She trudged behind heading for wherever it was that they were going in this part of Afghanistan. High above them the PIA flight to London left a white contrail. She thought of their flight to Pakistan in the PIA airplane from London, of being served delicious food by the stewardess, but fretting because she could not have a double vodka and tonic drink, or two. She remembered James saying, "If it gets too bad you can sneak one in the John." He had patted the small bottles in his brief case. Again she laughed; this time out loud as she slogged along the trail on her swaddled feet. The men turned to look at her, talking quietly with each other. "I hope a spirit has not caught her mind and made her mad."

☪

Dohst decided to wear his older soiled clothing to meet the owner of the small shop. He did not want the man to drive up the rent because he looked prosperous. He pedaled through the bazaar past companies that made tennis racquets, others that made surgical instruments and finally past the area of saddle makers to the bag-pipe makers. He could hear them before he saw them. One man stood on the street playing a bag-pipe, the strange wail with a constant lower groan of the instrument drawing the attention of a group of street urchins who crowded around to watch the demonstration.

The street where the vacant store was located was close to a number of run-down apartment buildings that needed repair and paint. Many of the apartments had been painted when they were new, but after ten or twelve years of neglect looked as if they had never been decorated. Many had long streaks down the walls where refuse water had run. The balconies of these apartments were used as storage rooms, junk piled high in each, others were used to dry clothing, or a place for women to sit and prepare food. At the base of one of these buildings, store front shops had been constructed. He almost missed the place but the Motor Oil sign reminded him where he was headed.

An elderly man with a beard dyed orange-red wearing a white cap sat on the platform in front of the store. He watched people moving by as if to identify the person he was scheduled to meet. Dohst stood in front of him and the man waved him aside, as if he was in the way of his view.

"Are you the owner of this shop?" Dohst asked.

"Yes. Yes, move aside. I am looking for someone."

"I think you are looking for me."

He looked at the dark-skinned thin youth in front of him and frowned. "How are you supposed to come up with the rent for this place?" He stood up, gathering his things ready to leave.

"I think you will want one month's rent in advance. Is that right?" Dohst now held a roll of bills in his hand. The old man looked at the wad of money in amazement.

"That is usual. What is your name? My memory fails me."

"Dohst Mohammed. May I see the place? It may not be suitable for me. It looks very small."

"Yes. Come." He took out keys and tried them in the lock appearing to be unfamiliar with the mechanism. "It was my brother's place. Wait." The lock opened and he reached down to lift the folding metal door but it was stuck in place.

Dohst bent down to help him but the door seemed to be rusted in place. "It is not working well. It will need to be fixed. This is not encouraging." Dohst tried to look displeased, hoping to push down the rent.

The old man looked around for something to slip under the metal to pry it up. Dohst could see his intent. He walked to the Motor Oil shop and greeted the man and asked it he had a metal bar or a large screwdriver. He was given a screw driver to use.

Dohst pried the bottom of the door carefully, not wanting to bend the screwdriver. Finally it gave way and he was able, with the help of the old man, to lift the door with difficulty. The smell of a dead animal was strong.

"This is terrible. Is there a body in here?" Dohst made a real fuss now, holding a handkerchief to his nose, waving his hand about to disperse the odor. The old man mumbled to himself and moved into the store. Near the back entrance the decaying body of the cat lay, writhing in maggots. He opened the back door and took a cardboard and pushed the decaying mass into the small back courtyard.

Dohst saw that there were two wood crates pushed against the wall, covered with dust and bird feathers. They looked unopened. He remembered that the oil man had said that the store had sold Peacock air conditioners, a brand made in China. Now he hoped the old man would ignore these in his efforts to get rid of the dead cat and get outside as quickly as possible. He was right. The man moved to the front of the store, stepped out onto the street and glanced back at the open sliding metal door, the lock still in his hand.

"I don't think I want to rent this place. It is filthy, unclean and in bad repair. Thank you for coming to show me." He prepared to get on his bike.

"Wait. I will reduce the rent if you take it as it is, smell, rusted door, dirt and all. But you will have to agree today, now. I have the paper with me. I will reduce the rent five hundred rupees a month. But you must agree now."

"I will look around once more. Wait." Dohst went back into the store and looked at everything carefully. He pushed against the two crated air conditioners to insure that they were indeed in the crates. He saw an old desk and chair and a box with dusty papers in it that looked like receipts. The back yard was enclosed with a cement block wall. A door at the back of the enclosure led to an alley that was choked with weeds. The air conditioners he figured were worth at least twelve hundred rupees each if they worked. If he could sell them he would have R24,000, a small fortune to him. He would invest this money in the oil business. He would hire two sweepers for two days and have the place cleaned, ceilings, walls and floors as well as the back enclosed area. He would be in business.

"I have looked at the place. It is terrible. I would have to hire a crew of men to come and clean it up, paint it and make it suitable for my use. I would have to hire a *mistiri* to repair the door and lubricate it. It looks like some rollers need replacement. No. It is too much of a problem. Look, if you would get it all set up for me, I would give you a list of the things to do then I will rent it. Otherwise..." Again he walked to his bike.

"All right, I will reduce it by R600 per month."

"Write on the agreement that I accept the place, as is, and that all the things inside it, the old chair, hanging light, desk, you know everything in the place that is not attached to the walls or floor I can have or dispose of. Then I agree." He took out the roll of money again, then put them back into his pocket, as if changing his mind once more, shaking his head.

"Agreed." He began to write on the bottom of the paper under "Conditions of rental" that all the junk in the room could become the property of the renter or the renter could dispose of it as he saw fit. He read this to Dohst.

"Change the word junk to moveable items not attached to the walls, floor or ceiling."

This time Dohst looked at the lease document carefully, thinking that Meher Jamal would look at it when he got back. He checked each line, each item very critically. The old man became impatient.

"Look, it is not as if you are buying it. Sign it and give me my money."

"Do you want to sell it to me instead?" Dohst now looked interested.

"It would be too much. No, my brother's family needs the income now." The old man smoothed the rental document, stroking it like it was a cat with his nicotine stained fingers.

"It will not be too much. I am a business man. I own property in Sukkur. I am going into the oil business soon. I have enough if the price is right. I will rent it for one month. At the end of this period I would like to buy it from you. If I do, this rental fee would be subtracted from the total price. I will check on other stores for sale and get an idea of a fair price. I would buy it as is, not fixed up, like it is now. I would need all the ownership papers for it. One month." He took out the roll of bills and peeled off the amount for a month's rental, but held it in his hand as the man reached for it. "Give me a receipt."

"I don't walk around with an entire office. A receipt? Oh, all right. He turned the rental agreement over and wrote on the back, the amount paid in full, and signed it. He handed it to Dohst.

"There is no date. Put a date near you signature."

Now the old man was getting shaky and very irritable. "Young man, I hope I don't need to deal with you again soon. You are like the coal man, when he handles money it turns black. This deal is filled with problems."

"Honored sir, it was the smell of a dead cat that greeted my nose this morning. My cash that is now in your hands smells clean. In one month you will see me again and your brother's family may rejoice to receive cash for his decrepit place. My cash may have my marks on it, but it may remove the blackness from the sorrowing faces of your in-laws."

The old man put the rental money in his pocket and was about to leave.

"Wait!" shouted Dohst.

"Allah! What is it now?" The old man was now very cranky.

"The lock and key. They are part of the deal." He pointed to the lock in the old man's hand, who looked at it in surprise. He handed it to Dohst and turned away again. "The key, The Key."

There were two identical keys on his chain. He took off one and handed it to Dohst. "The other as well. Both keys are to the same lock." He held out his hand. The old man looked at the key, then handed it attached to a little chain to Dohst.

Now he stood waiting. "Anything more?"

"Yes. Talk to your in-laws about the sale. I am serious. Give me your address. I can come to see you in a month to bring the next rent, or to sign purchase papers." The old man wrote his address on the back of the rental agreement.

"Excuse me sir. Do you drive a car?" Dohst asked.

"What has that to do with this? Of course I do. It is in the repair shop now. I have driven for ten years!"

"Good. May I see your driver's license to verify that the person I am speaking to is in fact who you say you are, please. I would hate to have given a month's rent to the wrong person." He laughed happily, seeing Meher's face.

The old man took out the small cloth-covered red booklet which had his picture and the license authority stamp on it. Dohst looked at it and then wrote the serial number on the back of the rental agreement. He was smiling. Meher would have nothing to suggest he thought. He saw now that the license had expired. "Excuse me *hazoor*, this is no longer valid. You have not renewed it. Please renew it or you may have trouble with my friend Feroz Hakim the Deputy Superintendent of Police if you ever travel to Lahore." He smiled broadly, hoping the man would see the devil in him. He handed the document back. Meher would be impressed, he thought.

The old man adjusted his bi-focal glasses and read the information and nodded. "Yes, yes. I will get it renewed." He walked away rapidly and yelled at a passing horse carriage which stopped to pick him up. He sat facing backwards and stared at Dohst, shaking his head as the vehicle moved forward, the horse depositing dung as it trotted away.

"Come over. I have tea prepared. Come. So you are friends of the Deputy Superintendent of Police in Lahore? I am not sure I want to do business with you." The next door shopkeeper laughed.

"Let me lock up this place and I will be right over." He closed and locked the back door, pulled the sliding metal door across the opening, snapped the lock in place and walked to the Motor Oil seller next door. They shook hands.

"I am most interested to know about your friend the policeman in Lahore." He handed Dohst a cup of tea.

"It is a long story that will take weeks to tell but let me begin with my stories of importing Persian carpets and forgetting to pay the Pakistani customs at the border. How I eluded the law and inherited a great fortune and how I lost most of it."

☪

"Sahib-ji, it is done. She is now in your compound in Tangi. All went well. The girl is with your aunt who will look after her well until you arrive. The car was returned. There were no witnesses." He stood proudly.

Sahib-ji reached into his pocket and peeled off ten one hundred rupee notes. "Just a little bonus. Buy yourself a new coat. The weather is getting cold. Has there been any action from her uncle the mullah yet?" Sahib-ji took out his cell phone and dialed a number. He waited for a connection, then when it came, waved the young man away.

"So the phone system works there now? Good. Are you going to be able to move the bathroom sinks as you planned?" He listened to the voice on the other side for a minute and then interrupted. "I have my own problems and deadlines. You get the materials to my warehouse when we agreed and you have a deal. If you have to castrate someone to make it happen, then do it. I will have the cash in dollars. If you fail me I will not buy from you again. My representative where you are now, will give you an Afghani cash advance for travel and transportation. Remember what I said about buying and selling." He hung up.

"Bring the car around. I am going to visit a certain mullah and enquire about his brother's marriage contract." He laughed and heaved himself to his feet and moved toward the door.

☪

The old family home in Peshawar was gloomy. The drapes were pulled over the windows. Mahtari was inconsolable. She cried quietly all day, refusing to eat or drink. Finally her brother-in-law Mohammed Rafiq became impatient.

"Get up and prepare food for the family. Chamuck is gone. It has been twenty four hours and there is no word. I know who arranged this, but I can not prove it, but it will do us no good to spoil the rest of the family with your sobbing. Even the children are affected. Get up!" He stood over her threateningly.

Mahtari got up and walked stooped over to the kitchen area. Two other of her younger co-wives met her and tried to comfort her. She began to cut onions and tomatoes, sniffing.

"I cannot believe it happened to Chamuck," she sobbed. "Her father set this all in motion and I can not make my heart forgive him for his act, signing her off as part of a business deal. It is fitting that his body was desecrated, eaten by dogs and vultures. He acted like them when he was alive!"

The women around were appalled at her words and told her to keep her voice down. She replied, "Why should I be quiet? He is no longer here. His brother hates him just as much as I do. He will get no gold for her and he has lost the car as well. Nothing I can say will bother him. He has been made into jackal dung." She reached for another onion, sniffing now from the strong onion fumes.

"It is the spirits. We must not disturb the dead," said one.

"When is the last time you saw a spirit jumping around. Chamuck is gone. It's worse than death. I will never hold the children she bears and care for them. I will never see her face again. Yet, I know she lives somewhere and she will never see my face again. Half way between us our grief will meet and forever it will meet, her grief and mine, joining and weeping with no end to it." She put her head back and groaned.

"Perhaps she will escape. She is a clever girl. Perhaps she will let us know where she is and we can call the police." The youngest wife took the knife from Mahtari and chopped up the onion.

"If she escapes, how does she travel halfway across the country to get here? She has no money, no identification. If she sends us a letter, how will she know her address?

If she does, how will the police become involved? Since when do the police enter the tribal territories and go behind the mud walled villages of northern chieftains? She is lost. I would rather stand by her grave this day than think of her alive and with that gas inflated devil Sahib-ji. In one month if she were to return, like a miracle, what would her uncle do with her? What man will take a girl for his bride who has been abused by another? Virginity is what sells the bride. That insures the honor of the family." She sat on a stool, hunched over, blowing her nose. "Virginity, our only value," she sobbed. "Sold and used up in a moment's time." Her head was now settled to the table next to the cut onions. The other women quickly lifted her up, protesting.

Outside there was a commotion, much pounding on the metal gate. Mohammed Rafiq reached for his rifle and fed a cartridge into the chamber and got up. He looked through the window and saw that the car of Sahib-ji was parked by the gate and that his driver was pounding on the door.

"Keep quiet. Stay in the kitchen. Make no noise!" He walked to the front door and yelled to the sweeper. "Open the gate for the car to enter."

The gate was opened and Sahib-ji's car driven in and parked in the shade of a tree. He got out clumsily, placing both feet on the ground next to the car and hoisting his bulk up with his hands on the metal above the car door. He walked toward the house, waddling from side to side to compensate for his fat thighs which rubbed together.

Mohammed Rafiq watched carefully. Sahib-ji came alone. He had no armed men with him. He placed his gun behind the door and waited.

"*Salaam alaikum.*" He extended his hand toward the mullah.

"Why are you here? Your life is in danger here." He glared at the man.

"I come as your guest as before to discuss the matter of the document signed by your brother. I have come to make arrangements for the girl that may be more suitable to you." He smiled and looked at the chair.

"I do not take you in as my guest. No arrangements would be suitable. I despise my brother for being so insensitive for the family." He shouted this out.

"I am prepared to honor the contract as if it were a regular arrangement. I can provide your family with heavy gold ornaments, cash to you and a wonderful wedding feast. I am not a selfish man. I wish to marry the girl, obviously, but want the family to have the benefit of their beautiful virgin daughter. I would wish that in future years she and her children can be visited by her mother." He stood on his feet outside the door uncomfortably, not used to being treated like a common visitor.

"It will never be possible. I would never agree to you as her husband. You must know. I must consider her happiness and her unwillingness to agree to such a union. She would never agree." Muhammad Rafiq could not get himself to invite the man inside his home. He had been surprised he had shown up at this time, right after the abduction. He had thought that Sahib-ji had arranged it. Now he had come to make regular arrangements which surprised him.

"I hope you daughter is well. She is attending classes is she not?" Sahib-ji spoke smoothly his voice flowing like oil.

He hesitated, not knowing how to reply. "No. She is not well. She has an ailment that she may not survive." He had used the words *tabiyat na-saz hai* which spoke of an ill condition. He had not lied about her.

"I am sorry to hear this. Nonetheless, she is mine, whatever has befallen her. I will have my lawyer bring official notice to you for a court hearing tomorrow. Since you have not shown me the courtesy of entering your home as your guest and inviting me in, I understand your feelings. Understand mine. The paper of your brother was not coerced, it was witnessed and it is legal and it will be carried out. The girl will be mine." He paused as he turned. "The servant I sent to give you a message, the one you shot did not die. He will live. He has told me that you owe him blood and that he too will collect." He returned to his car and was driven away; he did not look back.

Mohammed Rafiq sat on a wood chair in the front room of the house, his rifle still in his hands, the bullet still in the chamber, the safety off. He was not aware that he was holding it. His mind raced.

Then he spoke in a half whisper. "You son of *shaitan*, I understand your game. You are the one who took her. You are covering your trail with the tantalizing smell of gold jewelry, coins and an offer of a formal wedding while even tonight she may scream in loathing when you approach her. Before Allah, you have so violated my family, have been responsible for my brother's death; your blood is forfeit, yes, before Allah justice will be done and the family honor will be preserved. A life for a life. I will be avenged!"

The women looked out from behind the kitchen door at him sitting with his gun, mumbling to himself. The youngest wife dropped a plate on which the chopped onion was placed and let out a yell. The mullah jumped, his hand still on the trigger guard, but his finger slipped and a shot rang out like thunder and a framed religious carving on the wall crashed to the floor.

☪

The trip to Sukkur was expensive and time consuming, but Ikbal thought it would be the only way to find out more about Deputy Superintendent Feroz Hakim's claim that there was physical evidence about Maria Bernard. He also could learn of the whereabouts of the once accused Dohst Mohammed and interview him. The newspaper's senior editor gave him a week leave to pursue the matter. He enquired about fast buses that were air-conditioned and booked a trip from Lahore to Sukkur on the Sammi Daewoo Express Bus.

Once more he went to the police headquarters and asked for Feroz Hakim and was informed he was not in but to leave a message. He spoke to the officer who issued driver's license permits. He introduced himself and showed his press card. "Do you remember issuing licenses to two American US-HELP workers?" he asked.

Immediately the man became voluble. "It should not have happened. I was over-ruled and they got their licenses. The Senior Superintendent personally issued them over his signature. They had drivers for their cars. No, I would do the same today, except I would be stronger. It is not that I do not like American people, but they send their women here who do not respect our religious dress codes, who go to places no woman should travel to, including Mohenjadaro which is dangerous for men." He stepped outside of the office and paced back and forth in frustration, smoking. "Why are you interested in these women?"

"Actually, I am not. They had a friend who disappeared and I am trying to see if I can develop a feature article on her and the problem of abduction of women in Pakistan. Her name was Maria Bernard." He smiled at the clerk.

"Her husband was issued his driver's license through my office. An elderly man. Kind person. I think his wife accompanied him. Yes. Very young and pretty. Problem, always a problem to let beauty warp your reason."

The clerk stopped in front of Ikbal and confronted him directly. "Do you not agree that beautiful women are a problem for most men? Personally, I have been content with my wives. Allah spares me. What about you?"

"I agree. I have but one wife, a good and plain woman and fine children. Yes, I would agree, strikingly beautiful women exposed before men's eyes present real problems for most men. Cover them up. Do you agree?" He tapped the man's arm with a familiar gesture.

"Of course. Cover. Cover. Perhaps the Taliban are right. We must return to Sharia. Pakistan has moved away from Allah, from the teachings of the Prophet, blessings are upon him."

"So, your new boss Feroz Hakim is different from his predecessor, more fundamental in his approaches?" asked Ikbal.

The man paused, turned his head sideways and looked at Ikbal, a bit suspicious. "If you were not a reporter I would give opinion, but I must be careful. All I can say is that the late Sher Khan was a loner, one who kept all information to himself, shared nothing with anyone, and made all the decisions. He was feared." He smiled.

"Strange you respond with a question about Feroz Hakim by talking about his dead boss. All right. I see your point. May I ask one question? Does your present boss delegate well, whereas Sher Khan was a person who did everything alone?"

"The new man delegates. He has people in his office giving them things to do, even myself. He does not like to use a driver however, nor a police car with the lights on it. He is a private person. He hires people to help him to do things, whereas Sher Khan did things himself." The clerk sat on the railing on the verandah now, more relaxed.

"Oh. Interesting. Like what kind of person would a policeman hire?"

He stopped to think for a moment. "All I know is that he hires our police handyman we call Mistiri, to do odd jobs for him after hours and ..."

"But he is available to do things all day without being paid extra. I don't understand." Ikbal sat next to the clerk now.

"I saw Mistiri bring a large green trunk to the late Senior Superintendent's office and give it to Feroz Hakim. Another time I saw Mistiri sitting in his personal car driving in the bazaar. That is strange, to drive with a low caste person like Mistiri, one of the Hindus who stayed after the Partition. Very strange."

"Is he that old? My goodness he must be an old man.?" Ikbal laughed.

"No. Mistiri's father stayed on here. I think Mistiri still lives in a small village where mostly infidels live. I am not sure." He looked at his watch. "It is time for me to go home."

"I have not had tea this afternoon, or anything to eat. Would you let me order tea and some hot bread and chick peas for us? Please. I am starved."

The clerk smiled and yelled for his peon who was instructed to bring tea and food quickly.

Ikbal slept a good deal on the air-conditioned bus trip to Sukkur. His own car was old and unreliable and he hated long trips on Pakistani roads which in many places lacked maintenance. The bus pulled into the Sukkur bus loading area. He got out with his single suitcase, a simple pressed cardboard affair he had purchased years ago, but hated to abandon in favor of the more expensive luggage with wheels. He had fashioned his own shoulder strap from an old belt. He walked to the taxi area, blending in well with others traveling. The taxi took him to the local government rest house where he had booked a room for two nights rather than pay for a local hotel that would cost him more. He could do with less luxury. Why pay fifty rupees more when all one did was shut one's eyes in sleep.

Early the next morning he ate a breakfast of greasy fried eggs and rubbery toast washed down with a cup of tea. The waiter of the rest house provided the service with a grumpy face and his uniform was not clean and neat. Ikbal decided to write a brief feature article about the inefficiency of Government Rest Homes in Pakistan and wrote a note to remind himself. He left his suitcase in his room but took his valuables with him. The sun had risen as he walked toward the river, trying to locate a boatman to take him across to the island. He passed food stalls along the way and paused to purchase a package of sweet biscuits in case he was without food on the island. He was informed where to go to get a boat and as he walked along the road that paralleled the river he looked out toward the island which was his destination. He saw boats on the water. The fishermen threw their nets and drew them in but from what he observed they only caught a few finger length fish.

The boat trip was a problem for him. He hated boats because they felt insecure as the river moved under them. He held to the sides of the boat tensely. The old man who was his boat operator was in a talkative mood.

"The island is a popular place. I have transported a Lahore policeman, two buffalo bulls, a pregnant woman, a young man with dirty clothes from Sialkot, my son Jhika who seems to have developed some sort of attraction for the place, and now a visitor from Lahore. Did you tell me what your business is?" He adjusted the sail to catch the breeze and paddled the ancient wood boat as well to keep it moving against the current.

"No I did not tell you. Just say that I am a writer. I write about lots of things such as Government Rest Houses, transportation systems, efficiency of boat operators, island life. Lots of things." He smiled, his crooked, long, stained teeth exposed.

"Well if you are interested in writing about the boat operator, you can write that I got a new woman, me an old tired man who recently is now even more tired." He laughed as well, revealing two missing teeth in the front which made him lisp.

"The people who read books and magazines and newspapers don't care about your bed life, unless it deals with murder or blood feuds."

"What about river dolphins? Write about them. The government seems to care more about saving dolphins than saving starving people on the streets of Sukkur. One man who came to investigate the recent death of a dolphin told me they were 'endangered'. He explained that if they are hunted any more there will be none left. I told him that they tasted good. He was surprised. If a dolphin gets caught in our fishing nets it drowns. We cannot help it. So we eat it." He grunted as he paddled hard to miss a log moving on the surface of the water. "Our people do not have the same food restrictions as you Muslims. We eat almost anything." Again he laughed, sticking his tongue out between the missing teeth.

The barking of the dogs alerted Ankh that a boat had pulled up on the sand. She did not expect her sales agent Jhika so she stepped out of the gate and looked to the base of the island. A tall man with European pants and shirt, who had large ears that stood out, walked up the trail toward the walled compound. She got a shawl to cover herself wondering who this visitor could be. She had to call the dogs back as the man came closer. He stood uneasily waiting for her to control the dogs, but because they stood near her he did not move forward. He had an unnatural fear of dogs.

"Salaam. I am Ikbal. I work for a newspaper in Lahore. I am called a reporter. May I speak with the woman called Ankh?"

"Come forward. We can sit in the courtyard of the walled compound in the shade and talk. Come." She did not cover her face, nor avert her eyes as he walked up. He did not know whether he should extend his hand for her to shake, so he just nodded.

"I am Ikbal from the Dawning, a newspaper. Do you read?"

She shook her head. "I am called Ankh. Please, we have few visitors. I will ask the caretaker to make us some tea and ..."

He interrupted her. "I have some biscuits that we can take with the tea." He took them out of his pocket and handed them to her.

"May I ask you some questions first?" Her initiation of the conversation surprised him, but he nodded.

"Has the policeman Feroz Hakim written anything about me or my friend Maria in the newspapers? He said he was going to write something. I want to know what he wrote."

"Did he say he would send it to you?" he asked.

"No. I don't read, but I could give it to my ...the owner of the island when he comes. His name is Dohst Mohammed. He would read it and tell it to me. He gave me a paper on which he wrote some words. Could you read it to me, please." She dug into her pocket and took out the paper on which Dohst had written a few words. She handed it to Ikbal.

He read it quietly, turned it over, then read it again. "It says that you are no longer a slave of his family. It says he sets you free. That is all. It has the marks of fingerprints on it that he says are witnesses."

She reached for the paper, then she changed her mind. "Do you have a pen with you?"

He took out a pen. "Please write on it that you read it to me on today's date and sign your name. It may help me some day."

He thought for a moment, wagged his head from side to side and wrote a few words and signed it. "Why do you want me to do this?"

"Because I don't read and I want to make sure that he wrote what he said. You are a person who writes so now I know it to be true and that you have told me. Thank you."

"How do you know this person Dohst Mohammed?"

She hesitated, placing her hands on her bulging abdomen. "He is the father of my child."

"Oh, so you are his wife? I see. I understand now why he freed you, though Muslim men may keep women slaves within their harem." He looked at her pretty face, her big eyes and curly hair spilling out from under her shawl. "His father is dead. He died in Karachi. I should say he killed himself. He was accused of kidnapping a woman called Maria Bernard. That is what Feroz Hakim wrote about. He said that he talked with you and that you told him things that convinced him that Maria was at the border village that was bombed, and that she is now dead."

Ankh had tears in her eyes. "Yes. The entire village was destroyed. Her room was next to the big house and that was nothing but a big hole in the ground. She is gone."

"Did you give the Deputy Superintendent any thing that belonged to Maria? Like a piece of clothing or a letter with her signature. Anything?"

The tea arrived and they glanced at each other as they ate Digestif Biscuits. Maria dipped hers in the tea. She left the first one in the hot liquid too long and it disintegrated and slid to the bottom of her cup. She dipped more quickly and ate one after another. The package of twenty was half empty before they continued to talk. Ikbal almost regretted having supplied the biscuits, watching them disappear one after another so quickly.

"I gave him a small pocket comb that Maria had given me. That is all, nothing else. Just a comb, the kind that folds together." She ate a few more biscuit and picked up the remaining three and held them in her hand.

"Why did she give you that?" he asked.

"Why do you give people you love presents? I loved her."

"You loved her? Did she speak Urdu? How did you talk?"

"At first with our hands, then using words we learned. She wrote some down on paper on a notebook. She took out the paper with the drawing of an eye on it next to a picture of an eye. Maria had written in large letters, ANKH. He looked at it and handed it back.

"You said she had a notebook. What did it look like?"

"This wide." She held up her hands. "It had a red cover that was shiny, like a book. It had a black cloth to hold the pages together. It was like a school note book used by secondary school students."

"Ankh I am going to tell you something I have not told others. Two weeks ago an Afghani horseman went to a small town on the border and tried to sell a book like that to a merchant. The merchant looked at it. It was water-stained and many pages were stuck together so he only gave him a couple of rupees for it. The merchant called his local newspaper and told him about it and that it was found in the snow by horsemen fifteen miles from the Pakistani border town that was bombed. That newspaper man called my office in Lahore and asked if I would like to buy it. It had words written in English and in Roman Urdu and pictures of cats, dogs, beds, many pictures and a diary written in English that could barely be read. Water had blurred the ink on some of the pages. I did not buy it. But I still have the man's number." He paused to look at the face of the young woman in front of him. Her eyes were huge. She was breathing hard.

"Maria is alive! I knew it. She is alive. She carried the notebook with her wherever she went. That is why she wanted to have me give her the old *burkah*. She escaped and never told me. She escaped before the bombing." Her face broke into a huge smile. She got up and walked into the house. She raised her arms up and made funny sounds. "Alive!"

Ikbal smiled. I was right. The stupid Deputy jumped the gun. The case is not solved. When he sees the new headlines he will be demoted. He looked at the pen in his hand. He said, "Yes!"

Ankh returned in a few minutes and sat facing him. The scarf slipped from her head. She ignored it. "Maria is alive. She is walking in the mountains of Afghanistan. She is like me, with child and someone should help her. It was cold. There was snow."

"When I return, I will inform the authorities. May I ask you a question now?" She nodded. "Did Feroz Hakim come with anyone to the island here?"

"No, he came alone. He said he left his helper, a man he called Mistiri to look after the vehicle, sleep in it while he was on the island. That is all."

"Do you have enough to live on here? How do you get food, soap, kerosene?"

"When we have money, the boatman brings it here for us. We have no money now."

Ikbal took out his billfold and counted out five one hundred rupee notes, then reconsidered and made it three and handed these to Maria. "Use this money. I will get a message to you in the future about Maria if anything is discovered about where she is. Dohst sometimes comes to Lahore. If he does and I see him I will tell him I saw you. You have helped me and Maria. Thank you." He got up to leave, the boatman still waiting on the beach. "Keep the rest of the biscuits."

Maria was chewing the last of them. She stood on the path and watched the reporter climb into the boat. She called out shrilly to the boatman. "Tell Jhika to come. I am out of supplies" She held up the money in her hand and waved it at the boatman.

☪

Atiqullah had pressed his little group to move as rapidly as possible, but Maria held them up. The bindings on her feet came loose. Maria sat on the ground and tried to re-tie them. Atiqullah kneeled in front of her and undid the bandages from both feet and held up Maria's feet and looked at them. She had stone cuts and her feet were swollen. He took off his own shoes and stuffed the toes with cloth and pulled them on to Maria's feet. Marie looked down, and in spite of her discomfort laughed again. Charlie Chaplin, she thought. Ridiculous! He ignored her laughter, tied the laces tight and pulled her to her feet. He motioned for her to walk. She did and the shoes many sizes too large looked like the feet of geese. She imitated Chaplin, feet splayed out in an exaggerated fashion. He smiled, and laughed as well. They trudged up the hill more slowly.

They did not arrive in the village until it was dark. Maria was exhausted and was assisted by Atiqullah. He put her arm around his waist because he was so tall and reached over and supported her with his hand across her back. His own club foot was aching and he limped heavily. On the last leg of the trip the two of them clung to each other for support. Again Maria laughed, remembering the bag races at the high school in the Philippines. He patted her back and said something she did not understand as they moved toward the small town. He was worried she was going insane, she was laughing as they struggled forward, leg against leg.

Twice his companion had told him to leave her alongside the road. She was nothing but trouble. He had refused and became angry. Now, having arrived at their small compound Atiqullah gave orders to an old woman in the compound. Tea was prepared and fresh bread smeared with ghee was brought over. Atiqullah took Maria into his own room and gave her the food, motioning for her to remove her *burkah*. She pulled it off over her head and sagged back on the bed. He pulled her up to a sitting position and held the tea for her. She drank and then began to eat with a ravenous appetite. He smiled and left. Minutes later he returned with a small bottle of Aspro-codeine, took out two and gave them to her, pointing at her feet. She put one in her mouth and swallowed it with tea and lay back and was almost instantly asleep. He covered her with a quilt and left. Twice in the night he returned to look at her. She slept like one dead.

The call to prayer awakened her. She sat up and looked around at the unfamiliar room, at the quilt, the tea cup and tea pot. She poured a cup of cold strong tea and drank it and tried to get up, but her feet hurt terribly. She was trying to stand when Atiqullah returned. Knowing where she was trying to go, he supported her to the small room at the back of the house and left her. She washed her feet with icy cold water and soap twice, then took off her own clothing and poured the cold water over herself, gasping as each cupful poured down across her skin. The toilet-hole in the cement floor and a jug of water for washing herself were a luxuries compared to the leaves she had been using.

She made it back to her room, leaning against the wall. Two women glanced at her and left quickly, mumbling, foreign infidel, foreign infidel. The bottle of pain killers was still on the table. She took out eight tablets and wrapped them in the corner of her shawl, in case she needed them later. Then took another tablet and lay back again.

The bed was a luxury to her. The cotton pad under her was soft, the quilt warm and she again slept for hours. It was noon when he returned, this time with a dish of hot goat curry and flat breads. He squatted next to her bed and pointed at her feet. She stuck them out from under the quilt. He nodded and smiled and left again to return minutes later with bandages and a pair of slippers. She smiled and said "Joe? Thank you." He repeated the only English words which he knew. He said, "Thank you, Joe."

When he had come into the room he had placed a package wrapped in paper on the chair. Now he retrieved it and gave it to Maria. She untied the string and removed a set of Afghan women's clothing, including a head scarf. On top of the set of clothing was a bar of perfumed LUX soap. She pointed at herself. He nodded yes and said the clothes were for her. He touched the clothing she wore and made a face and shook his head. She understood. "Thank you, Joe," she said.

He looked very pleased as he hobbled from the room, in spite of his bent clubfoot paining him. He turned and motioned for her to put on the new clothes. He closed the door. Maria took the bar of soap and walked to the bathing area. She washed herself thoroughly and rinsed off, standing on the soiled clothing she had come with. She kneaded the wet clothing with her feet trying to get out some of the filth. Finally she rinsed out her old clothes and wrung them as dry as she could and dressed in her new outfit. Though her hair was still wet, she covered her head with the scarf and stepped out into the hall leading to her room. An old woman stopped in her tracks, looked at her and went away mumbling. In the room where she had been placed was a wood bookcase. On it was a plastic comb and a small hand mirror. She smiled and worked on her knotted hair, then put the scarf on her head again and looked at her reflection in the tiny mirror. A beautiful Afghani woman looked back at her. She whispered, "James, if you could only see me now."

☪

Sardar did not return for two days. Tur-ali was given food and drink. Bored, he began to explore the Afghan village within the walls. He wandered to one stall where a blacksmith was working and greeted him. The man welcomed him in to sit and watch him work. They talked for more than half an hour, the muscular iron worker smiling and taking special care to treat his young handsome guest with respect.

"What place is this?" asked Tur-ali.

"This is Narang. This household is not in the village itself which was bombed by the cursed Americans. It is in the Narang district. Our people are dedicated to one thing, to ridding our country of the scourge of the infidel. Our *jihad* is to ensure that we and our children will see the day when not one cursed American walks our soil. We, here in Narang have been the spring from which heroes have emerged to drive infidels out of our country. I will tell you stories of our people and how they drove out the British, killed them in their forts, women and children alike, all the infidels, how we drove out the Russians. Now we will get rid of the vermin Americans as well. We have never been a subjugated people. We are Afghani, proud followers of the Prophet, peace be unto to him. Narang's history is one of pride. Every death of one of our people by infidels seeds their own death, one hundred to one. Every one of us is willing to die for the cause."

"You sound like my father. He also hated the Americans."

"The Americans think that they will force democracy on the entire world. The Russians tried to force communism. The British tried to force their great Raj. All of them failed. Do you know their weakness?" The iron worker dipped a red hot piece of metal into water. "You don't know? Look at my hand. It has one piece of metal in it. I heat this one, pound this one, and cool this one until I am satisfied. Imagine if I heated six and tried to pound them all, cool them all at once. Some would not be red hot when I tried to form them, others would be hot but not enough for the work. There is a saying in Urdu and in our language. *Jiske pas bahut kam honge koi na koi bigrega.* If you try to do too many things at once, some will be neglected. Do you understand?"

"I think so. America is trying to control Afghanistan and Iraq at the same time." He laughed.

"Exactly. And they have a hot iron in Iraq and a cool one here. They even want to heat up one in Iran. Korea. Crazy. We will hold <u>our</u> elections in October, <u>they</u> say. Then we will see about their irons here." He hit a hot iron rod and the sparks flew.

"What is Democracy," asked Tur-ali.

"I will tell you. We will play democracy. You and I will vote on how best to form this piece of iron. Do you know anything about it?" The boy shook his head. "Good. How long should we leave the iron in the coals being heated by the bellows? Two minutes or four? Vote. Hold your fingers behind you back. All right. We will show each other." Tur-ali had two fingers showing, the blacksmith showed none.

"Why did you cheat? You showed none."

"Because it does not go by minutes but by how it appears, so I said none. You see if you vote on everything, then a leader's knowledge is meaningless. That is why we have chiefs, people who have lived a long time. That is why we have the Holy Koran to tell us how to do things and what to believe. How can you vote on what Allah says?" He laughed. "Do you want to learn about the Taliban? Do you understand Allah's will for his people?"

Tur-ali replied, "I have read much of the Holy Koran and can recite some of it already. Yes, teach me about the Taliban. I am interested. My father wanted to drive out the infidels as well before he died" He shook his finger at the huge man. "I think you did cheat. Whatever number I said would be wrong. You should say, choose any length of time up to five minutes. "

"Good. Democracy means the majority rules. Like in America. But they should really try it sometime."

Tur-ali frowned, "I thought Bush ruled there." He looked confused.

Now the blacksmith laughed hard. "Exactly! You understand democracy. Bush knows. He preaches Democracy and rules like an emperor. He makes the decisions, his generals all follow his lead. He is called their Commander in Chief. He tells his congress to act, then changes what they decide. Yet he exports Democracy by force, by the sword. You see, Democracy is a lie. The leaders tell all the others what to do. Then they vote and he says he will do the will of his generals. Then the generals decide and he doesn't like that either and he does what he wishes. It sounds like all the leaders in the rest of the world."

He asked Tur-ali to operate the leather bellows to heat the next iron rod. It was hot work but fascinating as the metal heated up, red, yellow and then almost white at the tip.

The boy was now puffing from the effort. "How many Taliban are here?"

"Allah only knows for sure. Taliban means student. We are all students of the will of Allah. Listen, five other young men of your age are learning from our Taliban leaders in this village. They are learning about the most effective personal *jihad,* ways of destroying many of the enemy and gaining eternal glory with Allah. Tomorrow we will meet after the evening meal. I will come to tell you." He reached over and put his arm around the boy's shoulder. "You would be Allah's perfect and most beautiful vengeance against the ugly Americans. Perhaps you will be given the chance to piss on the grave of one of these who are bringing us their brand of democracy. Inshallah. "

☪

"Jack Sprat could eat no fat; his wife could eat no lean, and so betwixt the two of them they licked the platter clean." Jasmin stood in front of Feroz Hakim, his wife and her father Mistiri. She looked up at the Deputy Superintendent for a moment to see his reaction, and then glanced down at her feet in respect.

"That was very nice. Do you have any questions?" He wanted to hear her talk.

"Sir, what is the meaning of lean."

He thought for a moment. "Well, it has been many years since I was in school, but I think it means thin, like a lean man. So she could eat no... yes, yes, meat that was thin. Without fat." He smiled at his clever answer, but wanted her to do the talking. "Why did you choose this poem from the English Reader?"

"It was the second one in the book and it was not very long like the others. English is very difficult." She glanced up and then away.

He wanted to see her eyes so he asked, "What is the picture behind my head about. Tell me a story about the picture." All he remembered was that it was a picture of mountains, streams and red and yellow-leaved trees.

She looked up now at the picture intently. He looked intently at her eyes and her earnest expression. Without knowing he did it he took a deep breath and sighed.

Her eyes did not leave the picture. "It is strange. I see trees that are the wrong color, yellow and red. I see mountains that are not brown but white on top. I see a river that is not brown but looks like clear drinking water. It is a strange picture." She glanced at the Deputy Superintendent again.

"Look again. Is there an animal in the picture?"

Without thinking she stepped a pace forward and stared hard at the picture. "Yes. There is an animal standing on a rock. It is a horse, but it has strange horns like tree branches on its head. Perhaps it is an imaginary animal drawn by the artist."

"Yes. The animal is called an Elk by Americans. The picture is real. It is a picture of a part of America." Without thinking she looked at him as he spoke.

"Is America so beautiful with such colors and such trees, sir?"

"I have not been there but I have been told that some parts are as beautiful as our own Azad Kashmir. Have you seen Kashmir?" Now he too was having a conversation with the girl and they were both talking to each other, oblivious of the others present.

"No. I have never been. I would like to go. I have not traveled outside of Lahore, sir." She did a tiny dip with her knees, and then realized she was not talking to a female teacher but to a man, a male, the Deputy

Superintendent. She became shy and turned half away and covered her head carefully.

"Well, perhaps some day you shall, that is, if you study hard and get good grades and ... are careful." He turned to Mistiri her father. "She will do well. Here is receipt that I want you to sign that you received the money for her school fees for a year and that after that time she will come back here to me for decisions I will make about her future."

Mistiri was unable to write and stood quietly not knowing what to do.

"Oh, I see. Make a mark here. I am writing that that is your mark. Put your fingers here on this pad and you can press your prints on the paper. Here."

Feroz looked at the paper and smiled. "Here is the check to give to the school bursar. I want regular reports on her. Every six months, no, make it four months. I will have her come for more questions to see how well her English is improving. At the end of the school year she will come here again with you and I will decide her future."

"Thank you, Sahib. I wanted to tell you that my new name is Ahmed and that Jasmin will be called Jamilah, sir."

"I see. So you have converted to Islam. Good. He glanced at the girl and said Jamilah. She turned and looked back at the Deputy Superintendent and rose to leave.

Mistiri ushered the girl out of the room.

Feroz Hakim's wife cleared her throat and got up and moved into the kitchen. All she could see in her mind was the lovely, fresh and pretty face of the girl staring intently at the picture on the wall, and the face of her husband as he stared at her face. She knew she would dream of that face and those eyes. She would hear his words again," Well perhaps some day you shall see...." All these years, all these years I have served you and now you are thinking of bringing a school girl into your bed. Well, some day you shall see!

CHAPTER SIX

Joto ya na joto lagan dena parega. (Urdu Proverb)

Whether you "plough or you don't plough", you still have to pay the rent.

Two of the shutters at the back of his house had broken hinges. Ikbal's wife had mentioned this many times, however he never seemed to have the time to do it and he had no tools in his house. It was a windy night in Lahore and the windows rattled and eventually one of them was caught by the wind and sagging on one weak hinge banged against the side of the house. Ikbal got up and tried to pull it shut but in doing so, the remaining hinge pulled loose and the shutter fell to the ground. He cursed.

On his way to the newspaper office he made a detour to the police headquarters. He spoke to the officer who issued driver's licenses and asked if Mistiri was present. Minutes later the handyman came, looking worried, wondering why a man in foreign clothing, wearing a tie would want to speak to him.

"So, you are Mistiri. I have heard that you know how to fix things. Would you consider a small job after you have finished work today? It has to be done today. I need new hinges put on shutters on my house. Can you do that?"

"Yes, Sir. That is my specialty. Hinges and locks. Where do you live, Sir?" He scribbled down the address, a place along the road near the Ravi River. "Must I buy the materials?"

"No, I will get these myself in the bazaar to save you time. Show what I have written and anyone can tell you where I live. Four o'clock?"

The man nodded and bowed, pleased to have a chance to earn a few extra rupees.

It turned out that there were six shutters and windows that needed work and Mistiri stayed until after dark, working with a Primus lantern. When he was putting in screws on the last hinge, Ikbal strolled over to watch him work.

"You do other types of repair work, plumbing, carpentering, car repair, cement work, brick laying?" He watched the man's face carefully.

"I do not repair cars or lay bricks, but I am an experienced cement worker," Mistiri replied.

"I see. Where did you get your experience?"

He hesitated, "In different places, such as the homes of some of the policeman that had work for me." He smiled.

"Do you also help others to purchase things in the bazaar so they do not have to do it themselves?"

"Yes. I am experienced at purchasing and get a good price for what I am sent to buy. I once purchased a tin trunk for a customer and he was pleased with the price I got and he gave me a small *bakshish*. I also purchased cement and cement tools for a customer. I know the sales people in the bazaar well, sir." Mistiri finished his work and turned to look at Ikbal.

"I have been thinking about a tin trunk myself. What sizes do they come in and how much do they cost." Now Ikbal took out a cigarette, hesitated because they were an expensive variety, but gave one to the worker.

"The biggest one costs about R900 or perhaps a bit more."

Ikbal held his hands apart. "About this big?"

Mistiri held his arms out his hands wide apart. "Bigger than this."

"What could fit into such a big tin trunk? It seems to be very large to travel with." Ikbal sat on the steps leading to the kitchen.

"Storage. Most people use the large one for storage. The metal is waterproof and so they store clothing, books, and family treasures. It has a lock on it as well."

"What do you think your clients used it for?" He looked bored.

Mistiri thought for a moment. "Well, whatever he stored there he put into his safe, so it must be valuable."

"A safe? Who in the world has a personal safe nowadays? We have banks to keep our money." He turned and looked at Mistiri in a challenging way.

"I think the tin trunk is used to store papers from the office. But that is a mystery to me as well." Mistiri was getting into deeper water, but felt that since he had not named any names that he was not telling any secrets.

"I have other friends who may like you to do work for them. They will want to know the type of people you have worked for. I mean are they doctors or politicians or what?"

"People that have money, that have their own houses, which work for the government like the police or like yourself for a newspaper. Important people. I can be trusted to do a good job."

"See if you can get a letter of recommendation from these people. I will give you one for doing good work on the hinges. If you have letters from people you work for then others will be more willing to hire you. We are finished here. Here is your money. Tomorrow you can come and I will give you a letter you can use."

Ikbal's suspicions began to be verified. Sher Khan had kept secret and personal files locked in his police office. One such file had information about himself and Piari from so many years before. There was no possibility of any other record; there were no newspapers that had reported the incident. The girl Piari, he had lost track of, but he had heard gossip that she had been in her twenties before she had been married off to an elderly suitor as a co-wife, but it was only gossip. Mistiri had bought a trunk to transport material from Sher Khan's office to Feroz Hakim's home. In all likelihood Feroz had had a safe installed in his own home. He could visualize it now and in it documents which could ruin the lives of many people. His own file was probably the top one which Feroz had read and used to threaten him.

He had combed the archives looking for information about Feroz Hakim and had come up with nothing. The man had been a nobody, a yes man for Sher Khan, had quietly gone about his work and had not become known to the public until he wrote his article about the mystery of Maria Bernard's abduction being solved. Ikbal's own article which accused the policeman of jumping the gun had infuriated Feroz who now was seeking revenge. One thing was clear, Feroz was not a very clever man, perhaps, thought Ikbal, and he had barely passed his courses along the way. He jumped to conclusions without having sufficient evidence.

He began to draft a new article about the Maria Bernard case, based on information he had gleaned from his visit to the island home of Sheikh

Mohammed in Sukkur. After an hour of writing and re-writing he had a draft which he typed up and printed to take home. His habit was always to sleep on a new idea for one or two nights before embarking on it.

DEPUTY FEROZ ACTIVITIES REVEALED

Feroz Hakim's report of two weeks ago stated that the case of the abduction of Maria Bernard had been solved. New evidence has come to light which shows that Mrs. Bernard had left Bahadur before it was bombed! She escaped into Afghanistan on foot wearing a burkah. One of her personal artifacts has recently been put up for sale by an Afghani merchant. The article is a personal diary, which is almost surely to have been owned by Mrs. Bernard. A witness, interviewed by this reporter possessed an article, a page ripped from this document which will be matched against the new evidence.

The Deputy Superintendent of Police, Feroz Hakim who has taken over the work left by his predecessor, Sher Khan, informed reporters that all the papers and current files in the office of the late Sher Khan, related to police business. What is strange is that two eye witnesses have stated that a tin trunk of materials was moved from that office to the home of Feroz within two days of the time when Mr. Hakim occupied the office of his deceased boss. Not only this, one confidential source interviewed by this reporter informed him that one of his clients had a safe installed recently. If this was installed in the home of Feroz Hakim, then the question that needs to be asked is, what does that mystery safe contain?

It is hoped that regional law enforcement offices will look into these mysterious matters in order to shed light on the mystery of the large tin trunk.

The article appeared in The Dawning the following morning and telephones began to ring in many offices in Lahore. Reporter Ikbal's phone never stopped ringing. After the sixth call in an hour, the last from the U.S. HELP office in Lahore, he stopped answering calls and turned on the answering machine so he could screen and delay enquiries. Not only was the fire burning hotly but the smoke screen it was causing blinded Feroz Hakim as he sat in his police office reading the headlines.

Ikbal's cousin in Peshawar had met with an Afghani merchant and had purchased a bedraggled red note book for five hundred rupees. He had called Ikbal's private cell phone to verify that the purchase had been successful. A page had indeed been torn from it.

C*

Never before in his life had Feroz been frozen with terror. Now he sat with the newspaper article in front of him and shook. He dripped sweat. His hands shook. He took no calls, turned off his telephone, locked his door and refused to meet any appointments.

His mind raced from one thing to another. He could not decide which way to move. The tin trunk! The damn trunk painted with a huge Pakistani flag now sat in his living room covered with a blanket. If the Regional Police issued an order, his house would be searched and the trunk discovered. Mistiri, damn talkative man had helped Ikbal set the trap against him; the stupid ignorant man! His lovely daughter, now with her school fees paid for a year, what of her? What of her? Soft eyes, gentle voice. Damn Mistiri! The safe in the bedroom closet. Allah. It is impossible to remove easily, impossible to move. Move the contents of the safe before there is a police search. Where? How? The tin trunk? Allah, the stupid tin trunk. The contents of Sher Khan's files. Ikbal's files. What about other information from the files? His list of names and contents in code? That list sat now on top of the safe for his easy reference. Now he began to sweat again and his hands shook so he was unable to continue to write notes. The deed from Sher Khan's file that he had given to Dohst Mohammed's slave woman Ankh, piqued by kindness, would hang him now if it came to light. Could he get the paper back from her and destroy it? How much time do I have? His bowels became a problem for him now and he rushed to the latrine, locking up his office. He sat with his stomach aching. Ikbal, the bastard, the low bastard who had raped a school girl, now sits in his office writing about ME! He must be silenced! How? Now all he could think about was Ikbal; he cursed and made an oath of vengeance against this enemy. If another article was written he would be damned, lose his position. Damn, the latest article may doom me and my career. Allah. I will kill the stupid bastard and shut his mouth forever! He has ruined my life. Vengeance is mine.

The telephone rang and his immediate superior from the Regional Police Hdq. was on the line.

"Is it true? Is it true what the newspapers say? Did you remove material from Sher Khan's office soon after his death?" The man was shouting.

"Nonsense! It is true that I took a tin trunk that I purchased in the bazaar to my home at the end of the day. There is nothing wrong with taking an item one purchases and bringing it home later. Allah, sir! This reporter, like so many, tells half-truths to make his stories interesting and to sell more newspapers. You can come to my home today, I welcome you to drive over; I will meet you there. The trunk is filled with cold weather clothing covered with moth balls." He was sweating.

"I can't come over now. Listen, you must interview another reporter from a different competing paper and give your entire story. I am sure my boss in Islamabad will be calling me soon about you. Police should only be in the news when they make news about their success. This report fans the flames of those who hate us. I will call tomorrow." He hung up.

He did not hurry. He stopped in the office of the Automobile License first. He greeted the man who looked nervous. On his desk was a copy of the newspaper and the article about the tin trunk and moving files. There were only two people who could have given the information, this bastard and the stupid Mistiri.

"I see you have read the news." He said it like a challenge.

"Sir! Oh, yes. Terrible sir. I am sorry sir." The man stammered.

"Think carefully before you answer because I have witnesses. Did the reporter Ikbal visit you here in your office within the last seven days? Do not reply yet. Think. If you give a false answer you will be fired, lose your pension and become my enemy. Think carefully. Did you visit with Ikbal, here or anywhere during the last seven days?"

The man began to cry. "He comes here frequently when there are news items related to the police. We frequently talk and I serve him tea. It is not unusual to talk to the press in an informal way. Yes. I spoke to the man."

"Then why are you weeping? Are you remembering the words you spoke that damned me? Are you remembering why you said them? Are you remembering the quiet bribe you received for the information? I have often wondered who the mole was around here. Now I know who the rat is." He adjusted the gun in his holster.

"Sir! Please do not speak such words. I am a long time veteran of the police service sir and have nothing against my record, sir. I talked to the reporter about family, gossip about Bollywood, my recent purchases in the bazaar. Common things, sir." Now, he remembered his sharing information about Mistiri who brought in a tin trunk and that later he saw it being loaded into the boot of the Deputy's car.

"Did you mention a tin trunk, one with the Pakistani flag painted on it?" Feroz reached around and picked up the newspaper and read the offending article.

"It was not on purpose sir. We were simply sharing small-talk and I may have mentioned how hard you worked, what late hours you kept, that you always drove your own car without police lights..." He felt he was heading down a dangerous slope.

"Go on! More about my driving habits, my after-hour activities, my personal life. Go on!" He was livid with anger.

"I did mention about Mistiri being of personal service to you sir, because Ikbal wanted to find a handy man to do jobs for him and I brought him up. It was nothing sir." His eyes were big and tear-filled.

"What more about Mistiri? Oh well, I will talk with him too after this and the entire story will come out. You are aware, are you not, that the handyman has the habit of sharing everything he hears with his friends in his village, with other handymen in town. He is a weak low-caste Hindu, an uneducated person who finds some satisfaction in knowing people who have power. He thinks that if one works for a king, one becomes a kind of king. You understand." He pushed his face close to the clerk's face who backed away.

"I would suggest that you make a phone call to Mr. Ikbal at his office and tell him that the way the story was written was not correct, that he did not remember well what you actually told him. Remember, it is his word against yours. If he gets you to testify, which he won't, because you are a confidential witness, all you need to say is that he jumped to conclusions about what you two talked about and that he needs to write another article which clears up the accusations that I stole material from Sher Khan's files." He now talked more softly. "If you do this, now, while I am listening, I will not file a formal complaint to have you fired from your job and lose your pension. I mean now! I am waiting."

The clerk picked up the phone and looked at a pad of paper, read a number and dialed it. "May I speak to Mr. Ikbal please?" He cleared his throat. "Mr. Ikbal, this is Karim the Licensing clerk at the police station, sir. Yes. Good morning sir. Sir, I am very sorry to tell you that the article you wrote in the newspaper contains information that was not correct. It was not what I told you sir." He waited while Ikbal talked loudly on the other end. "Sir. I am so sorry but the information was not correct sir. I never said he took material from the office of Sher Khan, I just said he took a tin trunk from that office and put it into his boot sir." He waited for more than a minute before he could say something again. "Sorry sir. Sorry sir." He hung up and looked at Feroz Hakim staring at him.

"You may have kept your pension, I am not sure. Hand me that pad of paper on which a number is written." He pointed to the pad on Karim's desk.

He looked at it and tore off the first page and threw it into the waste basket and handed him the pad with a clean sheet of paper on the top. Feroz took it and quickly walked to the waste basket, retrieved the crumpled paper, smoothed it out and put it into his pocket. "So, a common clerk working for the police keeps the number of a reporter from the Dawning right on top of his desk, ready to report any and all newsworthy items. Is that a new suit coat? So. There are rats everywhere." He smiled and got up to leave.

"Please, sir, this job and my pension are my life, my whole life, sir. Please in the name of Allah, forgive me, sir. He bent down to put his head on the Deputy's shoes. Feroz stopped him and pulled him up.

"Yes. I will consider your plea. Rats and moles are usually dispatched. Vermin are not tolerated. I will consider it. I am sure Mr. Ikbal will make a personal appearance to your office very soon. How you deal with him will indicate how serious your intent is to keep your job." He turned and walked toward the door, then paused and tossed the small note pad onto the top of the desk and smiled.

☪

Dohst had left the rental agreement on the table in the front room after Meher and he had discussed it. He went to his back room to retrieve a file from his box and she went to make tea. Pagali picked up the paper and squatted on the floor. She creased the paper, folding it in half. She creased that half and then carefully tore along the crease lines. Her favorite toys were cloth which she folded repeatedly, and paper which she enjoyed tearing up into progressively smaller pieces. The thin paper of the receipt was a delight to her. She now had eight pieces and these she lay out in a row on the floor in a straight line, then starting at the beginning she once again began to fold and tear each of these into ever smaller pieces.

Meher Jamal almost dropped the tray with tea cups on the floor when she returned to the room and saw the destroyed receipt for the rental of the new shop. She let out a screech and rushed forward and pushed Pagali away from the papers on the floor.

"Stop! Get away. You have ruined it!" She bent over and began to pick up the small squares when Dohst returned and rushed over and began to help her.

"Stupid girl! Don't ever rip up any paper unless I give it to you. Stupid!" He almost struck her. "Now what are we going to do?"

He and Meher lay the small papers on a table and began to assemble them, fitting the tiny squares like a jigsaw puzzle together.

"If you buy clear tape I will carefully join them together. At least you will have a record of your payment and the agreements you made with the old man."

"Let us learn from this. I will lock all my papers in the little metal box. You know what I mean. It has money in it and a deed of my Sukkur Island property. I carry the key with me."

"I fear to ask, but could you take us to the bazaar so I could purchase food. We are short of almost everything. If there is money perhaps you could buy a bag of rice, a bag of *ata* for making bread and another of sugar for tea and sweets. I forgot, lentils and onions and..." she stopped when she saw impatience in his eyes.

"Three women to support, they do nothing but eat."

"There are only two of us, but it is true the Pagali seems to eat for two because of her pregnancy." She was surprised that she had replied so quickly.

"Three. I have a slave, no a servant girl on the island that I support as well. But she is clever and grows things, takes care of animals, milks the buffalo, and even sells a few unnecessary things in the house for cash."

Meher did not immediately reply not wanting to challenge or offend. She looked at the back of Dohst's head as he bent over placing squares of paper together and was amazed that the night before her own hands had been on that head, holding it in the darkness. "How did you obtain a slave?

I have not heard the use of that word for a long time? Our government has forbidden us to formally have slaves."

"She belonged to my father who died. He had bought her. Now she is mine, but I..." He looked up into her face and saw tears in her eyes. "I freed her. She is no longer a slave, just a servant like you." He thought about his reply for a moment. "I have given you a marriage contract. I have not given her such a contract."

"Is she young and beautiful?"

Dohst looked at Meher's plain, thirty year old, serious face, at her eyes filled with concern. He sighed. "She is beautiful, just a girl and is pregnant." He had not thought about the implication of what he said for a moment because of Pagali. Her pregnancy was advanced and he was the father of that child as well. He seemed to forget that he could be responsible for Pagali's child, but there had been no other man but he in the house. He seemed to forget that the episode of love making on the sand beach on the island had caused Ankh's pregnancy. He some times wondered about it because among his friends it was rumored that it took many sexual episodes to make a woman pregnant.

Meher Jamal left the room and went into the bedroom and closed the door. She put her head in her hands and cried softly. Three women! Two pregnant. Whenever she looked at Pagali she could hardly imagine that she and Dohst had been together. Whenever she looked at Dohst she could hardly imagine that the two of them each night held each other's bodies in sexual embrace in the darkness.

Dohst waited for half an hour for her to return, then picked up the small table and carried it to the back room and locked the door, not wanting Pagali once again to play with the paper squares. He took two pages from a Bollywood advertisement that he had in his room of Indian women and on his way out of the house, gave them to Pagali. He decided that he would teach her a new game when he returned that evening, that is, putting a picture back together.

He bought grease, a screwdriver and hand brooms and pedaled to his newly acquired vacant store. On the way he passed a group of men who clustered together near the entrance way to the Sialkot Tennis Racquet factory seeking manual labor. They crowded around him shouting at him, telling him what they could do, what good workers they were. He looked at them all, trying to find two people who were physically fit but not aggressive and pushy. To the surprise of the young eager workers, he selected two men who had been pushed to the back. One had a drooping eyelid; the other was heavily pockmarked with evidence of small pox as a youth. He pointed at them to their surprise. They trotted after him as he slowly pedaled his bike to his new holding.

He supervised as they swept out the place, the ceilings, walls and floors. He borrowed a bucket from the oil seller next door and the men washed the entire place, throwing bucket after bucket of water in which he had poured a liberal amount of Izal, while one swept the filthy water away. By noon the place was cleaner and he set the men to work in the back courtyard, burying the remains of the cat, pulling weeds and grass with their hands and then sweeping the courtyard clean and dumping the trash across the back fence. While they labored he used the screw-driver and worked at the metal bands that held the boxes together until they snapped. Then he pried the lids off and eagerly looked into the boxes. Carefully protected in blocks of white Styrofoam, the portable air conditioners looked like new. He removed the front of the box and saw the attractive machines, their shining paint and the label, Peacock Machinery Works, Taiwan. He covered the machines but did not pound the nails back.

The laborers were exhausted and filthy and stood waiting to be paid. He told them that he would use them again in the coming week if they did not have employment. They left looking at the money in their hands as if they were disappointed. He sighed and took out two ten rupee notes and gave each of them a small tip. They moved away, pleased.

"The first rule of business is to save every rupee along the way. A soft heart makes for a soft wallet." His neighbor who watched the process of cleaning up the next door store shouted to Dohst in a friendly manner. "Whether you plough or don't plow, you will still have to pay the rent."

"Allah rewards the merciful. Allah sees the just master who treats his slaves and servants well." Dohst replied back.

"So we have a reader of the Holy Book. I will have to watch myself. I was not aware that I was getting a Taliban next to me." He laughed again. "Nowadays students are everywhere."

"No, not that, but a neighbor who may become a business partner who now knows a secret." He smiled.

"A secret? Already? You hardly know me."

"My business neighbor loves to hold tight to the *paisa*. If I do business with you I will have to be careful for myself, wondering if my penny is being spent wisely." Dohst sauntered over and shook the man's hand. "Dohst Mohammed."

"Abdulhassan," replied the other. "Have you considered investing into this business? See how many tins of T2 discount oil I sell a day. Good money." He ordered tea to be brought to them.

"I have decided to wait a couple of weeks. I have another business deal to complete and then I will talk with you again." Dohst sounded very professional.

"And what kind of business deal are you into, kind sir?"

"I would rather not say at this time. You know, the competition." Dohst sipped his tea.

"So you are going into the oil business behind my back because of what I told you?" He tried to look offended.

"No, another matter. Not oil. I don't know oil. To me oil is a slippery business, however..."

"Slippery? Oh, *chikna*, I understand. Of course you mean smooth, not slippery. Take care when you lock up, that a cat or dog is not hidden in your store. The last tenant was a rotten neighbor." They both slapped each other's hands, enjoying their Urdu puns and banter.

☪

Half of the men stood up and began to shout, "Jihad! Jihad!" The room was crowded; officials were seated on carpets on the floor around a central area where they had spread their papers, or had put their weapons. Behind them stood men, all carrying their weapons. The leader raised his hand and waited for the room to quiet.

"The opium survey that was done a few months ago in October by our Government of Afghanistan Narcotics Directorate and its findings were sent to Kabul and to the Americans. We know it was not accurate, but accurate enough. We can be proud of the numbers. I was surprised that so much had been grown and harvested. The opium crop was good, very good. The opium needs of other parts of the infidel world remains strong. Support for our causes comes from these sales. The West is dependent on opium products and every kilo we grow is sold to a hungry infidel market.

It is hard to imagine that Americans use tons of opium every year. It makes one wonder about their civilization. You have heard about the ancient Chinese who also were addicted to the drug?" He looked around at the attentive faces which looked blank "The West drinks the oil that Iran, Iraq, Saudi Arabia produce. Their beautiful huge cars guzzle oil. We rejoice." There was murmuring. He raised his hand again. "Listen to me. Return to our people and encourage them to grow more in every tiny place poppies can flourish. We do not have oil under our soil like Iraq and Iran. They do not have our opium. We have opium that the enemy needs and will pay for at the price of gold, while they officially curse us for growing it. The crop this year should be even larger and our work, the Taliban's cause to bring the rule of Sharia here and in Pakistan, will be served by their addictions."

Someone shouted, "What about what happened in Chaman?"

"Yes. Chaman. Our border town is more vulnerable than others. It is indeed a tragedy that Maulvi Abdul Mannan was arrested. May Allah be merciful to him and grant him glory and peace. Any one of you may be arrested. As servants of Allah we must expect persecution, but through the fire of persecution we will become red hot and burn them. Our Jihad is sanctioned by Allah. There will be many martyrs. Blessed are you if you are persecuted, rejoice, die for His sake. If you are chosen to be one, rest happily in eternal peace in *asman*. We, people of Islam are not afraid of death!" The young men sitting in front of him glanced at each other. "But they are terrified of death. What does that tell you? We fight with our bodies covered with a shirt; they hide behind tanks, behind head-to-toe body armor. They get a scratch they whimper and get a Purple Heart and head home to show their whoring wives their talisman. We know that our days are numbered, that the time of our death is ordained. We are fearless under Allah's merciful will for us. But remember this, they are terrified of catching one of <u>our</u> bullets because they think <u>they</u> control life and death; that they can cheat the time of their dying. They do not know that the very minute and second of the time of their deaths is ordained."

"Their rockets hit Narang only last week. How should we react?" Another shouted from the group standing.

"Be cleverer than they. Pass information of their coming and going to each other. Use your cell phones. Avoid their attacks; attack them at their weakest points. A rocket launched at a group of their vehicles pulled up

along-side the road when they take out their binoculars to scan the countryside, when they are resting and having an energy drink, eating specially
packaged foods filled with vitamins, a single rocket crashing down on them
can destroy many lives. Then the news reports about our attacks will stream
across the world while they shudder. Terrorism! We number in the millions.
One by one we will attack them. Even an elephant does not stand a chance
when millions of ants are on the march, and just a few climb up its trunk
to drive it mad. They have now appointed an interim leader, Karzai, with
his green cape. We are not fooled. He wears the green of holiness, of the
chosen. But he was not chosen by us!" The crowd of men shouted and
cheered.

"We will meet in a different place in two weeks. Already there is probably one among us who has used his cell phone to call a friend to tell them
where we are now meeting." He looked around and they avoided his gaze.
"They put this on their GPS and soon a rocket will quietly come down and
blast this place. Our worst enemy is our own traitor, one of our own people
who for dollars betray us, our cause. May his eternal state be of torture, fire
and pain. Keep your lips sealed, your phones turned off about where you
meet and your ears open. If you hear someone betraying us, though he be
your father or your brother, report him. Even if it is your bearded grand
father. The devil takes many forms."

"No. No one here is a traitor. Impossible!" A tall young bearded man
shouted out bravely.

"Let us see who survives during the next month. We will know. Have
ears, big ears, listen, and keep your mouths shut. Listen and if you have
news of any one who betrays us do not hesitate to extinguish his lights.
Vigilance for Allah!"

The group began to disband, as if mention that someone had already
informed the enemy of where they gathered was a reality. The men left
in groups of twos and threes, heading in different directions muttering to
themselves.

The Taliban leaders talked to each other, making arrangement for the
next meeting. A man with a crippled foot, turned sideways like a club, tall
and gaunt with large protruding ears called out.

"I have a small matter to bring before the council. Can you give me five
minutes of your time? I need your leadership to do the right thing before

Allah." Atiqullah stood away from the wall where he had been standing during the meeting.

The Taliban leaders turned and looked at the man, crippled from birth with a club foot by the will of Allah. They knew him well, a bright man, but because of his malformation one that had been taunted as a child by other children, and rejected as a suitor by parents who were not willing to give their daughters to such a man, fearing that the children born to such a one would also be abnormal.

"Yes. We are leaving, but if it is a small matter, speak." The leader turned to look at Atiqullah impatiently.

"It is a very strange happening. I have taken an infidel woman, an American who escaped from Pakistan as my personal prisoner. We are against the infidel and in a war against Americans on our soil. Yet, here one of their women was captured by me on a mountain trail. I wish to claim her as my slave, taken as a prisoner in this holy war. I have no woman of my own. I wish to keep this one as my own. There is a complication. She is pregnant. So I also wish to claim her child as my *dhimmi* slave as well, whether it be a male or female. She was brought into our town, covered in a *burkah*. No others have seen her."

"This is a truly amazing request. You say you have taken a slave woman, an American? Where is she now?"

"I have put her into my own room. She slept there last night. I have given her food and have clothed her. Allah has heard my prayers. I have been given a woman slave to help me. I claim her and request that she be excluded from Islamic functions because of her slave status." His speech surprised the religious leaders because of his reference to taking captives, prisoners in war.

The leaders now spoke amongst themselves, arguing points of the *Sharia* while Atiqullah stood patiently listening. One turned to him now and asked a question.

"Do you wish to bring this slave before us so we can see her?"

"What would you see of her except her eyes, and the bulge of her stomach under her clothing? I do not understand. Only I have seen her when I clothed her. It is not suitable for others to see her. She does not speak a word of our language except that she says, 'Allah bismillah' from time to time. No, I do not wish to display her, shame her and me."

Again the men talked, looking back at Atiqullah from time to time. One elder stood and faced him. "We have decided that it is not for us to judge against you on this matter. We agree we are in a state of holy war. We agree that you captured her and can, under war, claim her as your slave. She is an infidel, but we encourage you to teach her the language and perhaps she will revert to Islam in due time. The teachings of the Prophet, blessings be unto him, relating to how to treat slaves apply in this case. Treat her with understanding; feed her as you would anyone in your home. Be merciful as Allah is merciful."

A second leader stood. "I have heard that a number of Pakistani Christian children, both boys and girls have been abducted in Pakistan and brought to Peshawar and have been sold as slaves to those who have wealth to buy them. Many Christian organizations are working against this practice, some even pretending to be buyers and purchasing them only to free them. It is not against the customs of our people to own slaves. We have done so throughout our history of the Holy Prophet, peace be unto him. He has spoken about the need to treat the slaves in our homes with honor. He has told us not to call them slaves, rather refer to them as the man servant in our home, or the woman in our home who is under our hand. Treat this woman with mercy. In six months return to the council and tell us about her condition. Until then she must always remain in complete seclusion behind the walls of your home, under your care. What is the woman's name?"

She has the name of the mother of their Prophet, Jesu. Her name is Maria."

"This is a good omen. We have advised you well. Treat this Maria with respect and provide for her physical needs, feed her, clothe her and tell her of the one true faith. *Inshallah*, she will revert from her disbelief. You could have taken her into your care quietly without telling us, but your decision to inform us is good. *Sharia* and upholding the holy law will only occur when true believers in Islam submit to the holy teachings and the leadership of the Taliban. Others who hear will only respect you for coming to us."

"I thank you for your decision. I will return in six months as you request. I will tell all in my village about your decision so they do not treat the woman badly though she is an American. I failed to tell you, she is not white. She is of our color and appears to be one of our own race, but I do not understand how this came about. I also failed to tell you that she is not a girl. From her appearance she is getting older, perhaps thirty or more."

"Six months. Yes, in six months." The men rose and left the house.

Atiqullah opened the door of his room and stepped back momentarily. Maria stood in front of him, her mouth open in surprise at his entry. Her new clothing fit her well and with her head covered with a scarf, her face was framed, enhancing her beauty. He looked at her and his heart was overwhelmed with joy. She looked at the man, his clothes wrinkled and soiled, his club foot sticking out sideways, his smiling face and she turned away embarrassed at the intensity of his gaze, his admiration so transparent that he looked boyish. She had seen that look only once before. James, when he had first seen her working as a secretary in Cebu had stood as one transfixed with a look so openly admiring that she turned away then as well. James, thirty five years her senior, balding, with sparse white hair, dear James with his rounded tummy had remained silent for a moment, then aware of his own staring had introduced himself. 'Hi, I am Dr. James Bernard.'

"*My name is Atiqullah.*" She turned to see her captor pointing at himself. "*You are dhimmi, the woman of my hand. I rejoice to welcome you to my home.*" He made a sweeping gesture around the room. "*I will care for you, Maria. I will keep harm from you. It is my solemn oath; I will kill any man that touches you.* " His face looked fierce.

Maria stood and looked at the earnest man before her and nodded, understanding only his intent; understanding that she was his and under his care. Without thinking she nodded. He saw her gesture, not a sweeping one like his, but one of understanding. He took out a prayer rug, spread it and gave thanks to Allah while she watched in amazement.

When he had finished giving thanks, Maria reached under the small bed and pulled out a pair of his boots, those she had worn on her grueling hike to this place. She reached in and pulled out the material from the toes of the ugly, worn boots and handed them to him. She said " Joe. Thank you Joe."

He took the boots from her, his face wreathed in smiles and replied, "Thank you, Joe." He knelt in front of her and picked up her foot and looked at the bottom of it carefully, and to her surprise laid his cheek against the sole of her foot. Then he stroked the soft dark down on her leg.

☪

Dohst spent the better part of the day looking for Peacock Air conditioners. In Sialkot, no one sold that particular brand. Dohst questioned various shopkeepers and found out that the brand was one of the least expensive of the window type machines but that they knew one merchant had sold them two years ago. He found out that the price for such machines was less than he had hoped, but about $300.00 or R18,000 each. He returned home and decided to talk to Meher about his find.

Before he could begin to discuss his business Pagali came to him with a small stack of carefully fashioned squares of paper. She smiled and held them in her two hands and dropped the papers in his lap. He started to pick them up and was joined by the other two women.

"Bring the papers to the table. I will teach her to put them back so she can see the picture." They spread the papers and carefully turned each of them over so the colored picture showed. Dohst sorted through the squares and found two corner squares and put them on the table, searching for the other two. Pagali found them and handed them to him. He nodded and put them in place. Now he began the more difficult task of matching the parts of the picture. He and Meher placed a dozen or so and the mouth of one of the Bollywood singers was filled in. Pagali watched with her mouth open and then moved forward eagerly. For the next half hour she worked diligently.

Meher opened the front door to get some air into the hot and stuffy room and the slight breeze blew the papers from the table. Pagali let out a yell. Her picture had been spoiled. Meher quickly shut the door and Pagali began working again, making small grunting sounds each time she put a square into the correct position.

"I have rented the shop and had it cleaned. It is empty and I must soon put it to use. I did not tell you before, but the owner rented it to me with the agreement that I could have everything that was in the store, the table, a chair and two boxes covered with filth and dust. He was not aware of the boxes because of the rotting body of the cat." Dohst was hurrying trying to get to his search for Peacock Air conditioners in Sialkot.

"A rotten cat? What do you mean? In the store?" Meher sat across the room from him leaning forward in her chair as if to hear well.

"The previous owner died a few weeks ago. He had been ailing and had not used the store for some time but came to get some papers or do something and had felt ill and closed up the shop and left. He died. His

brother did not keep track of the store and did not know that a cat had
jumped into the store to look for mice when his brother had visited it last.
Well, the cat died of thirst and hunger and when the brother opened the
store to show it to me the smell was terrible. Enough to make one vomit.
The body was writhing with maggots. The older brother held his breath,
entered, took a cardboard and scooped the rotting remains and threw them
in the back courtyard. He came out and hardly looked back at the place as
we negotiated the price of the rent. He did not see the two dirty boxes in
the corner. He rented it to me with the agreement that everything moveable
in the store I could have or dispose of."

"Did you know that there were air conditioners in the two boxes?"
she asked.

He was anticipating her question and was already impatient. "Of
course, I went in to inspect the place and held my breath and pushed
against the boxes and knew there was something in them. Why?"

"Did you tell the man that there were boxes with machines in them in
the store?" Now she saw the look on his face and decided to keep quiet.

"Do you think I am crazy? Of course not. If the stupid man was such a
poor business man as not even to know what was in the store he was renting
to me, then that is his problem and a gift to me. Pure business. Nothing
less!" He got up and went to the toilet, now not pleased with himself that
he had told her. He returned and looked at her expecting more comments.
She looked at the floor and said nothing.

"He was lucky I came along and paid the rent that I did. The store
could have remained vacant for a year. He was lucky! So, I spent the day
going around town seeing if there were dealers who sold Peacock Air
Conditioners. I found none. I want to sell these older models but like new
machines to another dealer. With that money I will invest into the T2 oil
business. I will make part of my business deal with my neighbor to use my
store for storage purposes so we can buy larger amounts of the oil. In fact,
I may just buy many tins of the oil myself, store them and sell them to my
neighbor for a small increase. I have not worked this out yet." He looked
excited and she was pleased that he was trying to set up a business on his
own, being so young.

"Have you checked out where your neighbor gets his cans of oil from,
how much he pays for them, and how much mark-up he makes when he
sells them to people on the street?" She remembered her uncle's deals with

sugar cane and sugar manufacture in a small mill he owned, how he always wanted to know what the today's price for raw sugar was.

"I was going to do that today but I don't have a telephone and I don't know where to call to find out." He bit his lip.

"If you buy one tin of oil to pour on the runners of the sticking door of your store you will be able to find out." She smiled.

"I do not understand you. You talk in circles. How would buying a tin of oil to lubricate the rollers in the runners of the door help me to get information about T2?" He lit a cigarette, something he frequently did when he was thinking or when he was not thinking but looking like he was thinking.

"I remember that my uncle used to pour oil in his machine that crushed the sugar cane. He tossed the tins aside. I collected them, cut off the tops with a can opener, washed them with detergent and sold them for drinking containers or storage containers for two rupees. On the tins were many words that many children could not read. I could read and there were words written in small letters about the name of the company, who to contact and such things." She looked at his face and decided she had talked enough.

"Oh, I see. Of course. That is a beginning. I can buy a card and use a pay phone. Yes. That is what I will do. I am leaving now. I forgot to tell you that I was going to the store to work on the door. I will return before dark." He started to gather his things to leave.

"I forgot to tell you that when you get home that you will have to eat lentils cooked without salt. We have nothing else to eat in the house. We need many things so I can cook for the three of us. Tomorrow is the day to collect the pension money from your dead aunt's husband's account." She looked down at the floor.

"Yes. Yes. I will be hungry, but that is not a problem. I can eat something from a seller on the street. Tomorrow I will take you both in a Tonga to the vegetable and meat markets to buy things for the house. We will get the pension money first." He turned and left. A vendor passed him selling *aloo chole,* a favorite dish of potatoes and chick peas, spiced and tasty. He bought four servings in disposable clay dishes and returned to the house, walked to the kitchen and put them on the table. Pagali and Meher looked at the food, then at Dohst and they both laughed.

C☪

Four young men sat on a carpet in front of Sardar and a Taliban leader. The two older men passed the mouthpiece of a hookah back and forth to each other. When one was speaking the other smoked. Sardar took the pipe and inhaled deeply and held his breath for a long second, then blew out the thin smoke, his eyes red.

"The greatest service any of us can do is to please Allah by bringing about the rule of Islam on the entire earth. The time of the infidel is now over. We are in the last holy war fought to ensure that our children inherit a better world, one ruled under Sharia. The great difference between the forces of evil of the infidels and ourselves is that we do not fear death. We welcome death and the prospect of eternal glory in heaven with Allah! This life, which Allah gave us is not our own, our birth was not something we did or deserved. It was the will of the almighty that we are here. Every one has his purpose. Every one is ordained to live and die by the will of Allah." Now he paused and took the pipe and inhaled deeply and sat back, the sweet grass-like smell of the smoke filling the air.

"The Hakim speaks the truth." Sardar turned to Tur-ali and looked at him, then at the other young men. "They fear pain, they fear death. All those who do not know what will happen to them after death, or know that hell awaits, are terrified of death. They think that everyone of them will somehow cheat the death of a bullet heading their way, that their 'buddy' as they call them will catch it, not they. They are always so surprised when the rocket hits their vehicle, that the bullet tears through their neck where there is no protective Kevlar. Surprised at the messenger of Allah that stings them, making them consider the reality of life on this earth, a life they have abused, a life full of blasphemy." He reached for the pipe.

Hakim now spoke. "They have technology, they have planes, and they have helicopters, bombs, rockets. Yes, they have these devilish means to kill and maim children, to occupy lands that are holy lands of the faithful. But they lack one thing. They lack what we have. We have the knowledge that we are correct, we are right; we are on the side of Allah and doing his will. They are paid soldiers, paid with high salaries, so high that a captain in their army gets more a year than our interim president, than our highest leaders. They think only of what drives their economy, oil. Oil runs their planes, their cars, their tanks, and their entire country. Who has the oil?

The blessed people of Allah have the oil. Why was oil put under the sands of the faithful of Islam? To ensure their victory. Why are there thousands of infidels working desperately to find more oil on our lands? To get rich, get more power of course, but that is our oil. Those are our lands. Saudi Arabia tolerates the infidel so their leaders can stay in power, but they too are weak with the lust of material things, Mercedes cars and such power that they do not have to do a day's work, just watch the money come into their bank accounts. They are worse than the Americans because they do this, yet call on the name of Allah. Their land is filled with foreigners at their invitation. Osama was right. They have lost their way because of the greed for money, the abuse of the use of the power that is the oil beneath their feet." He began to cough and took in more smoke to ease the tickle. "We do not fear death; we welcome death because we are the true believers, the true servants of the almighty. We have something that terrifies all of them. Do you know what it is?" He looked at each of the earnest young faces in front of him. They kept quiet. Tur-ali shook his head.

"They fear our faith. They fear people like us, the glorious Taliban who destroy the colossal evil statues in the Bamiyan Valley. Allah abhors idolaters. I was there when they were blown up; oh how the infidel world shrieked when Buddha was defaced. They are terrified of people who will die happily for the only great cause of the universe, the bringing of a universal caliphate of Islam to pass. You have heard of our martyrs who flew the jet-liners into the Trade towers and changed the course of history! Martyrs whose names may some day be forgotten generations from now when Islam rules, but never forgotten by the almighty. Thousands of infidels died in the Nine Eleven attack, but that was not the major victory. It was terror! Terror. They are in terror. They have declared war on terror, but terror is in their own hearts." He now laughed.

Sardar stood up to stretch. "They are in terror because when they look at the thousands that walk the streets of New York, they all look the same, but among them may be two, perhaps three common looking people, beautiful young people, even women and girls who may be willing to die to bring down their empire of fear. Each day I read of martyrs in Iraq, in Indonesia, in India whose deaths begin to erode the foundation of the infidel civilization which is based on greed. America is not the same. They go to bed knowing what level of fear alert exists for that day, yellow, orange, red: what level of fear they should have because they just might die in their soft

beds and not awaken to drink their Starbuck coffee, but die in an explosion
that seemed to come from nowhere."

He strode to the door and called for tea and food for the young men.
The young men asked permission to get up to stretch and relieve themselves. They talked with each other softly as they moved toward the latrine.
They returned to be fed a meal of soft white basmati rice, meat with gravy
poured over it, raisins, almonds and apricots blended into the pilaf. They
ate with their hands and shared food with the two elders, shy to look at
them sitting fierce and powerful, with their big black beards, a talisman of
their zeal.

Sardar again spoke. "Did you hear the words of Bush right after Nine
Eleven?"

The boys shook their heads. "You must hear them and see that face."
He turned on the TV set and slid in a cassette. President Bush was speaking in English and Sardar translated roughly. 'It is not only to those who
do acts of terrorism that we declare war against, it is anyone who supports
those who do such things.' Look at his face. Is it calm? Is it the face of one
who knows victory before the battle? No. Look. And learn. Soon after this
he gave his crusade speech. His advisers tried to downplay that and told
him not to say the word crusade again, because the crusades were against
Islam and were believed by the infidels to be their holy cause, that if they
killed Muslims their god would take them to heaven. They did not want
to inflame all of Islam, only those who acted unreasonably with a warped
faith, the terrorists." He smiled sardonically.

Hakim took up the litany. "They fear that if other weak nations get
the atomic bomb they will use them. They call us rogue states, like mad
dogs foaming at the mouth. Yet America has hundreds and hundreds of
them. What they really fear, that is stronger than the atomic bomb, is that
in every atom of every true believer of Islam is a *jihad* that allows them to
die with their atoms for Allah, happily. Not hundreds of atomic bombs,
but hundreds of millions of the faithful all over the earth looking for the
coming of the kingdom of Allah's rule through the deeds of His faithful
who submit to his will. Islam!" He shouted this out. Now he turned to the
young men in front of him and looked at each of them in their eyes. Three
of the sets of eyes wavered and looked down. Tur-ali stared at the Taliban
leader's eyes with a gleam of belief, a spark of pride that the others did not
yet possess. "What is your name?"

"I am Tur-ali."

"Allah has great plans for you. You will be a prince among men, one whose names will be on the lips of the faithful. You will be a warrior for Allah who will ensure that our cause will prevail." Hakim turned to the other young men. "Learn from him. He is younger than you; so beautiful in his fervor that the angels have marked him for glory. Learn to kindle a fire in your hearts against the evil ones of the world which will become a flame that consumes them."

C*

The rains ceased and the island was drying out. There was a chill in the air and the old caretaker went to get fire wood. He put his hand into the wood pile and the cobra struck it. The old caretaker cried out and held his hand in front of him and saw the fang marks and screamed. "*Nag! Nag!*"

Ankh and the old woman rushed to him; lifted him up and took him to his bed. Ankh tied a string around his wrist tightly trying to cut off the poison.

"It is no use." The old woman sat on the floor and cried. "It is no use. The poison is already in him. He is old. He performed some terrible deed in his youth. Terrible."

Ankh had seen two others die from snake bite. The very young and the elderly died quickly. Strong men would fight the poison for hours of misery, struggling to breathe. The old caretaker had been bitten on the top of the hand where his own blood vessels stood out and the venom had raced to his heart and from there to the rest of the body. He was already breathing with difficulty, his diaphragm becoming paralyzed. He looked at the two women standing near him and tried to talk but he did not have enough air in his lungs. It was over in twenty minutes. They watched him as he went into a small shaking spasm, then was still. They stood next to the body of the caretaker and stared at it, lying so still. His mouth was wide open as if trying to get air.

"What do we do with the body?" asked the old woman.

"Was he a Muslim?" asked Ankh.

"He never did daily *puja*. I thought, perhaps he was a Muslim. He has been here so long I never thought to ask him. I thought every one on the island was a Muslim until you came."

"We don't have enough spare wood to burn him to ashes. We do not have the iron tools to dig a deep grave in the rocky soil. I think we should remove all his clothing, his boots and drag him to the water and let the current take him downstream. The crocodiles will find him." Ankh was already beginning to unbutton the dead man's shirt. The old woman did not assist. She just stood and shook her head watching. Ankh checked the pockets of the dead man and found something that surprised them both. It was a woman's ring made of gold and set in the top was a white jewel that shone softly like the moon. They both looked at it surprised.

The old woman spoke. "It comes from a clam. I heard that those who catch clams in the ocean cut them up to take out the meat. Inside the some of the clams there is a white shiny round thing like this which our fathers, from the time of the Moguls, called *moti*. What was the old beggar doing with a gold pearl ring? He never goes to Sukkur. He has remained here for years. He hates boats. Where did he get it?" She put out her hand to Ankh to receive it.

"No. It must be from here. He was the servant of the father of Sheikh Mohammed who killed himself. Perhaps he stole it from one of the women many years ago. It remains here until Dohst returns." She slipped the ring onto her middle finger, thinking that the first owner of the ring must have had fat fingers. "Help me pull off his pants."

The women pulled off the old man's pants and looked down at his sagging, shriveled genitals. The old woman began to laugh. "Imagine, when I was a young woman I worshipped that thing, I thought it was the answer to all pleasure, to heaven." She laughed so hard she began to cough. "It was the ruler of the household. That thing."

"Help me pull him to the water's edge." They placed the body on an inverted *charpai* cot and each held to a leg of the cot as they dragged him to the water's edge.

The corpse remained in the shallows for a time, hardly moving, and then as if it had heard some distant caller, made a complete circle in an eddy of the water, headed down-stream, the nose, the toes and the penis showing above the water.

"Let us go and find the snake in the woodpile and kill it," said Ankh.

"Let it be. It was a messenger. Shesh Nag is the protector of the Shiva Linga. It will leave by itself. The old man's time had come. I will put out a small saucer of milk for the snake to drink as it leaves, near the wood pile by the gate. It will no longer bother us." The old woman tottered away to get a saucer. "He must have done something very evil in this life," she muttered, "or perhaps in another."

"I don't understand," said Ankh. "How could a snake protect anything?"

"You said your mountain people had many Gods. I don't understand them either. Our people have Ram. You don't understand. It is a story told within the family. The old man died because he knew, he knew, but he never once did *puja*. He always took the last spoonful of tea, the last of the sugar. Always. He was selfish. "

Jhika arrived by boat in the late afternoon, something he had never done before, wanting to be able to return by the time it was dark. His arrival surprised the women. Ankh was sitting in the courtyard cleaning a chicken when he appeared at the gate of the homestead.

"What are you doing here at this time of the day?" shouted Ankh.

"Do you want to know the real answer or the good answer?" Jhika smiled and walked to where Ankh was working, pulling out the guts of the bird, her hand reaching into the warm cavity to pull loose the gizzard and liver.

"I really don't care, except that you had better tell me about what you have found out. What you can get for the coin? Tell me and then get on your boat and head home again. I have no extra food to share with you. We lack supplies here and I am sure you would eat a lot." She did not look up.

He had been carrying fish behind his back and now with a flourish he displayed them as well as a handful of tamarind pods. "Look. Caught this afternoon. So fresh that they are still opening their mouths and crying for help." He laughed. "You said you wanted fish and tamarind curry."

"Thank you. You remembered. Good. I will finish cleaning the chicken and you can have the knife to clean the fish. Wait." She cut off the feet and the head to soak in boiling water to remove the hard cuticle. She gave the knife to Jhika. She got the kettle of boiling water and poured it over the head and feet. The hard scaly substance on the feet softened and she wiped the scale-like skin away. Then she pinched the beak and the hard outer layer came loose. She tossed the head and feet into the pan to cook with the rest.

"Do you make your visitors also clean fish?"

"Yes, if the visitors brought them. I will bring the chicken to the old woman who will soak it in boiling water and then pull off the feathers. Wait. I have news."

She hurried away, conscious of his eyes on her back as she moved. She wondered what it was. When she was alone she never thought about how she looked, how her body appeared when she walked. With Dohst present or as now with this impudent Jhika here, her body could feel their gazes as if it had eyes. She turned to confirm her thinking and looked into Jhika's eyes the instant she turned her head. She looked away again and hurried to the kitchen. He had not been smiling. His eyes were misty.

He cleaned the fish and was almost finished when she returned. "What is the news?"

"The old caretaker died last week. He was bitten by a cobra on the hand and was dead in about half an hour. He couldn't breathe."

"A cobra? Amazing! There has not been a cobra death around here for a long time. How did it happen?"

"The cobra went into the wood pile when the rains came. He was pulling out wood and not looking. It was coiled on a flat piece of wood where he was pulling out kindling. It struck his hand and I heard him cry out, Nag, Nag. Then we watched him die."

"Where did you bury him?"

"We put him in the river. We have no wood for cremation and no shovel to dig a hole, so, I pushed his body in the river. The crocodiles will eat him" She made a face.

"No, the catfish will get to him first. They begin to pull at the eyes, at..." he paused. "Did you wrap the body?"

"No. He went into the river naked as the day he was born. All we could see in the water was his nose, his toes and ..." She laughed.

"The catfish will get him." He too laughed. "Once the skin has been broken it is easy. A hundred mouths nibble away and that attracts other fish and soon everything is eaten except the bones. The river dolphin was the same. I left the skeleton in the water and watched the fish clean it. It was amazing."

"Come sit in the meeting room while I cook. The old woman forgets to put in salt, or puts in too much. Smoke and wait until the food is ready." She left him sitting on the carpet.

She served his food to him on a tray and moved back into the kitchen where she and the old woman ate the fish curry and the chicken with rice. She had forgotten how good tamarind fish was. The old woman, lacking teeth, loved the white fish meat and carefully removed the bones with her fingers before each mouthful. She retrieved the brass tray in front of Jhika and noted that he had eaten everything.

"Tell me. What did you find out about the little white elephant with a howdah and the coin? Did the merchants recognize the picture of the coin from the pencil rubbing?"

He sat back and belched looking at her quizzically. "How did you know about the coin?"

"Know what?"

He nodded. "Know that it would have value. I would never have even picked it up. Now I am going to tell you the truth and when Dohst returns he can verify it in the market. That coin is old. Very old. Have you heard of Ranjit Singh, the Maharaja of the Punjab when the Punjab was a country?" She shook her head. "Well, the merchant says the coin is from the time more than two hundred years before that. About 1500 years ago. Some of the small countries ruled by Rajahs made their own money. That is what the coin is." He laughed.

"Well?"

"Well what? Oh, money. You always think of money. It is not worth much. Only about five hundred rupees!" He watched her expression.

"Good. Take the coin and go back and show it to the man. Do not put it into his hand, just hold it and show it to him and say, One thousand rupees. If he refuses, bring it back and I will give it to Dohst. The elephant?"

"Six hundred rupees if it is perfect and the tusks are not broken."

"Only sell the coin. I will show the elephant to Dohst when he comes. We can live off of the coin. We need onions, spices, tea, sugar and a bag of rice that has no mold. I need vegetable seeds for radish, beets, carrots and spinach." She looked around her, as if surprised. "It is dark. I will light the lamp." She returned in a minute with a lit kerosene lantern. "Where will you sleep tonight?" She turned the new ring on her finger, enjoying the feel of the pearl.

"Where will I sleep tonight?" he responded. He smiled at her broadly. "Yes, where?"

CHAPTER SEVEN

Kushi ki gharyan chhoti hoti hain. (Hindustani Proverb)

The enjoyment of pleasure is short-lived.

The twin towers are struck with two airliners. Then as Tur-ali and four other young men watch as the scene is described in Arabic, the announcer is shouting and is excited, the first tower collapses. There are cheers and shouts of "Death to America!" and "Allah's blessings to the martyrs!" Pictures of the martyrs are now playing on the screen and scenes of devastation in New York are spliced between the descriptions of each martyr's life. The last is shown with his new wife and child before he left for America to receive training as an airline pilot. Now the presentation moves to Iraq, to pictures of burning military cars, men pulling out burned blackened bodies of Americans and desecrating them shouting, "Allah Akbar!"

The room remains dark as the instructor moves to turn on the light. The five men sit quietly, not talking to each other, looking still at the now dark television screen as if it still was speaking to them.

"Before you there is a long line of those who are known in the entire Islamic world as heroes of the faith. These men and women, whose courage is heavenly, inspire us to join them in heaven in our efforts to create such terror in the hearts of the invaders that they leave our soil. Afghanistan has not only the devil Americans but their henchmen, those who have betrayed us and our country. The new Afghanistan army with their new uniforms paid for by Americans, and their new weapons, shiny and bright and boxes of ammunition made in USA. These men are now moving among us, looking for us. We are invisible. We, the Taliban, rise like *jinns* in the night and attack them when they least expect it."

Tur-ali stood, wanting to ask a question. "How are we to learn how to use weapons, bombs, rocket-launchers? How are we going to afford buying rifles and ammunition?"

"That is why you are here. We will train you; train your minds to be like steel, hard and unyielding, train your bodies to be strong and lean, able to move like wolves after their prey. You will be given weapons and bombs when you are ready. In one month we have a secret campaign against the nearby town of Kohst which is smothered with the new army and supporters of the Americans. It will be your first real attack and you have been chosen to carry it out. Each of you will become an avenger. Allah Akbar!"

They all replied, Allah Akbar, God is Great, they shouted again and again.

Before dawn the group was up and drank tea, performed their prayers and by the time the sun could be seen as a bright ball on the tips of the mountains to the east, the young men were running a four mile course, carrying weights equal to a gun and a full pack and ammunition. Their thin legs were soon aching and they slowed their pace as they came to the end of the run, panting and holding their sides.

"Tomorrow the same and for two weeks the same, until you will hardly pant when you run. Now we will practice distance shooting. The one with the lowest score will clean the guns and the boots of the others, and I will inspect them. After the third call to prayer we will study the Holy Quran for two hours and hear a lecture on Surah II 90-91 on war. The holy words are, *Fight in the way of Allah against those who fight against you, but begin not hostilities. Lo! Allah loveth not aggression. And slay them wherever you find them, and drive them out of the places whence they drove you out, for persecution is worse than slaughter. Slay them. Such is the reward of disbelievers."*

Their leader looked at the young men and was rewarded. Their faces shone in holy zeal.

☪

Peter Slough stood in front of the staff members of the US-HELP project. The street outside the office building in Lahore near to where the group was gathered was noisy. Protestors were carrying homemade placards denouncing Musharraf's continued assistance to the United States in the fight against the Taliban. One placard painted in red and black read, 'Pakistan for Islam, not America'. The noise of the passing crowd came to the ears of the dozen staff members sitting in the room. Peter paused to let the noise subside before he continued his briefing.

Celia and Gretchen sat together at the back and glanced at each other as he continued his briefing, picking up with the last sentence he had spoken a minute before.

"Our work here is not political. Our work here is to provide assistance to the Government of Pakistan so that the lives of thousands of women and children in this country can be improved through better health, better child care and a diminution of the threat of AIDS. It is a big order but we have begun to make an impact. Our work is to bring an improvement of relations between Pakistan and America through the person to person humanitarian efforts we make." He stopped to take a drink of water.

"I will speak briefly of the President's address to the nation just yesterday, but let me once again refer to the matter of Dr. James Bernard who died many months ago from a heart ailment augmented by the sad disappearance of his lovely wife Maria, who you all knew and met. There is news that some of you may not know that has been reported in the Urdu press as well as in the Dawning. Briefly, the spectacular news is that Maria did not die in the bombing of the village on the Afghanistan border but that she escaped before that into Afghanistan."

Those gathered began to talk with each other excitedly. He waited until the news had sunk in. "She carried a notebook, a diary of sorts in which she wrote about her abduction and in which she began to write words in Urdu in a kind of rough dictionary. Her notebook, it is reported, was found sixteen miles from the border months ago and just recently was purchased from a trader. The reporter, Ikbal from the Dawning personally traveled to Sukkur and met with a young woman called Ankh, also a sex sl... I mean prisoner, against her will in the village. She had a page of the diary given to her by Maria, ripped from the notebook that matches the torn page of the diary. In all likelihood, Maria Bernard is alive! She has survived. I have to add, however, that her lot is a very difficult one, if she is still alive, because she traveled in winter, in snow. She, according to her friend in Sukkur became pregnant during her stay in the border village. So it is good news but sorry news as well." He reached for the glass of water again. Gretchen stood and without being acknowledged began to speak.

"If she traveled only fifteen or so miles on foot beyond the border, why couldn't a search party, say of our military in the area, be sent to look for her?" Gretchen, always impetuous, did not sit again but continued to stand, waiting for Peter to swallow.

"It has been months, Gretchen. Months! Think about the countryside there, the rough terrain, the snow and the real threat of local natives, perhaps Taliban as well in the area. No, that would be a useless effort now. If she is still alive, she would have to be with local natives. The nearest settlement to the Pakistan border from where she escaped is about forty miles through god-awful terrain. I thought you all would be interested to know this information since we all were guests in her home last Thanksgiving."

The group of people began to talk and whisper to each other animatedly. Peter let them speak together for a few minutes before he tried to bring the meeting to order. "Hello! I wanted to brief you about our President's Address to the Nation yesterday. I took a few notes and these may not be exact but he said that, let me see, that the terrorists have lost the shelter of the Taliban and the training camps in Afghanistan. He said that they have lost the safe haven in Pakistan. Please understand that he speaks from information given by Rums... by his advisors. From what I read in the local newspapers, from what the Urdu newspapers report locally, there are still very hot and active cells that support the Taliban, particularly in *madrassas*, you know, religious schools. Such schools are all over the place here and in Afghanistan from what I have heard. I am bringing this up to remind you that you must be circumspect and careful in your work, avoid conflict situations, do not become involved in political discussions. A low profile is what would serve our project best. Be professional, personal but not in their face. In the same press conference, April 13th the President gave sound words of advice to us all. I quote, "A desperate enemy is also a dangerous enemy and our work may become more difficult before it is finished." He said, "We will succeed in Iraq. Iraq will be a free, independent country."

I want to end the briefing with words from a recent Newsweek article with Michael Hirsh et al byline. "So elusive is the terror threat today—so deeply burrowed in the globe's darkest crannies—that even a wily old commander like Pervez Musharraf seems confused about exactly which bad guys his soldiers had cornered last week." We go about our technical assistance duties in an environment which is tough to psych out, to understand. Be careful. I know you are all doing a terrific job. I am proud of your work and from my point of view, this kind of American assistance is what makes our country great. Honestly, I don't know who the," he made quotation marks with his fingers in the air, "bad guys" are. I suspect that right at this minute there are meetings being held by these bad guys to plan additional terrorist acts against us, against democracy." His audience was fading, looking out of the window and a few whispered to each other.

Gretchen stood again. "What would you think of some of us trying to give a helping hand to the young woman in Sukkur who was said to be Maria's friend? I bet she is really hurting."

"Interesting. Not really a project agenda, but maybe something personal, like we make donations or something personally to send to her? Gretchen, lets talk about this after the meeting. Thanks folks." Peter finished the water in the glass and packed up his notes. He muttered to himself; how in the hell did we end up with a woman on an island at Sukkur? God! We have a whole country of them out there that need help so much more.

Gretchen and Celia conferred together quietly, thinking of Dohst and his womanizing and children and the lonely woman in Sukkur.

"What the hell. Should we take part of our holiday trip to that island and meet the girl called Ankh?" They continued to talk as they left the room, but Gretchen was now shaking her head negatively. Peter watched them and shook his head. Trouble, he thought, trouble when it comes to those two.

☪

Maria was amazed! Atiqullah pulled the old burkah over her new clothes and motioned for her to follow him. She had seen other Afghani women following behind their men, so she kept a few paces behind him. He carried his automatic rifle and glanced over his shoulder from time to time and said her name softly. She responded as best she could and said, yes. They walked for a goodly distance in the small town until they came to sellers of various kinds of foods. Here he stopped and pointed to one food or another. Again she said, yes. He bought small quantities of rice, oil, a little piece of goat meat, and oranges. Maria said, yes, yes, and he doubled the quantity of these. These purchases were all put in a stiff basket that Maria had to carry on her head. She looked around for grass to make a pad to place against her skull. He understood and helped her fashion a round and firm pad of grass. She placed the basket on her head but could not balance it and had to keep one hand lifted to hold against the side. Her arm tired; she used the other. He ignored her problem and continued to move through the market, buying one small item after another and placing them in the basket. Maria spoke to herself, "I have become a damn grocery cart. Oh God. What next." He turned and spoke to her; she shook her head.

The area for cooking was shared by other women in the cluster of small homes. She watched how they prepared the food and tried to mimic them. They laughed as she worked. The first meal she set before Atiqullah was only a partial success. Now he laughed and talked, pointing to the dishes of food. She sat outside near the cooking area and ate her food alone as the other women were doing, but they all ate together, looking over at her. One young woman stood and waved Maria over even as the others objected. Maria picked up her food and joined the group and smiled at the young woman.

He handed her a short broom in the morning and motioned for her to clean up. There were little bones and hard pieces from the food which he had dropped onto the floor. She swept the floor and under the beds, moved the boxes and cleaned under them. When he returned he nodded and handed her an armful of his clothing, those used on their trek. Again she followed him, all covered from head to toe, as he walked to the local stream. He sat and smoked while she washed the clothing with soap. She watched the other women and saw that they beat the clothes with a flat stick. She had none so she did the best she could with her hands, rolling the clothing into a sausage like shape and hitting it against the stones. He stretched out in the shade of a tree and lay back and fell asleep. She spread the clothes on large rocks heated by the sun and waited for them to dry.

The next day she followed him to a rock corral where goats were kept. He handed her a bowl and said something she did not understand. He shook his head, walked to a goat with huge udders, held its head under one arm and proceeded to milk it with the other hand. He pointed at the next animal. She struggled with the animal, but finally subdued it and pulled at the udder. He laughed and made a squeezing motion with his hand. She milked five goats while he waited. Again he slept in the shade of the wall and awakened when the last goat was milked.

Each day Atiqullah taught her new tasks to perform while he watched. Each day he accompanied her to different parts of the village. Now he pointed at objects as they walked and named them. She walked behind and repeated the names. The second day he pointed and did not name them, expecting her to do so. For two weeks, she was never out of his sight except for the times she bathed and used the latrine. He seemed not to have any other companion, and most of the others ignored him. He talked constantly to Maria as she worked.

The first night he had crawled into the bed next to her. He had talked again, his hands reaching out to feel her back which was toward him. He stroked the back of her head and talked. He ran his hands down her spine and was then quiet. She wept lying with her back to him. Then he patted her and lay his face against her back, mumbling and pulled her toward him.

Each night he shared the narrow bed with her. At dawn he prayed as she watched, then she went to bathe. The pattern was repeated day after day. On one day of the week he did not leave the room. He took out a deck of cards and spread them on the bed and motioned for her to take one. It was a strange game which seemed simple at first, but she could not win. They played and he talked. Then he went to the mosque to pray while she stayed behind. It was her first time to be alone in a week.

She sat on the bed and thought about her friend Ankh; she thought about her thanksgiving party in Lahore with more than fifty guests in the huge house with its empty bed rooms; she thought about James, now alone in that house or in his home in La Jolla. She sat hunched over on the bed and wept, tears falling to the earth floor that she had swept. In the distance there was gunfire and then an explosion that sounded like the one she had heard over Bahadur, a rumbling, deep sound that shook the earth.

☪

It took Feroz Hakim the Deputy Superintendent only ten minutes to pack the tin trunk with all his winter clothing and to pour moth balls on top of them and close the lid. He did not cover the trunk with a blanket as usual, rather left it exposed with the Pakistani flag emblazoned on it.

He got a basket from the kitchen and piled ten files into it, including the file relating to Ikbal, then covered it with towels. The others he wrapped in old cloths in two bundles and pushed them under the bed in his own bedroom. He carried the basket with him to the office and entered unseen. He placed the ten files in one of the existing filing cabinets, putting them on the bottom of the drawer so the hanging files hung above them. He locked the file and put the key on his personal key chain. He called to the peon to bring Mistiri to him.

Mistiri stood in front of Feroz Hakim's desk. His lean frame seemed to shrink in his too loose clothing, as he listened to the Deputy Superintendent talk.

"Were you hired by Ikbal to do work for him in his house?"

"Yes, I worked for him, installing hinges on his windows. I did not think there would be any problem with my finding a little extra work after my work was done here. We are poor folk...."

He was interrupted by the Feroz. "I am sick of hearing those words, poor folk, *garib admi.* Being poor does not excuse stupidity! What did you two talk about? Was my name mentioned?"

"Sir, before Allah, I never mentioned your name, not once, I swear an oath on my father's..."

"I am sick of hearing people swear on their father's this and that. If I was not mentioned by name, what did you talk about? Think carefully, Mistiri Ahmed." He used the man's new name, perhaps being the first one ever to use it.

Being called Ahmed confused Mistiri more because it brought up old issues and the matter of the scholarship of his daughter to the girls' school. "He asked me if I had letters of recommendation from other people that I had worked for. I told him no, but that the people had been pleased with my jobs."

"His next question was, what kind of jobs? Correct?"

"Sir, yes. How did you know?"

"And you replied; jobs helping people move things, repair things, install things, doing cement work." He shook his head knowing what was coming.

"Sir, he asked about cement work and I told him some of my customers had steps to fix, one even asked me to install a safe." He now put both hands next to his head in fear and frustration.

"Did you tell him the registration number of the safe, how much it cost, where he could buy one? Allah man. You told him everything he wanted to know. How many customers have you had in the last month, Ahmed?" His voice was filled with sarcasm.

"Just you, sir. Only you. I did not mention helping with the car on the trip to Sukkur."

"Get out. It is my own fault to hire an idiot. My enjoyment of the pleasure of being in charge of this police station was surely short lived. I hire a fool and get fooled. Get out of my office," he shouted. Then he thought of the beautiful young Jasmin with her new name of Jamillah standing in front of him, talking to him about the beauty of the American picture and his heart softened. "Wait! If Ikbal comes to you again, tell him you are under orders not to speak to him alone. My orders. Do you understand?"

"Thank you, sir. You are kind. Thank you." He hurried to his work.

He picked up his office line phone and booked a call to the Sukkur police and hung up. He made another call but the number was busy. Then the operator called him back.

"I have the Sukkur Police on the line sir." He heard a voice on the other end shouting Hello, Hello.

"Is this the Chief of Police of Sukkur," he asked.

"No sir, this is Detective Mirzah. To whom am I speaking please?"

"Mr. Mirzah, we have met I think when I was last in Sukkur and stayed in the Government Rest House and I had to fire my pistol into the ceiling to get your attention. Do you remember?"

"Sir. Yes. Yes. Deputy Feroz Hakim from Lahore, is it?"

"Your memory serves you well. I am sure that you will be able to handle this. I need you to perform a service for the Lahore police. Hello. Yes. A service, man, I want you to go to Khawaja Khizr Island to obtain a document for me. Hello. Hello. Yes a document, man. Listen! Are you writing this down?" He paused and waited for the man to get a paper and pencil. "Yes. Hello. There is a woman there whose name is Ankh. She is pregnant. She has a small yellow colored paper which is a deed to the property there. Ask her for it. She may not want to give it to you but you must be firm. I do not mean to beat her, do you understand? Make a photocopy of the paper. Yes. Then send both of them to the address I am going to give you. It is my personal address. Send them registered mail. What?"

He listened while the man requested money for the boat trip, for copying the document, for the stamps and registration costs and for the trouble.

"I will send you a Money Order for two hundred and fifty rupees in your name. After you cash it, go to the island and get the paper and there should be enough left for you to eat a good meal of *siripai*." (Head and feet stew) Again he waited and wrote the man's name on paper. "Finally, when the document has been copied, and when it has been sent to me call me at this number to let me know that all is accomplished. I almost forgot; this is highly confidential detective work. Perhaps it could be done after your regular work hours so that the matter is just between us. I promise not to shoot into the ceiling again." He hung up.

He drove his personal car to the street where the reporter Ikbal lived. He slowed down to observe the reporter's house and noted that the huge rambling structure was probably built in pre-partition years. It had a look of neglect about it. The trees were overgrown and hung across the top of the walls which were cracked and in need of repair. Old money, he thought. Old family, probably with ties to India. He pulled the car over a block away and returned on foot. He stood in front of the metal gate and noted that the bar had not been slid into the lock from the inside. He pushed against the gate and it opened easily. He walked back toward his car and stopped in front of a man selling potato and chickpea curry in small baked clay dishes. He purchased one.

"The guard in the second house down the street wants to have four of these dishes. He left the gate open. Just walk in and go around to the kitchen, he is waiting for you." He had his back to the man as he began to eat the food.

The man picked up his wicker stand and tray with food on it and hurried toward the open gate. Feroz got into his car and drove away, smiling, thinking about the reception the merchant would have as he entered into the house of his enemy.

The merchant walked boldly into the courtyard, looked around for the kitchen, strolled to it and opened the door of the kitchen and shouted, "The potato chick pea man is here." There was a noise of a woman's voice shouting and screaming, that a thief had entered, "*Chor, Chor!*"

☪

It was not a good time to travel. The bus he rode in was not air-conditioned and the smell of diesel and fumes from the exhaust made him dizzy. He mopped his brow. Early summer days were steaming hot. He arrived in the Lahore lorry park and got a horse carriage to take him to the bazaar where air conditioners were sold. Dohst paid the man off and began his search for Peacock Air Conditioners. He located two shops that sold the machines. At the second shop he saw exactly the same units that he had in his empty shop. He priced them and was pleased to hear that they sold for R19,840. He asked to have the machines turned on so he could see if they worked properly. The shopkeeper looked at him and shook his head and told him to cool himself somewhere else. He was too busy to talk to him as he had customers to attend to.

"Actually, I would like to sell you two machines, just like these. Identical in fact, even the same year of manufacture. I would sell them to you at a reduction from the price you are asking, even deliver them to your shop myself, and you can try them out." His stance puzzled the man.

"You are joking. How could you own such machines?" The man waved his hand at him dismissing him.

"I inherited them. My old man died and left these in his shop which I am now making into a store to sell motor oil. I have two machines, still in their wood crates. How much would you pay me?"

"Perhaps R10,000. One has to be careful with older stock. The tubes dry out, mice get into the electrical fittings. Very careful."

"Yes I agree. There was a dead cat in my father's store. He must have come there for a reason. Look, if they are in as good a condition as the two here in your store, exactly the same, not a scratch, how much?" Dohst ran his hand over one of the air conditioners and his finger stopped at a scratch in the paint.

"Bring them over. We will talk then."

"I live in Sialkot. I would have to hire a truck to bring them. If you give me a decent price I will bring them, but otherwise I will go to the man down the street who also sells them." He moved as if to leave.

"R12,000 last. No more. They are difficult to sell. Half when delivered and half in one month." He spat a mouthful of orange betel nut juice onto the street.

"R15,000 and cash on delivery." Dohst stepped down into the street and headed for the next store.

"R14,000 last price, if perfect."

Dohst returned and asked the man to write down the name of the shop, his address, telephone number and the amount he had agreed upon. Then to the shopkeeper's surprise he asked to see his driver's license. The man laughed.

"What does my driving have to do with the sale of these machines?"

"It has to do with who you say you are and who you really are. That you signed your actual name on the paper. That the picture is the same as your face. I don't want to go to all this trouble and when I get back here find that you don't remember who I am and what you said." He smiled broadly and shook his head as if to make a joke of his statement.

The man took out the red booklet and looked at the picture of himself. "Good? Much younger. When I am married. I did not have a picture when I got license. I use wedding picture." He admired the face looking back at him.

"Let me see. Yes, good. *Jivan*, young and handsome fellow. I would like to meet him." Now Dohst laughed seductively.

"Come. Sit. We drink tea and not talk business. We talk of the pleasures of life, of being young like you, of beautiful girls who go to private schools and long to meet fellows like us. Come."

Dohst remained in the shop until it closed in the evening. He and his new acquaintance walked to a nearby food seller and sat at a small wood table and smoked, looking at the electric lights come on and people strolling by. They ordered food and tea. Two American women walked together with a bearded Pakistani man walking directly behind them. One woman had black curly hair the other had blonde hair. Dohst started.

"Gretchen and Celia." He murmured their names under his breath. He stood to watch them walk up the road and stop at the air conditioning shop near to the one where they had been. It was still open. They were invited to sit and he could see the man was ordering tea for them.

He turned to the man with him. "Wait here. Here is my chance. I have to talk to the American women. I will be back in a minute." His new acquaintance looked at him as if he was crazy.

He walked to the store and stood in front of steps looking up at the two women. They glanced at him but did not recognize him and continued to talk to the proprietor.

"Miss Gretchen," he said, his voice pitched high and far too loud.

Gretchen turned and stared at Dohst. "Oh my God. Dohst! My God. Is it you?"

Celia stood up and walked to where he stood. "You look so different. Hi, Dohst. I am glad to meet you again. Come up. Sit with us. We are looking for an Aircon. Ours gave up during the last hot season." She patted a vacant chair next to them.

"Miss Gretchen, have you heard anything about Maria? Has there been any news about her?" Dohst leaped into what was on his mind the instant he had seen them.

They were both quiet and serious and looked at each other. Celia spoke. "We thought she was a captive somewhere or dead and had given up on her. It was as if she had disappeared from the face of the earth. After her abduction there was a bombing of a village on the Afghan border and Sher Khan the Senior Superintendent was killed. Everyone assumed that Maria had also been killed, since one witness said she had been there with him. We thought she was dead too. We just heard that she may have escaped into Afghanistan. Imagine!" She became emotional as she spoke and took a deep breath. "Did you hear that her husband James Bernard also died?"

"Allah. No. How did he die?" Dohst could hardly believe his ears.

"He died of a heart problem. We think it came about because of Maria. He looked for her everywhere." Gretchen now spoke while Celia composed herself.

"Madame. This is the best one and it is imported from England. Sorry to say but the units made here in Pakistan, though cheaper, don't hold up. Avoid the one made in China..." The shop keeper stood in front of the intruder, Dohst, as he spoke.

"Excuse us. Sorry. We have just met someone we knew before. We will be with you in a minute," said Celia.

"Shop closing in twenty minutes Memsahib." He stood at the back of the store and glared at Dohst.

Celia looked at Gretchen. "We can do this later. Let's find a place to eat and talk and catch up on our lives. Dohst, are you free to have dinner with us?" He nodded.

The three left the shop and the proprietor began to swear at Dohst in Punjabi, calling him the offspring of an owl, *Uloo ka phata!* The three walked past the other storekeeper who was waiting for Dohst, the food now on the small table. He glanced at the man, and raised his eyebrows at him and as he passed he said in Urdu, "I've got one for tonight." The man stood and pointed at the food but Dohst kept walking with the American women. In the distance he could see that their car was parked in an open area and that a young man stood by the car watching it. Behind them walked a man with a dark beard, looking out for them.

They sat at a table with a white table cloth. The waiter was dressed in starched white clothes. This restaurant, the Kababeesh on the Main Boulevard, Gulberg, served good Punjabi food and was their favorite place.

"So, Dohst? Are you a married man with a bunch of kids by now? What have you been up to?" Gretchen looked over at him and she thought that he blushed.

"I have been taking care of my aunt's home and also my father's place in Sukkur. My aunt died leaving me the house, but she had a daughter, though a woman, who is like a child. She does not speak. I am trying to start a business selling motor oil."

"What about the carpet business you worked at before with your father?" asked Gretchen. Now she remembered that he had committed suicide. "I am so sorry Dohst, I forgot. Sorry. Your father died." She shook her head.

"Yes. Since his death I have not dealt with carpets. Most were stolen by Sher Khan and the rest were sent to my uncle in America. So I am starting my own business."

"How will you fund it? I mean where will you get the money to start a business of your own?" asked Celia

"I sold my father's truck and I am selling two air conditioners, new ones, left to me. They are still in crate." He looked at them eagerly.

"We are looking for the portable window-type of air conditioners. Is that what you are selling?" asked Gretchen.

"You were looking at same thing in shop when I met you. Same thing, exactly. I will sell them to you for good price, better than in shop. Only R19,000 each. First class, imported quality, Peacock brand, made in Taiwan. Still in crate."

☪

Mahtari, the wife of the late Abdul, the mother of Chamuck who had disappeared weeks before, tried to maintain the household, requesting funds for food from the brother of Abdul, the mullah named Mohammed. He had taken temporary residence in his dead brother's house as it served his purposes to do his business. The wives and children of his late brother were in mourning for the father and the daughter and hardly communicated with Mohammed. He was served food and drink and left alone. He watched a small television set in the evening after the last prayer had been said and wrote letters to his relatives in Lahore about his brother's death. He called in Chamuck's mother and gave her money to feed the household and enquired about the location of his brother's bank and savings. He was told they did not know. He then searched his brother's rooms and found records which linked him to the arms dealer, Sahib-ji. No cash was found, no check books, no banking records, not even a billing or an invoice of any kind. Once again he called in his brother's wife Mahtari.

"Who would know where Abdul kept his money?" he asked.

"He did not talk to us about that. When Chamuck needed school fees he left the house and returned later with the money. He did not say where it came from. She once told me that he kept records of some of his business deals in the glove box of his truck which he kept locked. That truck was never returned after his death. Sahib-ji has taken it now, so if there were things in the truck at the time of his death, they are in his hands." Mahtari stood facing at right-angles to her brother-in-law as she spoke.

"Your daughter is gone. She will never be heard from again. Somewhere there is a village with high mud walls owned by Sahib-ji or his family and she is there, Inshallah. If she is not she is dead. It is the same." He looked around him, seemingly not focused on the death of his relative. "This house was one of three that our ancestors left to the family. The one I live in is larger than this but there are no papers of ownership for it. We lived in it, as did our forefathers, and those before them. It has always been ours. I will keep it for the male children born into the family." He looked at Mahtari critically as he talked. "How old are you?" he asked.

She was surprised at his question. She faced him now as she replied. "Could it be that I am thirty six? There are no papers. I was sixteen when I bore her. Chamuck was sixteen when she disappeared. Perhaps only thirty two. I do not know." She watched his eyes which now looked at her plump body from her feet to her head. She felt uncomfortable with his gaze and pulled her scarf over her head and turned away again.

"I am going to arrange to have three of Abdul's women to be married to me according to the laws of Islam. These will not be regular marriages, as I already have three wives, but special temporary marriages of inheritance and mercy. I will include you as well, though you are getting older. It will be done by the end of the month. Here is money for the household. I will return next week and see how you are managing this place." He put the money on the table.

She turned to him and asked softly, "I have heard you preach that the women of husbands who die, inherit a part of his property. Did you not say this?"

"You may have not understood. Yes, there is clear teaching about inheritance under Sharia. I will support you in your right to inherit your portion of your dead husband's wealth. The truck was expensive and it was there he may have put most of his money. It is gone, signed away by his own hand, with witnesses. This house is from our ancestors and will remain for the family, the next son to hold it, possess it. If you have found a box of money, perhaps it would be wise to say nothing to me about it and just keep it quietly, because any money that is located, in a bank or hidden somewhere will be used to pay debts and then the remainder will be distributed to the relatives who line up for their share of the spoils." He shook his head and glared at her. "Inherit what? Who is paying for your food now?" He got up, picked up his gun and walked out the door, irritated that she had asked. She stood dejectedly for a moment, sighed and walked toward the kitchen thinking thoughts of becoming the concubine of a mullah. She did not realize it but she was shaking her head from side to side as if saying no, no. She heard the truck door slam, the engine start and the truck drive away. It had an unusual squeal as the clutch was let out. The mullah was a bad driver.

Late that night the body of the Mullah Muhammad was dumped on the outskirts of Peshawar city next to the Christian Cemetery on Sahib Zad Gul Road. It was naked and bore no identification marks or jewelry. Its front teeth had been knocked out and the beard had been shaven roughly while he was still alive as there were wound marks with scabs formed from razor cuts. The hands were cut off. The evidence that an honor crime had been committed was that there was a bullet wound through his lower back which passed through the bladder and had severed a portion of the lower femoral artery which had been his cause of death due to blood loss.

The Peshawar police had been informed of the presence of this body near the Christian burial ground and assumed it may have been the body of an infidel cast there by a family that did not have the funds for a burial or cremation. Two laborers working for the police force were assigned to dig a grave next to the Christian Cemetery at the edge bordering the road where the body was found. The corpse was buried. No notice was put in the newspaper. No service was held, no holy words were said over the body. It was just one more body found in the city that day. Six other bodies had been found in four days and all were simply buried, having no way to identify them. The bodies were not kept in refrigeration in the city morgue which was reserved for special victims and special high profile cases. Hundreds of bodies a year were simply buried.

Two weeks passed and Mahtari had heard nothing from Mohammed. She sent a servant boy to the mullah's home to enquire about him. When he returned he said that the mullah's own family and servants had not heard from him for twelve days. They had called the police, however, they were informed that no one of the description they gave had been found and that all the unidentified bodies had been buried the same day. The police told them that since had they waited a week to report a missing person, the likelihood of finding such a person was near zero. Bodies decomposed rapidly in one hundred degree heat and were buried quickly for health reasons.

They were all worried that something terrible had happened to him. There was no news. The eldest son of the mullah, Haider, told the servant that he would come to Abdul's house and speak to Mahtari on Friday.

Haider, a young man in his twenties sat in the same seat where his father Mohammed had sat two weeks earlier. He called the entire family to come and sit on the carpet. The women and children of various ages came in and squatted. Mahtari the senior wife sat on a small wood stool near the door.

"We fear that he is dead. We fear it may have been an honor killing, since he shot the man who came to the gate. My father always keeps his word. The day he disappeared he said he was going to check the city records in Peshawar for information about his family. He took his truck, parked it near a small tea shop on Police Road near the High Court. He locked the truck but must have carried his rifle with him when he walked to the offices he wished to visit. That is all we know. He was parked near to where the Khyber Road meets the Police Road, so it may have taken him at least ten minutes to get to the High Court. We have contacted the police. The truck was located on the second day after he disappeared and had been held awaiting further developments. I have papers and spare keys for it and drove it back to the house." His eyes roved around the room looking at women and children, some of whom he had not seen before. He was surprised that his uncle had two very young and attractive wives.

Mahtari spoke. "Are you now the person in charge of the two households?"

He nodded his head. "There is no one else. I have been going through all the papers and possessions of my father and have found records of land purchases far away from here that I knew nothing about. I have found records of savings in two banks but I have not found credit cards. I saw him use them many times. Perhaps if he..." He sighed. "Perhaps these have been stolen. I will go to the banks to see how to get his money out."

Two of the small children began to cry and their mothers quickly unbuttoned their blouses and pushed nipples into their mouths to quiet them. One of the boys of about the age of eight shouted out, "Uncle, we are hungry!" His mother tried to quiet him but he persisted. "Uncle, we have no food and no tea!" He began to cry.

"I know. In my own house it is the same. I am trying to find money, trying to understand how my father did business. When I find money I will bring it so you can eat."

A donkey brayed in the back courtyard. He smiled. "I have found some money. The *khota* will provide. I will sell it in the livestock market tomorrow and bring money back for food. I want you all to think about what else there is that is worth something. Did you not raise chickens? Are there extra things of value in the house not being used? Think. I will come back tomorrow after I sell the *khota*." The small television set was on with the volume turned down. The news in Urdu was being read. "Now listen to the news", she was saying. The woman announcer in a green dress and scarf held a paper and began to read. "There were six more deaths reported in the city of Peshawar in the last two weeks, however, none of the bodies of the men could be identified. One of the men was recently shaved, his hands had been chopped off and he was shot through the lower abdomen..."

"The television set. The television set." The eight year old boy cried out, pointing at the picture of the woman.

"What about it?" asked Haider.

"If we can eat the donkey, we can eat your father's truck and the television set as well!"

☪

During the night there was a small earthquake in Sialkot that had not awakened Meher. When she got up and began her day she thought the house to be small and drab. She had not noticed how dark it was with its three small windows. She had not realized that the bed was so large and lonely. Meher found herself staring out of the grimy window wondering what Dohst was doing. Ever since he had left she had thought about him. While she prepared food for Pagali and herself, she no longer hummed and sang. Twice during the day when Pagali had come close to her and tried to stroke her arm she had been impatient and had scolded her, telling her to go and rip paper. She hung out the laundry on a string and smoothed the wrinkles on Dohst's shirt, pulling it taught so it would dry smooth. She held up his trousers and was surprised at how large they were.

The first day that Dohst was gone had seemed interminably long. She finished all the chores around the house. She took out her religious books, sat near the window and opened the Holy Book and began to read in the first place her eyes looked. It was her habit to open the book in a different place each day, hoping for a special message that would come to her eyes the minute she began to read. Her eyes settled on the text.

Surah V5

This day are all good things made lawful for you. The food of those who have received the Scripture is lawful for you, and your food is lawful for them. And so are the virtuous women of the believers and the virtuous women of those who received the Scripture before you (lawful for you) when ye gave them their marriage portions and live with them in honour, not in fornication, nor taking them as secret concubines. Whoso denieth the faith, his work is vain and he will be among the losers in the hereafter.

A dog barked outside incessantly. Meher could not concentrate. She sighed and closed the book, marking the place with one of the tiny squares Pagali had torn. She kept thinking of the phrase, *nor taking them as secret concubines*. Pagali made a strange moaning impatient noise. *Secret concubines*.

Pagali cold not finish her picture. One square was missing. She made a moaning noise again and waved her hands around as if by doing so the small paper would appear. Meher glanced over at her, and then remembered the tiny paper she had used as a marker for her reading. She pulled it out and went to the table where Pagali sat despondently. She held out the square of paper in her palm. On the paper was the picture of the eye of the actress. Pagali looked up at Meher and waved her hands and then quickly took the paper and put it in its place, upside down. She stared at the small picture, then at Meher. *Not in fornication, nor taking them as secret concubines*. She reached forward to reverse the picture but Pagali's fingers were quick. She picked it up gently and carefully placed it right-side-up, then delighted with her work, lay back and squealed. Her abdomen swelled large as she lay on her back, and Meher could not take her eyes away from it. Dohst's child, with this secret retarded concubine, she thought. Allah help her.

Meher went into the small back room where there was a cot and a tin trunk in which Dohst kept his papers. She looked on top of the trunk and found two more new movie magazines she had not seen before. The actresses were stunningly beautiful, they were smiling and their teeth were white as milk. Their breasts bulged hugely. She carefully tore off the cover of one of the magazines and brought it to Pagali. She sat up, her face one huge smile and reached for the new treasure. Meher gave it to her. Pagali placed the paper against her cheek and rocked backwards and forwards in an unconscious sexual gesture, making soft sounds in her cheeks.

The dog no longer barked. She went to the side window and watched three dogs cavorting, two males and a bitch in heat. She looked at the animals and frowned, shook her head and went to her bed, lay on her back and stared at the ceiling. She closed her eyes. She could see herself bathing and Pagali walking into the room naked and bathing with her, pouring water over her and then rubbing her back with soap. Now from the sitting room came the sounds Pagali made as she folded the paper and made the first careful tears in her new puzzle. She opened her eyes. There was a long crack on the ceiling from one side to the other she had not noticed before. She stared at it wondering how long it had taken to form. It looked fresh. She touched it and sand adhered to her finger. An omen, she thought, an evil omen to see a newly cracked wall.

She turned on the small, cheap pocket radio that Dohst had left in his room to listen to music, but the news came on instead. "Yesterday, October 8, 2005, a massive earthquake struck Pakistan leaving more than seventeen thousand dead." She sighed and turned to another channel and found Indian music which was broadcast across the nearby border. She listened for half an hour.

She had no one to talk to; even the reading of the Holy Book did not seem to give her hope. Her uncle had agreed to two thousand rupees for her, a sum which separated her now from her extended family to become Dohst's... What did he call her? Servant. Meher turned on her side and her tears wet the pillow.

She awakened and looked away from the wall. The room was small and dark. She wondered about her mother and the family she had left. She decided that when Dohst returned she would leave Pagali with him and cover herself up and return home and stay for a day. No one. She had never been disturbed about Pagali, a child-like person under Allah's care, but as she listened to the sounds coming from the adjacent room she frowned, sighed impatiently and wept again. No one. If Dohst had not moved into this room, she thought, she would not have noticed that it was so bare and that she had no one with whom to share even one single thought in the entire day. Her head turned on the pillow and she smelled Dohst's hair, a faint odor of sweat with the coconut oil hair cream he used.

Two thousand. Two thousand rupees! The cost of a *shalwar-kamiz*. Her uncle had allowed her to become Dohst's woman for a shirt and pants. She groaned and turned over on the bed and looked at the crack again. A new patch on a cracked wall never held, her father had always said. It always cracked again later. She shivered in apprehension.

CHAPTER EIGHT

Kali ma ke gore bachche. (Urdu Saying)

A black mother bears a white baby.

Or

A black chicken lays a white egg.

Sukkur city was beautiful in the late spring. Trees that had been without leaves were green. Mulberries hung in clusters to be eaten by birds before the children could pick them. Under the trees the ground was purple from squashed fruit and bird dung. Cheels nested in the top of a large tree and brought their babies small chickens that they had swooped and caught. It was a time of plenty for man and beast. It was a time of birth, fruit and the mustard fields were waving yellow hope.

Detective Mirzah cashed the money order and put the two hundred and fifty rupees in his billfold. He walked to his brother's tea house and drank tea and forgot to pay for it. His brother called out. "So, it costs me two cups of tea to see your face?"

"I provide police protection to this cheap place and all I get is two cups of tea a day?" Mirzah waved as he left the shop. His brother swore under his breath but waved at his departing brother who walked toward the Indus River where the Mohanna boat people kept their boats.

There were two boats available. The smaller one was operated by an arrogant young man called Jhika who Mirzah did not like; however, since his boat was cheaper he decided to put up with the man for a trip to the island and back. The day was heating up already. Mirzah looked at his watch. It was nine o'clock and the sun beat on the surface of the river reflecting back blindingly. There was hardly a breeze. Jhika paddled steadily and talked without stopping.

"This is your first time to the island. The island attracts police. You are the third that I have taken there this year. What is it that brings our local Sukkur police to the island?"

"Official business. You would not understand. Official." He looked away from Jhika to the island looming in the distance.

"What does it mean when you say detective?" Jhika grunted out his words in rhythm to the paddle.

"It means that the officer gets more pay than the patrolman on the street. It means he gets to ride in the police car with the blue lights. It means he does not have to answer questions of this sort from anyone on the street or in a boat." He lit a cigarette and saw that Jhika was holding out his hand. "It means that people think I have a high salary and can pass out free cigarettes." He handed one to Jhika.

"There are only two people on the island. Only women. One a young woman with a beautiful face and beautiful...," he paused to see the reaction on Mirzah's face. "The face is like the pictures of Indian movie stars, big eyes, full lips, curly black hair. She is an infidel and does not cover her head. She is also *bardari*." He stopped paddling and held his hands in front of his abdomen. "Her name is Ankh. She came here as a slave girl bought by Sheikh Mohammed from the Black Infidel tribe. Now, in her belly is the new master's offspring. Imagine. Serviced by both father and son. Ever hear of that before?" He laughed and missed a stroke, making water splash up which landed on the detective's legs.

"Watch out. Pay more attention to the boat. When you mouth works your hands stop." Mirzah wiped his pants with a small handkerchief.

"If she were the wife of one of your faith she would be covered from head to toe and hidden away like a treasure. This one now rules the island. I wonder what her baby will be like. Perhaps not like her. You know, black chickens lay white eggs." He stopped paddling and swatted at insects that swarmed near the boat. He continued, "Official business. This is my official business, Mohanna monkey business."

"Well, I am interested to meet this slave woman. Did you know her picture was in the newspaper?" Mirzah turned around to look at Jhika.

"Why? How could that be?" he asked.

"She survived the bomb blast. She was down in the well when the Americans bombed the village and killed most of the people, Taliban, according to the Americans. They killed the Lahore Senior Superintendent of Police. Katush! Fire and ashes. It is amazing how they get their information. I have heard they even bombed a *madrassah* school because they heard they were training Taliban militants." Mirzah reached down to the surface of the water and pulled a green weed out of the water on which there was a purple flower. He plucked the water hyacinth flower and threw the leaves back. He held it up for Jhika to see.

"Sometimes it comes down the river in a raft of green. If it comes near the shore we pull it in and feed it to our cattle."

They approached the south side of the island. The dogs were already on the small sandy beach barking at their approach. No one appeared as they disembarked, which was unusual. Jhika handed a paddle to the policeman and the two of them moved toward the mud walled compound brandishing these as weapons against the aggressive dogs which came at them.

The gate was shut; the metal bolt was pushed closed from inside. Jhika pounded on the gate with his paddle and yelled trying to get Ankh's attention. No one came to the gate in spite of the commotion they were making.

"I will climb over the top of the gate. Hand me the paddle when I get to the top." Jhika scrambled up the gate, took the paddle and then dropped inside and slid the bolt open and let the policeman in.

As they moved toward the house they heard the scream, a long anguished cry coming from the front part of the house. They hurried forward, pushed open the front door and almost knocked over the old woman who was carrying a bloody towel.

"What is it? What has happened," shouted Jhika.

"A girl. She has borne a girl baby. Just a miserable little wrinkled useless girl." The old woman hurried into the kitchen area.

The two men stood uneasily, not wanting to go into the room where Ankh lay. The sound of a baby's weak cry came to them, and then Ankh's voice. It was a low wail.

"No. Not a girl! No. Nothing but *bipta*, misery, pain and labor." They heard her weep, sob out the words in a voice of anguish.

The two men returned to Sukkur soon after, telling the old woman they would come back the following morning. The old woman had not answered them, had not seemed to hear them but muttered. "There will be no son to inherit this place. No son. No little Malik. Sheikh Mohammed's women never had more than one child because of *suzak*, his disease." She held her hand to her crotch; then waddled off on sore feet.

They left Sukkur at dawn and were at the island as the sun came up over the trees, casting long shadows on the river. Flights of ducks winged their way west. The dogs emerged from the gate when they arrived, and then with tails between their legs retreated to the area where the buffalo cow was tethered. They made half-hearted barks and growled as the men entered.

Ankh was sitting in a chair in the meeting room. She was breast feeding the small child, looking at it sucking, its cheeks moving up and down.

"I will leave as soon as I have finished what I have come for. My name is Mirzah I am a policeman who works in Sukkur. The Deputy Superintendent of Police, Feroz Hakim called me and told me to get a paper from you which he now needs." He stood uncomfortably to the side of Ankh, glancing at her as he spoke.

"I know the Lahore policeman. He was here. He took away my friend's comb. I have nothing else to give him." Ankh looked at Mirzah openly and shook her head.

"He says he gave you an old paper, yellowish in color on which was written information about the ownership of this place. Give it to me and I will leave." He put out his hand.

"I told you that I have nothing more to give. That paper was given to the father of this little girl. His name is Dohst Mohammed. He was here two months ago. He has it. It belongs to him." Ankh looked at the two men as they stood near her. "Jhika, come back tomorrow for something else. Bring all the supplies that we talked about. Bring back the paper that you made of the image of the coin. I want to show it to Dohst when he returns." Ankh stood up stiffly, walked to the old sagging divan and placed the child there.

"What paper is this that you gave to Jhika?" Mirzah looked very official.

"It is something that I drew. A picture of a coin. Nothing. I have thrown it away already. Nothing." He was uncomfortable to be the focus of the conversation.

"I will have to search the entire house for the paper. I can't go back without it. Do you understand? If it is not found we have ways of making people talk." He stepped toward Ankh.

"I do not swear to your one Allah as I am a *kaffir*, but I swear oaths on thirty-three of my gods, that I gave Dohst the yellow paper in trade for this paper." She took a folded paper out of her waist band and held it up for him to read. He reached for it but she backed up. "Do not touch it. You can read it from where you stand. This is the paper of my freedom. I am not a slave. I am a free person like yourself. I am the wife of Dohst the *zamindar*, owner of this island property and house. I know what the yellow paper contained. It was the paper about *zamin*, land. Feroz Hakim read it to me when he gave it to me. It is the paper of inheritance of all the land owners of this place in the past with their marks on it. My child is not a son, but under your law of *Sharia* she will inherit one half of the share she would have had if she had been a boy." He leaned forward and looked at the paper. She stood poised ready to move her hands back in case he lunged forward. She was smiling now, smiling at the lie that came so easily to her lips that she was a wife.

He stepped back and looked at the face of the woman in front of him. Her huge eyes burned with resolve. Her lips were pursed in concentration. Her hair was wild about her face. In all his life he had never seen such a woman who confronted him openly, challenged him. He looked at Jhika as if for confirmation of what the woman had said.

"She speaks the truth. Dohst mentioned the land deed to me when I took him in the boat. She does not have it." Jhika walked over and looked down at the fair face of the sleeping child. He turned to Ankh. "The *kala kafir* infidel lays a white egg, indeed. What is her name?"

"I will call her *bipta* for all my calamity and misery. Her name is Bipta." Tears streamed down her cheeks. "You have called me the black infidel. Does clothing make the person?" She stared at the black coat worn by the detective.

No more words were spoken as the men retreated from the room and the house. On the boat both were silent most of the trip. Mirzah saw the wilted purple flower on the seat of the boat and threw it overboard. "Bipta.

I have never heard of this name before," he said. "It is not our custom to name a child a sad or bad name lest the meaning of it attaches itself to the child and it becomes like the name. We like names such as sun, star, moon, jasmine, rose and other perfumed flowers, sweetness, complacency, joy and grace. Bipta is a terrible name to give so beautiful a child even if it is a girl."

"Don't worry about it. The mother may be a black infidel, the child is fair. Like we always say, "The black chicken lays..."

"Paddle your boat. I know the saying. It changes nothing. If she is his wife, why does he not protect her and take her with him?"

"She is not his wife. She was a slave girl of his father. She needs no protection, she is like a she-bear with a cub. She growls." He laughed and made a deep sound.

"I am very happy that our women know their place and that they are kept in seclusion, away from the eyes of other men." The policeman looked very wise.

"I have often wondered if the reason why Muslim men keep their fat wives draped from head to toe is that they are so ugly with bulging folds, that to display them would make the husband ashamed." Jhika again splashed water.

"You are a *badmash, badmunh*, a naughty person with a dirty mouth."

G

The rifle was not new, but it had been well cleaned and oiled. It was an old 303 Lee-Enfield, made in 1916 with the 'volley' front sights. Its box clip carried ten rounds of ammunition. These old rifles had been brought to Afghanistan during the time of the war with the British. In Peshawar, exact copies of this weapon had been made by the thousands over the century and it was difficult to tell if a given weapon was a copy or an old original.

Tur-ali held the heavy weapon in his hands and examined it carefully. This was his first weapon. It looked very old. On the stock there was an old initial carved. OJS. His finger ran over the black marking, wondering who the soldier had been and whether he had died in Afghanistan far away from his home in England.

"Remove the bolt as I instructed you. Now hold the gun up to the sky, the barrel toward your eye. What do you see" The Instructor watched as the six young men held up their guns. "What do you see?' he asked again.

"I see a shiny tube with lines that snake around on it." Tur-ali was usually the first to respond.

"Those marks are called rifling. This is what makes the bullet spin around as it leaves the barrel and gives it accuracy. Is there dirt in the barrel?"

One lad called out. "Mine seems to have many black specks in it."

"I will show you how to clean the gun to remove the dirt and specks of burned powder and streaks of lead. Point the gun at the ground in front of your feet, not at your feet." He waited for them to comply. "Pull the trigger back all the way. Insert the bolt carefully and release the trigger." One lad had trouble lining up the bolt in the receiver. "Like this. It is not difficult. You will do it one hundred times today until you are so familiar with it that you will dream about it. Now, listen. This is the part where these pieces of steel and wood become messengers of death." He walked up and down behind the young men. "Push the lever which releases the clip." He demonstrated.

They all pushed the lever. Two clips fell to the ground and became covered with sand. "You two will clean the clips and take them in and out one hundred times. Sit over there and wait."

He took out a handful of bullets and walked to the four young men who waited eagerly. "I am giving you each one bullet. I will demonstrate how you insert it into the clip and how you put the clip back, and finally how this instrument becomes the messenger of death."

He demonstrated how to push the shell into the clip. The young men seemed to know how to do this, having seen their brothers and fathers do it hundreds of times.

"On the side, here, is a lever. It is the safety. If it is back toward you the gun should not fire, Inshallah! Pull the lever back toward you."

The boys did so holding the guns awkwardly. "Turn toward that huge rock over there about one hundred meters away. Do you see it? It has a small bush growing in a crack. Lift your weapons. Place the butt against your shoulder like this. They all did so, the barrels wavering around unsteadily. "Push the safety forward."

There was an explosion and one boy dropped his rifle and held his hands up as if seeking mercy.

"Good. You had your finger on the trigger, pulling back on it when you pushed the safety forward. Of course your rifle was happy to fire the bullet. If someone had been in front of you he would be dead. Your fellow soldier, your brother would be dead!" He handed him a second bullet. "Re-load. First pull the safety back!"

"Lift your rifle and point it toward the rock. Do not touch the trigger. Push the safety forward. Look down the sights and see the bush at the end of your rifles. Pull the trigger." There were crashes like thunder that echoed in the valleys around them. "I saw that all four hit the huge rock. Only one hit the area near the bush. Tur-ali, go run up and put a chalk mark around all four marks." Tur-ali shouldered his weapon and jogged up the hill toward the rock. The instructor shouted at the other boys. "Keep your weapons pointing at the earth near your feet. Lower them!" He manually pushed two of the barrels down. "Never point your barrel up or in front of you unless you are going to take a life. Never!"

Tur-ali returned and handed the instructor the chalk. "Since you made the first chalk markings you get the first shots. Tur-ali, right above the small bush is a black spot on the rock. Do you see it?" He nodded. "Here are four bullets. Take your time. Aim at the black spot. Do not pull the trigger. Squeeze it as gently as you would a nipple and you will be surprised when it goes off. Do not jerk back or the gun will be pulled off target."

Tur-ali stood with the rifle to his shoulder, already feeling the dull pain of the bruise he had received when the first shot went off. Without thinking he held the rifle away from his shoulder to avoid the recoil impact. The instructor kept quiet. The rifle crashed. And Tur-al almost dropped the gun, his face in pain. He reached over to rub his shoulder.

"Weapon pointed at the earth!" The instructor screamed at him. "You are in pain because you did not hold the butt tightly against your shoulder. If you do, your whole body will move back with the recoil." He looked at the other young men who were now perspiring, anticipating their own turns.

"Unload the empty cartridge and put in the second one. Point at the earth. Good. When you are ready you may fire." He waited while Tur-ali got his rifle in position. He saw the lad wince when he pushed the butt against his sore shoulder. Tur-ali began to squeeze the trigger gently but it refused to give so he pulled back harder. Then he remembered the safety.

He glanced back at the instructor. Then quickly pushed the safety forward and again positioned his weapon. He sighted along the barrel for the black spot but could not keep it in his sights. The weight of the weapon made his arms tire and it began to weave around. Then when the spot came in sight he quickly pulled the trigger. He could see now, more than two feet above the spot, there was a white mark that the bullet had made.

"Never pull that trigger unless you know exactly where your bullet will go. The black spot is the face of an American who wants to kill every Taliban. You! You jerked the trigger and the gun shot high, missed the enemy. That bullet cost fifty rupees. Make your shots count."

Tur-ali was breathing heavily when he put up the rifle again. He could see that every time he took a breath the sight wavered from the targeted spot. He held his breath. Then he saw that the sight moved up and down at each of his heart beats. He sighted, slowly let out his breath and when the black spot was in his sights he squeezed. He reared back at the recoil. There was a white spot in the center of the black mark. The instructor said nothing. Again he sighted, breathed out and found the spot in his sights and squeezed. He lowered his weapon and stared at the black spot and saw another mark, almost over the other. He stepped back and tried not to smile.

"Fifty percent! Failure! The Americans spray bullets. They are not sharp shooters and rely on hundreds of bullets to do the job of one well placed bullet. Make every shot count. I have seen their movies. They shoot a thousand shots and kill one enemy. Know where your bullet will hit! Tomorrow you will be given a chance to try again. Tomorrow we will not average today's score. If we did and even if you did shoot perfectly tomorrow you would receive only a passing grade. Tomorrow is another day. *Kal kis ne dehki hai,"* he said in Urdu. No one has yet seen tomorrow and what it will bring."

The second boy was handed four cartridges and the process was repeated. After all four had fired their trial shots he pointed at a rock high on the hill more than a quarter of a mile away. "Do you all see the rock that looks like the hump of a camel? When I fire my rifle at it all of you are to run to it and make a chalk mark around the spot where my bullet hit, and then run back again. You will carry your weapons with you. Right behind you is an American who has a knife and he is chasing you to kill you. The last one back here will be the one who is dead." He put up his weapon and shot high on the camel rock and his bullet hit it in the center. The boys all took off running. The larger and oldest of the group who had bullied the smaller youths took off at full speed, looking back over his shoulder at his more puny opponents. He ran almost as far as the first rock which had been used as a target and started to slow down. Tur-ali jogged along keeping a steady pace as he climbed the steep incline. His breath came in aching sobs. In five minutes he passed the larger boy who stood bent over, holding his sides, gasping. He looked up to see Tur-ali pass him and cursed and again sprinted, but there was shale underfoot and he slipped. He had forgotten that an American was following him with a knife. All he could think about was the word *khar-gosh*, hare, dreading the name, turtle (*kachva*) that he would be given behind his back. He became angry in anticipation and ran more steadily trying to catch up to Tur-ali who was far ahead.

Tur-ali came in second. On his return trip he also slipped on shale and hurt his knee which was bleeding as he limped in. The 'turtle' did not bother to run on the return trip. He strolled back, his face angry, his lips pursed. His gun was not pointing at the ground.

"Give me your weapon." The instructor put out his hand to receive it. He hesitated, still not lowering it. A shot rang out and gravel flew near the feet of the young man. "You made me the enemy. You pointed your barrel at me. Do you hand a knife to someone, point first? You do if you are *dushman*! Listen to me. I have killed more than fifty men who became my enemy. Fifty! If you want to challenge someone you must do two things to survive. Make sure you have a loaded gun, and know how to use it well. Second, make sure you are not angry. Anger will kill you. Screaming anger is pure suicide. I am Taliban. Our mission is to kill the invader, a holy *jihad*. We have no place for the bully, the violently angry one. Many times it is the small one who thinks carefully, who is cool in his actions that wins the battle. America! That is the real bully! America the violent one! America the angry one, the huge and powerful who fears nothing! Afghanistan, is small, careful, patient with the knowledge that Allah supports us. Afghanistan, Taliban, only a few of us, but we will prevail."

He took the rifle from the young man and looked at his eyes. For a moment the lad glared at the instructor, and then he lowered his eyes.

"You were wise to lower your eyes. Do you see where the gun in my right hand is pointing?" The boy looked at the barrel which was aimed directly at his chest. "You may leave and go home and tell you father whatever story you decide to tell. Or, you may stay but know this well, that here I am your father. These others here are your new brothers. Any harm that comes to them becomes my blood debt against your real father and his family. You may not stay as *dushman*, or in anger because the anger is against yourself and that will destroy you. Choose. You may leave now and go home. You may stay but recognize me as your father. Which is it.?" The barrel of his rifle was slowly rising.

The young man sank to his knees and reached for the shoes of the instructor who lifted him up. "None are servants here. None are slaves unless of Allah. We are one family in our fight against the invader, the infidel Americans. Inshallah we shall win! We have never in our entire history lived under the rule of an invading conqueror. We are Afghani! We are Taliban." He handed the rifle back to the young man.

"You are to run up to the camel rock. On it you will find the mark of my bullet. Circle it with a chalk mark and return. No American is following you. Follow your own mind, your own desire to serve Allah and submit to his will."

The young man whose name was Gulami (slave born) turned and jogged away. The instructor looked at the remaining young men. "Next week we will learn how to use explosives, make bombs and how to infiltrate into the camp of the enemy unseen. This week we have the simple lessons of rifle use and the use of our energy. Tur-ali will be the last to fire his gun tomorrow. He who is first will be last. Each of you will be given four more chances to make your mark."

☪

Two representatives of the Central Police Office, one the deputy Inspector General Masood-ur-Rasuul and the other his assistant Zaherudeen Khan, booked into the Intercontinental Hotel in Lahore. From their room phone they called Feroz Hakim.

"Mr. Hakim? Yes, this is Masood from the CPO. Good afternoon. Mr. Khan and myself would like to meet you in fifteen minutes at your private residence. We wish to keep our activity discreet while we are here. Yes. Your own home. We will take a taxi right now and see you in a few minutes." He hung up.

He turned to his companion. "We should probably beat him there. The Intercon is close to where he lives in Gulberg. Let us go. Let me do the talking. Please be the witness and take notes where needed for the report." They hurried down to the lobby and saw that the taxi was already waiting. Ten minutes later they arrived in front of the gate. Feroz's car was not there so they sat and waited. In five minutes, Feroz drove up, parked his car and came over to the taxi.

"Welcome. This is indeed a surprise. I am so surprised you wanted to meet here. This is official business, yes?" Feroz shook hands.

"So far yes. It is in regard to the newspaper articles Feroz. The Inspector General has asked us to come and talk to you personally. May we sit in the privacy of your home?"

"Come. Come. I have phoned my wife. We have not prepared a meal for you. Sorry. Come." Feroz wondered how the Deputy Inspector ever got into such a high position. He was short, dark skinned, bald and wore thick glasses. His ancestor must have been an Indian Bengali Baboo, a shopkeeper!

They sat in the sitting room. Feroz walked about fussing with pillows, walking to the kitchen to order tea. "Gentleman, please excuse my wife. She has a headache. I will bring tea in a minute."

"Sit down man. We only have a few questions." Masood pointed at a chair. "The matter of the disappearance of the American woman, Maria Bernard; have you found any new evidence and if so what is it?" He sat forward on the edge of his chair and looked at the intimidated Feroz intently.

"Yes. Wait a moment please." He scuttled into a back room and came out with an envelope. "This. Please do not touch the item." He opened the envelope and slid a small plastic pocket comb onto the glass-topped table and stood back triumphantly.

"What? I do not understand. It looks like a folding comb. Is that correct?"

"Yes. Yes. This was given to me by the woman Ankh who survived the terrible bombing of the village by the Americans. She was in a *baoli*. Ankh told me that the American woman, her close friend in the village, both of whom were sex slaves of Sher Khan, gave the comb to her. Look closely. There are three curly black hairs in the teeth of the comb. DNA evidence will prove they were her hairs." He took a deep breath.

"I do not understand. DNA does not have a person's name written on it. It has to be compared to another part of her body, her skin, blood, even a mouth swab. How do those three hairs prove anything? The woman was blown up, burned to ashes." He sat back and looked at Feroz and wondered how the man could ever have attained the rank he had. He was of lowly origin, the son of immigrants from India from before the partition, surely not a native Pakistani by origin. His thoughts must have shown on his face because Feroz became nervous and carefully slid the comb back into the envelope and put it in his pocket.

"We will get something from the two other American women who were Maria's dear friends here in Lahore before she was..., before she disappeared." He went to the kitchen and returned with a tray with a tea pot and three cups. He poured the tea while the others watched.

"What item do you think these women would have of a friend? How would they know for certain? This is very unusual. Since it is your great hope, yes, pursue it and let us know the results of your enquiry." He picked up his tea cup and sipped noisily. "The piece in the paper suggests you 'jumped the gun' with your report. How do you respond?" Mr. Khan now spoke to the surprise of his superior who frowned.

"I did not jump the gun. An eye witness survived. She saw the American woman frequently, was her friend and she survived. She and I both think Maria did in fact survive for good reason." He scuttled away and came back with a postal package, the stamps still on the wrapping paper. "This!" He peeled back the papers and revealed a water ravaged notebook with a red cover.

"Allah, man. You never cease to surprise me. What is that?"

"It was delivered to the reporter, Ikbal. I had an around-the-clock watch over him and when it was delivered to his home I was called. Using police authority, I confiscated it as evidence in an unsolved police case. He was furious. It is Maria's personal diary and writing book. It was found in the snow eighteen miles inside Afghanistan territory by horsemen. The horse's hoof skid on the slippery cover." He took a ruler and opened the book. The first fifteen pages stuck together, but the sixteenth page showed a crude picture of a dog and the word DOG in English, a cat with the English word CAT and a picture. He pointed at the pages. "There is proof! She had the book with her all the time. She escaped before the bombing and walked into Afghanistan in a *burkah*. She must have dropped it and did not notice, or she was getting weak and discarded it. Ankh saw her draw those pictures."

"Feroz, you do understand the meaning of circumstantial evidence?" He was trying to be patient.

"Not! Not circumstantial, sir. No. Look." He pointed at the book where a page had been torn away. "Look carefully. Do you see it sirs?" His hand shook.

"See what? No I do not see anything. What are you so excited about?" Again Mr. Khan, his subordinate asked a question. His superior cleared his throat but the man did not seem to notice.

"A page was torn from the book. The woman Ankh showed me that very page on which Maria had written ANKH and had drawn a picture of an eye and written the word in English." He looked almost smug.

"Well, show us the page." Masood stood up impatiently.

"She has it. She treasures it dearly. She now knows her friend is still alive. She keeps the paper folded up in a pocket over her heart." He was almost in tears.

"Why in God's name didn't you take it from her?" Again Khan butted in. Now Masood turned toward him and said, "Man, stick to our agreement. I am the Deputy Inspector here. Do you understand?" Khan shook his head slowly and sat back and took out a cigarette.

"I did not have the heart to tear the only article this poor slave woman had from her friend... tear it away from her. At that time neither of us knew that the notebook would be found. We both also thought Maria was dead."

"You are going to have to go back to this woman and get the sheet to see if it matches the torn segment. There is no other way. Pray, man, that she has not used it to roll a cigarette. So, on this evidence you have solved the case. Maria is alive. She is in Afghanistan. She lost a notebook and her friend has a slip of paper. Perhaps. Perhaps. When you get the information about the DNA and the mysterious torn paper with an eye on it, come to Islamabad and show it to me. We will then issue a press release."

"Yes. Yes." He poured more tea. "Is that all gentlemen?"

"No. We have hardly begun. Sit down, you make me nervous." He pointed at a large tin trunk in the room on which there was a picture of the Pakistani flag printed. "Open that!" He sauntered over to the trunk and looked at is more closely.

"It is not suitable. Sorry. I do not wish to open it. It is a personal item in my house. No. I do not wish to open it at this time."

"I have an order from the Senior, right here. You are ordered to open it!" Khan stood up and also walked over to the trunk.

Feroz's hand was shaking as he tried to unlock the box. The two policemen looked at each other meaningfully, smiling. The lock was opened. He pointed at the box and said, "Gentlemen, *zen...zennanah*! I will not open it and shame my household. You will have to do it and take the consequences."

"Move aside!" The lid was laid back. They were staring at four rather large brassieres, the cups pointed upward, two in pink and two in white. Next to them there were six sets of women's underwear, also of a rather large size, all in black with lace on the tops. There were pictures of a wedding with the woman sitting staring at the ground, she was plump and covered with gold jewelry. Next to her sat a young Feroz.

"You have violated the privacy of my home. You are not a Mr. Huge Heffner to come and spy on the secrets of my wife. I shall report this to the Senior Inspector himself." He was so upset that he left the room running and bent over.

Khan looked at the large cones, trying to imagine what they would fit over. In fact he was amazed. He had not known that women had such huge breasts. He looked at them without touching them, a small smile on his face.

The Deputy Inspector slammed down the lid. "What are you thinking? He is right. This is very awkward."

"I was thinking, what a wonderful way to put us off the track. Pile a bunch of female unmentionables on top of Sher Khan's secret files. We take a look and walk away and he has fooled us. That is what I was thinking. I was smiling because I was beginning to admire the warped and strange way of thinking of the Lahore Deputy." He reached for his hat to leave.

"Wait. You are right." He opened the lid and looked at the objects, then reached in and carefully removed them one by one and put them on the couch all in row, followed by the panties which he draped on the back of chairs. He saw a blanket in the trunk covered with moth balls. He lifted this up and stepped back. There was an entire row of women's sanitary napkins laid out as well as a bottle of Vaseline, partially used. He recoiled and looked at his Deputy.

"This is terrible. Quickly man, feel along the sides to the bottom to see if there are any files in this box."

Khan pushed the row of sanitary pads to the side, picked up the bottle and looked at it muttering, 'DNA' and reached down along the sides of the box and felt only clothing, heavy wool coats. There were no files. "Nothing. He was right. I hope he does not have a gun with him."

"Quick. Repack it with me. I can not touch the items again. Hurry before he gets back. The Deputy used the ruler to pick up the bras and to push the sanitary pads back as they were. That done, he closed the trunk, locked it, and sat on a chair to think.

Feroz returned and stood in the doorway looking at the two strangers in his house with hatred. "You said you came on official business. What more?"

"Yes. I have an order for this as well. Do you own a safe?" Masood asked the question very softly.

"What? A safe? Oh. Yes, I had one installed. Why? Do you have a safe in your home?" He was becoming braver.

"Take care Feroz. We are not being investigated here, you are. Your newspaper article spilled the can of worms. Show us the safe." Masood stood up ready to follow.

"Please. With all due respect, I wish to ask both of you, do you have a safe in your homes?"

They both nodded.

"Why?"

"To keep valuables in. Children, servants, friends of my wife coming and going. Yes, valuables."

"My safe is the same. Valuables. Please leave it alone. You do not need to open it. It has my valuables and I do not want you to see what I have. Would you like me to see how much gold, how much money you have? Your private letters?" He stared at the two men.

"Sorry. All you have to do is open it and we will peer in quickly to see if you have stored ..." He took a breath.

"Stored what, sir? What do you think I would store in my safe. I do not understand." He looked offended.

"It was in Reporter Ikbal's article, you know, files of the late Sher Khan." He pointed at the safe. "Open it, please."

It took Feroz a minute or two to open the locking mechanisms with two sets of keys. The safe, though new, was crudely made and the handle had to be pulled back at the time the keys were turned. He opened it and handed Masood a torch and stood back embarrassed.

There were a number of letters, some official papers in envelopes tied with string, six gold bracelets and a gold filigree necklace in an old jewelry box, a cheap looking ring with a red stone in it and his police revolver in its holster. To Feroz's horror he saw now that he had left the table of contents of Sher Khan's files, in code, in the safe on top of the envelopes, in full view. He had not seen it. He had totally forgotten it when he moved some of the files back to the police HDQ. The men looked at the contents, then at the hapless man standing there and stood up and moved toward him with their hands outstretched. He avoided their hand-shake, looking angry, looking at the gun in front of him in his safe. He reached into the safe and took it now and strapped it on. Their eyes moved away from the contents of the safe to his strange action. They watched as he hooked the belt around his waist.

"Sorry. Very sorry. It was our duty. Following orders. You understand. I will issue a statement today to Ikbal the reporter, a strong statement about his using hearsay and circumstantial information given by dubious witnesses to besmirch the good name of a trusted police officer. Sorry. I never trust the motives of the press, particularly that Ikbal who has shifty eyes. Always seeking for a story! And if his story puts the police down; all the better he thinks. "

The two men left Feroz standing at his front door. They got into the taxi and it drove off. Khan now began to laugh.

"What is so funny?" asked Masood.

"Size 40E."

☪

The Taliban trainer repeated again what he said each time they used weapons. They had heard it a hundred times. Do not jerk the trigger. During the third week of their training the men had learned how to handle and fire shoulder held rockets. Because of the expense of these, no live firing occurred, however, their training with rifles had taught the young men to hold the weapon steady, to sight it carefully and to squeeze the trigger.

"The national election will be held in October. We must do everything to disrupt that process. The enemy says that Al Qaeda are present in this area and they will cause some trouble. We will not disappoint them. They see 'Al Qaeda' everywhere. If one of their toilets does not flush, they look around for an Al Qaeda terrorist. We will help them to see its power." The instructor, who had never given his name to the young men, motioned for all of them to surround him at the table. "This is a map of the Kohst Air Port. The enemy airplanes use this as a staging area. Our first battle in our *jihad* will be here." He pointed at the map of the air field. "We will try to take out helicopters and airplanes that are parked here. To do so we will fire rockets from the low hills here near the airport. We will infiltrate into these hills during the night and at dawn when all are still sleeping, we will form a rough half circle, twenty yards apart from each other. There will be five teams of two each. A senior warrior will lead you. Each of you will carry your own rifle and three rockets to supply your leader. Watch exactly how he loads the rockets and how he fires and selects his targets. If the rockets are shot up into the sky at an angle they go a considerable distance, however, it is impossible to shoot a target that way. They go where they go. If the distance is less than 500 yards, it is possible to hit an object as small as a tank. If the distance is over a thousand yards, about what we will be firing, it is more difficult to hit the target, but by the second shot an experienced man will hit it, especially if it is as big as an airplane."

The young men stood uneasily and they had the look of a bridegroom who has not yet seen the woman he is to marry; they looked curious but worried. "The Americans are not good spotters of the fire flash of rockets because they use electronic eyes and hate to get up at dawn. Israelis are trained fighters who know how to set artillery fire minutes after a rocket is fired at them. We are not dealing with cursed Zionists. All four of your rockets will be fired within two minutes time. Then each group of two will run to the left, not going uphill, for ten yards, and then run straight up the hill for thirty yards and then again to the left. If there is mortar fire from the airfield soon after your salvo, by running thirty feet to the left and then straight up the hill will probably put you out of the range of the exploding mortars. You will have to be quick. There are round-the-clock sentries at the Kohst field at all the gates and near the control tower. These will immediately rouse the others that there is an attack. In five minutes time how far can you be from the place you fired the rockets? Almost a mile.

Helicopters will be warmed up and within ten minutes they will be heading for the coordinates they established at the beginning. If you hear them coming, lie down under a bush. Stay still. I have been in helicopters and it is hard to see an individual person lying down in a gully or under a bush. Movement is what attracts the pilot."

He became increasingly more excited as he talked. "We will begin firing at the targets on the ground at exactly 5:15 a.m. Then each team will take time to fire their remaining three rockets at targets in front of them. Listen now. We will not join up after that. You all know the rugged countryside. We will climb up the rocky hill behind us and head due west. You will each have water for one day and food for a day. We will meet here twelve hours later. Talk to no one on the way. Your first day of great service to Allah will be at Kohst. In all the newspapers of the world there will be the story of the rockets raining down on Kohst airport, stories of the Al Qaeda attack and your *jihad* will have made history! Allah Akbar."

Just before sunrise the land is bathed in a pink-gold color. The higher ridges and hills catch the light first as the sun's rays beam up from the eastern horizon, gold plating them. Crows awaken and swoop from their roosts into the valleys seeking, looking for food, crying to each other. A breeze on the slope of a hill gives them lift and they rise on the air current, playing with the wind, calling out in warbling alto notes during their acrobatic swoops. Partridges begin their rasping territorial calls. A long tailed Tree Pai leaves its tree perch and with jerky flight, swoops to the next tree calling out a high pitched, **ko-ku-la, ko-ku-la.** In the distance there is the comforting sound of the *muezzin* as he makes the first call to prayer of the day, invoking Allah's blessing, reminding the faithful to submit to the will of the almighty, the merciful. The high tenor notes of his voice carry faintly over the land, bathing it with sounds of praise which are answered by the call of the crows soaring high.

The men stood on the slope overlooking the airport. They began their private prayers, the *Iqama* and brought their hands to their ears, palms forward, thumbs behind the earlobes. They murmered, *Alluhu Akbar. Subhaana ala humma wa biham dika...*

In the semi-darkness the men finished their prayers and took their positions waiting for the sunlight to appear over the eastern horizon. Each team leader had already loaded the rocket in the shoulder-held rocket tube. The men sat and did not smoke. At 5:10 there was sufficient light to see the parked helicopters which looked very small in the distance, like black bugs against the light-colored cemented airfield. Only two fighter jets were on the apron of the runway near a metal hangar almost beyond range.

Tur-ali and his leader stood poised, waiting for 5:15. Alum, the senior man aimed his rocket at the helicopters. At exactly 5:15 he pulled the trigger and watched the rocket streak toward the target and fall far short. Three other rockets screamed on their way and landed on the runway, making orange puffs followed after a couple of seconds with the puny thuds of the explosions. Tur-ali passed on the next projectile, it was loaded and Alum raised the sights and fired. The rocket hit on the airstrip closer to the target. Again he loaded and lifted the sighting mechanism aiming toward the hangar and fired. He was directly on target in terms of distance but the rocket hit more than thirty feet to the left of the helicopters. He fired the last and watched in frustration as the missile again missed the target, hitting slightly to the right, the wash of air of the explosion making the rotors tip and sway. He swore, shouldered the tube and ran uphill. Tur-ali ran after him. Now they jogged to the left and ran again, then uphill. Alum ran like one possessed. They ran for about five minutes.

Tur-ali could not keep up but was almost at the top of the rise when the entire hillside erupted in explosions. He threw himself to the ground but the earth around him was lifted in an explosion that scattered parts of his body across the hillside. His head, still attached to part of his torso stared with open eyes at the golden sky.

Helicopters lifted off the ground and rose vertically from their position, then angled toward the hill, the sound of their rotors thumping. There was the sound of their canon fire as they searched the hillside. Alum lay hidden under a shelf of a rock, deafened by explosions all around him. He abandoned the rocket firing tube as the helicopters moved away from him and crawled on his knees up the slope and again hid in a ravine. His last view of the Kohst airport was one which reminded him of a hornet's nest. The hornets were swarming out of their slumber toward him. He looked back for Tur-ali and saw only a ball of hellish fire for an instant.

☪

Pagali had no idea what was happening to her when the labor pains began. She shrieked and held her abdomen. Meher was terrified. She had never seen a birth before and did not know what to do. She could not leave to find help and abandon Pagali in the house in this condition. She knew about labor pains, so she decided that each time Pagali had one she would sit with her and pat her back and talk to her and tell her that it would be all right.

Pagali's labor was difficult and long. Meher fell asleep between the contractions. She put a blanket on the floor and a cushion for Pagali to lie on. She sat on the floor next to her and held her hand and talked. Then she began to recite from the Koran from memory. Pagali became exhausted as labor progressed for hours. Just as the first call to prayer was heard from the nearby mosque, the child was born. Pagali was unconscious as Meher pulled the child away, but stopped because of the umbilical cord. She had a razor blade in the bath room. She got it and cut away the cord and was concerned that it leaked blood so she tied a string around the cord tightly near the abdomen of the baby. She cleaned the infant and wiped away a membrane, a caul, from its face and then lay the child on a tattered cushion and covered it with a towel. She then tended to Pagali.

Pagali was bleeding steadily and was not moving. Meher placed a towel against the vulva to stem the bleeding but it continued; the placenta was still retained. The baby began to cry so Meher picked it up and saw now that it was a boy, a healthy boy. She rocked the child, wishing she could feed it and looked toward Pagali hopefully. There was a huge puddle of blood under her. She was no longer breathing.

Meher sat for a long time looking at the body of Pagali, trying to think of what to do. Finally she stood up, wrapped the child and threw a shawl over her head and left the house, forgetting to lock the door. She made her way to the mosque and then to her parent's home behind the mosque. Her mother screamed when she saw her, covered with blood on hands and clothing. When she saw the child she screamed again.

"What are you bringing here? Whose is this?"

Meher was so tired that she sagged into a chair and handed the child to her mother. "It is the child of the young woman of the house I lived in. The woman died giving birth to it. She bled to death. Help me."

☪

It was the first time that he had eaten in an expensive Lahore restaurant. He was amazed at the variety of food on the table.

"Dohst you are looking thin. You need some one to fatten you up." Gretchen passed the bowl of aromatic *basmati* rice to him. He heaped a huge portion onto his plate.

"It has been a strange time for me, Miss Sahib. I was being sought by Sher Khan for Maria's abduction and had to run and hide. I went to Sialkot and hid at my aunt's house. I even changed my name, my clothing, shaved my head and took a job as a currier delivering letters. It was terrible work especially in the hot season. I have heard that Sher Khan is now dead and so is Maria." He talked with his mouth full.

"No. Haven't you heard? There have been newspaper reports that Maria had escaped from the village that was bombed and that she hiked into Afghanistan and was not killed. One of her friends, a Pakistani girl by the name of Ankh reported that she had been with her and had some things that only Maria could have had."

"Ankh! When I spoke to her..." He looked around at their surprised faces. "Yes, Ankh is now at my father's island home. She was his slave. After he died in Karachi I visited the island near Sukkur and saw Ankh who had been taken back there by the Red Crescent. She thought Maria had been killed in the bombing. Amazing!"

"Were you able to talk freely with a woman from your father's... you know, his harem?" Celia frowned.

"Yes. My father was dead. She is with child." This admission surprised them. Their faces were blank as they stared at him. He sighed. "My child. She is due to have the child very soon. It is a long story. I must return to Sukkur after this trip to Lahore to see her. She was my father's slave. I freed her and ..." He shrugged.

"So, you are going to be a father! Wow. Fantastic, Dohst! When are we going to be able to see your little woman?" Gretchen extended her hand to shake Dohst's. He did so tentatively, not quite understanding their enthusiasm.

"She is not my little woman, like being a wife. She is from an infidel tribe and is not a Muslim." He looked around at the two faces staring at him, now thinking that they were both infidel Americans and became a bit flustered.

"Why not?" Celia shook her head. "Why can't you marry her? Don't you love her? She is having your child, right?"

Dohst put down his fork and wiped a grain of rice from his lips. "I do not understand your question. Sorry."

"I see. You had a quick affair with her, she got pregnant and then you, what? What happens to you and her now?" Gretchen frowned.

"I set her free. She is no longer a slave. She is staying in my house in Sukkur now and I will provide for her food and clothing and the child's." He bit the inside of his lip, thinking about how to make these women understand.

"Is she beautiful? Is she young? Is she smart? Do you like her? Do you talk with her?" Gretchen pushed for Dohst's level of commitment.

"Yes. Very beautiful. She has huge eyes, the color of your eyes." He pointed at Celia's face.

Dohst now thought about Meher and that he had given her a secret marriage. Perhaps these American women would be pleased that he actually married and they would then not be concerned with Ankh. "I have a wife in Sialkot who is living in my aunt's house there with... She is taking care of the place while I am gone." He smiled.

"I see. I see. My goodness this has been a busy, busy year for you. Will we get to meet this woman? Tell us about her." Celia seemed pleased.

"No. I mean, I don't think it will be easy for you to meet her. There are other problems in Sialkot that I am trying to work out. I am trying to start a business to support my family and make money. I want to go into selling oil. I am going to sell two new air conditioners that I have in order to have cash to get started. Very nice. Still in the wood boxes." Now he smiled and thought of the Mullah, Meher's uncle's words, that smiling was the sign of the devil.

"That's right. We almost bought one when we met you. The guy was not happy. So do you want to give us a good deal? We will buy your machines, one for my bedroom, the other for Celia's." Gretchen smiled broadly.

"Yes. Yes. A big reduction. Only 19,000 Rupees each, like I said. You will save hundreds of rupees." He was still smiling.

"I tell you what. Since we will buy two, sell them at 18,000 each and you've got a deal, that is if they work when you turn them on. Of course, this price means you will install them for us and give us a one year guarantee." Gretchen stared at him intently, enjoying the bargaining process.

"Install? Guarantee?"

"That is what the man in that shop was saying. Yes." Gretchen took a sip of tea.

"Of course. What he says I will do. I can bring them when you tell me. They are in Sialkot. I will have to rent a car or a truck."

"Heh. We have never been in Sialkot. We could go back with you, drive you there and pick them up and then see where you live. We have two day's off. Do you want to go tomorrow and get them?" Celia looked over at Gretchen who nodded.

Dohst was not used to such quick decisions. He looked confused. He was thinking of the women seeing his small house and wanting to meet his wife. He was thinking of Pagali and what they would think of her with her huge belly. These thoughts made him sweat. He thought of 36,000 Rupees and what a huge pile of money it would be and how he would get into the oil business.

"Thank you. I agree. I agree. Thank you. One can go to the back seat, the other into the boot of your car with the trunk tied down. Yes. It will be suitable. Tomorrow?"

Celia drove as Gretchen looked at the map and Dohst, from the back seat interpreted road signs. It took them almost two hours to make the short trip to Sialkot. Dohst decided that they would drive to the store and pick up the air conditioners first and then from there stop by his house briefly. He would tell the women to wait in the car while he checked on what had happened to Pagali and Meher Jamal while he was gone. Then he would tell the women that they both were very sick and that were coughing terribly. Then they would leave.

One of the machines fit into the boot but the lid could not be shut so it was tied down with a string to keep it from bouncing around. The other did not fit through the opening of the door. Dohst took the screwdriver and pried off the wood crate and was able to pack the machine still in its white foam protective wrappings into the back seat of the car.

They drove to Dohst's house and he got out and told them to wait. Dohst did not realize that his house was so small and that there was trash in the street in front of it. He had not remembered that there was little paint on the outside walls and that the small gate was lacking a hinge. He did not remember that the front door which was once painted a light green had smears of what looked like dark dried blood over it. He did not want the American women to get out and see the burning trash in the ditch and the body of a dead crow covered with flies. He opened the door and closed it behind him. The room was dark. He opened the window to let in light and then heard the sound of a baby crying from the kitchen. He hurried into the small kitchen and surprised Meher who was mixing powdered milk in a bottle. A tiny baby was lying on a cushion on the floor and was crying.

"Aziz! You frightened me, Aziz!" She began to weep and set the bottle down on the table. The baby cried more loudly.

"Whose baby is that?" he shouted.

"Yours. A son." Now she could not continue speaking, picked up the crying baby with her good arm and supported it with her flipper arm from beneath. She hurried to the bedroom. Dohst followed her, shaking his head.

"Where is Pagali?" He shouted to be heard above the weeping of the child and Meher.

"Dead. She died when the child was born." She rocked the hungry baby but it continued to wail.

He stood confused. Died. Pagali was dead? He felt confused, but somehow felt a relief, then guilt at his relief. Outside he could hear the sound of the car's engine. He had not yet been paid for the air conditioners.

He turned and rushed to the front door, paused then stepped out, shaking his head. "Terrible news! My wife died in childbirth." He lied easily, calling Pagali his wife, lied to cover his immediate situation with Meher of whom he was ashamed because of her flipper arm and because she was an older woman, as old as Celia and Gretchen. That thought made him guilty again for writing Celia a love letter which, according to his dead father had attracted the attention of the police which had ended up with the suicide of his father. His mind whirled. He turned to the women. "The baby is alive. A servant woman is taking care of the child. Terrible." He placed his hands on the front fender of the car, his head hanging in apparent dejection.

The women got out of the car and both put their arms across his shoulders. "How terrible that your wife died while you were gone, Dohst. So sorry. So sorry. What can we do? How long ago did she die?"

He shook his head. He did not know when she died. "I can not invite you in to my humble home. Perhaps..."

"Look, here is the check for the air conditioners. You can deposit it into your bank account. It will take about one week to clear." Celia handed him the check.

He looked at it as if it was a foreign object. "I have no bank. I am sorry. Please, I will need cash. No bank."

"Dohst, if you are a business man you will need a bank account. Do you have the time now to go with us to your local Barclay's Bank? I know it is a terrible time. We don't have cash. We can help you set up an account and have this money deposited to it. Then you can draw against the account later. Let us help you."

His thoughts of the pile of money energized him. "Wait. Let me go tell the servant woman who is caring for the child, that I will come back soon. Wait." He rushed away.

Meher was sitting in the tiny front room feeding the child when he returned. "I will be back in one hour. I have to get money from the bank. Wait. I will be back soon."

She looked up at him, tears streaming down her cheeks. "What will you call your and Pagali's son? Do you want to look at him?" asked Meher. "It is time to name him."

He still could not admit to the fact that he was the one who got Pagali pregnant; that he was the father of a son. He stood uncomfortably. He stepped to where she was feeding him and looked at the child. The baby was beautiful, with a fair complexion. "Just call him *Malik*, king." He hurried out, the check still in his hand.

CHAPTER NINE

Sher bakari ek ghat pani pite hain. (Hindustani Proverb)

The lion and the goat drink from same source.

Jhika brought sweets from the bazaar in a small paper box. He bought two bars of fragrant soap and a small vial of perfume, Oriental Jasmine, made in Egypt. When he pulled the boat up on the sands of the island the dogs came running but greeted him with wagging tails. He strolled up to the walled compound and called out.

"Is there any one here?"

"No one is here anymore except two women and a girl child." The old woman was grumpy as she opened the gate. "Why are you here again? You were here four days ago."

He did not answer but took a pound of Yellow Label Tea from his satchel and two tins of condensed milk and handed them to the old hag. She did not thank him but waddled off with the gifts making small sounds like one would make when stroking a kitten. He walked to the front door and called again. He could hear a baby complaining so he waited and sat on the steps and smoked. After a few minutes the door opened and Ankh stood above him with the child in her arms.

"Again? Are you here again? Does no one cook for you in your father's home?" She moved into the living room as he followed. He did not respond but took out the gifts he had brought and handed them to her. She put the baby on the sway-backed divan. She opened the bottle of perfume first and smelled it. She put a drop on her palm and rubbed it on her forehead. The soap she set next to the baby. Then taking the box of sweets she walked to the window for better light and opened it. She stared into it for a moment and took out a square of white *barfi* which was covered with thin silver foil. She held it with her thumb and index finger and looked at it for a long moment, then took the tiniest bite and put it back in the box. There were four kinds of sweets. She savored each one, taking tiny bites with her pearl colored teeth while Jhika watched her. A ray of sun came in the window and played on her hair, raising reddish-purple hues in the black curls. She turned to face him with a round candy, a *ludoo* the size of a golf ball in hand, took a big bite and laughed as she chewed.

"What did you do with the old woman?" she asked.

"The same as with you. Gifts. She is now cooking herself a batch of strong sweet tea, enough for five people, which she will not finish off by the time it is dark." He walked to where the baby was lying quietly and to Ankh's surprise picked it up and looked at it carefully. "Bipta, little misery, what a name for such a beauty. You rival your mother's beauty. When you grow up a Malik will seek you out and make you a queen. Queen Bipta." He brought the child closer and smelled its soft cheeks. He turned toward Ankh. "Smells better than you too." He laughed and put the child down.

Ankh chewed her sweets, smiling all the while. "It is late. You will not have moonlight to light your way home with the boat. I have not prepared food. You had better leave now while you are able." She was still smiling.

"At the first hint of dawn I will be away. I cannot leave. I am a captive of the mother of all misery that smells like Jasmine and has sticky fingers." He did not smile.

"Eat one of these or you will be hungry." She handed the box to him. He shook his head and handed the box back and when she took it he held her hand tightly. Ankh looked at him with a serious face, sighed and put her other hand over his.

"Dohst Mohammed told me that he would return here during this month. He could be arriving tomorrow. Your coming here is dangerous. He would kill you. He would cut me up and maim me as a matter of honor." She pushed Jhika away, but he pulled her back.

"He does not even know he is a father. He has granted you freedom from slavery but that was done cheaply for him. He can come here and expect you to be here, to take care of this property, pay you nothing. You are no better than a slave to him." He pulled her closer and looked into her worried eyes. "Tell me. When he comes next time what are you going tell him?"

"What do you mean? I will tell him nothing. He has not married me, yet he is the father of this child and he would be furious if he knew you came to the island to see me. Nothing. I will not say anything." She looked angry.

"What if I said that I was interested in marrying you and would pay..."

She cut him off. "What? You have not even spoken to me that you would be interested to marry me. I am not interested in marrying you. No. That idea is impossible." She pulled away from him.

"Why? Then why have you let me come and be with you here on the island?" Now he was angry. "I want to marry you. You know that. I am asking you, please, Ankh, let me marry you."

"I will tell you if you first tell me why you wanted to come to see me." She stepped back.

"I...you know why. I think you are beautiful. I do not have a girl friend, I have no wife. I wanted to ask you to be my..." He laughed now. "You have no family to ask, so I ask you."

"You wanted to have sex with me." She used the crude term for it, *jor lagana.*

"Yes, of course. That is a reason. Tell me your reason." He was laughing now thinking of the words she used. He had never heard a woman speak such words.

"Then you have my answer as well. For the same reason. Leave now while there is a little light. Perhaps he will come tomorrow and we both will suffer. Leave."

He looked at her in amazement. "The same reason?" He nodded his head. "What about the sales of items from the house?" He swept his hand in an arc.

"That is finished as well. If the old woman wags her tongue when Dohst arrives there will be terrible trouble for me. Go!"

"I will leave now, but I will come back. The same reason? I came to ask you about marriage. I like the smell of the baby's cheek." He picked up his bag and left, walking jauntily into the semi-darkness with the dogs following close behind, gamboling playfully. "But I like the smell of your cheeks better!" He sauntered toward his boat.

☪

When she walked, she waddled. The child she was carrying seemed huge to her. The skin of her abdomen was etched with stretch marks. Her appetite was huge. She ate all that 'thank you Joe' brought her. Maria had never eaten so much goat meat in her life; however, the spicy food was palatable to her as long as she had oven breads to sop up the gravy. She longed for fruit. One day she drew an apple and a cluster of grapes on a paper and pointed at herself. Atiqullah nodded. He returned with two clusters of grapes, one dark red the other a greenish yellow in color. Maria said "Thank you, Joe."

Her daily excursions and language lessons finally came to an end. She felt too uncomfortable to walk and shook her head when he suggested they go to the market to buy fruit. She pointed at her stomach indicating discomfort. He misunderstood and thought she was in labor.

An hour later a small, bent over woman accompanied him when he returned. She talked constantly as she examined Maria. She felt her abdomen and then called for tea. After half an hour she again felt Maria's abdomen and shook her head as she talked to Atiqullah. He paid her a 50 Afghani note and pointed at Maria again. She nodded.

The next day at noon Maria went into labor. She lay on the hard cot in the windowless room and stared at the ceiling anticipating her next contraction. At first she became afraid of the intensity of the contraction of the muscles in her lower abdomen and placed her hands on the surface of her belly as it hardened. She had heard her mother speak about bearing four children and that each time she had been surrounded by other women of the family who were experienced with childbirth. She wondered if she would die alone in this drab dark room and not a person in the entire world would know of her suffering or even think of her.

In the periods between contractions during the first three hours her mind returned over and over again to family, to Manila, to her mother. She wept hopelessly and fell asleep exhausted from her emotions only to be jarred awake again as another contraction began. She groaned and called out her mother's name. Atiqullah looked in and said words she did not understand, her mind focused on the intensity of the contraction.

She sat up at the end of a contraction and got up to go to the latrine. When she returned she sat glumly on the edge of the bed and stared at the floor between her feet, dejected. Near her on a small table she saw a motion and stared at a little creature there. She wondered about its strange appearance and then recognized it as a large cockroach. Its body pulsated with a rhythmic motion and Maria watched, fascinated, as it struggled to expel a huge egg capsule from its behind, its body arching in spasmodic motions. The egg-sack seemed immense compared to the size of the insect. As she watched, the egg-sack was delivered and dropped to the table top. The cockroach sensed the noise of Maria's slippers against the floor and scuttled away quickly, leaving behind a brown egg sack. Another contraction gripped her.

The old woman, a *qabilah* was summoned and was pleased that Atiqullah had called for her early in the labor process as she would be paid more at the end. She cooked food for Maria, set it out on the table and lay back on the bed to nap. When she awakened she examined Maria and nodded, seeming pleased. She pointed at herself and said *qabilah*. Maria thought she was telling her what her name was and called her Qabilah, though the woman was telling her that she was a midwife. The midwife came and went from the room during the hours that followed. Whenever Maria cried out loudly, she patted her arm and nodded. As the intensity of labor increased Maria became exhausted and fell back on the bed. The woman chatted incessantly, seemingly telling Maria stories. Her old arthritic hands stroked Maria's abdomen, patted her shoulders and massaged the small of her back.

Atiqullah absented himself now, visiting tea houses and wandering about the town. He tended to his flock of goats, accompanying the lad to the nearby hillsides where the animals were grazed. He returned the next day after the last call to prayer and was relieved to hear the sound of a baby crying when he opened the door to his outer courtyard. He carried a gourd of fresh goat milk which he set down on a table. The old woman met him and told him that the foreign slave woman had borne twins but the male child had been stillborn.

Maria lay on the cot, her tiny daughter next to her, cradled in her arm. She looked at the child and leaned over it to kiss its forehead, baptizing it with tears falling from her own eyes.

"What name do you want, little one? Will I call you by a Filipino, Tagalog name? What about Mata? Will I call you by some American name such as Iris, or will you be happy to have an Afghani name?" The baby responded by pulling a face and looking up at her blindly for a moment. Her eyes were grey. "None of these! None of these. I am going to call you Ankhi, for my friend who died when the bombs fell on Bahadur. Ankhi Bernard. Yes, it suits you well." She shook her head, remembering that Sher Khan was the father, not James.

Yes. Ankhi Bernard, 'conceived and born in sin' as her catholic father always said when she misbehaved. Fathered by a Pashto policeman, born in Afghanistan to a slave mother, the concubine of a Taliban peasant, without a country in a place that has no name.

She tried to feed the baby, her tears falling onto its cheeks. Her milk did not let down. The child, after a moment of sucking, seemed to have little interest, and moved its lips away from the nipple and cried. "Later. Give me time, little one. We have each other. Perhaps, Ankhi, some day the two of us will somehow be able to leave this place and find our home in ..." She paused, " Home. Where ever it is. Manila, La Jolla, Lahore, wherever home is." Now her tears fell again, streaming down her cheeks onto the child.

Atiqullah pushed open the door and hobbled in on his club foot. His face was wreathed in smiles. He sat on the edge of the bed and picked up the tiny baby and began talking to it. Maria understood that he was think-ing of a name, but he was describing the child's face, that it looked like a little monkey, a little shrunken monkey, fathered by a despised Pakistani.

"Ankhi." Maria tapped the baby's chest. "Ankhi." Atiqullah nodded and repeated the name good naturedly, put the child down and said he would return in the morning with food and cloth rags for diapers. Maria did not understand.

She learned to carry the child with her wherever she went, watching how other women tied the child to themselves as they cooked, drew water, swept the courtyard, gathered fuel. She fed it whenever it cried, but it was a placid child and seemed to thrive.

Atiqullah slept elsewhere for the first two months. One evening after dark, as Maria slept; he entered the small room, lit a kerosene lamp, took the baby from the bed and placed it on a quilt on the floor. He took off his clothing, and slid into the bed next to Maria. She lay rigid, having anticipated that he would eventually return. He did not touch her then. He lay looking at the ceiling, the shadows of the guttering lamp playing on the ceiling. He talked, a rambling speech which she took to be a portion of the Quran because of the lilting way he intoned the words. He lay on his side and faced her, reached for her right hand and entwined his fingers into hers.

Maria looked at the rugged face, orange in the light of the lamp, a scarred, weathered, smiling, and kindly face. She looked at the black piercing eyes of a man who was her captor, for whom she was but a slave, a prisoner of war. But she could see reflected in his eyes a look of amazement, a look of astonishment with his mouth partly open. His eyes roved over her face. He reached with his index finger and traced the outline of her eyes, the ridges outlining her lips; he felt her ear lobes with his thumb and finger and made a small clucking noise in his throat. He placed his hand on her curly black hair and said softly, "Allah Akbar."

In the far distance there was the sound of bombs exploding; a deep penetrating sound, more a vibration than a noise and it shook the foundations of the house.

"America," said Atiqullah. His eyes were filled with hatred.

☪

Dohst looked at the check book entry. Rupees 38,000. He flipped through the pages of checks, all blank, ready for him to write any number up to the amount of the first entry. He still did not trust it. He had watched his father deposit American checks at a bank in Lahore, but at that time it did not make much sense to him, nor did he really have an interest in what his father did. It amazed him now, that by writing on a line on a piece of paper that someone else would accept it as money. He decided that the next day he would try it out in the bank and write a check to himself for Rupees Two Thousand and see what would happen. His plan was to get some cash, take the bus to Lahore and go to Gretchen and Celia's house and ask if he could sleep in the kitchen for one night. Then on the next day he would install the two air conditioners. He had no idea how he would do this. He got his bicycle and pedaled off to talk to an air conditioner salesman and ask many questions about installation, as if he was an interested customer. He would hold the checkbook in hand so the man would know he was serious.

He purchased a few tools and amazed, got cash from the bank by exchanging his check for money, returned home to Meher and his son Malik. He bought six different sweets, savory snacks, biscuits, a *ser* of sugar and Red Label Tea for Meher.

"I will go to Lahore to install the air conditioners for the women as I promised. Then I will go to the Lahore Barclay's Bank to see if they will also exchange money for a check. I will take the Sammi Daewoo Express Bus to Sukkur to visit my other home there and see if it is being cared for well by the two women living there. The trip should take ten days." He looked at Meher who was nodding.

"Who are the women that live there?" she asked.

"One is an old hag, a left-over servant from my father who has lived there most of her life. The other is a slave woman of my father." He looked uncomfortable.

"How old is the slave woman? What is her name? Your father is dead, so is she your slave now?" Meher watched his face, reading its thoughts.

"I do not know ages. I do not know how old you are. Her name is Ankh. She is an infidel, not a Muslim. No, she is not my slave now. I gave her a letter of freedom. She is about to have a baby." He spoke quickly as if to get rid of the information.

"Is the baby yours?" Meher already knew the answer and was shaking her head.

"That is what she says. It does not seem possible. Yes." Now he took out a cigarette and smoked, looking at the glowing end accusingly. "Look, I am tired of talking and answering a hundred questions. Malik is sleeping. I have to leave tomorrow. Let us go to our bed." He sounded like he was giving an order.

She got up and took another sweet, frowning as she ate it. "I am thirty one years of age. How do you speak of me when you talk to others about me? Servant?"

He was amazed to know her age, so much more than his own. He had not thought about her as a person of age, simply a female that lived in his house, with whom he slept, who was taking care of his baby. Her admission startled him. He thought about other women he had looked at and had desired and wondered now about their ages. Maria. Gretchen. Celia. His letters of love and wanting to do dating to them came to mind and now he actually smiled, thinking about his eager focus on women without realizing they were people who had an age, people who had a life. He turned and looked at Meher Jamal, still standing and looking at him after asking a question.

"Thirty one! It is a strange thing to think about. You were a little girl in Islamic school before I was born. Amazing. How do I speak of you? I have not spoken about you, but now I will think about how I will speak of you. How do you want me to speak of you?"

"I will answer you with another question. When you hear the sound of my name, Meher, what is the first thing that comes to your mind?"

He looked at her with a frown on his face. "It is strange, but I thought of driver's licenses and the small lettering on T2 oil cans." He laughed and got up and headed toward the bed room.

C⋆

Piari read the newspapers each day, both the Urdu and the English versions. Her father, Osama, a business man in Lahore worked in what he called the 'export-import' business. He humored his daughter, a beautiful woman of twenty five who was frequently house-bound, taking care of her younger brothers and sisters. She was now his receptionist and bookkeeper, spending many hours each day in the home office for his T2 import business.

Ten years earlier Piari had been raped but she did not become pregnant. The entire matter had been kept quiet with a vain hope that Piari would be able to find a husband. Initially her father had been furious with her for what he called 'her part' in the rape; that she must have enticed Ikbal, but worse that she got in the car with him alone, and without a chaperone. No decent girl took a ride with a single man. She had protested that Ikbal was a family friend who they all knew, that they had frequently been in each others houses socially with their parents, though never together alone.

Osama had struggled with his daughter's problem for more than six months, keeping her in utter confinement. He feared that if the matter became public, religious leaders would condemn her, possibly sentence her to death. The reality of the Hudood Ordinance loomed large in his thinking. Even if a girl was raped, she was often sentenced to death for *zina*, adultery. Though she had always been his dearest love child, one he spoiled with affection, now he threatened to kill her to maintain the honor of the family. He appeared to be insane in his ranting, in his silent dark periods of depression when he walked about the house, his head down muttering and withdrawn. Piari avoided him and kept to herself in her room when he was home. His anger slowly shifted away from his daughter. His wrath turned against Ikbal and his family. He now spoke an oath of vengeance against the one who had spoiled the family name, who had dishonored a generation.

He visited the Senior Superintendent of Police, Sher Khan in the hope that the young man could be arrested and punished. He hoped for some type of financial payment, of recompense from Ikbal's family and he warned, if it was not forthcoming, the family of Ikbal could be assured that he would not stop in his plans for revenge until Ikbal had been killed. He began to plan how to kill Ikbal to preserve the honor of the women of his family. Zen!

The police officer Sher Khan had heard the same litany many times before; men who came to him with the look of hatred on their faces, seeking openly to defend the honor of their family through the shedding of blood. This was a welcome sign to Sher Khan because it was at this stage, desperate for revenge that his intervention paid off handsomely. He took an immediate interest in the case and persuaded him to keep the whole thing as quiet as possible and seek a financial settlement behind the scenes with the family of Ikbal. He assured Piari's father that the matter would be dealt with, but that great care must be taken to maintain records of all the family actions. But the matter had leaked out from the school friends of Piari who whispered about what had happened to their school mate. The scandal of rape could not be kept quiet. In dozens of kitchens where women prepared food, tongues wagged furiously. On the flat roofs where people dragged their light cots to catch an evening breeze while they slept, Piari's rape was whispered about. Families that had previously greeted Piari's mother now shunned her because of her tainted daughter. It was as if Piari had been painted black and would never be able to wash away her stain, a stain that rubbed off on her entire family.

The accused rapist, Ikbal Sufi, a bright young man who was beginning a career in the newspaper business had privately said he would be willing to marry Piari, but his own parents were aghast at the idea, having a daughter-in-law who was tainted, about whom all the people spoke in whispers. Piari heard of Ikbal's willingness to take her quietly, but she had said that she preferred death than to marry a man who she loathed, the one who had ruined her by force, who she thought looked like a monkey with his huge ears and whose teeth were crooked. The mere mention of the name Ikbal brought tears of hatred to her eyes. She refused marriage to the man who forcefully violated her. His name brought back dark visions, nightmares of screams and sorrow. For the first dreadful year she remained at home, isolated, not able to complete her senior year of schooling because of the scandal. The father had requested books and assignments from the school, but the Principal had told him that the reputation of the school would be ruined if it were known that a *zani* girl was still enrolled and allowed to study and take tests like other decent girls. An envelope with money appeared on his desk with the words written, "Home examination fee." Later he relented and corrected the girl's examinations.

When the matter had come to the attention of the police Sher Khan the Senior Superintendent, he investigated the matter quietly. He found that no charges should be leveled against Ikbal and his family as the girl Piari had enticed the young man by getting into his car. There was, of course, the need to have four witnesses to the alleged crime. Ikbal, a young and active man should get on with his life and know that no court would condemn him without witnesses. However, if the matter came to court, Piari would be the one to suffer, perhaps even face a death sentence, since the charge she leveled against Ikbal was in itself an admission of having had sex outside of marriage. Sher Khan played his role well, seeking benefit from Ikbal's family and seeking payment from Piari's father because he had advised that the matter should be wrapped up and put away.

The threats of violence against Ikbal Sufi from Piari's father continued. Meetings were held in Sufi's house with three representatives of Piari's family present. After bitter arguments and threats, the family of Ikbal had eventually agreed to the payment of a substantial sum of money, in one ounce gold bars to the family of Piari. They had insisted on gold, not cash. Ikbal's grand father had ended up having to sell one of his homes to finance this and had traveled to Karachi to find the one ounce gold bars. He suffered a heart attack and died two years later. This new wealth that came to Piari's father Osama, had been the impetus for him to begin his dealings with Iran to import motor oil called T2 in bulk to be repackaged in Lahore.

There had been no suitors. What young man would marry a woman who had the reputation of being raped? What true *Muslim* man would take a non-virgin for a wife? Virginity was what the gold dowry paid for, that and family honor. How often her grandfather had shouted out the three words which were the badge of honor to every family, Zar, Zan, Zamin! How could a husband live with and honor such a wife in front of their children? It was unthinkable.

Piari remained at home and helped her mother. She had been good at mathematics in school so she was given duties related to her father's business, ordering materials, checking payments, even keeping the bank accounts in balance. Each day she checked the newspapers for items relating to her father's area of business, importing oil to be processed, packaged and sold in Pakistan. Her facility in Farsi was excellent and she handled basic invoices and billings with supply agents in Iran. Within five years her father decided to establish a branch office in one of the rooms of the rambling house in Model Town in Lahore where they lived. Piari ran the office for him. Telephone lines were installed and she was given a cell-phone as well to communicate with her father who traveled a great deal, especially to Karachi.

Piari's eyes fell on the article by Ikbal regarding the Deputy Superin-tendent of Police, Feroz Hakim. For years, for some strange compulsion, she had clipped all the articles written by Ikbal, the man who had raped her. She kept the items in a paper file-folder, sorting these by month and year. From time to time his picture also appeared in the paper and she kept these as well. She smiled when she read the article from Ikbal accusing the Deputy of acting prematurely in his declaration that the mystery of the abduction of the American woman Maria Bernard had been solved. She read about the death of Sher Khan, that his vehicle, a Humber, had been destroyed in the bombing. The vehicle mentioned had been in the family of Ikbal for some time, a cherished possession kept in immaculate condition. It was in this Humber Sedan that she had been raped. She remembered occasions when the two families interacted that they had come in a Humber sedan, a strange make for Pakistan. It was even stranger, she thought, that this vehicle that had been in Ikbal's family had ended up being burned up in the bombing of the border village where Sher Khan lost his life. She clipped the article and put it into the folder.

The telephone rang in her office. She put down her newspaper files.

"PB Oil Distributors," she replied.

"Good morning. I wish to start a retail oil shop in Sialkot. How would I find out more information about this?"

"Thank you for your call sir. Where did you get this number? How did you come to call PB Oil Distributors?" She was very professional and encouraging.

"My friend is selling PB Oil and I saw the address and number on the tins of motor oil. Is this the right number?" He was pleased that a woman was talking to him. Seldom did women answer the phone when he called other businesses.

"I see. Yes, this is PB Oil Distributors branch office in Lahore. We would be very interested to help you to set up a sales branch in Sialkot. We already have one there, but it is a big enough city to have two or three, depending on the location. Please give me your name sir, so I can send you information."

Dohst had decided to use his fake name for the new business. The name he had used to inherit his aunt's property was Aziz Shabash. "Yes. The name is Aziz, Aziz Shabash. I have not yet got a telephone. I am using a pay phone. The address of my shop is Allama Iqbal Chowk, Number 93, Sialkot, Pakistan."

The address was familiar to her. Number 95, was the location of their only retail customer in Sialkot. She decided not to mention this. "Mr. Aziz, in order to set up an account you will need to fill up documents and set up a way to pay for your oil shipments. Is it possible for you to come to Lahore to fill forms? At that time all the details of becoming a retail sales agent could be explained." Her voice was soft and persuasive.

"May I know your good name, Madame?" asked Aziz.

She hesitated. "You may refer to me as Miss Piari. I am the daughter of the owner of the PB Oil Distributors which handles T2 lubricants. I am managing his Lahore branch office. Would it be suitable for me to send a letter to your address at Number 93 with information about PB, our street address, FAX and e-mail addresses so that you can gather the information you need before coming to Lahore?" She paused.

"Yes. I will wait for the letter." Dohst wanted to talk more to this young woman whose voice was like honey.

"Mr. Aziz, what day can I expect your visit?" she asked.

The question pleased him." I will come one week today, at noon. Excuse. I meant to ask for you to send me the wholesale prices I would have to pay as a dealer." He listened to her reply and hung up. He was now eager to receive the letter. Talking to a woman on the telephone was something totally new to him. He had pictured her beautiful face as her gentle voice came to his ear. He could almost see her mouth speaking the words, 'Mr. Aziz'.

C*

Feroz had wrapped Sher Khan's extortion files into two bundles. Two blankets that they used in winter were in the tin trunk. He had used these for wrapping up the files and smiling, replaced the files once again into the tin trunk, placing them at the bottom. He remembered a detective story he had read in which Sherlock had said that often the most obvious place is the best place to hide something. On the top he arranged the brassieres and women's underwear and sanitary napkins in the way they had been before when the regional police inspectors had come to his home. If the trunk was again opened, the same strange view of white and pink cones looking like small mountains would be seen. The most obvious was the best place to hide them now.

He stood back and looked at his handiwork, then he got an inspiration. In the bathroom under the sink were new boxes of Tampax, still unopened. He took out the tampons and slid his hand down the side of the trunk like the inspector had and secreted rows of tampons in the area next to the files. He tried it and reached down and felt the tubes, retrieved one and laughed. His files were secure, guarded by rows of tampons which men never handled, and did not even like to think about. Unclean! He frowned, thinking about the times his wife had been careless and had not disposed of pads and tampons carefully and how angry he had been. He had shouted the words to her from Surah II, 222. *They question thee (O Muhammad) concerning menstruation. Say: It is an illness, so let women alone at such times and go not unto them til they are cleansed. And when they have purified themselves, then go in unto them as Allah hath enjoined upon you. Truly Allah loveth those who turn unto Him, and loveth those who have a care for cleanness.*

He sat at his desk and wrote on a yellow line pad. On the third try he felt he had said the right words.

FAX: To the Deputy Regional Inspector of Police, Islamabad.

Since your last visit here, new information has come up regarding the matter you wanted to explore in my trunk and personal safe but did not find. Since it is sensitive, I do not wish to share the matter by phone for obvious reasons. I would be happy to come to Islamabad to your office to apprise you of this new development, or you may wish to come to Lahore and we could discuss the matter here.

Feroz Hakim, Deputy Superintendent of Police, Lahore.

The following morning he called the Motor Licensing Division and asked the clerk to come to his office.

"This is the description of the car that was burned at the time of the border village bombing by the Americans. It is an older Humber car. This is the identification number and the current license number. I want you to trace back to the time when the last owner transferred ownership to Sher Khan. It may be more than ten years ago. Find out who the last owner was and if possible how much the late Mr. Khan paid for the vehicle. You are to consider this work secret and of high priority. Do not share the information with anyone else. I need the information by this evening." He looked at the clerk who stood uneasily in front of his desk and noted that his pants were stained and that the strap on one of the sandals was torn. "You look terrible. Don't come to work in dirty old clothes. Consider this to be a first warning."

The upset man left his office rubbing his pants mumbling about his low salary. He returned to his small desk and prepared to carry out his assignment. His office mate looked up at him and asked him where he was going. He replied that it was a very secret mission. His friend replied that he would see him later about it.

The phone rang and the Deputy Inspector Masood-ur-Rasool from Islamabad was on the line. "Feroz, what is this secret mysterious thing you are talking about. This is not an Agatha Kristeen mystery, man. Tell me what you were thinking about and I will give you an answer now." His voice was impatient and authoritative. "Oh yes, I have called that reporter chap Ikbal and gave him a verbal drubbing. He was not happy."

"Sir, do I have your permission to drive up to Islamabad to show you personally what I have found. It is rather a serious thing that involves the very person in question that you have been speaking about. I do not think this should be shared on the phone." Feroz was enjoying his small day of mystery.

"I see. Yes. If it involves who I think you are alluding to, yes, drive up. Is this physical evidence of some kind?" He kept pushing.

"I would rather not say now sir; I will brief you and show you when I get there and then you can decide what action needs to be taken. I will be in your office at two in the afternoon tomorrow. Thank you, sir."

Feroz took the file from the bottom drawer and went through the material once again, planning his strategy with the Deputy Inspector from the CPO in Islamabad. He read once more the complaint from Piari's father. "My girl, Piari, reported that Ikbal had driven to a deserted area near the Bari Doab Canal, parked the car and got in the back seat with her. He then began to fondle and kiss her. She had shouted and resisted, however, he was very strong. He removed her lower clothing and raped her. Then while she was crying and trying to dress herself again, he smoked a cigarette and told her to take off her blouse and bra. She refused. He told her that she had no choice, and that he did not want to harm her. Weeping, she obeyed. She stated that soon after that she was raped again. Then, strangely, he told her to get out of the car and arrange her clothing properly. He told her that he had wanted her from the first time he had seen her in her father's home. He said that he could not sleep at night thinking about her. Then he apologized for forcing himself on her, saying that he had been driven by lust, *Ishkh*. He drove her back to the spot where she had got into the car, a stone's throw from the gate of our own house."

There were other documents. One was a signed statement from Ikbal Sufi that he had not in fact had sex with the girl; however, she had been the one to greet him as he sat parked in his car and had asked if he could take her for a ride. She had made advances to him in the car when they parked and had taken an active part in the romantic encounter. He denied that rape had occurred and said that he had been seduced by the young woman's charms, in fact that she had exposed her breasts to him in the car which resulted in the sexual fondling. Being a young and active man what was he to do?

The other document was signed by Sher Khan himself. It was a copy of a statement from his office to the parents of Piari. It stated that the evidence was strong that the girl had been a willing partner in the sexual act because she entered the car alone eagerly. If the matter was pursued farther it stated that the girl herself would be charged with violating a number of civil and *Sharia* laws placing her in jeopardy of being tried with possible dire consequences to her, perhaps even death. If no formal public charges were brought forward to the police, and the matter was not reported to the press, it could be filed and forgotten.

The last document was one with Ikbal Sufi's signature agreeing to transfer a car to Sher Khan. It did not mention cost. It was an older Humber Sedan, but in mint condition.

Feroz had a FAX machine in his office that had a copier. He spent the next few minutes making two copies of the material. He did not intend to give the original copy to the Inspector in Islamabad. He wrote notes; 1. Present material to CPO and let him read it. 2. Suggest that since the late Sher Khan's office is 'too close to the scene' that CPO, Islamabad, handle the matter as it will create a scandal since he is a well known reporter. 3. Reopen the case charging Ikbal with rape and molestation of the girl and bring him in for interrogation. 4. Payment to Sher Khan of the Humber car pushes guilt on Ikbal for creating a cover-up to get a favorable reading from Sher Khan on the case. 5. Present new information about the Humber car and its change of registration to Sher Khan.

He called the peon in and requested that Mistiri come to his office. The man came in and stood just inside the door.

"Come in man. Don't stand there. Have a seat. I have asked you to see me to remind you that in two weeks I would like to have another meeting with your daughter, a progress report. We can meet in my home again. Ask your daughter to prepare a longer reading this time and dress in her school uniform. We will meet after school."

"This is only three months since the last meeting, sir. But, yes I will arrange it."

"At the end of the school year you have agreed that I will make the first payments toward marriage arrangements with your daughter. I thought it a good idea to have an opportunity to see if my interests in her education and in her as a future member of my household is still positive." He gave the information in a matter-of-fact manner.

Mistiri stood dumbstruck, literally shaking. He stared at Feroz Hakim in consternation. "I do not understand what you have said, sir. About marriage to my daughter. I understand you have a wife. Please explain." He sat on the ground near the door.

"Oh, you know the statement you signed when we met last. The statement about her scholarship and that you agreed to consider my taking your daughter into my household. You signed it. Your finger print." He lit up a cigarette and took a document from the top of his desk. "This. You remember?"

"I do not read well, Sir. Yes. I thought it was about her schooling only." His voice was shaking.

"Yes, I am married. I want another younger woman in my household. Of course, I am not talking about a registered marriage with *mahr* dowry, gold and money. I wrote on the paper you signed that it would be a *nikah urfi* contract, that is, unregistered. You can understand that the status of our family is vastly different from yours, particularly the Hindu immigrant background. Such a marriage for your daughter would lift her from poverty to living in a wealthy home with a motor car, servants and possessions." He looked up at Mistiri and was surprised to see the man in tears.

"I am very willing to provide some gold to her and considerable money to you for such an arrangement. There would not be a formal wedding, however, as I do not wish to make this a public event. Considerable money, many thousands of Rupees. I do want to remind you that in spite of strange and difficult actions made by you that you still have your job." He stared at Mistiri. "Your conversation with Ikbal about me has created much trouble."

Mistiri looked up. "Hazoor, be merciful to me and my daughter. There is already one who has been speaking for her from my village. It is a family I know from our people. My daughter was not pleased with it, but she would have had to obey me in this matter. Now, this is very difficult for me and for the family. How would she see her mother, her relatives in such an arrangement? Our families are not the same. They could not interact. Hazoor. Please, please!" He hit his head on the floor.

"Stop that! You will have much more wealth than you do now. You would have your job to continue to support your family. Your daughter would be in a home where the children would have schooling, opportunities, a home where there is a television set, books to read. Your daughter could visit her family from time to time under my supervision and agreement of course. That is not a problem. Think man. Think carefully. It will be up to you to persuade your daughter and be firm. I think you noticed that she enjoys talking with me. After our next time together we can make the final decision. Now, just wait. Let her continue with her schooling. Tell her nothing. We will meet and you can see if she and I seem to be agreeable." He folded up the document. Then he changed his mind, took it to the FAX machine and made a copy. He walked to Mistiri and handed it to him.

"What is this, Hazoor?" Mistiri stared at the copy. He took it with shaking hands.

"It is the agreement you signed. It is good for you to have this to keep. It mentions your agreement to the engagement." He made a motion with his hand that the man was dismissed.

☪

The newspaper office was stiflingly hot. The ceiling fan was off balance and as it spun around it emitted a noisome creak that was reminiscent of a dying animal. Ikbal loosened his collar and lit a cigarette and called for the peon to bring him tea. The phone buzzed. He waited until the third buzz hoping the caller would get discouraged.

"This is Ikbal speaking. Yes. Who? Did you say from Islamabad CPO? Yes, I will speak to him." He looked at the phone for a moment, remembering how the man had scolded him for writing what he had about the police. He put it back to his ear. "Yes, good morning Masood-ur-Rasool. How can I be of service to you... sir?"

"Mr. Ikbal, I think it would be helpful if you came to see me in my office on a matter that relates to you. Since at this time it is only an item of enquiry, I felt that due to your position with the Dawning and your reputation, we should speak privately." Masood's voice was grating.

"What is this in reference to sir? Of course I am willing to come to Islamabad and speak to you privately but it would be helpful to me to have some information so I can prepare myself." Ikbal's voice rose to high tenor when he was upset. Many of his past experiences with the police had been unpleasant.

"The only reference that I wish to make here should suffice. The vehicle of Sher Khan that was destroyed in the American bombing of the border village."

"What? I do not have a clue about what you refer to, but I will drive up to see you and hear what you have to say. Tomorrow? Good. At two in the afternoon. Yes, goodbye."

He set the phone on its cradle and stared at it. His heart was pounding furiously. The damn Humber car! Damn Feroz Hakim! So it has begun, he thought. He called the Vehicle Licensing Office of the Lahore Police.

"This is Ikbal from the Dawning. I am calling for a piece of information. I wish to know how far back, the sale and purchase records are kept for each licensed vehicle in Lahore." He listened for the reply. "Thank you."

He sat back and tugged at his rather large and hanging earlobes. Five years from the time of re-sale, he thought, however, there is really no firm national policy on filing vehicle registration records. Computer based records on vehicles purchased eleven years ago would be impossible to access since digital copiers had not been widely used. Paper records in large pink files with a string around them were used in many offices. He seemed to be in the clear, he thought. It would be difficult to show that Sher Khan did not purchase the car from his father without any records available. His father was dead. The car was destroyed. Sher Khan was dead. No one could be called in except perhaps, himself.

He got up and walked to the window and thought of what Feroz Hakim had said, "Do you know the name Piari?" This had been solved a decade ago. Sher Khan had suggested that because of the Hudood Ordinance that zina could be charged against the girl with dire consequences. Her accusation of rape, zina-bil-jab against him could not be brought forward because it required four male witnesses for the offence. His thinking was scattered. He was sweating in anxiety. Bringing all of this up again at this time would kill his career. Damn Feroz! I should kill that stupid policeman. But why did the CPO make it their concern? Certainly the girl would not bring it up again. The family had been paid off handsomely. There would be no reason for her to again accuse him. She could endanger herself and even now be charged under the Hudood Ordinance. Of course! Of course!

He was nodding to himself. Of course. Feroz Hakim took over the office of Sher Khan and he must have found his personal files, the damn incriminating file with signatures. Allah! What could he do? Of course. He could stop writing things that made the police look bad. Stop accusations. He entered a few search words into his computer, 'Reporters Abducted by Police' He waited and then began to be amazed. In the early part of the year 2004 a reporter had been abducted and held for five days by the police, or whoever, for speaking against the government. His eye caught another entry relating to reporters in Karachi speaking about Taliban in Pakistan. He changed his Google entry words and included Taliban and then saw a pattern emerge in the reports. The administration was very strong and controlling about any news that was reported about Taliban activity, particularly training in *madarassa*, the Islamic religious schools. Reporters of Urdu newspapers had been brought in for questioning when they spoke of Pakistan's involvement with support and training of terrorists. One reporter had been held for weeks as he had been heard to mutter words which could be interpreted to be blasphemy.

Ikbal began to sweat. It then occurred to him that he had better inform others about his trip to Islamabad in the event that he was held after the questioning. The power of the pen was weak, he thought. In fact he wondered if the pen had ink in it. One had to be careful not to write words against the present political administration and its leaders, its relationship to the bloody Americans, or any references to *sharia* that countered the statements of leading mullahs. There were so few English language newspapers in the country as it was and the readership for these was a small fraction of the total population, very small. So many millions were basically illiterate and relied on government radio and television for their news, if any. Others relied on word of mouth reporting of national incidents or trends from the mullahs in the mosques. A small group read Urdu newspapers, but these too were under close scrutiny from the government. He mopped his brow.

He wrote a detailed memorandum relating to the events of the past two months and the recent request of the Regional Police to have him appear in Islamabad for a discussion. He put this in an envelope and wrote the address of his elder brother on it and walked to the nearby branch post office and mailed it.

He made a call to his brother and informed him that an envelope addressed to him was on its way and not to open it, but hold it for him. He told him that he would be traveling to Islamabad at the request of the police.

His brother became alarmed and obviously concerned more for himself and his family who could possibly be connected to his brother in some sort of scandal. The incident of the rape ten years earlier had sensitized the entire family against Ikbal because it had placed them in negative focus with their friends and family in spite of the fact that it had been covered up. His brother pushed for information and the possible reason for his being called in by the regional police, rather than the local superintendent at Lahore. Ikbal replied that all he knew is that it related to the old Humber car that had been given by their deceased father to Sher Khan. Its burned out frame had been identified at the bomb site as belonging to Sher Khan. Now they were checking to see how and when he got it and what he had paid for it. His brother began to curse.

"It is no problem," he shouted. "I still have the fake receipt that was given to Sher Khan, a copy of which is in our father's files. He was given a receipt for Rupees 60,000 for the car, which was used at the time the ownership papers were processed. Don't worry. Tell them Sher Khan <u>bought</u> the *Shaitan* car. I hated that car from the beginning. It looked so black, so official, so *pukka* English. It still haunts us."

"I am so glad you told me that. I had no idea that a fake receipt for purchase had been drawn up. Sher Khan, a jackal. Good. I am clear. My interview will end with my being forceful and strong about the matter, knowing full well we can clear ourselves that the car was not given as a bribe. Good!" Ikbal was greatly relieved and stopped his pacing.

"When do you leave?" his brother asked. " I warn you now that if you are in trouble you will have to bail yourself out. I want nothing more to do with your impossible life!"

"I will leave tomorrow. It is better to take care of this matter as soon as possible." He hung up and walked to the window and looked out on the courtyard below him. To his surprise he saw two men standing in doorways looking toward his building. Police, he thought. Again he began to sweat. Was he being shadowed? He had been surprised when the package that came in the mail to his house had been confiscated immediately. He had not had time to open it and look at the notebook that Maria had written before there was a hard knocking on his door. The police had an official order to take the book. This had surprised him. Why would they still be observing him? He decided to see whether his observation was accurate. He wished to appear cool, in charge of the situation.

He left the building by the back door and walked rapidly toward a crowded market place. Immediately he noticed that first one man, then later two others began to follow him. He now tried to shake them. Scenes of American movies where police tailed suspects came to mind. His heart beat faster.

Ikbal walked into a small alley that he knew had a blind end, except for a two feet wide flight of old cement stairs that led to the first level of a roof. He climbed the steps and hid behind hanging laundry to watch what would happen. In less than a minute the three men entered the alley. They saw the staircase and two of them climbed it cautiously. One of them, obviously an officer, wore a service pistol and snapped the cover open. Ikbal hurried to the other side of the roof, tried a door leading to a pigeon coop. He entered the room and the birds fluttered about. He threw them grain and they settled down to feed ignoring him. He squatted behind two large sacks of bird feed and watched, now becoming alarmed for his life.

The men approached cautiously, looked at the pigeons that were feeding calmly, then moved away to the other side of the roof where there was another cement staircase that led down into a private courtyard, obviously belonging to the owner of the pigeon loft. They disappeared down this and almost immediately there was an outcry from two women below who screeched that their privacy had been violated. Their cry brought the cook from the kitchen with a huge knife in his hand. The men retreated and left the roof.

Ikbal sat for half an hour, looking at his watch impatiently, waiting for a sufficiently long time for the men to leave and return to report that they had lost their tail and report that certainly Ikbal had something sinister to hide as he was actively avoiding the police.

While he waited he looked up at the sky above Lahore. He had almost forgotten, it was Basant, the spring holiday. He looked at the hundreds of colorful kites flying in the sky and directly across from where he sat he could see a father with two of his boys on a flat rooftop, flying their kites. One kite was cut as he watched; the ground glass on the string of another kite flyer had sawn the string. The children shrieked as the kite was taken by the wind. On the ground there were already boys running underneath the spiraling object, yelling at each other that they would be the one to get to the kite first. These kite runners sped away between the streets but the kite became snagged on one of fifty electric wires that hung above the street, seemingly woven by a drunk spider. The kite hung down, its tail spinning crazily in the wind. The boys gathered beneath it yelling, frustrated, then in anger at their luck they picked up stones and pelted the hanging kite until it was in tatters. Competitors now walked hand in hand bragging that their stone was the first through the thin paper of the kite.

Ikbal made his way to the parking area of the newspaper office and got into his car. As he left the lot he saw a police car with blue lights on top start up and begin to follow him. He pulled over and parked his car and went to the boot and opened it and took out a water bottle as the police car passed him by slowly. He took a drink, taking his time. Now he resumed his trip and headed for the trunk road that led toward Islamabad.

The streets were festive at this time of *Basant*. Decorations were hung in many stores and there was music, obviously Indian music, rising from a dozen competing loudspeakers. Children in tattered clothing were wandering around in groups scoping the scene for any possibility of a quick snack to be taken from an unwary vendor. One small group made their way to a tea stall and stood innocently while two fat men finished their tea. They left cold fried breads and half-eaten sweets on the plate. Before the proprietor could clean up, the boys snatched the left-over food and shrieking with pleasure trotted off with their treasures, stuffing their mouths. Ikbal leaned on his hooter to warn the boys of his approach. The urchins stood in a defiant phalanx across the road as if to oppose him, mimicking the hooting of the car's horn and did not disperse until the car almost ran into them. One boy held a half-eaten orange in one hand and as the car passed he smeared the side windows with the orange leaving streaks of dripping orange juice on the glass windows. Ikbal swore and speeded up, knowing that if he got out, chasing them, they would blend into the crowd.

Twenty miles outside of Lahore on the Grand Trunk Road heading north there was a police road block, which was very unusual he thought, unless there was to be a visit by Musharraf in the area. He slowed down and stopped behind a row of about four cars. Two policemen walked to his car and asked for his identification papers. He looked around to see if there was a cross-road in front of them. He noticed that the area was rural and fairly deserted. He reached into the glove box for his car identification and spoke to the police officer as he leaned down.

"So, what is the road block for? Trying to catch some criminal?" He retrieved his package of papers. On the top was a card identifying him as a member of the press. He took this and put it on the dash board. The officer looked at it without expression and did not reply to his question. When his papers were read the officer asked that Ikbal step outside of the car.

"What is this about? Do you realize I am a member of the press?"

"Yes. Hand me the keys to your vehicle first, then walk to the police van next to the road." He stared at Ikbal fiercely, his dark mustache accenting his drooping lips.

"This is very strange. On whose orders are you asking me to give up my car keys and be hauled over like a common criminal? Whose?" He did not give the car keys to the man.

The policeman waved at another officer who strolled over and stood next to him. "Do not cause trouble. Do what you are told and come with us quietly." He held out his hand. He held a stick in the other hand.

Ikbal began to shake. This made the policemen smile. Ikbal handed them his keys and stumbled behind the first officer as he was led to the police van. The back door was opened and Ikbal was made to crawl in. The door was slammed shut. One officer returned to Ikbal's car. The other went to the road block, removed the barrier sign and got into the van and started it up. Ikbal sat dejectedly in the back and looked out through the mesh reinforced window at the rear. His identity papers had not been returned to him. He sat without his billfold, without cash, without identity in the back of van like a criminal being hauled off to jail.

The metal bench he sat on was cold, dusty and hard. He gritted his teeth each time the van hit a pothole. In his mind's eye he could see another of his countrymen who must have had a similar experience. The late Zulfiqar Bhutto had also been captured, imprisoned and made to languish in a prison in 1977, held on a murder charge. In Lahore he had been sentenced to death and had been hanged in 1979. He remembered reading the story many times, particularly when Bhutto's daughter Benazir had become Prime Minister and the papers had been filled with the history of her father. He could see himself thrown into a prison and languishing, his family not even knowing where he was, and ... He became physically ill and began to retch. He tried to control his nausea but after the vehicle lurched around to avoid a buffalo on the road, he vomited onto the floor of the van and then sat back and groaned, hating the sickening odor of his own discharge and began to dry-heave unable to control his retching.

An hour later the van pulled into a parking lot. The back door was opened and the policeman backed up, appalled at the mess and the smell. Ikbal sat hunched over, his head in his hands, groaning.

"The Deputy is waiting for you. Come this way." He was handed his car keys and his billfold and identity papers. His own car was parked next to the van. They had arrived in Islamabad. He staggered from the van, tripping as he exited, falling to his knees. The officers did not help him because of his soiled condition. His shoes were splattered with filth.

He was led into an office that had a large Shisham-wood desk on which three impressive buzzer buttons had been installed, each a different color. Aside from that the room was bare. After a few minutes a short man in a dark suit, starched white shirt and shiny black shoes entered and sat down opposite Ikbal.

"Mr. Ikbal, we thought you were trying to escape. You eluded some of our best men. You may recall that I asked you to come here to discuss the matter of the Humber car. That information certainly put you in a royal spook, it seems. So why don't we just get to it. Oh! You smell terrible. Wait, until I open the windows. Terrible!"

"Why am I here? I will not let this matter rest! You have detained me unlawfully!" Ikbal shouted at the Deputy.

"An old file of the late Sher Khan was discovered at the bottom of a filing cabinet. It contains a rather sordid story of your activities about ten years ago, rape, bribing a police officer and conspiring to elude the consequences of the law. There was this girl called Piari. I presume you recall what I am talking about now?"

"The matter was resolved. She withdrew her complaint. She could have been found guilty under the Hudood..." He paused. "Just tell me what you want. Why am I here?"

"Mr. Ikbal, I will just ask you a simple question. Would you be willing to write an accurate and unbiased newspaper article about this matter which brings to light the truth of the matters that occurred ten years ago? You know how powerful the pen is. What is written can not be erased. It remains in the memory of those who read, it remains in the archives, as if the very words are inspired. Would you write a clear article about this matter for me? I will give you paper and pen and half an hour to write. Do you agree?" He smiled broadly. "I have searched the archives for your writing about police matters, alleged police brutality, police interference with the sacred work of the press to write the truth. You have certainly enjoyed your position of power behind your miserable little dusty desk as you dig up half truths, innuendo, and publish these to the world at large; the thoughts of your small, yet inflated little mind." He pressed a white buzzer button on the desk. A man appeared at the door almost immediately.

"Bring foolscap paper and pen."

The man scurried off and returned momentarily with the materials. "Do not let it be said that the police interfered with your mission. I will leave you to your work, reporter Ikbal. Half an hour should do it. Be succinct please. Only the facts. Oh yes, do include the matter of the old Humber sedan as well in your account. Good day. Remember, the truth. The lion and the lamb drink from the same source."

He left the room and the door was closed behind him and locked from the outside.

CHAPTER TEN

Gusse men a-kar jhunjlae jab ape men to
apepe jhunjlae. (Hindustani Proverb)

An angry man is again angry (with himself) when he returns to reason.

Dohst had installed the two air conditioners for Gretchen and Celia, however, he did not know how to seal the area around the window and eventually hired a person to come and do the job for him. The machines worked well. He stood in front of one of the machines and shivered as the cool air passed over his body. In his entire life he had never felt such coolness, he thought. It was even colder than the February night his father had taken him on a trip at midnight across the city to the edge of the Ravi River to look at the moon and see its reflection on the water. There had been no wind that night, but the air rising from the river was cool as they stood looking up at the sky, shivering. Strange, he thought, that he should think of his dead father as he stood in front of the newly installed air conditioner. It was an omen. He had cursed his father saying he would become the shit of crabs. He shivered and reached up and held both ear lobes.

"Dohst, come on the porch for a cup of tea, hot tea, when you are finished." Celia called to him from the porch.

He turned off the machine and went to the porch and sat uncomfortably with Celia, alone. Gretchen had not come back from work yet and Celia had arranged the meeting so Dohst could attend to the *aircons* as he called them. "Thank you, Miss Celia. In our country it is unusual for a man to have tea with a single woman alone."

"Dohst, we have gone through hell and high water together, man. Anyway, thank you for the compliment." She poured tea in his cup and pushed the creamer and sugar bowl toward him.

"Hell and high water? I do not understand. Compliment?"

"I keep forgetting. It is a compliment because you were thinking about me as a desirable woman in whom you had interest. Right? Hell and high water means that since I have known you we have, well, we went through the hell of Gretchen's attack at the Mohurram, Maria's abduction near the place where we went to buy carpets, the police searching after you and your father, you know, lots of stuff that was really difficult. Hell and high water." She laughed.

"My father told me about deep water as well. He said that when I contacted you and Gretchen with the letter pasted to your gate, that I had stepped into high water and that it pulled me under into all the trouble. Yes I understand. Yes." He sipped his tea.

"You know, I still have the copy of that letter. I loved the part where you said you wanted to make dating with me." She laughed loudly.

He was so embarrassed that he spilled tea and set his cup down and looked crestfallen. "Sorry. I thought that American women would like..." He looked down.

"Dohst, do you know what dating is?"

He nodded his head, not looking at her.

"Well?" she asked.

"It is activity of the sex." He blurted it out.

Now she laughed again, this time reaching over with her hand and patting his. "Dating means that you ask a girl to go with you, to a show or to eat dinner or take a walk and have fun and get to know each other." She could see he was still confused.

"Yes. I understand. In Pakistan if a boy and girl go alone together they would be doing sexual things together. I understand. That is why all fathers keep their daughters away from men and do not allow them to be alone in a room with a man, because if they are then they have..." He glanced up at her. "If a girl is seen talking alone, even meeting at a gate with a boy, she is punished, sometimes even killed by her father for bringing shame to the family. It is a matter of honor that the girl only knows the man she marries. Only!"

"I see. Well dating is..." she paused and smiled. "Dating could be just walking and talking and stuff, but I see your point. Dating is also to find time alone together and you are right, lots of kids do have sex as well. But dating and sex are not the same. It is a way to get to know a person of the opposite sex." She shook her head.

"It is not our custom. I only once did dating with a girl. We walked on the sand on an island. I gave her a gift. We talked and then ..." He got up and took out a cigarette and lit it. "She is now going to have my child. My father wanted to cut off her nose. Dating is very terrible trouble, I think."

"Are you saying that in the letter you sent to me that all you really wanted was to have sex?" She lowered her head and stared at Dohst.

He got up, bowed his head slightly. "Thank you, Miss. Thank you for buying the air conditioners. I must go to another person now to purchase tinned oil. Thank you." He walked off quickly and waved at a passing *tonga* for a ride. He glanced back at the porch as the vehicle moved away. Celia was standing on the steps staring after him, her tea cup in her hand. She was shaking her head slowly from side to side.

☪

Meher had dressed herself in her only full *sari*. It was one that her aunt had given to her when she reached her twenty first birthday. The pink color of the fabric was wound around her rounded form. She wore a white cotton blouse under it over which the *sari* was spread. Such dress was only worn in the home, not for the eyes of other men because the blouse revealed a section of skin at the waist and her ample breasts swelled obviously under the material. She watched Dohst as he packed his satchel, hoping for him to see how beautiful her clothing was. He glanced up at her standing near him but his eyes did not rove over her body or note her clothing. She had even put a hint of red on her lips and had put dark kohl on her eyelids.

Dohst glanced up again at Meher. "Look at this. It is called a check book. Look. See this page. On the top is written how much I put into the bank. On these pages I can write any amount up to the amount on the top and the bank will pay the person who gets the check the amount of money. It is amazing! A thief can not steal my money. It is in the bank." Dohst sat across the small table from Meher Jamal. She held his child Malik and was feeding him with a bottle.

"What if the person who you want to pay does not want to accept the check? What can you do?" she asked.

"I would go to the bank and draw out the amount in cash and then pay him. But most business people now know about check usage. They collect many checks each day and take them to the bank and have the money transferred to their account. It is wonderful." Dohst smiled broadly.

"What if a person, a stranger from out of town wrote you a check for some oil, but did not have enough in his account in the bank and when you came to get it they would say that the check is not good?" Meher held the book of checks in her hand and flipped through them with her good hand, the baby in her lap now sleeping. What if the check was written from a bank in Karachi? How would the bank in Sialkot know that the amount in Karachi is correct? Would the banks talk to each other? If they had a thousand checks each day, how would they make a thousand phone calls to verify that the money was present in each account? It seems very complicated to me."

"I see the problem. How can I trust a person to write a check and not have the money? I will think about that. It seems that I would need to know the person and have his address and even..." he paused. "Even see his driver's license or some kind of identification." He looked up at her as if the idea were a new one. "I did not think about a check from Karachi. Now I wonder if my check from Barclay's Bank will work on a Bank of Pakistan. How will they exchange money with each other?" He blew smoke rings one after another.

She smiled and nodded. "I think the check system will work if you are dealing *bhai-bhai.*" He nodded, thinking that he had no brother. "I noticed when I was in the bazaar with my uncle and with you when we went to get the retirement money from your uncle's fund that the clerks had huge piles of rupees and paid with these rather than using checks. Perhaps the use of checks is more common among folk in America where the women came from who bought the air conditioners from you."

"Well, tomorrow I will go to Lahore and meet with a woman who runs the wholesale part of the T2 oil business. I will fill up forms and find out how much everything costs, and perhaps even write a check for my first shipment." He put out his cigarette and leaned back feeling good with the turn of events that launched him in his new business venture.

"Why would you buy the tins of oil before you talk to the man who will be your new partner? How will you know which ones to buy, how many to buy and whether he will sign papers that make you equal? It seems a complicated affair to me." She put the baby over her shoulder and patted its back and smiled at him, enjoying talking to Dohst. During the day she was all alone with the baby in the house. After the death of Pagali she had been lonely, wishing to be home with her mother and family and watch the children fly kites and cook special dishes for the spring festival.

Dohst smoked another cigarette and blew smoke rings toward Meher. "Can you write numbers and add and subtract?"

"My uncle the mullah told me that I was better at numbers than most of the students that came to the mosque school. He told me I could have been a teacher for the other girls if I had not had my arm..." She was displeased with herself for bringing her impairment to his attention again. "Yes, I can add, subtract and multiply, first class. I even know the numbers in Arabic and English."

"When I buy things you can enter the numbers in the check book so I always know how much I have left. I am hungry. What is there to eat?"

"There is boiled rice. You were supposed to take us out shopping but you were very busy. Tomorrow you go to Lahore and again I will eat boiled rice. The dried powder for making milk for the baby is almost finished as well. Do you want me to walk to the market and buy what we need?" She did not look angry, standing sideways to him, her scarf hanging loosely about her shoulders, her bodice exposing the flesh of her midriff.

"We will eat boiled rice and have tea. Then first thing, before I leave we will go and buy many things and I will write a check for all of them." They both laughed. Now he noticed her colorful clothing and the red on her lips. The skin of her mid-riff was creamy brown and smooth, indented a tiny bit where the bodice was snug. A tiny smile came to his lips. She moved closer to pick up his tea cup. His hand moved to the skin displayed just below her breasts.

☾

Dohst looked at the address of the oil company that Miss Piari had given him on the phone. It was in Model Town, an area he had once been before, hoping to see girls from the American school ride their bikes. The house was huge and sat well back from the road behind a high wall on which cut glass had been imbedded in the cement. He glanced through the space between the gates and saw that the compound was not well kept. Plants of all kinds seemed to have taken over. There was evidence of little care. A hoopoe bird wandered around looking for bugs and paused when it saw Dohst's face. The crest on its head rose and settled back, then rose again. With a small cry it flew to another part of the compound. Dohst pulled the rope and heard a bell ring. No one came immediately so he pulled the rope again. A man in a *dhoti*, the cloth of which appeared almost like a large diaper, ran to the gait and asked his business. He showed the name of Piari and the oil company and said that he had an appointment. He was told to wait, however, the gate was not opened.

He smoked while he waited and wondered how such a place could be the headquarters of a wholesale oil company. Finally the black metal gate was drawn open and he stepped inside and walked up the bricked path to the main entrance. The verandah was large and cool. Here, a number of pots had been placed and in each there was a lily plant, many of which displayed their white faces with greenish pistils sticking up in what Dohst thought to be a most sexual display. He stooped to look at one of the strange plants when the door opened and a young woman stood in the entranceway and motioned for him to come in.

"Do you like my flowers? This time of the year their flowers are so white and pure, the flowers soft and waxy. Did you notice?" She smiled at him as she moved to her office. A clerk, a middle-aged grumpy looking woman sat at a small desk putting papers in envelopes looked up at him as he entered.

"Yes. Yes. The flowers are very... white. What are they called?" He glanced at the clerk, and then again at the young woman now sitting at her desk, his eyes roving over her hair, her scarf, her bodice. He caught himself and looked up into her eyes. She had been watching his eyes and her face was serious. She extended her hand.

"You may call me Miss Piari Sufi, please."

Her fingers were limp and cool in his hand which held them too hard. He nodded as he shook them. "My name is Dho... Aziz Shabash. I was the one who called about opening an account and starting a retail oil business in Sialkot." He stood uncomfortably in front of her.

"Mr. Shabash, please be seated. May I ask a few questions before I give you forms to fill up?" She paused and then asked, "How old are you Mr. Shabash?"

"Miss, does my age have anything to do with my purchasing oil wholesale from your firm? I do not understand."

"Let me begin again. Do you have any identification, official, like a driver's license or some other official document about yourself?" She smiled at the young man in front of her, enjoying his small discomfort.

"Oh, I see. Yes. Yes. Identification." He withdrew his driver's license and passed the little red colored book to her. Meher Jamal came to mind every time he looked at a driver's license. She took it and stared at the picture, then at his face. "So you are twenty six years of age. I would not have recognized you from your picture. It must have been taken some time ago. You look like a school graduate. Are you?"

"Yes, of course. I have matriculated." He got a terrible itch directly under his belt and it was distracting him. He stood up and adjusted his garments, muttering.

"I have checked your address in Sialkot and noted that it is right next to our other customer there. Right next to it, neighbors. Is that so?"

"Yes. I had hoped that he and I could become business partners together and share some of the costs and maintain a larger inventory to improve our sales. Partners, perhaps."

"Mr. Shabash that is unfortunate. You see, I do not wish to speak behind the back of any of our most valued customers, but since you mention partnership, I must tell you that we will have to refuse your enquiry and not allow for you to purchase oil from us. I am so sorry, ... sir."

"Allah! Why? I do not understand. I am not his partner yet. He suggested that I invest money in his, I mean our business and share the profits. I have not yet drawn up any papers yet, you understand. I am actually checking carefully about prices so that I may understand his level of profit on each tin of oil. It is like that." He was almost tongue tied and his hands fiddled in his pockets. His fingers touched his Barclay's check book. He pulled it out and placed it in his lap. She looked at it, resting directly above his crotch and frowned.

"I see, Mr. Shabash. Well, may I tell you something in utter confidentiality?"

He nodded and leaned forward and glanced at the clerk who was watching them.

"She has a severe hearing problem. Your neighbor, no name mentioned, who wants you to become partners has been negligent in paying his bills. We will no longer supply him with any more oil until all accounts have been paid in cash. No more credit. His bank checks also were not, you know, were refused by the bank for lack of funds. He was overdrawn. I see you carry a check book from the same bank." She looked at his lap and he took the check book from there and held it in his hand and adjusted the cloth covering his genitals.

Dohst sat in amazement. The information had caught him totally off guard. The oil *wallah* was such a handsome and pleasant man and he had observed that the business was active; people stopped and purchased oil. His mind raced, trying to remember the exact words that the man had used to encourage him to purchase oil and store it in his own empty store. He must have been thinking for rather a long time. Miss Piari broke the silence.

"I would like to warn you that if you have not yet become his partner, to check his particulars, his credit, his business activity and know accurately the stock he has on hand. I see you have been taken aback by the information I provided in confidence. You appear to be a fine young man, Mr. Shabash, and I would hate to see you loose money on a bad venture." She looked into his face with great sincerity.

Again Dohst said nothing, but stared at the beautiful face in front of him, the large dark sincere eyes that sought his own. Thoughts of business and oil vanished and his open admiration of the young woman in front of him caused her to become nervous. "How old are you Miss Piari?" he blurted out.

Now she was caught off guard. She stammered, "Mr. Shabash, what does my age have to do with our setting up a business account with you?" Now she could not help but smile. "About the same. Perhaps the same as yours, Mr. Shabash. Women do not tell men their age."

The clerk got up and pulled a drawer of a filing cabinet open, making a grating sound. She took a file and sat down, then got up again to push the drawer closed, again creating a loud grating sound which she seemed not to hear. Piari's eyes were drawn to the checkbook and then she glanced quickly at his lap where the check book again rested directly above Mr. Shabash's genitals.

"Miss, I am totally confused. You are a most beautiful young woman, talented, business-like and obviously capable. One hundred thousand young men just like me would seek you for marriage. Miss?" He was shaking his head from side to side, staring at the young woman who now blushed.

Her eyes now filled with tears. She got up and walked into the next room and was absent for a few minutes. Dohst was amazed. What had he said to create such a display of emotion? He had only complimented her, mentioning that she was beautiful and that...perhaps she had some hidden defect, some fault that was not visible like Meher's deformed arm. His imagination ran wild trying to think what strange hidden defect would prevent her from marriage. She was pure beauty, he thought.

She returned somber-faced and sat opposite him. "I am so sorry. Something must have got into my eyes. Sorry. Thank you for your kind words." She adjusted the cloth around her head as the clerk coughed and snapped rubber bands around a pile of envelopes. "Mr. Shabash, if you wish to continue the application process, these are the papers that need to be filled up. Would you like me to help you with them?" She passed a folder to him.

He looked up at her face again reading only softness, beauty and a great sense of personal sadness. "Please, Miss. I would like your help. Yes. Yes." He walked to a large table and spread the papers. She walked over and sat across from him.

"The first four questions deal with family matters. Your father? What is his business, Mr. Shabash?" She glanced up at him and saw that his face had taken on a look of unhappiness.

"He is dead. He was an importer and exporter of carpets when he was alive. He died in Karachi. Sorry. I was not expecting to give information about him." He smiled wanly. He wrote Sheikh Mohammed on the line.

She looked at the name and saw the disparity with his own name, Aziz Shabash. Instead of commenting on that, she spoke to what she perceived as his discomfort. "Each of us has our areas of pain, Mr. Shabash. Each of us carries memories of suffering. Just write in; Deceased-merchant in the space provided. The next line is your address." She wondered what the circumstances were of the death of his father. She saw unhappiness in his face and a look of regret. "May I ask Mr. Shabash if your father is your blood relative?"

"Of course. He is my father. I am a child of my father's first wife. The only son." He was defensive.

"Yes. His name and yours are not the same Mr. Shabash. Usually you would carry one of your father's names, like Mohammed in your name. Is that not so?"

"You have caught me up, Miss. Caught me up. This will be difficult to explain to you. Actually I have two names." He looked embarrassed.

"Two identities? You mean like they say in the films, aliases? But why? Usually persons with two or three names are trying to hide something, is that not correct?" She was now genuinely interested in this new line of questioning.

"Caught me up. Amazing. You are very clever, Miss. I never thought that filling up a form could be such a problem. May I speak confidentially?"

She nodded and made a noise in her throat with her tongue against her palate which gave assent.

"My father was suspected by the police of smuggling carpets into Pakistan. The police caught up with him in Karachi. He was terrified of being tortured so he..." He looked disturbed and wondered if he had said too much. "He killed himself, jumped into the ocean and died. So I was afraid that the police would look for me as well with my name being Dohst Mohammed. I changed it to Aziz Shabash and fled to Sialkot and began a new life there. Yes I was hiding." Dohst expected the interview to end.

"It is like a mystery book. Amazing! So you have two names, a real one and now a business one?" She shook her head.

"Yes. My first property in Sialkot is under my Aziz Shabash name.

"Oh. Do you have another?" She had not spoken to a man for such an extended time in years and was enjoying the interaction and the flow of emotions.

He hesitated. "I have two. Which one is the better one? Should I put my ancestral home in Sukkur which is on an island in the river, or my small home in Sialkot which I inherited from my aunt as Aziz?" He looked up at her.

She looked at the young man sitting in front of her and could not imagine that he was a multiple property owner, obviously a man of some means.

Her father would be interested in this information. Two properties, two names, she thought, and I have none except that given by my father. She smiled and pointed at the blank line. "Just write the Sialkot one because that is where you want to open a business. Sialkot will do." Her scarf kept slipping from her head and Dohst looked at her dark shiny flowing hair with interest, a cascade of glistening ebony that fell around her shoulders. He thought he could smell a certain fragrance the very moment she lifted both her arms to adjust the scarf. He could see that the garment was moist in her armpits which surprised him and he was surprised at his immediate arousal. The fragrance of acacia blossoms in spring on the island in Sukkur, a sweet heavy earthy odor came to him across the desk as she raised her arms. The memory of Ankh now came to his mind, standing near the beach with acacia blossoms blooming on the small trees behind her, her arms raised as she put them around his neck revealing the soft black hair. He wrote Sukkur on the line, making sure his handwriting was clear.

"Mr. Shabash, did we not agree to Sialkot? I do not understand." He looked at her now in surprise, then back to the page and was amazed that he had written Sukkur instead of Sialkot. "I do not understand,' she repeated.

Now he could see Meher sitting in front of him holding his drivers license and looking at the picture. "I do not understand. What if a person writing a check lacked funds in the bank? Should you ask for identification?" Dohst pushed his chair back and stood up saying, "May I take a smoke, please."

She nodded as he took out a cigarette. She noted it was a strange brand with a camel on it, Turkish tobacco. She watched him light up and the aromatic smell of the smoke came to her, overwhelmed her. She could see Ikbal sitting in the car, the door open as he invited her to come inside for a ride. He was smoking a Turkish cigarette of the same kind. The memory of the sweet odor of this smoke had remained with her for years, triggering thoughts of that terrible day. Again her eyes filled with tears and she too stood up and retreated to the small room behind the office.

The clerk got up and hurried to follow her and their soft, controlled voices could be heard in the background as Dohst smoked. He shook his head, wondering at the strange effect a beautiful woman had on everything. A simple application form had taken on such strong meanings with a woman assisting. His father's warnings about stepping into deep water again came to him. His father was correct in saying that Dohst drew trouble to himself in the form of women.

Dohst decided that he would spend one night in Lahore and see if he could meet with his friend Ali. He would return in the morning and again have a chance to meet with this attractive woman and she would once again help him fill up the form. The idea of another meeting was compelling. He finished his smoke and sat at the table and began to write in the information, but paused as Piari returned.

"Miss Piari Sufi, I have another appointment soon and must leave. May I return tomorrow and complete the application? I would like to come back tomorrow." He smiled openly, showing his teeth. The mullah's speech came to him again. So be it he thought. She is beautiful.

"Tomorrow will do. Could you come when the office opens at exactly eight o'clock?" She was thinking that the clerk her father had placed with her to be her assistant was also a chaperone who made interactions with the public suitable, and that she did not arrive until a quarter to nine.

Dohst stood and gathered the papers together and put them in his satchel. He looked at Piari standing in front of him. Behind her the sun light shone in through the window and he could see the faint outline of her legs through the material. She watched his eyes, now aware of what he was seeing and moved sideways and extended her hand.

"Until tomorrow at eight, then."

"I will be here right on time." He shook her hand and noticed that it was no longer limp and cool. Her fingers curled around his.

Maria's life was confined to a couple of gloomy rooms except for the times she was taken to the market with 'thank you Joe' in the lead. She carried Ankhi in a shawl knotted about her neck which hung down like a small hammock in front of her. She did not want to carry the baby on her back as some women did because it made her perspire.

She looked forward to these outings and kept her eyes open for possible means of making contact with the outer world. Atiqullah did not carry a cell phone. He did not get mail. He had family members that he met from time to time, but basically he was a loner. Other times he spent hours teaching Maria various card games and always took her to the stone enclosure where the sheep and goats were kept at night. She helped him milk the animals and became adept at squirting milk into the gourd while she held the animal's back under her arm.

There was no calendar that she could use to understand the passing of time. Ankhi, however, was her time marker. The child grew well and was fair with beautiful features. It was not passive as many of the small children she observed were. Its eyes followed her every motion. As it grew she thought of months that had passed and was surprised that she had begun to adjust to her new village life as the concubine of an Afghani peasant. On one excursion they passed the post office and Maria strolled to the opening and looked in but Atiqullah sensed the reason for her interest and spoke to her sharply, shaking his head. Since the bombings of their neighboring village a couple of months ago, he seemed more careful, not giving her the freedom to stroll alone nor explore anything more than their immediate environment in the large walled compound.

Near the small post office was a store that sold newspapers and a few magazines. Maria pulled on Atiqullah's sleeve and pointed to the store indicating her interest to walk there and look at the display. He paused, and then nodded yes. She stood in front of the stall and picked up one after another of the newspapers all written in Farsi. She looked at the pictures of the destruction of villages. There were pictures of American soldiers in a Humvi vehicle riding into a village. She stared at the images of these Americans, the first pictures she had seen of anything to do with home, America. Under the last section of papers was a red color peeping out. She looked and saw it was an old Time Magazine, dated December 29, 2003. She picked it up and asked the proprietor how much. He laughed and waved his hand and said something that made Atiqullah frown. He gave it to her, laughing pointing at the foreign words and shaking his head that he could not read what was written. He pointed at the cover, at three American soldiers of apparently different ethnicity and held his hand like a gun and made explosive sounds. Maria stared at the Person of the Year. In her pocket she had a strange artifact from her other life, an American dime. It had been in her dress pocket when she was abducted in Lahore. She took it out and handed it to the man and said thank you. She pointed at the dime and said, "American money".

Atiqullah became impatient at her interaction with the merchant and took the magazine from the man roughly, put it into her hands and steered her away. She made a tube of the magazine and stuffed it into the side of the baby carrier and followed him as he limped away to the vegetable and fruit dealers. He bought dried tomatoes, dried apricots, dried okra and four small dark-skinned potatoes. He was about to leave when he looked at the small coins in his hand and turned and bought two onions as well.

Sitting alone with the small kerosene lantern she read the magazine from cover to cover. Then she read it again, savoring each word, each piece of information. Tears filled her eyes as she read about Christmas. She put it down and lay back on the hard cot, memories of family gatherings in Cebu, in Manila and the one she had enjoyed in La Jolla with James were in front of her closed eyes. Loneliness now overwhelmed her and she wept openly, sobbing into the pillow to keep from wakening the baby.

She stopped crying and picked up the magazine and looked on the cover. It bore an address: US Army Reserve 452 Combat Support, Bagram, Afghanistan. The magazine she held had been sent to Afghanistan, had been read by Americans and had been discarded or taken away and passed along to a variety of Afghani people until it somehow reached the tiny market where the shopkeeper had displayed it, hoping for someone to buy it, but keeping it concealed because of the picture of the American soldiers on the cover. American soldiers! Bagram. Where is Bagram she wondered? How close am I to Bagram?

A small seed of hope germinated in her heart. She could feel the joy of thinking of somehow getting away, going home. Home, she thought and again tears filled her eyes. James always used to say, "We are home! Home sweet home baby. Nothing like home! Home for the holidays!"

☪

Deputy Feroz Hakim stared at her intensely, forgetting that anyone else was in the room. His eyes roved over her, took in her tiny shoes, her hands holding a book, her neck exposed just below her chin, a wisp of hair creeping out from under the dark scarf which covered her head, her dark eyes filled with concern and fear. For an instant she moved her eyes from the book she was reading and glanced at Feroz Hakim, sitting in front of her in his police uniform. She read the words out loud.

"His eyes met hers, that smile was gone, and bursting into heart-felt tears

Yes. Yes, she cried, my hourly fears, my dreams have boded all too
right

We part, for ever part, tonight. I knew it could not last
Twas bright, twas heavenly, but tis past."

She stumbled on the words, on *twas*, not understanding their meaning
and pronouncing them as at-was. She dropped the book to the side of her
body and stood straight and stiffly, avoiding his gaze.

"Very nice. Much better than the last time with Jack Sprat. Better. You
are making progress. Who wrote this poem?"

"The English Reader Number One, sir."

"No, there is the name of person above the lines you read. He was the
one who wrote the poem."

She glanced again at the book and nodded her head. "Thomas Moore,"
she said quietly. "It is sorry story. It has tears and she cried about her fears.
That is why I chose this to read."

"I see. What makes you happy?" He leaned forward as he asked the
question, hoping that she would look at him when she answered.

"My little brother. *Basant* celebration and kites flying. Ten rupees."
She glanced at him when she mentioned money.

He reached into his pocket and removed twenty rupees from his billfold. He stood up and handed these to her. She took the money from his
extended hand and smiled revealing her very white and even teeth. She
made a tiny courtesy of thanks and then laughed and moved to a seat next
to her father, Mistiri.

Feroz turned to Mistiri. "I have decided that we will conclude our
business with your daughter when the school term ends. I will send you
money for her in two weeks."

Behind him he heard his wife sniffle, heard the sound of her feet as she
shuffled out of the room. The door to the kitchen shut with a bang.

"Yes. When the school term ends it will be arranged. There is no need
for a longer waiting period. I am satisfied. Very satisfied. I will formalize the
engagement with you next week." He turned and picked up a large package, carefully wrapped in red and gold paper. He handed this to Mistiri
who stared at it, his mouth hanging open in amazement.

"What?" he stammered.

"For her. Twenty meters of special silk cloth to make her dresses and
money for the *darzi* who will tailor them to fit her. Two boxes of assorted

242 Harold M. Bergsma

sweets as well." He stepped toward the entry door; Mistiri and his daughter followed as he ushered them out. He handed the handyman money to hire a horse drawn carriage, a *tonga*, then taking one more glance at the young girl he entered the house. He watched them through the window. The girl was bent over weeping. The father was speaking to her, his face serious and impatient. He tried to hand the presents to her, but she walked away toward the street.

"You had better build an addition on to this house for her. She is not staying with me here. She is hardly older than our own daughter. Can she cook the food you like? Can she keep the home clean and orderly as you insist? Can she wash your clothing and iron them without a wrinkle? Can she listen to you snore loudly every night and say nothing? Can she listen to you clear your throat like a buffalo each morning and spit loudly? Can she stand the smell of your farts?" She became increasingly angrier as she stood in the doorway and questioned him. Her hands were on her ample hips, her heavy breasts swaying as she waved her arms about. He looked at her and his face became clouded with anger. He moved quickly to the closet and took out an umbrella and moved toward her. She shrieked and ran into the bedroom and shut the door, putting her back against it to keep him out.

"You are spoiled. I should have taken a concubine many years ago. Get away from the door, or I will beat you harder. Now!"

☪

The police interrogation room was airless and stuffy. He sat bent over like a monk and read the manuscript he had written once again. Ikbal liked it. While he had the time, he now copied it by hand so that he would have a record of what he had written in the event that the matter was brought up again. He completed writing the copy and folded it and took off his shoe and put it under his foot in the shoe. He now read his masterpiece.

Gusse men junjlae jab ape men to ape pe junjale.

An angry man is again angry (with himself) when he returns to reason.

Yes, angry! I was furious to have my car stopped on the road and to be packed off in a police van like a common criminal. I was angry to be hounded by the police for some trumped up charges against me regarding my having spoken the truth about matters related to the over-zealous hand of those who are paid to enforce the law of this land, who have themselves been destroyed in the hell of a bomb. Then when I sat down to write this essay I was angry with myself for not having written more lucidly with evidence for what my pen put on paper about Sher Khan and Feroz Hakim.

"Half an hour should do." Let me give it a try.

There was an old saying from the Prophet Jesus that is quoted even by our people. It was the time when a woman had been charged with adultery and was about to be stoned. The prophet Jesus stooped and wrote in the sand. 'He that is without sin may cast the first stone.' He was not just defending an unfortunate woman who had been offended, perhaps violated against her will by some man, perhaps standing in that very crowd with a rock in his hand, trembling. No, he was pointing to that part of the life of each and every man when his weakness, his sin, his lust is exposed in front of his own eyes, that what comes before the harsh justice of stones smashing into flesh, there exists the justice of the Almighty One which reveals that mercy should abound among those who judge and among those who carry out the penalty for breaking the law.

I was angry with myself when I sat to write because ten years ago, as a young man with raging hormones and lust in my heart, starved for the touch of a woman, aching for a relationship with a female, one of those mysterious creatures that only the wild longings of youth can conjure up; I had acted upon these toward a young woman who was innocent and virginal in her very being. Now, ten years later, looking back I do not know that young man, though he lurks in my mind somewhere. Yes, angry at him for stupidity and impetuosity. But of course what I have just written is but out of my dream.

'Let he who is without guilt cast the first stone.' Indeed. The bearded elder who sits in judgment over such matters and enforces the Hudood Ordinances against a girl who has been raped against her will and condemns her to death, may be the very one who in his own household, behind *char divari*, those large mud brick walls, which gives him the illusion that he is the gatekeeper of all that is right, all that is just and all that is fair while violating the freedoms of all his women of whom he is sole and righteous judge; he commits any violation with those he controls knowing he is immune to the law because he is a man, biologically he has the penis, thus a male who interprets the Holy Laws. What man among us in our culture of Pakistan has not lusted after a woman, many women? What man among us has not in a youthful moment forgotten himself and tried to establish a liaison with a lover? What man among us has not gone to the street of prostitution and released frustration with some nameless painted, perfumed whore? So who is guilty of what? How many have never had any sexual experience before taking the bride that the family has carefully chosen, the virgin who comes to the marriage bed, truly a virgin, to the man who carries not only the memories of past sexual encounters, but the diseases which accompany them? How many have used the slave girls, oh no, we do not use those words now, the servant girls in the household as our own chattel and then in righteousness pray before Allah? The Prophet, peace be upon Him says, Surah XXIV, 33. *Force not your slave- girls to whoredom that ye may seek enjoyment of life of the world, if they would preserve their chastity. And if one force them, then (unto them), after their compulsion, Lo! Allah will be Forgiving, Merciful.* Yes, anger at myself, my stupidity, my lust and my cowardice of hiding behind law and convention which protects me, a man, even as I dream of my past. "Four witnesses of the act of *zinna* to be convicted!" There are not four witnesses, or three, or two. Yet, as a Muslim I stand before Allah and cry out my repentance. Vs.70, *Save him who repenteth and believeth and doth righteous works; as for such; Allah will change their evil deeds to good deeds. Allah is ever Forgiving, Merciful.*

I was reminded to write about the Humber motor car sedan that was found burned in the compound of the late Superintendent of Police, Sher Khan in his village Bahadur after the bombs destroyed it and him. The car was indeed held by Sher Khan for a decade, a symbol of an old power, of an old Raj, and carefully preserved and cared for as he drove with the flags of authority and power attached to its bumpers. Oh yes, the Humber car. How did he obtain it? He purchased it for Rupees 60,000 from my father. A receipt of that purchase is even now extant in one of the safes in one of my family homes. A careful search of rat-eaten files in the government's car registry department may reveal to you, to those who wish to spend the time to enquire, that a copy of that receipt of sale still exists unless the white ants have ravaged that particular page. But of course police records are never ravaged; only mice make their nests in the chewed papers.

My half an hour is up. The above is written with the full knowledge that it now becomes public record, as the files of the late and honorable Sher Khan should have been made public record by the one who replaced him, Feroz Hakim. Where have all the documents gone, similar to the one he held on me? Was mine numbered 32? Where have the others gone that reportedly filled a trunk held by Feroz Hakim? Why was an immediate warrant to search his house not made, rather than giving a brother a polite warning with a set time for fellow police to examine the trunk, now filled with who knows what. Why is it that complaints are often filed against some one in order to cover the actions of those in power? So be it; but the public should know about Sher Khan, a Superintendent of Police; he was the one who should have upheld the law. To date, it is known that he was probably involved in extortion, kidnapping, murder, sale of illegal arms and who knows what else. At least the Americans had the goods on him and took him out. Thank them for that justice. What a glorious record to be made known to the public.

Ikbal Sufi

Ikbal had just adjusted his shoe when the police inspector stepped in. The Inspector looked at the handwritten page on the table before him and picked it up and to get better light, walked to the window to read. He took out his magnifying spectacles and read quietly for a few minutes. Then, strangely, he stood and looked out of the window at two nesting Brahamini Kites, that raised their chick each year in the compound. The high piercing cry of the female while being mounted by the male could be heard in the room. He sighed, turned and walked toward Ikbal, shaking the paper in front of him as if it were a salt shaker.

"You should have taken the same course in logic that I did in England. Professor Benson had a way with words. He would have enjoyed this drivel. You are free to go. Do not leave the country." He now laughed. Two policemen entered the room and told Ikbal to stand. They ran their hands across his pants and shirt, they looked in his pockets and had Feroz spread their contents on the table. Satisfied they told him he could now leave.

Feroz walked to the window and looked up at the messy nest of the kite. He could see his car parked in the lot nearby. From where he stood he could see that there was a long white streak across the windscreen of his car where the bird had defecated and that one stick from the nest had lodged on the roof of his car.

CHAPTER ELEVEN

Maute ke age chote bare sab barabar. Urdu Proverb

Contemplating death, great and small are equal.

Sahib-ji sat in the back of his Mercedes sedan and watched the village people crowd around the car. A train was coming and the gatekeeper had lowered the bars to prevent road traffic from flowing. In the distance the sound of the train whistle could be heard, then the low rumbling, vibrating sounds of metal on metal, wheels clacking against the joins in the tracks. Two young boys tried to peer into the darkened windows of the car. Sahib-ji rolled the window down just as one boy was putting out his tongue to lick the glass. He was startled as Sahib-ji struck out with his umbrella, hitting the lad a blow on his arm. Villagers now became angry and began to shout at Sahib-ji.

"The day of the Rajahs is over, fat man. Just because you have a fine car does not give you the right to hit a boy!" shouted a farmer. "Stay in your shiny car. If you get out you will be in trouble. This is not your village." The men crowded around the car. The train began passing through the crossing as he spoke.

Sahib-ji spoke to the driver. "When I tell you, speed away." He opened the car door and the crowd moved back looking at him with hostile eyes. He stood in the shelter of the car door and faced the people, then reached down for his gun and took it out and leveled it at the last speaker in the crowd.

"The day of the Rajah is over. The day of the British Raj is over. The day of opening your mouth at anyone you think you can taunt and abuse is also over. Power has shifted to this." He waved his gun. "If you have this, perhaps, you can taunt another. Otherwise keep your filthy mouth shut. Do you want to die now?" He kept the gun pointing at the chest of the man who had somehow lost the starch in his spine. Others around him moved back and then began to run.

"Sahib-ji, be merciful. I was protecting my son. You understand how a father protects his family." He was shaking.

"Teach your son to avoid snakes. Tell your son to avoid mad dogs. Teach your son that his filthy tongue and dirty hands must not reach forward to touch what is not his or he may be bitten. He is an unclean little creature that must learn to fear for his life if he puts his hand into a tiger's mouth." He snarled at the farmer.

"He is just a child, sahib-ji." He squatted on his haunches and placed his hands together in supplication. The crowd stood twenty feet away watching.

A foot patrolman holding a stout stick stood at a distance across the tracks, saw the commotion and blew his whistle and began to run toward the Mercedes. As he approached he saw the gun and stopped in his tracks, then moved back toward the crowd. He continued to blow the whistle but mingled with the crowd keeping out of sight.

Sahib-ji got back into the car, rolled up his window and nodded to the driver. The vehicle sped off. As it left, the people flowed toward the road again, looking at the tail lights moving off in the distance. Everyone was talking and yelling about what had happened. The farmer stood up and looked for his son who was talking excitedly with another boy about what had happened, laughing. The farmer walked to the boy and cuffed him hard against his head, knocking him to the ground.

"Keep your hands and tongue to yourself. You almost got me killed." The boy curled up in the dirt and began to screech.

The policeman now walked forward. "Where is the other boy? He must also be taught a lesson. The man could have been a Minister or the very *zamindar*, the landlord that allows the boy's father to use the farm land." He looked around and saw the other lad running rapidly away into the cluster of adobe houses. The policeman brandished his stick, boldly putting on a show of law and order. The crown melted away, the people mumbling and shaking their heads.

It was dark when the car pulled up at the gates of a small village of which Sahib-ji was the patron and owner. Men ran to the car shouting their greetings. Others pushed the gate open to allow the car to enter the fortress-like walled compound, the *char divari*. He waited until the door was opened from the outside to slide his feet to the ground, grunted and as he rose farted loudly. No one smiled or commented, though they backed away while they gave their greetings.

The compound he had entered was as large as a football field. There was an open area in the center which the younger men and boys had used as a game field. A few boys were kicking around a tattered ball, moving around vehicles, ox-carts and bicycles. Around the perimeter there were a number of doors leading to various smaller compounds. The house of Sahib-ji was not evident, as part of it incorporated the thick outer wall of the compound; however, the door to his residence was more massive than the rest and was supported with black iron hardware. Animals were tethered here and there and chickens ran about looking for food.

Sahib-ji waddled to his door which seemed to open by itself as he approached it. A young man bowed and gave his salaams as Sahib-ji entered. The room he entered was mainly for visitors and was decorated in the style of the Yemeni. The floor was covered with Persian carpets and smaller *kilims* which one of the women in the house produced and around the room there were many cushions and pillows. There was no other furniture, except for a large and ornate *hookah* set off to the side. On one wall a calligrapher had painted the words, *There is only one God and Mohammed is his Prophet.* From the ceiling hung two sturdy hooks to which were attached Primus pump up lanterns which had been lit and gave off a hissing sound. The walls behind the cushions were painted in bright colors with geometric patterns. Here and there the paint had peeled on the walls and plaster was showing through. Moths circled around the lanterns and burned their wings against the hot glass, falling to the floor from where they crawled across to the walls and slowly climbed upward, unaware that hungry geckos waited, their tails slowly waving to and fro as they stalked their prey. The strong smell of burning moth wings, incense and sandalwood was in the air, a heavy sweet smell of opium permeated the cushions and the dusty, faded carpets.

Sahib-ji stood in the center of the room and glanced around, not having been home for more than a month. He nodded and moved through the next doorway to a hallway and a series of rooms from which came the sound of women's voices and children's high-pitched laughter. He moved to the last door along the hallway and opened it and entered his own private sleeping chamber, a large room which was decorated Ikea style, with ultra modern furniture, a California bed and a television set and VCR across from it. There was a modern light-colored desk and a swivel chair. A Dell computer was on the desk, next to which were a printer and a stack of papers. Sahib-ji opened the walk-in closet and took off his coat, the holster for his pistol, and his turban. He was bare footed having already kicked off his shoes when entering the first room. He put on slippers and a bathrobe, a thick towel-like garment he had rescued when staying in a plush hotel in Dubai. A servant knocked and entered carrying a tray with a tea pot and cups and a package of four chocolate sweets wrapped in shiny gold paper.

He sat in the only soft chair in the room, a reclining theater chair with a place for drinks, built into the arm. The servant set his steaming tea cup on this as well as the plate of sweets. He picked up the tea and took a sip and in the distance he could hear a small electric generator start up and as he took the second sip the lights in the room came on. On the table next to the bed was a light with a glass stand filled with colored liquid which, with the heat at the bottom began to rise slowly in a swirl of color. The flat screen television set on the wall came to life as he clicked the power button. The disc on the roof top was set to pick up a number of stations, including one from Kabul which he selected. The news was being read. The temperature for the night in Kabul was ten degrees Centigrade. The woman speaker did not stare directly into the camera but off to the side so that her eyes never looked directly at the viewer. She was covered with a green garment and a head cloth that revealed her pretty face. Her Farsi was clear and well enunciated.

Sahib-ji rang a small hand bell. The servant appeared almost instantly. "Tell the women to inform the newcomer to bathe and dress and come here at seven o'clock. You know, the one called Chamuck." The man nodded and left the room.

Chamuck knew the day would come eventually. She had been in the compound for almost two months, wondering each day when Sahib-ji would return, dreading the terrible moment when she would face her abductor. Her imagination knew no bounds as she thought about what he would do to her. She had tried in the past not to think of meeting the monster everyone called The Farter.

Her life had been one of total boredom. She had no reading materials and the women who were in the compound were all unschooled traditional women except one more elderly woman who would not talk to her but who worked a loom and made small *kilim* carpets. She wondered if the woman was Sahib-ji's first wife. She wore severe clothing on her thin frame and her long fingers pushed the shuttles of thread back and forth as if they had a mind of their own. She greeted this woman daily, trying to start up a conversation but she simply shook her head and remained quiet.

The day had come today! She had been informed to go to the room with the large door in the evening after the last call to prayer. The woman who told her, laid clothing on her bed and as she did so, shook her head sadly. Chamuck had bathed in the morning so she put on the clothing set out for her. She was surprised to see that the clothing laid on her bed was a dress of western design with a low-cut top and no sleeves. The shoes were high-heeled and colored blue to match the garment. She had never seen such clothing before and hardly knew how to put them on. She picked up the small mirror from the table and looked at herself and the dress. The bra she wore, a large broad cotton affair her mother had made for her in Peshawar, stuck up above the line of the dress and showed in the cut-away section on the back. Her hair was wild and uncombed and she ran her fingers through it in an unconscious gesture to tame it. She looked into her own tearing eyes and recognized fear and dread in them. If she looked terrible, she thought, all the better. She stood in her bare feet and looked down at the tight-fitting dress and at her toes. She was surprised how long her toe nails were and that her feet were covered with dust from walking around bare footed. She sat on the bed and pulled on the shoes which fit, to her surprise. Her uncared for toes were revealed, sticking out at the front of the open-toed shoes. She tried to stand and was not used to the effect the heels had, tipping her forward. She straightened up and felt tension in the muscles of her legs. She tried a few practice steps and learned how to walk. Her legs were well muscled. Long hours of practicing Badminton for her school team, had kept her lean and in good athletic shape.

She had no brush or comb. She had come with a school uniform on her back when she had been abducted. The uniform had been washed dozens of times and was now faded. The new dress she wore reminded her of those she had seen in a magazine that her father had brought with him in which American models posed. She ran her fingers through her hair again and again, and then wondered why she was doing it. Why should she even try to look attractive? She was about to face a monster. A murderer. She sat glumly, then lay back on the cot and stared at the ceiling, thinking of her bed in the deep basement room where she had read and practiced reading the strange words.

She mouthed the English speech she was to make in class the day she was abducted.

> *As she is mine, I may dispose of her:*
> *Which shall be either to this gentleman*
> *Or to her death, according to our law*
> *Immediately provided in that case.*

Or to her death. Or to her death. She repeated these words over and over again. Then she thought, *or to his death, or to his death.* She had never before thought of such a thing, but now a seed had been sown. His death. Stories told at home of "The Pigeon" came to mind, how an old Pathan woman had taken up arms to fight against those who violated the honor of the tribe. Her uncle's words come to her, "Women are weak!" She muttered, Zar, Zan, Zamin.

The call to prayer came over the loudspeaker in the small mosque in the village. She sat up, then stood up not knowing which way to face, looked down at her dusty feet, hoping Allah would accept her prayer without a ritual washing. She brought her hands to her ears, then with palms upward toward her head put her thumbs behind her earlobes and began the Iqama, the private call to prayer. "*Alluhu Akbar. Subhaana ala humma wa bihamdika...*" Her prayer was not a personal one for deliverance from evil, rather a prayer which showed her utter obedience to His will, Allah the all merciful. She began to relax, knowing that the very days of her life were numbered and the very day of her death predestined. Her father had gone about his business with no fear, saying always, that if it was his time to die he would die. He had died on the instant chosen for him in all time.

Chamuck now wondered when the time to die for Sahib-ji was recorded, wondered how he would pass from this life to an eternity in hell. She wondered who the instrument of his death was to be, and if that too was ordained, so that his evil life could be brought to an end to stop the suffering he inflicted on others. He was a dealer in death, in arms and ammunition. He was a creator of death situations for a number of women in the village who had been brought there and had never left, never tasted the joy of freedom. The picture of the thin woman who would not speak came to mind, passing the shuttle back and forth across the loom, back and forth.

His abduction of her was her death sentence. So be it, she thought. *As he is mine, I may dispose of him; Which shall be either to this man, Or to his death, according to our law, Immediately provided in that case.*

She looked around the room at every object in it. It was essentially bare except for a bed, a small table on which there was a picture frame and a portion of the Holy Koran in calligraphy under glass. She picked it up and turned over the frame and carefully removed the holy words, placing them on the bed. The glass came out and she held it in her hand, then wrapped it in a part of the blanket and broke it. It shattered into three pieces. One was an elongated thin triangle of glass eight inches long. She replaced the picture into the frame and put it back onto the table. The extra pieces of glass she put under the central part of the mattress. She removed the pillow case and with the sharp glass, sliced a portion and then ripped a hand-width of cloth into a long bandage. The rest of the pillow case was pushed under the mattress as well. She wrapped the top of the glass making a handle for her hand. With the weapon concealed in her left hand, held behind her back she now stepped out of the room and walking unsteadily made her way to the door of Sahib-ji's room. She knocked with her right hand gently.

"It is open. Come in." He called out from the bed on which he was reclined.

She entered and stood inside the door, her face a mask of fear and resolve.

"Walk around the room so I can see how you look in the new shoes and clothing I bought for you." He sat up in the bed to watch her. She kept the weapon concealed in her left palm against her wrist as she walked the length of the room as far away from him as possible. The high heels made her stumble, but she caught herself and glanced at him sitting staring at her. His mouth was open.

"Come and stand in front of me." His eyes looked like those of a cobra, black, glistening staring steadily at the low-cut bodice of her dress which revealed the swell of her large breasts.

Chamuck moved in front of him and stood three feet away. When she glanced at him, all she could think of was the toad at home that ate white ants until it could no longer hop away, swollen and bloated with its food, sitting with its fat body splayed on the cement.

"Come closer."

She moved closer and could now see the veins in his eyes, smell his garlic breath as she stared at the top of his head which was slightly bald. She looked at his neck and could see the artery throb. He reached forward with his hands and lifted up the dress until it came to her knees. He stooped and held the dress up with one hand and moved his right free hand up between her inner thighs. He was not looking at her face, only at his own hand and its progress as it slid upward. His mouth was wide open, his tongue slightly extended. No man has ever touched me before this, she thought. Zen! Family honor for the women of her household.

Her left arm swung in a short arc. She was surprised at how easily the glass slid into his fat neck under his right ear, how easily it cut through flesh and veins as she pushed and sliced with it. She could hear her classmates shouting as she struck the shuttlecock a hard blow with her left hand. "Kill it!" The glass was imbedded all the way past the wrapping. She stepped back two paces and looked at Sahib-ji. His hand went to his neck and grasped the wrapped portion of the glass and he pulled it out. The severed artery and Jugular Vein gushed blood over his shoulder. He tried to stand but was obviously dizzy and sat back. He looked at the object in his hand, dropped it onto the floor and lowered his head, looking in amazement as his blood flowed onto his chest and lap. He made no sound. He glanced up at Chamuck and saw in his last instant of conscious life that she was smiling. She spoke only one word, "*Shaitan!*"

He fell back onto the bed, his eyes glazing over. She studied him and thought of the hundreds of sheep that had been slaughtered in her compound by her father and how as a little girl she watched the knife slice the neck and how quickly the animal lay still with a huge pool of blood forming. Her father told her each time, as if she would forget, that an animal had to be killed this way while the holy words of thanks were spoken for the meat to be sanctioned and made *hallal.* Sahib-ji's legs began to jerk and shake, blood rattled in his windpipe and then he was still. Chamuck exhaled, not realizing that she had been holding her breath.

Her mind raced. Either I died to this world, forever, hidden away in this remote village, a sex plaything for this devil or he died. If this means that I die too, it is better than being here with my family not knowing where I am and I as a dead person to them; no more education, no more books, no more friends, sports, no anything except Sahib-ji. She picked up the instrument of death, wiped it off on the bed spread and held it in her left hand again. She was an *anari* and her parents had not been able to correct her left-handedness. Her teachers shook their heads but admired her beautiful writing, bending her wrist around and above the line of words being written so as not to smudge the ink when she wrote from left to right in English.

She stood for a long moment looking at the dead man. Her legs felt weak and she settled down on her haunches, shaking visibly. Her mind raced, thinking of what she had done. She thought of how her father had died working for this man, who drew up a marriage contract based on the death of the one who made it. This was a devil that sat and ate sweets and counted money and cared nothing for the lives of those who worked for him; looking at his gruesome corpse made her fearful.

She turned and glanced at the door, then went to it and pushed the lock closed. She now examined the room, wondering what she would do next. She knew that the household was aware that Sahib-ji had taken a new girl into his room and that he was to remain undisturbed until the morning. She had time, the whole night to make a plan. She used the remote control and turned on the television set and set the volume fairly high. The satellite disc was picking up a program from Dubai; the drums beat and a woman sang a song as an Egyptian belly dancer gyrated. She had never seen a woman act provocatively before and stared at the gyrating woman and at the movements she made with her belly and hips and pelvic thrusts. She watched the dancer and looked at her smile, a smile frozen on a face that did not match the hard vacant eyes that stared at the camera.

She went to the closet and looked through the clothing hanging there but saw no clothing for a woman. There were trousers, belts, shirts, jackets, various types of hats and shoes, many shoes of various kinds. A small mirror was on the dresser. She looked at it and at her long curly hair and put her hands to the side of her head and pulled it back. Blood was drying on her hand.

She leaned her head forward toward her knees and with the glass sawed away at her long hair, cutting it off roughly. She dressed as a man, pulling her hacked-off hair back and putting on a round Pashtun tribal cap. She gathered up the hair from the floor, went to the corpse on the bed and pulled back the vest and stuffed the hair deep inside the bloody clothing on his right side.

The clothes she found were much too large for her, but she drew the waist of the pants up into the belt, pushed the shirt into the pants. She put on a heavy wool shirt and then found a pair of shoes that were slightly large for her but with two pairs of stockings, fit her fairly well. Finally, over the top of this she pulled on a long tribal gown. She stood in front of the mirror and looked at herself and was surprised at the transformation. She looked like a sturdy teenage boy in badly fitting clothing. Her eyes fell on the rifle propped in the corner and near it a leather ammunition belt. She had watched her father clean and load weapons since early childhood. She picked up the weapon and slung the ammunition belt over her right shoulder. She looked for money but her search of the room revealed none. Finally she went to the bed and carefully pulled the blood-soaked vest away from the left part of the chest and saw the fat wallet in an inside pocket. There was also a shiny object that looked like a carrot with indentations on the side. She took the carrot shaped object and slipped it into her pocket and held the cool metal in the palm of her hand.

Chamuck glanced up at the television set from time to time as she sorted through the contents of the wallet, watching Egyptian belly dancers. She was surprised that for all the body movements the women made as they danced, their faces seemed to remain dead, expressionless, distant, and when they smiled it was as if that too was part of the dance, their teeth showing in a grimace much like the teeth of the dead man on the bed. Their eyes seemed to be looking elsewhere as they gyrated. She removed all the money and placed it in a small pile on the table. The red cloth-covered driver's license had a picture of a much younger man, of Sahib-ji when he was still somewhat lean. She took this. There were six credit cards. She had gone to the ATM at the bank with her father in his truck and sat in the front seat and watched as he had inserted a card, tapped in some numbers and had withdrawn cash. She searched now for the magic numbers to use with the cards and was surprised that these were neatly written on a business card of a firm in Lahore that sold T2 motor oil. The last four numbers of each of the cards' numbers were written, followed by four numbers which were underlined. She took all of the cards and the coded business card. A shoulder bag with a sling was the only thing she found to carry her treasures. The money she put into two different pockets of the clothing she wore. On the table near the bed was a plate piled high with different kinds of sweets. She wrapped these in paper and took them as well as two bottles of water. Now she sat and waited and wondered what time it was and how long she had taken to prepare. She glanced at the gold watch on Sahib-ji's wrist. She read the label of the watch but it meant nothing to her, Oyster Perpetual. She took it off the dead man's fat hand and put it on her own wrist where it hung loosely. It was nine o'clock. She knew that people moved around the house and the compound until ten or eleven o'clock. She had to wait.

At one o'clock in the morning she opened the door and looked around and all was quiet. She shut the door carefully, first reaching around snapping the inside self-lock. She tried the door making sure it was locked. She stepped out into the hallway. The generator had stopped at midnight and the television set was quiet. But the generator went on for two hours in the morning when Sahib-ji was in residence. The television set would again come on loudly. She moved down the hallway past two other doors and paused at the third door, hearing sexual sounds of moaning. She had heard such sounds many times in her own household from her mother and other women her father kept, when she had moved to and fro to the bathroom area past their sleeping rooms. She paused and listened to the noises, strange noises made by the woman, almost complaining whines and the deep grunts of the man. Strangely, she stood transfixed and listened, unaware that she did so, until the woman called out "*sand, sand!*" Images of the stud, an Arabian stallion that was brought to her father's household came to mind. She breathed deeply and looked about her. There was no other activity in the house.

The large entry room was occupied by one person, a snoring guard who lay sleeping sprawled on two cushions. The sweet smell of burning raw opium filled the air. She moved past him and stepped into the open field where the boys had played football. The night was clear, the stars were bright and the air very cold. She could see her breath, like smoke.

She walked next to the wall until she came to the gate and found it shut, locked from the inside by a wood post which fitted into a metal holder. She lifted it up and pushed the gate open, closed it behind her and looked around wondering where to go. There were a few distant lights burning in households on the far slope. The motor road led toward these. Another footpath angled across the countryside and she took this. She practiced moving forward trying to walk like a man in her shoes and clothing, her rifle slung across one shoulder. The cold was biting so she strolled along more quickly hoping to warm up from the exercise. She looked at her watch again, after what she thought was hours of walking and was surprised that it was only three in the morning. The path led downhill toward the dry river bed. She decided that downhill was the best way to go for her, downhill toward an unknown destination. The gun was very heavy so she shifted it to the other shoulder. At four in the morning she sat on a stone in the dry river bed and ate four large squares of sweets. Again she moved forward looking carefully ahead of her lest she meet another traveler unexpectedly. She decided that she would not speak, simply point to her mouth and shake her head and hold the weapon more aggressively if she was confronted. She looked at her outer clothing now and was surprised at how fine a garment it was, made of soft wool and embroidered at the neck and wrists. She saw that the shoes she had selected were of shiny brown leather and looked new. If she met someone they would look at her clothing and think that she was a rich young boy.

Chamuck continued to walk and then stopped abruptly. She heard stones rattle. She stepped behind a large rock and waited, gripping her rifle, pointing it ahead of her. There was a strange deep grunting sound. She waited fearfully, in spite of having a gun. In the semi-darkness she saw dark forms the size of large dogs moving in an area next to the mostly dry stream bed she was following. Pigs! She had only seen pigs once before as a child when she traveled with her father in his truck. These too had been in a deserted area. She shouted out loudly at the pigs and was amazed to see that the animals scattered and ran into the nearby bushes.

As dawn came she was walking on a path that led her uphill. The stream-bed was filled with huge boulders and walking there was almost impossible. The path led her to the top of a rise. She stood quietly and looked around. She could see for miles. The hills around her looked deserted, but then her eyes caught a plume of smoke rising into the still morning air.

In the distance there was a village located on a flat plain far below her. It looked to her as if a field was burning. Then she understood. Sugar cane. It was the season for harvesting sugar cane and farmers frequently burned the drying leaves and rubbish in the cane field when there was no wind before going in with their machetes and cutting down the blackened sweet stalks. She salivated, remembering the times that she had been given the freshly made sweet straight from the condensing pan, remembering the *gur*, an orange-brown lump she held in her sticky hand as she bit off pieces, licking the treat.

She moved down hill again toward the village and as she came within a mile of it she could see that two old trucks were parked in the courtyard and that a dirt motor road led to the village. Chamuck felt the money in her pocket, thinking of the trucks and that she would try to hire one of these to take her to a larger town where she could buy a ticket for a seat on a bus and head back home to Peshawar, to her family, to her basement room. They would not have to sell a television set to get money for food now, or sell their donkey. She had credit cards that could be used to draw money from the ATM booths found in most banks. She moved forward with large steps, almost loping on the downward slope, her rifle slung across her back, bumping against her buttocks as she moved forward. In her left hand she held the brass carrot, feeling the indentations with her thumb as she walked.

☪

Malik was a calm and pleasant child. Meher set him on the carpet and he did not cry, simply looked up at her. She responded and sat next to him and put three serving spoons in front of him and rattled them together. He looked at the spoons and reached out for them, putting himself off balance. He rolled to his side and took a spoon and pushed it into his mouth, his tongue licking the shiny surface. All the while he stared at Meher. She could not resist his stare and scooped him up and held the baby to her and kissed its face and ears.

"My little king. My sweet soft child. Come we will put heavy clothes on you and we will step outside for the first time for you to see there is a world out there." She wrapped the child in a heavy shawl and walked to the door.

She had not ventured outside for weeks. Now, carrying the baby she stepped over trash and the open sewer and walked toward the mosque about a block away. Flies and mosquitoes rose from the open sewer and she lowered her head as if to plow through the swarms. She was ignored by most. She made her way to a compound where her parents lived, walking with her head down, the scarf covering most of her face. The baby wiggled in her arms and she moved it up across her chest. She had not been home for many months and was excited at the prospect of seeing her sister and mother. She came to a wood door and rattled it calling out if any one was there. An old man, one who had served the family for decades looked out and opened the gate, cackling and smiling a toothless grin.

"You are back! Come, your mother is in the back cooking lentils. Come." He scuttled away and led her to the back kitchen area. Her mother looked up and shrieked.

"Daughter! Daughter!" She ran forward and held Meher in her arms, then looked at the child and her happy expression changed to a frown. "How? Is this the child?"

"Yes, it is the child of the woman who I worked for. She died and I am raising it." She held out the child to her mother. "Malik. His name is Malik. He is the king of our little household."

Her mother took the child and inspected it, then pinched its cheeks. "Beautiful. A boy that would make any mother proud? Isn't your *sahib* home now? Did he allow you to come unaccompanied?"

"He is on a trip and I was lonely. I came alone." Meher looked at her mother's wrinkled face and saw that she had lost a couple more teeth, making her look even more aged than her fifty years. She reached forward with her good arm and placed her hand on her mother's shoulder and tears came to her eyes.

"Don't stand here. Come. Help me with the cooking. Come." She moved forward still carrying the baby who stared up into her face.

"How is father?" asked Meher Jamal.

The mother stopped and turned toward her. "Oh, you did not know. He is dead. Has no one told you?" She began to weep. "He hurt his leg while chopping fire wood. He took care of the wound like he always did. He tore a piece of cloth from his shirt immediately, urinated on it and pressed it to the wound to stop the bleeding. He tied it tightly. For four days he appeared to be better. Then he could not walk, his leg became swollen, then when the urine bandage was removed it had a bad smell. It was his *kismet*. His time of death was written in the great book." She handed the child back to Meher and sat on a small stool and stirred the lentils, tears streaming down her cheeks.

"Who is in charge of the household now?" Meher squatted near her mother, putting the child in the apron formed by the cloth between her legs.

"It is the mullah. He has taken over. Your young cousin Gulabi is his newest wife. He took her soon after your father's death."

☪

Dohst sat in the bow of the boat and watched the water hyacinths float by, some with purple flowers, but most with green shiny leaves sprouting from the round stem floats that gave them buoyancy. His thoughts were on his trip to Lahore to apply for a merchant license and make arrangements to purchase oil wholesale so he could set up a shop in Sialkot. But his thoughts were not on oil, they were on Piari, the young woman he had interviewed. When he woke up in the morning and drank his first cup of tea he thought of her. When he traveled and saw other women walking in the *burkahs* he thought of her. When he saw the purple flowers floating by he thought about the scarf she wore which had paisley designs in deep purple. He sighed and reached for a floating plant and plucked it out of the water, dripping on to his pants.

"Poets write about it!" The boat operator shouted at him.

"About what?" Dohst turned in his seat and looked at the elderly sweating man paddling hard to move against the current.

"The poet Malik-ul-shuara, of course. *Ishkh, piar, mohubuth*. Wild desire, sweet love, worshiping love, all the stages of love suffered by the one who can not possess, can not hold the beloved. All the great poets write of the same thing." He laughed as he pushed the oar deeply in the water. "Yours is the worst kind. Purple or blood red, *khuni* are the colors of madness. Longing that is so insane that even when the man is holding his wife in his arms during sex, all he can see and think of is the purple of the forbidden lover's eyes, the purple glint of the sun on her hair, even the strange purple perfume of her body which is hardly noticeable but which overwhelms even the smell of sandalwood." He laughed. "The blossom. Pick it. Rub the petals between your fingers!"

Dohst looked at the blossom in his hand, then at the ugly old face of the oarsman and shook his head. Then, curious, squeezed a purple petal between his fingers. The petal disintegrated easily, leaving a purple mush on his finger and thumb..

"Smell it!" shouted the boatman.

Dohst lifted his finger to his nose and smelled, then looked back at the boatman.

"See. Purple is the worst. Smells just like your fingers after you have stroked her *harf-i-shafti*." He put back his head and laughed at the sky. "Now feel your fingers."

Dohst had already noticed that the purple pulp was slippery and sticky. He threw the flower into the water and rinsed off his hands and turned to the boatman. "You seem to know a lot about the woman madness. It is hard for me to imagine that you ever came close to a beautiful woman, much less courted one." He began to laugh derisively.

"Before you were born. In my village there were three girls that desired me so much that they braved death or having their noses chopped off to come and sneak into my bed. Before you were born." He reached under the boat seat and opened a small tin trunk and pulled out a tattered and worn book and held it out to Dohst. "Here, read it while you are on the island. I will take it back when I return to get you."

Dohst took the tattered book and looked at the cover. He read in Urdu, Aziz Luknawa, the poet Mirza Mohammed Hadi. He flipped to the first poem and read, **Gulkana.** He noted that the poet had resided in Lucknow and that he had died in 1935.

"I have never heard of him," said Dohst.

"I think that you have never heard of any poet, nor have read a single poem in your life. Man, your mind will now turn purple with the sweet fragrance of the words. Your mind will sigh and weep. Your eyes will tear and your vision will be blurred with the beauty of words. Young people don't read, except the sterile words of school text books in English." He now moved the boat across the current so that the small craft would be taken to the southern tip of the island. "Who are you going to meet on the island?" He laughed at the sky again.

"It is not your concern." He looked away.

"Let me see. There is an old cow buffalo. No. There are two people on the island. One is an old dry hag.. The other a young slave woman with eyes of purple who now has had a female child. Let me see. Yes it must be the old dried up hag that you are going to visit. Strange. So many men pay me for my work to come to the island, policemen, traders, other young men who pluck purple hyacinths from the river and don't know poetry." He laughed loudly and held up the paddle and allowed a trickle of water to run to his hand.

"You are a real old bastard. I would suppose that you also stopped by the island to visit the old hag. She is about your age, but all bent up from childbirth and arthritis. Just the kind you would desire." Now Dohst laughed.

The old boat man nodded. "Yes. I met with her when she was the new concubine of... of your father, Sheikh Mohammed. He was gone a lot in his younger years. He left his women here and there while he traveled. Over the years, many times I visited the island. Sheikh Mohammed forgot that those who have boats can come to remote islands. Once she was so beautiful that I wrote a poem about her. She had a *til* on her left breast which was so beautiful it did not need that beauty spot to highlight it. My poem is folded into the last pages of the book. When you see her now, old and lame, read my poem and know that we all were born helpless and bloody, grew a bit and dirtied our legs with shit, staggered around with our first steps, lost our milk-teeth, grew pubic hair and thought we knew the answers to all the mysteries of the world; discovered the pleasure of a woman's body, slippery with sweat, grew even older and had our food chopped up finely so we could swallow it because our teeth had fallen out; again we dirtied our legs with our shit because we could not contain our bowels, wet our pants because of our weakened bladders, staggered to take a few steps on shaking knees and finally lay on a cot, unable to care for ourselves, following with our eyes the movements of our caretaker; hoping that tomorrow, tomorrow Allah will take us to paradise where once again the fields will be filled with young virgins with purple eyes and we will be eternally young and potent. We will know that the world we have left behind was not a mystery but simply an illusion of passion, *ishkh* and pain. We will know that for the moments of pleasure we took to satisfy our lust we left behind worlds of misery, pain, children who cried for food and that which was once beautiful was squashed by time like the purple mush on your fingers." He lifted his arms up to the sky, very impressed with his own words. Dohst shook his head.

The boat grated against the sand and Dohst stepped out and took his bag; paid the boatman and said, "I didn't know you could read. Were there schools back then?"

The old Mohanna did not smile. "Youth always thinks it is the first generation to discover that the sun rises. My father taught me to read, to write. But he taught me to love words. Stop at my crude house on your way back. I will show you the books he left me."

Dohst paid little attention to the man's speech. "One week. Come back in one week, old man. I will read your poem. What is the name of your poem?"

The old boatman shook his head. "I already told you. You don't listen well. It is Beauty Spot, *til.*"

Dohst held out his hand to shake the hand of the boatman but noticed that his index finger and thumb were purple. Instead of a handshake he waved and stepped onto the sand.

"Her eyes were large and purple-hued. Her breath was sweet like honey. Her legs like those of a fawn. Oh, Ankh! Oh Ankh!" sang the boatman at the top of his voice as the craft drifted away rapidly on the down-current. "Oh eyes of purple!"

☪

Feroz Hakim sat in the police chief's office chair and glanced about the room. His eye rested on the picture of the tiger above the desk. Irritated, he got up, took the framed picture from the wall and turned it to face the filing cabinets. Somehow, the room now seemed smaller and more dismal. The ceiling fan squeaked at each revolution, an incessant repetition of pain. He got up and turned it off. A gecko crawled across the wall stalking a fly. He watched as it got close, its body moving so slowly that even the fly was not disturbed. The tip of the tail of the gecko undulated slowly as the last inch of the stalk was carried out. Feroz was then surprised that the fly was in the mouth of the lizard. He had not seen the last quick lunge. Now the room was stiflingly hot. He got up again and put the fan on, this time on high speed. The squeaking now was almost constant. He lit a cigarette and opened the file in front of him. In it was an essay that had been mailed to him by his superior officer in Islamabad, an essay written by Ikbal the journalist a week earlier. He read the essay again, and the note pinned to it by his senior officer which read, "He has a way with words. He has a point that you failed to discover. The Humber was paid for. As to the matter of the affair of ten years ago, perhaps you would like to cast the first stone. The newly appointed Lahore Senior Superintendent of Police, Ramesh Khanna, will arrive to take over the position vacated by Sher Khan next week. Prepare the department for his arrival."

He looked up as one of his patrolmen knocked on the door. "Yes. Come in. What did you find?"

"Sir, I have written all the particulars about Mr. Ikbal Sufi's travels during the last two days. He seems to have the same schedule and do the same thing. Most of the day he is at the news office; he travels back and forth. He stops at the Chemist shop and takes tea at the same place. I have written it all. He did not meet anyone on the street. He has a habit of parking his car inside his courtyard behind the gate but he does not drive in forward, he backs the car in. That is all I know." He handed Feroz Hakim the three page report.

"Good. There is no need for keeping a watch on him. The Islamabad office has cleared his case." He held out a cigarette to the man who declined, saying he did not smoke, then changed his mind and took one, thinking to give it to his friend.

Feroz closed up the office and drove his car toward the section of town where Ikbal Sufi resided. This section was an area near the new Ravi Road Bridge. A new Internet Café had been built and many of the university youth came to it to get on the internet and send e-mails. Since the internet café had been established, many young people were able to communicate with each other, especially young elite women who were at home where there was a computer. They now could 'talk' with young men in distant parts of the city with ease. Near the Internet Café was a tea house where many young men met to talk and walk along parts of the Bund Road near the Ravi River. Here and there were areas where cars could be parked overlooking the river. Ikbal's house was situated on a rise near the intersection of the road that came from Data Ganj. Strangely, the view of the river was occluded by the high wall around Ikbal's compound, which cut off the breeze from the river as well as the view. Instead of building the entrance gate at the front along the Bund Road, the Sufi family had placed the gate on the river side which required that the driver pull around the compound and up into the gate area. The road sloped uphill away from the river.

Feroz drove his car near Ikbal's home and waited for him to return from work. He sat watching from his car. It was almost dark when Ikbal arrived home. He drove his car around the perimeter of the wall and then rather than pulling up to the gate and sounding his hooter, he turned the car around and backed toward the gate which strangely seemed to open as if by magic, except for the hand that could be seen pulling the gate inwardly. When the car was inside the compound the gate was closed again.

At dawn, Feroz was again parked across the Bund Road overlooking the Ravi River. He was rewarded. The gate opened and the car rolled forward on the slope without the engine on, then jerked as the clutch was let out and the motor roared to life as Ikbal left it in second gear and moved away, smoke coming out of the tail-pipe of the car. Feroz now followed the car at a safe distance but Ikbal drove straight across to Anarkali road and turned into his parking space in the area behind the newspaper office.

Feroz drove back to the Bund Road home and sat and watched the goings-on in the household. During the day many people came and went, traders carrying cloth, carpets and even scissors. When these people came into the household they were admitted by the old caretaker or gardener who simply pulled the gate shut but did not slide the bolt home. In a period of two hours, six different people entered and left. Then occupants of the home, including the chubby wife of Ikbal came and went. It was a busy place. He was surprised. His own home seldom had a daytime visitor.

Feroz strolled along the Bund to get a better idea of the way the house was protected. To his surprise, there was a section of old wall that had collapsed and had never been repaired, leaving but three feet of wall for an animal or person to traverse. The rest of the wall was secure. He now returned to his office and prepared for the coming of the new police chief, which meant that his promotion had not been approved, in fact, it was a well known fact that such new chiefs frequently selected their own deputy from among other police offices or from the new office. Seldom did a deputy remain for long with a new boss. He knew his days were numbered. He thought of Sher Khan's files. They could be a possible source of income, or at least protection and leverage in the future.

Feroz left his house at midnight and drove to the Bund and parked almost a half mile away from Ikbal's house. He had a torch but did not use it as it was easy to keep on the tar road in the dim light. In his pocket he carried a small packet of wrenches, taken from the tool kit of his own car. He approached Ikbal's house and observed it for a while, then walked around the wall to the broken section and waited. The night watchman had moved his cot under the protection of a porch ceiling and had pulled a cloth over his head to keep away the odd mosquito. Feroz could hear his snores. There was no dog on the premises. He stepped across the low wall and walked quietly toward the car which was parked right inside the gate, facing outward. He slid under the car and now used his torch to locate the hydraulic brake fluid tube. He found it and followed it with his finger until it reached the rear brake area. He saw that the tube was fitted into the rear of the drum with a fitting like a sleeve over the tube and that it was threaded. He tried three wrenches before finding one that fit. It was difficult for him to loosen the fitting, but when he did it, fluid dripped down the tool onto his arm. He loosened it more but did not remove it from its socket. He set the wrench on the ground and reached up to hand tighten the fitting. More brake fluid now dripped to the ground, but not being under pressure stopped and developed into a slow drip. Feroz slid out from under the car and walked carefully to the wall, stopped, and looked at the watchman who was still sleeping and left to find his car. He put the small packet of tools in his pocket.

He drove across the city to the red light district, Hera Mandi and parked his car at an establishment from which the sound of music came. He walked to the door and tapped it four times. A middle aged woman came, greeted him and he moved inside and sat on a cushion and watched a slender girl dancing. He asked to use the wash room and washed his hands and arms. Later he returned to the front room. Two greasy-haired musicians with red, *pan* stained teeth sat on a platform; one playing the *tubla* glanced up at him, nodded and continued with his music. The room reeked of incense and strong perfume. He reached forward and pulled a stick of Shah-Jahan incense from its holder and played with the smoke, moving his fingers through it. The smoke rose up in front of him and clung to his jacket. After half an hour of watching the dancing girl, he rose and went to the toilet area again. There he looked at the bottles displayed in the cabinet, condoms placed in a cup shaped like an inverted breast, perfumes of various sorts and eye darkener. He opened one bottle of perfume labeled Sherezad and dabbed it on his collar. When he returned a new girl was dancing. She was slender but rather tall. Her clothes were multicolored with gold stitching. He noticed her ankles first. Each ankle was encased with a string of small silver bells that jingled each time she hit her foot on the floor. Her feet seemed to be apart from the rest of her body. They kept a jangling rhythm going as her hands snaked around and her head shifted on her shoulders as she moved her neck. The scarf slipped from her head and without losing a beat she reached up for it. Feroz held out his hands and she smiled and danced over to where he sat and with a soft motion dropped the Benarsi scarf onto his outstretched arms. He could see her face clearly now, even the small blood vessels in her eyes. He looked up at her and smiles and she returned with a smile, revealing her very white and even teeth. She looked to be about thirteen.

He watched for half an hour, then stood and put a small roll of rupees on the table in front of the girl. She smiled with pleasure and motioned with her fingers for him to follow her. He shook his head, smiled, got up and left, carrying the flimsy scarf in his pocket.

It was nearly dawn when he finally returned to his home. His wife heard him enter and shouted at him, wondering where he had been and that she had been worried. He waited to answer, went to the tin trunk and placed the scarf on top of the row of brassier cups. He entered the bedroom where she was sitting up on the bed.

"I received a call that I should go to Model Town to assist a family that had their car stolen." He slid into the bed.

The smell of perfume and incense on him was strong. His wife leaned over and sniffed his hair, then began to scream. "Get out of my bed. Out of this room. You go to filthy whores and then expect that you can come back to me. Get out!" She held her nose. "You smell like prostitutes." She backed away from him. "What has become of you? Seeking out a small school girl to be a new wife and now visiting whores!"

"So how do you know what a prostitute smells like?" He laughed and picked up his shoes and moved into the second bedroom. He could hear his wife weeping and muttering in the room next to him that she would kill him rather than living with the shame of a husband who was insane for sex.

She would make a fine witness for his alibi for Ikbal Sufi's accidental death.

☪

Ikbal the journalist ate his breakfast on the verandah. He slurped the hot sweet tea, chewing on greasy fried bread. On a plate there were a number of white radishes sliced into chunks. He picked up one and dipped it into the salt and red pepper condiment dish and chewed happily. His wife came and stood near him and asked, "Is the battery dead again? Why don't you use the starter?"

"All our neighbors have bought new batteries. This is the original battery of this car and it is still full of juice. I think I have saved four batteries already."

She walked to the kitchen muttering to herself, 'stingy'. She fingered her wrap-around scarf and muttered again that she needed two new garments.

At exactly seven thirty, as was his custom, he picked up his briefcase and left the house. He glanced toward the night watchman and saw he was still asleep under his cloth. Quietly he tip-toed toward him and carefully tied one end of the loose cloth near his head to the foot of the bed. He did the same with the cloth at the end of the bed. He walked to his car and turned toward the still snoring man.

"*Chor! Chor!* Thief, thief," he cried out loudly.

The watchman tried to sit up but the cloth across his chest held him down. Frustrated he rolled over and the bed tipped over onto him. He began to shout, not knowing whether the thief was attacking him. He yelled loudly, "Chor! Chor!" The alarm whistle hung on a string around his neck, and now still struggling with the bed he began to blow on it, the high piercing notes echoing from the walls.

Ikbal opened the car door and beeped his hooter. The frustrated watchman came running now and opened the metal gate. Ikbal, laughing at the good joke he had played on the guard pointed at him and shook his head in derision. He released the hand brake, put in the clutch and let the car gain speed as it rolled forward. He jerked the clutch and the engine came to life moving him rapidly down the slope in second gear. He put on the brakes and the pedal became soft and moved all the way to the floor. He pumped the brake pedal wildly screaming, "Allah!"

Now he tried to steer left on the entry road but he was moving too fast. The car bumped off the road and ran down a small hill toward the Ravi River, toward a drop-off of many feet. At last he remembered the emergency brake and pulled it up with all his might. The rear wheels skidded on the soft dirt and the car moved to the very edge of the drop-off, one of the front wheels now sagging in the soft sand. The car lurched forward in slow motion. The other front wheel slid down the edge but the rear brakes held by the emergency lever kept the car from going off the edge. The weight of the front of the car caused the car to move forward slowly, almost reluctantly through the sand. Ikbal opened the car door to leap out just as it plummeted down the twenty foot steep incline toward a huge pile of rocks piled there for use by the On Farm Water Management crew for making a flume. The car, still running, hit the rocks, the momentum carrying the front of the car past the pile, but crushing the rear end and the petrol tank. Fuel flew in an arc onto the rocks. The car slid forward, the metal grating against the stones, sparking. There was an explosion as the fuel ignited.

Standing at the top of the rise was the night watchman who was shrieking incoherently, waving his arms. Passing cars stopped and in a minute there was a crowd that gathered and stood watching the car burn brightly. The body of Ikbal was not seen. He had tried to leap from the car but the impact of its body against the stones had thrown his head against the doorjamb and he sprawled back onto the seat as the flames engulfed him.

"Whose car was that?" shouted a driver of a bus to the watchman.

"He was the *Sahib* who wrote for the newspaper. Ikbal Sahib. That is his great house." The man was weeping. "He will not have a burial like a good Muslim. He will be nothing but ashes like the Hindu corpses."

They watched the flames for a few moments and then the truck driver replied, "*Maute se age chote bare sab barabar.*" (At the time of death, the small and the great are all equal.)

The crowd replied, "*Wah!*" They were amazed at the poetic utterance of one so low. There was a smell of burning hair on the wind.

$$\text{☾}^{\star}$$

"Don't bother him. He has the new girl. The television set is on. They are probably...." The old woman bent over and cackled as she moved past the door. The other woman carrying a tray with tea and biscuits bent down and set the food on a low stool. The two women went off with their heads together, gossiping.

At ten in the morning the generator was turned off automatically. The television set was quiet. Twice, the women walked by the door and put their ear to it, listening carefully and hearing nothing.

"They are not talking. She is not crying. He is not yelling. Nothing!" Now she tapped on the door tentatively. When there was no response she pounded on it hard. She tried the door handle and found it was locked from the inside.

Two men worked on the door. It had been hung so that the hinges were concealed and the pin was only accessible from the inside. The latch was of metal and it slid into the metal in the door jam, making it difficult to break. The door was expensive and they were loath to ruin it but finally in frustration they called a carpenter. He drilled a hole, then with a key-hole saw cut an opening big enough for a hand to enter. He reached inside and pulled the lever back and door gaped open. Three men stood quietly, transfixed. The blood had already dried and was black on the sheets and the floor. Sahib-ji's body lay like a bloated dead toad on the Persian carpet.

Strangely, the men did not shout or carry on. They looked at each other, then tentatively, almost guiltily they stepped into the room as if they were invading another man's *zennanah*. None of them had ever seen the interior of Sahib-ji's room, though it had been the focus of gossip among them. They glanced at the body on the floor, bending over to see the wound on the neck, avoiding the blood on the carpet. Their quick eyes glanced at the objects on the desk tops, the table tops, at the briefcase pushed under the table.

"Ali, you and the carpenter go run and tell the others what we have found. I will wait here. Bring the other men." The oldest, heavily bearded one, a local mullah, spoke.

The others glanced at the wallet on the floor, at the brief-case, wondering, but they obeyed and then as they backed out of the room began to scream and shout the news. The older man immediately picked up the wallet and looked inside, scanned the contents, swore and disappointed threw it on the floor. He quickly went to the brief-case and tried to open it but it had a combination number lock. Frustrated, he pulled out his long knife, pried the latch back and rifled through the contents, all papers, files, lists, numbers on papers, e-mail addresses, and a few pictures of nude women at the bottom. He pulled these out and stared at the crude photos, obviously amateur efforts taken in Hera Mandi in Lahore or some other brothel. The frontal black and white pictures were of the young girls, standing naked. The black places seemed to be blots on the overexposed surfaces, hair, eyebrows, nipples, pubic hair. They stood with their hands at their sides staring at the camera and they had no smiles on their faces. Two were thin and angular, the third, overly large at the hip. He glanced at the dead body, then back at the photographs. He shook his head and threw these onto the pile from the case just as a crowd of men returned. They entered and looked at the body, at the pile of papers on the floor, the blood and the photographs. Three youths moved closer to the pile on the floor to glance more carefully at the nude photos.

It took more than an hour for the crowd to decide what should be done. They shouted and cursed and carefully looked over all the items in the room.

"He had a gun. A gun! Where is his gun?"

"He always carried a roll of money; where is all the money?"

"She should be easy to spot, long beautiful black hair, American clothes."

"No. She left the high heels and the clothing in the closet. What did she wear?"

"Where could a helpless girl go? We are miles from the nearest town?"

"Look! I found this under his vest. Her hair. Why would she cut off her hair?" the young man held a thick lock of Chamuck's hair in his hand and felt its texture with his thumb and his fingers and then smelled it and passed it to his friend Kemal.

"What time is it? When did she leave here? She had to walk."

"Get the Toyota four-wheeled-drive ready. Four of us will go up the dirt road and catch up to her."

"We will take our horses and explore the country-side. The demon girl must be caught. Do we kill her when we find her?"

"No! No! Bring her back here, you fool. We must try her. It is a matter of our honor. No reports to the police. Nothing. Here. We will behead her. Dishonor! She owes us a debt of blood."

The young man who had found the lock of hair, put it into his pocket. He went to the latrine and lifted the thick lock of curly black hair to his nose and smelled it carefully, his eyes closed. Then he took out his cell phone and called his older cousin, Sardar, who lived across the border in Afghanistan.

He had contracted with Sahib-ji to sell rockets and now he called to warn his cousin not to complete any shipments to Peshawar.

"Sardar, Sahib-ji is dead. Don't worry now. Do you know that girl he took from Peshawar, the one with the dark hair, the school girl with big breasts?" He listened for a minute still holding the hair to his lips and nose. "Yes, that one. She killed him and escaped. I can't talk more. Don't worry about the last shipment of arms now. He can't collect any debts owed to him now and he can't pay for any shipments." He listened carefully and was reminded to look out for a brief case that contained an orange-colored notebook that had the lists of all the people that owed Sahib-ji money. He was told to get that little book. He hung up and returned to the murder scene, adjusting his lower garments. Three men had cell phones against their ears and were talking softly. He sauntered over toward the pile of documents on the floor near the open brief case. He dropped his hat accidentally, stooped to pick it up and with the hat scooped up a small notebook.

One caller waited for his Peshawar number to pick up the phone, tapping his toe on the carpet. "Peshawar News." "Listen, this is Rafi. Sahib-ji was killed by a ...."

It was high noon before the various groups took off, shouting and yelling, brandishing their weapons in their right hands as they rode off on their snorting horses. "Honor!" shouted Kemal, the leader of the group of horsemen, wearing a beautiful new leather jacket and a brown colored beret placed jauntily on his head. "I swear an oath on the *Takht i Suliman*, that mountain there, a life for a life!"

CHAPTER TWELVE

Jan ki evaz jan; khun ke badle khun.

An oath: Life for a life; blood exchanged for blood.

Pretending she was mute presented problems. It was difficult to get her request across to the villager. She pantomimed but finally had to write her request on a wrapping paper. Chamuck only had to pay three hundred rupees to the villager to drive her to the nearest town where she could pick up a bus to Peshawar. She sat next to the driver and stared out of the window while he asked questions. She pointed to her mouth and shook her head, grunting in the lowest voice she could muster. He explained to her that their village of Kiyar was near the Lutkoh River which they would soon cross in the mostly dry river bed. The next larger village was Chitral where he would drop her off and fill his tank with petrol. He told her that there was a hotel there, the Shai Bazaar Hotel near to the bus station and that for about one hundred rupees she could get a sleeping room and eat there as the food was good, and to wait for the next early morning bus heading south toward Peshawar. She grunted and nodded and fondled the gun between her legs, her hands moving up and down the cool, smooth, black barrel. The driver was fascinated with her action. His eyes left the road as he glanced at the soft hands moving up and down, pausing to feel places where the manufacturer's insignia had been stamped into the metal. She was initially unaware that her actions had such a strong effect on the driver. Then she noticed his eyes on her hand as it stroked the black barrel.

"It is the only way. If your family has not arranged a marriage for you to some young woman, it is the only way. Before I had my four wives, I too stroked the barrel, for years." He laughed. "You will find that in Chitral there is a small pleasure house in the old bazaar where...."

Chamuck frowned, glanced at the man and shook her head and stopped stroking the rifle barrel, holding it now at a downhill angle toward her feet. The road was rough and from time to time the bumps were so severe that they were lifted off their seats. She hung on to the hand restraint, trying to look nonchalant as the driver roared across a mostly dry river bed and then gunned it up the other side, the sand flying.

Chital was a bustling place with many bazaars, jewelry stores, hat factories, and food stalls. There were people from many places, from Afghanistan, Kashmir and the Punjab. There were even American hikers, fair Kashmiri women, women dressed in black from Saidu Sharif, and mountain people from the Hindu Kush. She got off at the Bazaar Hotel and strolled through the crowd which ignored her. She paid for a room. The keeper said that Chamuck would have to share it with another man. She shook her head and held up one finger. He laughed.

"Pretty young boys like you need to be careful. Yes, very careful. But you will pay double for the trouble; a room with two beds." He leaned forwards and looked at her neck and ears, at the smooth skin of her face. She frowned and defensively adjusted the rifle and slung it across her back aggressively. The band of cartridges rattled against the stock.

"The food is good here. Do you want to have a brass tray of food brought up to your room tonight?" She nodded. "I will bring it personally." He gave her the key and he turned to the next customer.

Chamuck lay on the hard cot and stared at the ceiling trying to work out what to do next. Her first thoughts were of the executions she had seen on television. The picture had shown that the Taliban in Kabul had made convicted women kneel down in an open courtyard. These women, they said, had violated Sharia, the laws of Allah. She was quiet as she thought of the slumping bodies of the decapitated women. What, she thought, if she went to Peshawar? No. The people from the village of Sahib-ji would be waiting there, having talked to the driver who had brought her to Chitral. They would assume she would go to Peshawar to find the members of her family at her father's home. She thought, someone would be waiting for me there, expecting my return. They would beat the women to have them reveal where I was hiding. I would be caught. If they did catch me what would they do? Now her mind raced. When she was home the women of the family had talked about the executions and news that came of how the bodies of the decapitated women had been violated and not buried, the ultimate dishonor because they would not rise on the judgment day. The bodies had been stripped and thrown outside the city walls to rot to be eaten by vultures and dogs.

They would drive me back to Sahib-ji's compound, she thought, and the men of the family would meet and judge me. I owe them a blood debt. All the citizens of Sahib-ji's compound, women and children alike would be called together to witness my punishment and understand that it was a matter of honor. I would be made to kneel and one of the men would sharpen his sword in front of my eyes, then, cut off my head while they all cheered, "Blood pays for Blood, Life pays for Life!" Then my body would be hacked to pieces and taken to the wall of the compound where the stray dogs gathered. The last piece would be my head which they would impale on a post in the middle of the open area and leave it there to rot. They would place a long piece of bloody glass in my mouth. Young boys would use my skull for target practice with their sling shots, shouting happily when they shot out my eyes and knocked the glass out of my mouth. I would never be buried. No holy words would be said at a religious burial. In the Last Days of Judgment, my body would not be taken by Allah because I would be dog dung scattered across the hills, the wind blowing my dust to Afghanistan.

She thought about the look on the face of Sahib-ji as the long shard of glass knifed into his neck, his hand still up high between her legs. She smiled. Her father would approve. She had maintained the honor of the family. "That *Shaitan* does not have the right to live!"

She lay for a long time, unable to think of what to do. She had nowhere to go, no destination, and no home. She knew no one outside her own family except her badminton teacher. The lack of options left her with a feeling of such hopelessness that she turned on the cot and sobbed. Someone knocked on the door. She got up quickly, stood behind the door and when the servant entered with the food, she pointed to the bed. He set the tray on the bed and looked toward her. She handed him five rupees. He nodded and left.

In spite of her hopelessness, the aroma of the food made her realize she was ravenous. She hunched over the large brass plate and ate without stopping until all the food was consumed. She put the tray on the floor outside the door. There was a small table in the room. She pushed this against the door since the door had no internal lock.

Again she stared at the ceiling. She was a prisoner even though she was now free. Pakistan was her prison, *purdah* was her jailor, her gender was her chains, her ability to read and do sums her liability. The words of the poem she had memorized again came to her, *"Or to her death, according to our law."*

She fell asleep. She dreamed of pigs grunting, low ugly sounds. She was awakened by the grunting in the room next to her, the deep voices of two men who writhed on the cot next to the wall, shaking the thin partition. She sat up, breathing hard. Her school mates had spoken of this practice and the girls had all whispered together trying to understand the meaning and the possibility of men with men. *Adbhut walla.* Queer folk, they had muttered. The noises were intimate and seemed to be in the same room where she was trying to sleep. Finally they quieted and slept but she could not sleep. She tossed and turned restlessly.

Not Peshawar, she thought. Not Peshawar, but Lahore. I will go to Lahore where my uncle took us when I was a child. We stayed far out in the country in a small rest house, Changa Manga in the forest. Yes. He said the rest house was cheap, a place where the wealthy people of Lahore came for a week-end, to picnic and take walks in the woods.

Now she remembered the small narrow-gauge railroad that went through the park and their family sitting together in one of the carriages as the tiny train ran along crooked rusted tracks. Lahore. A train! Yes. She sat up and lit the candle. In her pocket was the packet of credit cards of Sahib-ji and the code numbers for taking money from an ATM. She looked at each one carefully and tried to match the card with the Pin numbers on the cards. She was so engrossed with her task that she did not hear the door being pushed open slowly. The table-leg caught on a crack and tipped over. She turned in panic, grabbed her rifle and cocked the gun, the bolt making a snapping metallic noise in the breech that everyone knew and understood.

"Take care! Sorry. I am in the wrong room. *Khabardar.* Take care." The proprietor backed out, muttering.

She sorted the cards again and counted her wad of money, more money than she had seen in her life. Lahore and Changa Manga. Her uncle had a phone. She would call him when she got there.

She wandered into the town of Chitral. People turned to look at her dressed like a man. She stopped at a store that sold small cardboard suitcases. She bought one. Then she went to a shop that sold ready-made *burkahs*. She selected two, both the most expensive in the shop with embroidering on the sleeves and hem. She bought two pairs of shoes in matching colors, not trying them on, knowing her own size. The proprietor nodded in understanding.

"For a big senior sister?" He laughed. Chamuck nodded.

She returned to the hotel, packed the men's clothing she could use into the suitcase with the second *burkah*, dressed herself in the second outfit, a deep blue one with the eye area open, rather than wearing the one which had the crisscross mesh. Under this she wore the pants she had worn with deep pockets, in which she carried her money and cards. This made her look bulky, almost pregnant, however, the very expensive clothing would elicit respect and people would avoid her as she walked the streets or rode on a bus.

The gun! What should she do with the gun? There was a large window in the room that looked like it had not been opened in years. The glass panes had been painted over for privacy. Two large spikes had been pounded against the window to keep anyone from entering. She was unable to move these aside. She had no lever, no bar, no hammer. She looked around the room and saw the gun. She picked it up and placed the end of the barrel over the top of the large nail. It fit. She leveraged the spike to the side with the gun barrel easily. She did the next. She worked on the window and it took her a few minutes to pry it open. Chicken wire was tacked in front of the opening. She moved it away with the stock of the gun. She pushed the gun and suitcase through, moved the little table and climbed on the sill and jumped to the ground. There was a drainage ditch in front of her where raw sewage and garbage fermented. She pushed the gun into this sludge, submerging it.

She walked to the bus station, her new blue high-heeled shoes clicking on the tarmac. Some men turned to glance at her, at her shoes and clothing and then quickly looked away. She looked at Sahib-ji's expensive watch. At seven in the morning she enquired for buses going to Peshawar, paid for an expensive ticket, which allowed her to sit on the front seat. She would tell the bus driver to let her off at the old fort. From there it would be but a ten minute walk to the railway station where she would book a Second

Class Ticket on the train to Lahore. No, she thought, a First Class Ticket. It was difficult for her to spend money, to buy the best, to act as a wealthy woman. She remembered the small dramas that the English teacher had made the girls take part in, where for various parts in the plays the girls took on deep voices, high squeaking voices, or seductive voices of a young woman. She decided to use a deep voice of a middle-aged woman of thirty when she bought the ticket.

"Don't forget to drop me off at the fort." She glanced at the driver. The brass carrot was in still in her palm, her worry stone.

"Ji, begum. Yes ma'am I will not forget."

C*

Smoke rose up from the river bed, black and acrid. Feroz Hakim pulled his car over and placed a blue police flasher on the top of his vehicle, jumped out energetically and blew his police whistle as he moved forward to clear a path among the crowd that gathered. He joined the crowd and looked down the incline and saw the car burning. As he watched, the tires caught fire and orange flames rose again, this time with the odor of burning rubber. Two other foot patrolmen joined him but stood respectfully back. He nodded at them and now they cleared a space around him, pushing spectators back.

He took out his cell phone and made two calls, asking for other police units to join him as well as an ambulance. He looked around to see if he could locate the night watchman who he could recognize because of his bright red Fez. He saw him at the edge of the crowd talking animatedly to a group of people around him. He strolled over and joined the crowd and listened in as the watchman spoke.

"He beeped his hooter. I was working on the other side of the house and ran quickly to the gate to open it for my master. He sat quietly in the car and he was laughing."

One bystander asked, "Why do you think he was laughing?"

The night watchman knew he had misspoken, remembering the joke that had been put on him. "Perhaps he was coughing, not laughing. I opened the gate and he let the car roll forward."

"Didn't he start the car?" One young boy was curious.

"No. No. I told this already the last time. He did not start the car! Instead he let it roll forward as he always did. At the end of the hill he let out his clutch and the engine started because the car's gear had been placed in second. He always did this. He was a battery saver. He hardly used his headlights at night when he drove, saying there was plenty of light from the other cars. Just his parking lights. He was a battery saver. It was six years old." He turned and looked at the faces around him. "Imagine, six years. A battery saver."

The boy called out, "How did he go over the edge into the river bed? Tell it again!"

"He let out the clutch, the motor started and the car moved forward in gear as it always did. He put on the brakes, I could see him put them on again and again, because the rear red lights flashed over and over quickly, but the car streaked downhill and he could not make the turn by the time he looked up. The car bumped off the road and went into the sand. Then he put on the brakes but the lights did not come on. The rear brakes locked and dragged in the sand but it moved forward, forward, slowly, until the front two wheels came to the edge. The sandy slope moved and the wheels slid over. The car hung there. I could hear him screaming. Allah. Allah. Then it went over, hit the rocks and exploded into fire. Katash!" His hands went up above his head. "Katash!" He stood back and looked at the effect he had on his audience.

Feroz Hakim the Deputy now moved forward. "Come with me. He held a pair of handcuffs in his hand. You were the last one to see your master. Laughed. You said he laughed. Come. Was he mocking you? "

The man cringed and moved back and away from the officer, his face now a mask of terror. "I have done nothing. I just opened the gate. Nothing."

Feroz looked at him sternly. "Put out your hands. There is a reason you said laughed. It was a slip, but all criminals slip. You are a suspect. This is a suspicious event. Very, very suspicious. Laughing, you say." He snapped the cuffs on the man.

"What crime sahib? He did not control his car and it went off the road and he died? What crime, Hazoor?" He was weeping. Feroz looked stern and distant.

The crowd moved away from their hero, now looking at him with their heads held to the side, glancing at him sideways to see if they could see him in this new light as a suspect. The boy shouted out, "Was the battery dead, disconnected, so he had to use his clutch to start the car?"

"You stupid owl's offspring. The lights would not go on if the battery was dead or turned off. You can't start a car with the key off!" A man in the crowd reached over to hit the boy on the head, but he ducked, laughing. Now the crowd began to murmur and a few called out the prisoner's low Christian caste-name, Joshua.

"But he told a long story about the battery. He was making a point about the battery. Why?" shouted the boy from the edge of the crowd.

Feroz pushed the man forward toward Ikbal's house and saw a group of women standing at the gate. One of them was a buxom woman who was bending over weeping, keening and falling backwards. The other women caught her and patted her, and then they too began to keen and weep loudly.

"Widow!" screamed the woman. "I am a widow! Allah help me."

"Get behind the gate," shouted Feroz. "Are there other servants here? Cooks, *dhobis*, gardeners?" He looked at the crowd of women. Now they became quiet, all except the wife who reduced her wailing so she could hear what the police office said, not wanting to miss any of the comments.

"Yes. All of them. Also there is a cousin living here who goes to college." The women moved back toward the house shouting information over their shoulders.

"Send them all to me. We will meet on the verandah and I want a statement from each for the FIR. All of them!"

The first to arrive was the cook, always the prime suspect in any crime. More crimes had been solved in Lahore with cooks, who confessed to almost anything, as their feet swelled from the interrogation, as canes hit the soles of their feet. They all were thieves because it was well known that they lived off the foods that were prepared in the kitchen. Two tablespoonfuls of tea a day, four of sugar, all the left-over chapattis, the bottles that were cleaned carefully and sold to the bottle *wallah* that came every Saturday.

"What is your name?" asked Feroz.

"Pindi Massih, Hazoor." He bowed a little as he said the last word.

"Christian?"

"My name is, but I am a believer, truthfully a believer. That is my father's name, Hazoor." He bowed more deeply now. His voice cracked.

"Did Sahib Ikbal give you a raise in salary this year?"

He remained quiet and looked around at all the other faces on the porch. It was a well known fact that Ikbal was stingy; he pinched his money, hated to part with even the money for a new battery in six years. The others looked away, not wanting to be implicated in the story the cook told. All who were gathered there took interest in the crowd by the river bank, ignoring the cook.

"I take your quietness to mean that you did not receive a raise. Did you hate your master because he did not give you raises? Have you argued with him?"

Again he was quiet. Now Feroz looked around at all the people on the porch and they avoided his eyes, confirming what the cook had implied. The master, Ikbal Sahib, was a stingy, selfish man.

"How many children do you have?" asked Feroz.

"Eight, and one soon to be born." He began to cry. "Yet the salary stayed the same."

"Has the sahib ever given you a big gift at the end of the year? Whiskey, that you Jesu followers love so dearly? New clothes and uniforms?" The cook sagged to the floor. Feroz turned quickly to face a man with wrinkled hands. "So. You wash and iron all the clothes. I won't even ask your name. You look like the cook's brother. Do you love the sahib?"

The man did not speak; he nodded his head up and down, then, rocked his head from side to side on his neck as if he had no spine.

"You!" He spun on his heels and looked at an old man with mud on his feet, his *dhoti* cloth pulled up between his legs. "Name?"

"Ram Das, Hazoor."

"Hindu?" The crowd members around him were all nodding their heads. He did not reply but dropped his head and rested his chin against his chest. He moved the toes of one foot over the other trying to dislodge the dried mud.

"Where do you do *puja*, Mr. Ram Das?"

"No. No *puja* any more. My father did, Hazoor, at the time of the Partition." Around him the crowd members smiled and shook their heads. From the back of the crowd the boy again shouted, "*Hanuman wallah*! Monkey worshiper! I saw the picture of the monkey god when I looked into the doorway of his house." This time a man in the crowd was able to connect and swatted the boy across the head.

"Both of you write your names here on this paper." The cook moved forward and scribbled his name, printing his name in large uneven letters. The gardener came forward and wrote his name in Hindi characters, then seeing his mistake, looked up guiltily and handed the paper back.

"This is Pakistan! You either write in English, the official language or Urdu the language of literature and commerce. Write your name in Urdu."

"I learned Hindi in school, Hazoor. I do not write Urdu."

He took out an ink pad from his pocket. "Place your thumb against this ink pad. Now, press your thumb on the paper."

Feroz turned abruptly and began to stride away; then he turned and pointed at the three men. "Do not leave Lahore." The unfortunate gate watchman stood dejectedly with his hands still cuffed. Feroz was almost at his car when he remembered he did not have the cuffs with him. He motioned for the man to come forward and he undid the cuffs. The crowd on the verandah sighed.

Smoke continued to billow up from the river bed as Feroz drove away toward his office. The radio was broadcasting the national daily news. The female broadcaster said,

"*A wealthy and well-known merchant named Sahib-ji was reportedly murdered in his remote border village in the tribal area, killed by a girl. Police have named the suspect as a young woman, a school girl and resident of Peshawar, by the name of Chamuck who, family members reported, had been abducted and taken to Sahib-ji's compound some months back. However, a representative of Sahib-ji's household stated that a signed and witnessed marriage contract for the girl had been made with the girl's father and that she had not been abducted. The school girl, allegedly the new wife of the man, escaped in the night, dressed in the clothing of a man and carrying a gun. She can be recognized by her hair which has been cut to look like that of a man. Anyone who sees her is asked to report to their local police so that she can be apprehended. The honor of the family must be preserved. Blood has been spilled.*

There was a rocket explosion in a madrassah near the Frontier. The origin of the rocket is not known at this time, however, it is believed that American forces in Afghanistan may....

☪

She stepped out from behind the wall into the path carrying the child in her arms. Ankh watched as Dohst got out of a boat and strode toward her. Her unflinching gaze disturbed him so he stopped and lit up a cigarette, turned around and squatted in the path and urinated. When he turned around, Ankh was still staring at him, her large eyes moving up and down his body as he drew near to her.

"Why? Why are you staring at me?" asked Dohst.

"Why? Why are you returning at this late date? You said you would come long ago. Look!" She held out the child.

Dohst looked at the baby now and noticed that the child was pretty, her skin fair and her body plump and full. "Oh. He looks pretty."

"She. Look at me now. What do you see?" Ankh seemed to be angry.

"I don't know what you mean. You look the same. What?"

She nodded at him. "Not the same. Do you understand about being alone? No one to talk to. No one to laugh with. No one to share food with. No one to whisper together with when the night is dark and the wind is blowing. Do you understand that the child does not speak to me, she cries. Do you understand that the old woman no longer talks, she just drinks her sweet tea and sits with her legs stretched out in the sun and hums and sings the same song over and over. Do you understand that the boat people, not you, have helped me to get food, to get the buffalo cow with calf, to buy a single dress to wear in the market across the river?" Now she began to cry and turned around, placed the child on the path and spoke over her shoulder. "A girl! Not a son! Yours. Take it."

She moved toward the gate of the compound. Dohst had never picked up a baby before, but he saw ants on the trail so he reached down and picked up the squirming child and looked at its face, then looked up at Ankh moving away from him. He followed her to the compound and seeing her waiting held out the child to her. She smiled but her eyes were angry. She took the baby.

"You have no idea what it is like to be alone and go through labor pains and bear a child. It is terribly lonely. Where were you during the last two months? You promised to return before the birth of the child."

He ignored her tirade." I have brought you a present. I bought it in Lahore." He reached into his pocket and pulled out a gold filigree necklace and held it out to her.

She stared at the shiny gold object and thought of her mother who had always worn a similar marriage necklace, day and night, even when she bathed. She took the gift and stared at it in her hand. Rather than put it on her neck, she draped it across the neck of the baby.

"Gift for a bride, little one." She held out the child to Dohst again. He took it and then was surprised to see Ankh undo the knots of a crude string that hung around her neck on which hung a tiny silver bell. She took the gold necklace and put it around her own neck, held her hand to her neck as if her splayed fingers had eyes and could see how beautiful it looked against her smooth skin.

She smiled broadly, tears filling her eyes. She handed him the little silver object. "I am angry at you but I am happy you thought about me. I am happy you came back. I have cared for your property carefully." She took the child again. "Let us go into the house. I have something to show you."

She turned and walked in front of him. Her slender female form moved under her thin cloth and Dohst stared at her hips and back as if seeing them for the first time. He mused, the child is mine, but I do not know the mother; I hardly recognize her; she is a stranger to me and such a beautiful one.

Ankh walked to the wall where a picture was hanging backwards. She turned it over and stood under it, her hand on the new necklace. She was smiling. He saw the crude letter he had written that had freed her from slavery.

"What shall I do? Where should I go? How can I live? I can no longer go home to my family. My father would cut off my nose or my head. I cannot eat unless I have work that pays me money so I can buy food. I have no husband. I have no home. I am not a slave, but I am a slave here, unable to move or live. Tell me Dohst Sahib, what am I free from? What shall I do?"

A shaft of sunlight streamed through the high ventilation window onto her hair. Red-gold rusty highlights shone from her hair and the gold on her neck seemed to burn. Dohst stared at her, his mouth open, struck by her beauty. He remembered the first time he had held her on the sand bank, her long girlish legs, her smooth skin and the flecks of gold shining from her purple tinted eyes. He sighed deeply and stepped forward toward her, aroused.

"Tell me first. Tell me what I should do?" She saw desire and intention in his eyes and now she held out her hands, palms toward him as if to fend him off. He reached out and held her hands in his own, palms to palms and moved forward toward her, pulling her to him. She was shaking her head.

"Dohst Sahib, please, do not tempt me again. The last time..."she glanced at the child. "You are the father of that child. Tell me what to do? Do you want another child from a woman who is not a slave but still a slave?" Tears fell to the floor.

Dohst reached forward and held her; put his arms around her and her body convulsed in sobs as she repeated again and again, "Tell me. Tell me." Her arms reached around his body and she held him momentarily and whispered, "Dohst, tell me."

He remained quiet. She pushed away from him with surprising strength and stood back looking at his surprised face. "You have nothing to tell me? I was hoping you would tell me some thing that could change my life. Nothing?"

He seemed confused. "What is there to tell? I think you are very beautiful. Even more beautiful than when I first saw you. I think that I want to hold you again."

"It is not a matter of beauty and holding. What should I do, Dohst? I cannot stay here alone with your child. How would I do that? You have not solved that part of my life and I understand now what I mean to you. Have you suggested that you would marry me? No. Have you suggested that you have affection for me, care for me, think of me, not just so you can have pleasure but because I am important for you, for your life? No." A river of tears streamed down her cheeks.

"You do not understand. You see I have two houses and..." he hesitated. "And I have a young son, younger than your daughter and I am starting a new business in Sialkot and ..."

"If you have a new son, you must have had another woman who means more to you. A son! Yes, now I understand. I suspect that she is not a slave women and that she is very beautiful. I suspect that the two of you talk of many things and that she makes you laugh." She moved two steps backwards.

The vision of Pagali, her mouth half open in a perpetual smile came to him." She died in childbirth. Another woman was caring for her and is now raising him." Dohst stepped forward.

"No. One. Two. Three. Another woman? You amaze me. So did you have two women in Sialkot at the same time or how did this other woman appear so quickly?" Her face was a mask of sarcasm.

"I hired her to take care of my cousin, my... wife who was not well. The servant woman is waiting for me to return." He was amazed that he was talking about Meher. He remembered her words, 'When you speak of me what do you say about me?'

"You were busy, two women and a son. What are you going to do with this island home of your father Sheikh Mohammed? Are you going to sell it? Are you going to keep it? How will it be maintained? Who will protect it from being vandalized by anyone who has a boat and comes to the island? Who will protect me? Is the paper I gave you about owning this island of any value? Will you some day give it to your son?" She spoke so fast he could hardly catch all the questions.

"I had not thought much about it." He laughed and took out a cigarette.

Her hand was on her new gold necklace now. "Why did you buy me this, then?"

"I thought that it had been a long time and that the only thing I gave you was a tiny silver bell the last time we..." he paused, "and that I should get a better present for you this time." He blew smoke.

"This time? What? This time so you can crawl into my bed for sex?"

Her use of crude words for the sexual act made him frown. He remained quiet and stared at her, thinking that when he bought the necklace he had planned to put it on her when she was naked and that she would be pleased with it and....

She undid the necklace now and placed it on the small brass table near him. "I will no longer wear it, but since it is mine, I will sell it so I can buy onions, meat and a bag of rice. I understand why you gave it to me. You understand too. I was to be paid like one of the women in Heera Mandi, a prostitute, I, the mother of your child, paid in gold filigree."

He moved toward the table to retrieve the necklace and she stood angrily in front of him. "No! It is mine. I earned it caring for this place. Look around you. Is it clean and sparkling? Has anything been stolen? Look around, Dohst. Are you a blind man who sees nothing more that a curved body, a beautiful face," she glanced at his hand, "a man whose fingers always have the smell of purple hyacinths?"

"So, what do you want?" Dohst looked about the room impatiently.

"No, man, what do you want? What is good for you and your children? What is good for your home here? Do you think I will be here the next time you simply decide to drop by on the island bringing another gold necklace?" She spoke in derision.

"Yes." He was thinking of the words of the American woman Celia. 'So Dohst, when you said you wanted to do dating with me you really wanted to have sex. Right?' He sighed. The face of the American School girl student, screwed up in distaste came to him now. 'You creep. Is this how you get your jollies?' His father's words of stepping into deep water came to him but his thoughts were interrupted by her voice.

"Once more, Sahib Dohst. What shall I do?" She watched his face and when he looked up held his gaze steadily until he dropped his eyes.

He thought of a solution, one which would make her available to him and which would also insure that the house would have care. "Could you stay here and take care of the place? I would pay you for your work each month and pay for the expenses of keeping up the place."

"No. Not like that. You will expect to return and bring me gifts and I will be lonely and our daughter will not have a father and I will be no more than a freed slave who you will serve you and your needs. No." She turned about angrily.

"All right, what do you want?" He was surprised at his own question.

She spun around. "Have you thought about taking me back with you to Sialkot to be part of your family there? Have you thought about me as a friend? A friend who you can trust, who confides in you and who you like to talk to? Dohst, I want to marry a man who admires me, wants to see me, talks with me, brings me food, and thinks my daughter is the most beautiful child he has seen." She turned away from him, but then looked back. "That man's name is Jhika. I laugh when I talk with him. He is clever with his hands and can fix anything. But most of all, me and my daughter are always on his mind. He is my only friend. I want to marry him. If you like, Jhika and I could stay here, use part of the huge house as our own, raise your daughter and then you would contract with us to care for this place." Her words flew from her mouth with emotion. When she said Jhika, her mouth smiled.

Dohst stared at the woman in amazement. At first he had a flash of anger when she mentioned another man coming to the island, but, he remembered, she was not his wife, nor his slave, but a free woman. She was alone months at a time and he hardly thought about her. But was she involved with *Zinna*, adultery. It was very confusing. He frowned and then sat down on the sagging couch continuing to stare at Ankh.

"*Nikah ek beri hai. (Marriage is a padlock.)* But it is the best way. I am surprised that you already have a man seeing you. Amazed! I have never heard of such a thing of a slave, infidel woman who has a man friend who makes her laugh." He shook his head from side to side.

"Why? How many women have you seen and lusted after in the last two years? Already you have fathered two children by different women. Why? Am I not a person? Do I not need love? Am I different from the buffalo cow that goes into season and needs the bull? Why?"

"In our religion women..." he was cut short.

"Is your child by me part of your religion? Is your child by your dead cousin part of your religion? Is your gold necklace part of your religion? Does not your religion teach that it is the responsibility of the man to treat all the women of his household fairly, even the slave women and to attend to their 'tilths'? Am I wrong?" She leaned toward him aggressively.

He held up both hands toward her now, palms forward as if to ward off her words. "I agree to your ideas. I agree to your ...," he could not finish. "I can draw up a contract with him for you to care for the house with him, your new..., husband and I will provide money for care and upkeep and his work. Yes."

"No! The contract is not with him, Dohst Sahib, it is with me. I am talking with you. I am taking care of your child. I love this place Dohst. It has become a home to me. That little yellow paper you have with you which gives you ownership of this place should go to your heir. Should it go to the child of your cousin who died or really should it go to your child by me if both of us die? I speak boldly Dohst, so that your daughter may have a life. Women can have lives. Remember, we had a woman Prime Minister named Benazir. Perhaps your daughter could become a Prime Minister." She was smiling now and picked up the sleeping child and uncovered its face. "Bipta. My little Bipta. Open your eyes and look into those of your father who has given us so much trouble, look for the first time." She rocked the child.

"Why did you call her Bipta. That is calamity and misery. Why such a strange name?" He looked from the child's face to that of its mother and had his answer. Tears filled her eyes and fell to the child's forehead.

"Yes. I understand now. Yes. Your plans are the best ones. Only, I am sorry that you ..." He reached over a finger and touched Bipta's cheek. He looked up at her and Ankh's beauty and did not want to let her go. "I am sorry that you and the child will be under the care of another man. It does not seem right to me now."

She remained quiet, staring at him steadily until he became uncomfortable, waiting for him to ask her.

"I have changed my mind. It would be better if I took you as a wife and then the child..." He paused.

Her temper flared. "What do you mean took me? You have not asked me. You never asked me, though that is what I wanted before the baby was born. You never considered marrying me. I was an infidel slave girl in your mind; your father's left-over *kutte ke patta*, bitch trash. Low and not worthy. How could you take me as a wife now? I do not want to be taken, Dohst. Do you understand?" She waited for him to reply. He stood mute, his face a mask. "I want it like when you first met me. You asked, 'Would you like to come to me tomorrow?' It was the first time in my life that someone asked me my opinion, asked about my will, asked my permission. Dohst, that question opened the door of my mind. My permission. I am a person, Dohst, like you. No, I wish to marry Jhika. He has asked me many times and says that he will continue to ask." The child awakened and began to fret. She opened her blouse and began to breast feed it, standing in front of Dohst, her legs slightly apart to keep balance.

"Yes. I hear you. But the fact is, you were my father's slave girl. No I never asked you. I did not think that I had to because ..." He stopped, looking at the expression of anger on her face. His fists were balled up ready to strike her. She stepped back seeing his intention.

"I will only say this Dohst Sahib, your words 'I did not think that I had to'... are sharp to me like a knife. They make wounds. I know you did not think that way about me, and those words could have killed me if I had not found Jhika. My last words to you, Sahib Dohst are, please think that way about your other woman, who now cares for your son. Think about her in a better way. What is her name?"

Dohst was at a loss for words. He had not thought of her as his other woman. He frowned and then said "Meher Jamal."

"What a strange name. A person with the name of 'dowry'. Is she beautiful Dohst? Is this new woman who is a servant caring for your son more beautiful than...." She sobbed. "So, what is your son's name?"

Dohst paused and then spoke with pride. "His name is Malik. King. He is beautiful!"

"How strange, Dohst. When Bipta was born and people saw her beauty they would say, some day she will be the bride of a Malik. How strange." She moved to the table and picked up a pad of paper and a pen and brought them to Dohst.

"Please, I ask you, please, write the words of a contract with my name. Write the name of your child, Bipta in it too and write how much you will pay us to care for your little empire here while you are away, and if you don't pay what will happen. Write it all and I will call in the old woman to witness your writing and I will make my mark with black pot soot, she can make her mark and the baby can make its mark with its foot, not its fingers, they are too small. Then I will put it into a frame and hang it on the wall next to the first paper you wrote which gave me my freedom. Please."

He looked at the weeping woman before him, so utterly beautiful, so defiant so strong. He looked and was again drawn to her and stepped forward moving his arms up. She stepped back seeing his mood shift. She shook her head and her eyes flashed fire as she reached for the cane.

Dohst took the boat back to Sukkur the next day. Ankh watched him go and returned to work on framing her new contract. She cooked tea for herself to celebrate. In the bedroom was a bed-side small table with a drawer. In it was another paper which she unwrapped and took out a gold ring with a beautiful pearl. She put it on. It fit on the middle finger of her right hand. She drank tea with a blue and white china cup with her left hand and admired the ring on her right hand. On the table next to her teacup was the gold necklace.

There was a commotion outside near the stable where the buffalo cow was kept. Her chains rattled and she grunted. The dogs barked. Ankh put a cloth across her shoulders, lit a lantern and walked to the stable, the dogs now jumping and whining around her. The light of the lantern reflected back in the eyes of some small animal on the ground. She looked closely and saw it was a calf. She quickly undid the rope tied to the ring in the nose of the cow buffalo and knelt next to the calf. It was trying to stand on wobbly legs. It was a girl calf she saw.

"What shall we call your baby?" she asked the buffalo cow. It shook its head and the iron chain rattled. Ankh looked at the calf again, its skin the color of a pot. "Well named. It is the color of iron. I will call you *loha zanjir*, iron fetters. Bipta and you shall be friends. I had hoped you would be a little bull calf, but we don't get our wishes."

☪

The household was in an uproar. The women sat in front of the small television set and listened to the news of the death of Sahib-ji. Initially, they all had clapped. Then the women and children looked at each other in disbelief. Murdered? By Chamuck!

"How could she kill such a huge powerful man?" said one.

"Why did she do it? Why?" questioned another.

"Where will she go to? She has no place to hide except here," exclaimed her mother, Mahtari.

"Here? If she comes here they will find her for sure and kill her. They will torture us to tell them where she is hiding. Who will protect us?" The youngest wife got up agitated.

Mahtari stood. "Everyone be quiet. Listen, we must first talk amongst ourselves and share ideas. How can we help? If she does return here what will we do? We can't desert her."

"She is a murderer and will be sought by the police, by all Sahib-ji's people."

"She is not a murderer! Have you ever heard of a woman being a murderer? She was probably assaulted by the master of farts and to protect the name of the honor of this family, shed his blood. Is the protection of our honor only up to the men? Why? They always speak of protecting us because of our weakness, our desires for other men. Can we not protect ourselves, our babies, our own virtue? Murder? Never use that word in this house again. She was avenged!" Mahtari glared at her youngest co-wife who had never become a real wife. "If someone was trying to kill your first born son would you have the courage to kill? A life for a life?"

"If we do protect her here she would become a prisoner in the house, not able to go out, to shop, to school. No one would ever approach the family to marry her. She is ruined. How could she get an inheritance?" Thirta, the *nikah mutah* marriage girl became bold, she knew she lacked status, but she had always been sought out by the master for his bed because of her beauty and her spirit and because she could read and write well.

"So, you think any share of the family wealth will be allocated to you? Your marriage was a secret one, not even recorded. What has Chamuck's problem to do with inheritance. Keep quiet." Mahtari walked toward the beautiful young girl as if intent on hitting her. Thirta held her arm in front of her own face protectively.

"If she comes back in the darkness we will take her down into the cellar room. She can stay there until we know what to do. We must buy new locks for all the doors and get the iron worker to install window protectors. We have Mohammed's guns and ammunition. We will protect ourselves and..." Mahtari waddled about in the room and all eyes followed her.

"Let us call our uncle in Lahore. At least he is a senior male. Perhaps he can advise us on what to do if she comes here." Again Thirta had spoken up, unable to curb her tongue. She looked around at the other women and in her eyes held them in contempt. Most were illiterate and only spoke of babies, pregnancy, and food, always food.

"Yes. That is the first good idea that any one has made so far. We need advice." Mahtari motioned with her hand for a young girl to run and get their cell phone.

No one spoke while she pressed the numbers. She set the phone on 'speaker phone' and when her uncle answered she shouted at the receiver.

"This is Mahtari. Yes, widow Mahtari. I am calling from Peshawar about...."

"I know. I know. I have heard the news as well. We are all in trouble. I will not allow the girl to darken my door here in Lahore. She is first of all soiled, tainted, raped by Sahib-ji and unfit to be in my household. I have many young men who work for me and there are other young male family members who would be affected by her. No. Never. I will not allow a girl who can be accused of infidelity to be part of this household. Why are you calling?"

"She is not accused of infidelity, but of murder. Can you imagine? How could a school girl kill a huge powerful man like Sahib-ji in his own compound? I think that they are making up that story because someone else, one of his hundred enemies killed him. She ran away. Fooled them and they pinned the murder on her. The police don't even go to such places, so far in the native territories. They make their own law and judgments. She is not a murderer!" Mahtari was shouting loudly.

"Stop screaming. I can hear you. Just talk. She will be accused of *zinna*, adultery, if she returns and since she has been in the news the mullahs, the Taliban, all the fundamentalist believers will cry for her to be tried under the Hudood Ordinance. Perhaps she is not a murderer. That does not matter. She is now unclean! A Pashto-family girl whose virginity was taken without agreement, without marriage, without any compensation. *Zinna*." Now he was shouting.

"How do you know she was raped or that Sahib-ji ..." asked Mahtari.

"She has been gone for many weeks. Can you imagine a pretty school girl not getting raped within a day of her being abducted? Do not speak rubbish. *Zinna!* Do not call me here again. I do not want contact with all of you until she is captured and she has been examined."

"Examined? Examined? By a woman doctor of course. Of course. Examined, so the family honor can be maintained!" She closed the phone, cutting him off. She glanced at the women sitting around her and it was as if they knew that she knew their thoughts. Examined? Each of them was thinking about that, even by a female doctor. Not one of them had ever been seen naked, down there, by another person since they became women except by the master and the mid-wives. Examined? They looked away embarrassed by her eyes on their faces.

They were silent for many moments. All then stared up at Mahtari as if expecting to hear what to do next. She frowned, understanding their faces. They all gossiped in the kitchens, when they cared for children, but who had ever asked them for an opinion about anything outside the walls of the compound, about purchases, about medical problems, about schooling, about anything, about being examined?

"This is the plan. If she calls I will speak to her. If she comes, we will put her into the cellar room and care for her. Then we will decide what to do. *Bachari*, how can she walk all the way from the Afghanistan border in a school uniform without being assaulted by a hundred Pathans along the way? *Bachari!*" Now she wept for her beautiful daughter as if she had died, knowing in her heart she would never see her again. Her voice rose up in a high keening shriek and the rest of the group joined her in grief, anguish and frustration.

Only Thirta sat quietly, shaking her head, remembering her talk with Chamuck about inheritance. What would Chamuck inherit now? Nothing but the storms of difficulty would engulf her. She walked down the long steps into the cellar and sat on the bed and looked at the goods stacked around the room, the huge box of sand that had oranges buried there, the sacks of rice held off the floor by blocks of wood to prevent moisture from creeping from the floor, tins of *ghee*, bags of small hard onions, pumpkins and hard-skinned squashes laid out row upon row waiting to be consumed. She lay back on the cot and breathed in deeply, smelling the comforting odor of foods, the slight dampness of the place and the old aroma of ancient wood. She felt a rumble and thought it was distant thunder but then sat up and gripped the side of the cot as the floor moved under her. *Zalzala*, earthquake she muttered. Upstairs dishes fell to the floor of the kitchen with a clatter and the women shouted in fear. Thirta stood next to the bed but quickly sat down as the floor seemed to rock. A crack appeared in the wall across from where she sat; a long jagged crack that ran from the cellar floor to the boards of the floor above. Earthquakes, her father had told her that earthquakes always came with shaking family news and life and death events. They were a portent of doom, certain death...

The women gathered in the kitchen area after the quake, each talking animatedly about what she had felt, how the plates had fallen from cupboard, how the Bulbul in the cage had stopped singing. They gossiped about Chamuck and that the quake was a warning about her. More than an hour passed and they waited for the next quake, wondering if they should leave the house. Then their small television broadcast the news. Pakistan in the area along the NWFP tribal border area had just suffered one of the most devastating earthquakes in its history, with estimates of twenty thousand killed and thousands left homeless.

Mahtari looked at the women around her in shock. "Our days our numbered. Our time of death already written. Our book of judgment, our personal augury will hang around our neck and all will be revealed about all our deeds. There is nothing you can do about it anyway so why not be comfortable and stay right here. This house has stood for almost eighty years." Mahtari glanced around her at the somber faces of the other wives and children.

There was a loud sound of clanging metal as someone pounded on the gate. The gardener ran to the gate and looked out and saw a government postal vehicle parked and a man in uniform waiting.

"Did you feel the quake? I have a parcel for a Begum Mahtari Moham-med. Does she live here? It is registered and she must sign for it."

Mahtari covered her head and waddled to the gate with two other women accompanying her. "What is it?"

"It is a registered package from Lahore for Mahtari."

"Me? Who knows me?"

"I don't care who knows you. Sign for it and I will be on my way. I have to deliver six more packages." He held out a paper and pointed to a line.

Mahtari signed her name in large letters. She accepted the package from the delivery man and walked back into the house with the women.

The entire household gathered in the kitchen. The package was put on the center of the table and they circled around the table and gazed at it.

"Who sent it?" asked Thirta.

"Look at the handwriting," said another.

"What do you think is in it?" It was the size of a shoe box.

Mahtari picked up a kitchen knife and carefully slid it along the area that was taped. "The only way we will know is to open it. I just hope some monster or some dreadful thing is not inside it, like a person's finger."

The children screamed. "A finger?"

They stood back as the paper was carefully unwrapped from the small box. Mahtari lifted the lid and bent forward and stared into the package, obstructing the view of all the rest gathered there.

"Chamuck " she yelled. "It is from her !" Again the children screamed.

She reached in and pulled out a cotton bra, one that she herself had sewn for Chamuck the year before, the one Chamuck had worn under her school uniform the day of her abduction. She held it up for everyone to see. Hands reached for it and they all verified that it was from her. Now, big-eyed they stared at Mahtari.

"Why was a bra sent to us in a package?" asked Thirta.

Mahtari looked at the bottom of the little box and saw there was an envelope. She took it out. In it there was a note in Urdu written in large characters.

"I have escaped and am in Lahore dressed in a burkah. I have withdrawn Rs5000 from two banks and purchased five money orders at the post office for Rs. 1000 each. Go to the post office to draw out the money, one each week. Go to different post offices. I am going to Lahore and try to contact our uncle there. I will stay in the Lahore Intercontinental Hotel until I know what to do. I am going to buy a cell phone and I will call you at your cell phone in about four days. Mama, be sure you ask Thirta to help you with the money. She seems to know about such things and always talks about money. Don't tell anyone outside the house. I am sending my bra to show you I am alive." Her signature was firm and clear.

The after-shock was not as strong as the first quake. It came as they stood around the table. Mahtari dropped the bra to the floor when the room began to shake. The bird cage swung back and forth, back and forth and the bulbul flew against the wires of the cage as if insane.

☪

The wholesale oil office was quiet. No one had called in for orders. Piari sat at her desk, arranging deliveries of oil to various retailers in Lahore. A boy stuck his head into the room holding up a newspaper. She nodded and he brought it over and she placed a few coins on the table which he took. She glanced at the front page and Ikbal's name jumped out at her.

"A local journalist, Ikbal Sufi, died yesterday when his vehicle went off the road over an embankment at the Ravi River near the Bund Road where his home was located. Police are checking the incident; however, it appears that he died as a result of an accident. The Deputy Superintendent of Police, Feroz Hakim stated that his inspection on the scene did not reveal any suspicious activity. The body of Mr. Sufi was completely burned because the car exploded into flames when it fell onto a pile of rocks which apparently ruptured the petrol tank."

Piari stared at the page for a long moment, then took her scissors and clipped out the notice. She sat at her desk and pulled out a scrapbook and opened it. She pasted the press notice on the last page, flipped through the entire document, glancing at the history of Ikbal's published news articles with the Dawning. She closed the book and put it into the drawer. "Take off your blouse," he had said ten years ago. Agitated, she rose and walked to the door.

"I am going to call the driver. I need to go to the bazaar to purchase a few items from the chemist. If anyone calls take their number and name. I will not return today."

Her assistant nodded, looked up at the clock and wrote something on a pad and continued with her work. On the desk lay the unfinished application form for Aziz Shabash to become a retail oil dealer in Sialkot. His address was highlighted with a yellow marker. In Urdu the words "check personal and family background and possessions including Sukkur island house" were written.

☪

Feroz Hakim's hands shook. He held the letter from the Regional Police Office in Islamabad in front of his eyes, but he could not read the entire memorandum. All he could see were the words, Immediate Transfer Notice for Feroz Hakim to Sialkot Police Office.

The phone rang. He picked it up. "Yes. Feroz here."

"You are on administrative leave until further notice, Feroz. A team of police investigators from Islamabad have completed their inspection of the burned vehicle of Mr. Ikbal Sufi and we have cause to re-open this case that you said was closed. There are two suspicious discoveries. Do not report next week to Sialkot. Remain at your own residence until you are summoned. The *chowkidar* discovered something near a section of the wall that had collapsed, a blue label..." he trailed off. "You are under house arrest until further notice."

Feroz stood up sweating and shaking. He tried to compose himself as he went to his vehicle. A few policemen noticed him and saluted. He opened the trunk of his vehicle and folded back the carpet over the area where the car tools were kept. The small bundle of wrenches was lying there. He breathed a sigh of relief and then picked up the tools. Each tool had a plastic tag with his name imprinted on it. It had been all the rage, years ago, to get a bunch of blue plastic strips with your name imprinted on them from a local merchant. He had bought a roll of these at the time and had stuck his name on all his possessions, including his tools. One of the wrenches was missing a name tag. He groaned as he stared at the tools. Then furiously he peeled all the tags from the rest of the tools and put these in his pocket. As he got into the car, Mistiri strolled up and greeted him. Feroz started the engine and rolled down his window.

"Yes. What do you want? I am in a hurry."

" Deputy Sahib, you had planned a meeting with my daughter for next week. What shall I tell my daughter..."

"No. No. Forget the meeting. Tell her to study hard. No meeting." He started the car, then rolled down the window and motioned for Mistiri to approach. "I have changed my mind. I wish to have her brought to my house. I will have a mullah present and he can perform the *nikah*." He took out his billfold and extracted three thousand rupees. He counted these and then leaned out of the car window and handed them to the carpenter.

"What is this sahib? *Nikah*? She is not prepared so soon. Her schooling sahib! What about her schooling?" He held the money in his hand as if it were hot.

"This is a bad time for me to explain everything to you. I wish to marry her now. It is convenient for me now and I desire to finish the marriage arrangement. More schooling for her is not necessary. She even says that she has trouble with English. Bring her to my house on Friday in the evening and prepare her for a *nikah* ceremony. She should bring all her personal belongings. A *nikah* is more convenient for me now. Yes. It must be now."

Now the carpenter tried to hand the money back to Feroz who refused to take it. "Remember, either this or you will have no work. Don't be foolish. The girl is ripe and my offer is a handsome one. She will have a television set of her own. Instruct her well. She will be asked if she is willing to become my wife. She only has to say 'yes'. Do you understand?" He started the car and drove off, leaving Mistiri standing at the side of the road staring at the money in his hand.

☪

She picked up the phone in the hotel room. Chamuck had never called the cell phone at the house in Peshawar, but she was sure she still remembered the number. She waited and when a deep male voice answered, she quickly hung up. She altered the last digit, dialed and waited again.

"Hello." Thirta held the phone to her ear as the other women gathered around her.

"Thirta? This is Chamuck. Chamuck. Do you hear me?"

"Yes. You are alive. She is alive. It is Chamuck. This is Thirta. Where are you?"

"I am in Lahore in the hotel. Did you get the package?"

"Yes. We got it. She asked if we got the package and I said yes." She repeated the conversation with the phone still to her ear.

"Thirta, listen, don't talk. I am going to contact my uncle tomorrow and see if he will shelter me there where no one knows about me."

"No! Don't call your uncle. We talked to him on the phone and all he talks about is that you committed *zinna* and that you were unclean and he did not want you in his household because there were lots of males there and that ... She is going to call her uncle." Thirta was interrupted.

"Thirta! You called him?"

"Yes. He does not want you around. You are unclean."

Chamuck was quiet for few moments. "All right, then I am coming home to Peshawar. I am wearing a new blue *burkah*. I will have a taxi drop me off at the house. Tell the gardener that you are expecting a visit from a rich aunt from Lahore and to let me in when I come. It will be at night just before the curfew. Few people move about then. Don't tell anyone that it is me. Even the gardener. Remember. A rich aunt."

"She says that she is coming home. What?" She listened to the phone.

"Thirta, tell them after we finish talking. Not now. Do not tell anyone that I am coming home. Anyone! Someone could call the police, or someone from Sahib-ji's group would come and take me away and kill me. Do you understand? Listen! Answer me."

"Yes. We will be careful. How did Sahib-ji die, Chamuck?"

"Keep quiet Thirta! I want to tell you one more thing. Wait, someone is at the door..."

The phone went dead. Thirta said hello, hello, but the phone was dead. She turned to face the others. "She had one more thing to tell us but the phone went dead. She said she is coming here disguised as a rich aunt. What shall we do?"

The children were now excited and ran around shouting. "Chamuck is coming home! Chamuck is coming home!"

CHAPTER THIRTEEN

Badla mitha hai. (Urdu saying)

Vengeance is sweet!

Mistiri could not control her. He struck her in frustration but that only heightened the problem. Jamilah his daughter laid on the floor and wept, curled in a ball. He tried to lift her but she remained stiff and screamed when he touched her. His wife sat on the floor next to Jamilah and stroked her daughter's head. She too was weeping and looked up at her husband with frustration.

"There is nothing that can be done about it. Nothing! I cry too, for my job, for my salary, for my very life and for you my daughter. Nothing. Feroz is a monster. I signed the school application paper but he had written that I agreed to give you to him in marriage on it. My finger print is on it. I did not know that it was a marriage engagement contract." He was shouting louder than their crying. "Friday. Two days from now. He has already contacted the mullah who will witness the *nikah*."

Jamilah sat up, her face blotched from crying and faced her father, challenging him for the first time in her life. "Will you allow it? Will you force me to go to him? He is as old as you. His eyes are like a mongoose, small and black. He is short and has a high voice like a monkey. Will you? I don't want to marry now. Please!"

"Jamilah you will have more than you have ever had before, your own room, television, fine food. He will provide gold bracelets and a necklace. He is a man of authority, the Deputy of the police in Lahore. He has a fine car. Please, listen. I do not want to beat you again. I have never beaten you in your life before. You are my only child and I want you to have a good life." He babbled on in his typical fashion and the women waited until he had finished.

"If I refuse?" Jamilah stood now, her body bent over, her face a grimace of frustration.

"If you refuse then I have no alternative. I will return the three thousand rupees and I will contact your cousin who lives near Changa Manga. He is also my age and his wife died leaving him with three children. He has already begun an engagement process. I will let him marry you. You can no longer stay at home here. You are..." He thought the word ripe but held his tongue. "You are a woman and must be wed. Must! I will not have a job, we will have no money. I will try to find other work. No school. We will be beggars." His voice broke and he began to cry as well his hands in his hair.

"I wish to stay home and continue with the school. Why must I marry? I am only sixteen. I don't want to be in the same bed with him." She approached her father, her hands held up in supplication to him.

"Because there is no other way. I must at least have my work so your mother and I can eat. No other way." Mistiri held his hands out to his daughter but she shook her head. "All you have to do is say yes, that is all. The mullah will ask if you agree to the marriage and you will say, yes. No more."

"If I keep quiet?" she sobbed.

She stood mute and stared at him hard. Her mother stood next to her and patted her arm again and made small sounds of comfort.

☪

Feroz and the mullah waited in the front room of the house for almost an hour. The mullah was about to leave when a *tonga* pulled up in front of the house and Mistiri and his daughter stepped down and moved toward the front door. Mistiri supported his daughter who had her head covered with a veil. Feroz hurried to the front door and opened it and stood aside as Mistiri and his daughter stepped inside. He pointed to an easy chair over which a gold and red cloth was draped. Mistiri helped Jamilah to the chair and she sat down at the very edge of it, bending over so that her head almost touched her knees.

The Kazi read four chapters of the Holy Koran in Arabic. Mistiri did not understand a word. Jamilah sat hunched over not listening to the chanting sounds. Feroz repeated sections of these. Then the Kazi turned to Feroz Hakim and asked him if he wanted to marry Jamilah and he replied he did. He turned to the girl.

"Do you agree to marry this man who has just agreed he wants you for his wife? He and I are both witnesses to your agreement." He waited.

Jamilah breathed in deeply and then stood up and looked at Feroz. He was surprised at her boldness. She began to speak in English loudly. "Jack Sprat could eat no fat his wife could eat no lean." She sat down.

The Kazi was amazed. "What is the girl saying? I do not understand a word she said. What?"

Feroz turned to Jamilah and asked her in Urdu, "Is that the poem you read to me six months ago?"

She nodded.

He said, "I did not hear you. Answer me."

" *Han ji.* (Yes. It is.)"

He turned to the Kazi. "She said, yes."

From the kitchen came the sound of a brass plate dropping and a loud shriek and then sobbing. Gulab, Feroz's wife blew her nose in her scarf loudly in the kitchen.

"What dowry are you paying the girl and her family?" asked the Kazi.

Feroz lifted a cloth draped over the table under which there was a gold necklace and six gold bracelets and a small bar of gold about the size of a large postage stamp. The Kazi noted the dowry payment and signed a paper. He congratulated Feroz who then gave him an envelope containing money as he left the room.

Feroz Hakim motioned to Mistiri to step outside the front door. Mistiri stood with his hat in his hand. "I have thought about this carefully. It is not suitable that you continue to be employed at the police office. It is unsuitable for the father of my wife to work for me, one who is in such a low, subordinate position and caste. You will have to find other work. Do not say anything about my marriage to your daughter to anyone at the police office." He handed him an envelope. "You are dismissed. I will inform the staff of your dismissal next week. Go now."

Mistiri stared at the envelope then at Feroz Hakim. "You can not do this sahib! You can not. You have stolen my daughter and now you have stolen my bread, my very life. I curse you and wish you dead. May you die the most awful death man has known." He spoke slowly and then his resolve broke and he turned his back to his employer and began to sob. "Sahib, I have worked for you for years. Do not do this to me."

Feroz spoke with authority. "There is enough in the envelope to last until you find another job. There is a small letter of recommendation in it as well telling how good you are at cementing in safes, fixing hinges, repairing windows and buying goods in the bazaar."

He turned around and entered the house again leaving the man outside. Jamilah was standing in the corner with her back to the wall. She had removed her scarf and was reciting a poem in English.

In the kitchen, Gulab, Feroz's wife, stood weeping over a pot of lentils and stirred the soup as it boiled. Her plump arms jiggled as she moved the spoon around. She was quietly mumbling one word over and over to herself. "*Arandi. Arandi.*" (Castor bean)

☪

Mistiri retrieved his tool box from the room in the police station. He tied it to his bicycle and pedaled home, hardly seeing the road. He took the tool box into the kitchen of his small house and removed all the tools and lay them on the table. There was a spool of fine steel wire in the box. He placed this on the table and then went to the corner where his wife kept a short broom. Its handle was only about a foot long but it served his purpose. He was sawing the handle from the broom when his wife came into the room.

"What happened? How is Jamilah? Did she agree to the union? What happened?" He continued to saw away as if he had not heard her.

"Why are you spoiling the broom? How will I sweep? What is wrong?" She moved around the table opposite him so she could see his face. "How is she?"

Feroz looked up at her. "She was tricked into saying yes. She defied me and him. She said an English poem as her answer. She became insane. She has gone crazy. But she did say yes and now is married to him." He sawed the second piece of wood.

"What are you doing? I think you have also gone crazy. How did she say yes? She told you she would not agree to the union before witnesses." She reached over hand held his arm.

He continued to work as she watched. He drilled a hole in the center of each piece of wood. Through each hole he pushed the wire and measured a two foot piece. He attached the wire firmly around the handle and held the garrote in his hands and snapped the wire tight. Now he turned to his wife.

"He has taken my daughter. He has taken away my job. He has taken my very life. I will take his head." He snapped the wire taught again and his lean and muscular arms bulged at the tension.

"What are you talking about? Have you lost your job?" She shouted shrilly.

He snapped the wire taught again. "I am not worthy to be his father-in-law. He has no intention of ever letting us see her again. I know it. I am not sure what his Holy Book teaches about a father's anger, but I know that in ancient India, my forefathers were feared dacoits who beheaded their enemies so they could not talk and tell. They lay in wait for an enemy (*dushman*) on a dark path and pulled a wire around his neck and took off his head. Revenge will be sweet. Very sweet."

☪

Gulab worked busily in the kitchen preparing food for Feroz and his bride who were ensconced in the small bed room. He had come into the sitting room briefly in the late afternoon and told her to make them evening food. He requested curried lamb stew, lentils, basmati rice and *khir*. He told her to put cardamom seeds in the rice pudding as well as chopped up cashew nuts. Then he left and went to the back of the house to join his new wife. He moved his clothing into the closet in the back bedroom as well.

All the ingredients were carefully prepared in advance of cooking them. The onions were cut into cubes, the lamb meat was sliced thinly, parsley was chopped and piled on a plate, lentils were soaked and the rice was carefully sorted removing small stones. Even the spices were prepared in advance and set in small dishes, ready for use when she began cooking. It was all orderly and neat as she usually cooked the Friday night meal.

Gulab went out the back door to their small yard to the back wall. She could hear their window air conditioner laboring in the room in which the couple was. It was rattling and dripping water from condensation.

There were six large castor bean trees growing where the grey water from the kitchen ran. They were filled with colorful red seed pods, spiky and defiant. A few had dried and turned brown. She picked these and with her fingers opened up the seed pods and removed the beautiful seeds. Each one, shaped like a bloated tick was spotted like a leopard. Dark brown and black marks dotted each of the attractive shiny seeds, the size of the end of her thumb. She selected a dozen of the largest ones and returned to the kitchen. Carefully, she removed the colorful spotted coverings from the seeds leaving a cream-colored nut. She chopped these seeds very finely on a piece of tile. She used the same knife to cut up the vegetables and meat.

The aroma of lamb curry and spices filled the house. The rice boiled on the stove. Gulab moved from dish to dish adding spices, salt and cilantro, tasting to make sure each was just right. The rice was done to perfection. She prepared the browned onions, raisins and nuts for the pilaf and topped off the mound of steaming rice with a fine edible silver sheet.

When the curry was done she tasted it once more, then satisfied that it was very hot and spicy and a little over salted, she added the last ingredient. She mixed in two heaping teaspoonfuls of the chopped castor bean and stirred it in carefully and turned off the heat. She did the same for the rice pudding and the lentils. Her own food had been set aside earlier, a huge plate of rice and a generous helping of meat curry. Her own bowl of rice pudding, in a red dish, cooled on the window sill.

It became dark and she knew that he would be calling for food. The television set was on with the volume high. Feroz had placed their only air conditioner in the window of the back bedroom. Gulab placed a pile of rice pilaf on a brass try and filled four small bowls with the condiments and stews. She made a second identical tray for the new wife. The smell of the *chapattis* was tantalizing, rolled up in steaming napkins set on each of the trays.

She knocked on the back bedroom door and Feroz opened it and looked out at the trays of food in her hands, took them and closed the door. He did not acknowledge her.

An hour later she saw that he had put the trays outside the door. One was completely consumed; one had not been touched except the bowl of rice pudding was not returned. She nodded and returned to the kitchen where she worked busily. She dumped the uneaten food in a bowl near the back door gate where stray dogs came daily for a hand out. She was humming a Hindi love song, 'Chup Chup'. (Keep quiet my heart)

☪

Mistiri waited twenty four hours before he made his move. His ex-employer had very regular habits which he had observed for years. Feroz always left for work at seven in the morning and drove his car to a small shop where he purchased two packages of cigarettes. Then he drove to the edge of the Ravi River on Bund Road and parked in a wooded spot to take a leisurely smoke and watch water buffalo wallow in the shallows of the river below him. His morning tea took effect and he squatted behind a tree and urinated, then adjusted his trousers and climbed back into his car. Mistiri had been with him twice when he performed these ritualistic movements, once when he had accompanied the Deputy to Sukkur.

Mistiri cycled to the place by the river and hid his bicycle. He took his place behind some bushes and waited. It was six thirty in the morning and the sun played on the surface of the water. The day was already oppressively hot. He mopped his brow and took out the garrote and practiced how he would slip it over the head and then pull it taught, slitting the throat, and if he had enough strength pulling through the muscles and sliding the fine wire between the vertebrae and decapitating his victim. A mangy, hungry dog moved near him and he tossed stones at it and it moved away. He tensed. A car pulled up and parked. Two people got out talking animatedly.

"Musharraf is a traitor to our country!" The taller man spoke earnestly.

"Why? Just because he plays both sides? He has to placate the Americans and he has to make sure he keeps his power base here in Pakistan."

"The Al Qaeda will try again. He was lucky that the explosives under the bridge did not detonate."

"Perhaps they will get him when he takes his next airplane journey. Remember Zia? Katush! To this day they have not figured it out, but at twenty thousand feet a very small bomb creates a very large accident. Katush! They found no actual remains."

His partner laughed. "You do that well. In American I heard them say Boom! Katush is more expressive."

"You forgot to tell me about your meeting Tuesday night."

"No I didn't and I don't intend to say anything about it either. After all she is the very pretty, eager, hot and willing daughter of a very high official not to be named and I won't say more. Only that Pakistani families that have lived in the United States for a while and then return to carry on their life here, return with liberated daughters with naughty ideas they pick up from TV and the web site. Or just watching their fellow American class mates making out." He laughed and they slapped hands.

The two men leaned against the front of the car and smoked, looking out onto the surface of the river.

"Today it will reach forty four degrees! I think I will drive up to our Murree bungalow and stay there for a few days. Coming?"

Mistiri looked at his cheap watch. Fifteen minutes remained. He had not planned on this car and these talkative people. They left at seven. He now readied himself for the act, resolved and tense. Now that he had made up his mind to kill Feroz he felt at ease and excited in a strange way looking forward to being avenged. The sun shone across the water brightly. He waited. It was now seven thirty. He pocketed his garrote and cycled home toward the railway station where his wife was preparing his breakfast. Tomorrow, he thought, tomorrow, or the day after that. I have time, he has little time left.

☪

Feroz Hakim was in pain and misery. He was doubled over with fiery cramps. His head ached and he felt dizzy. His stomach cramps were so severe that he broke out in a cold sweat, panting. The vomiting began at dawn. Already he had visited the latrine twice and had had violent diarrhea. The third time he noticed blood in his stool. He drank a glass of water and promptly vomited that. He called for his wife Gulab but apparently she did not hear him.

"Jamilah, go tell Gulab that I must have some kind of food poisoning. Hurry!"

Jamilah sat on the edge of the bed and stared at Feroz, loathing him, hating him, almost feeling ill when she looked at him, remembering what he had done to her, again and again. He had left the lights on. She had struggled when he began to take off her clothes, but he persisted, patiently at first, then almost violently. She still could not believe what had happened to her then, but the dull pain between her legs reminded her that it had been real. She looked at her legs and could see bruises forming on her thighs. She shook her head. Seeing him suffering now, pleased her. His new groaning made her smile, thinking of his groaning and sighing during the night.

She did not respond to his demand to go and get his wife. Frustrated, he got up and staggered to the door, opened it and shouted for Gulab. She did not answer. He stumbled into the front room and looked for her there. There was a notebook paper on the coffee table. He picked it up and read her scrawled Urdu writing.

"I have gone to be with my mother. I will be back after three days if you need me. Ask your new bride to cook for you now. You can come and get me at Aama's house in a few days. Gulab"

He staggered into the large bedroom and saw that she had packed her clothing and had taken a large suitcase. He cursed. A cramp doubled him up and he staggered toward the latrine, groaning. He was unable to make it there before he became incontinent and dirtied himself and the carpet. The telephone rang. He could not move quickly to get it and after six rings it stopped. He did not return to Jamilah but fell onto his own bed and groaned loudly as he lay back. The heat in the room was oppressive, yet he began to shake as if he was cold. He was terribly thirsty.

Jamilah was hungry. She looked at the dish of rice pudding that Feroz had set aside for her. She reached for it but then remembered that he had shouted that he had food poisoning. She got up and went into the kitchen. It was clean and tidy. All the dishes, pots and pans utensils were clean and put away. The bowl for left-over food outside the back door had been licked clean by stray dogs which Gulab fed every day.

She opened the fridge and saw a bowl of mangoes. She took two large ones. There was a plate with flat breads. She took two. Back in her room she turned on the television, sat on the rumpled bed and ate her breakfast. When she had finished, she picked up the bowl of rice pudding, poured it down the sink, rinsed the dish and returned it to the kitchen sink, filling it with water and a drop of detergent. She could hear Feroz groaning.

Bored, she wandered around the small house looking at its contents, comparing them with her own home. There was a large tin trunk which she opened. In it there was women's clothing and underwear and blankets. She wandered to the small spare room and noticed that there was a safe cemented into the wall. She squatted down and tried the handle but it did not budge. She looked around wondering if a key had been left somewhere in the room. Her search did not reveal anything. Then she noticed the shadow of the light on the floor and looked up. On the hanging light fixture were the keys. She reached up and took them down and fitted the keys in the safe and turned them. She opened the safe. On the first ledge was an ornate but faded jewelry box of the type used to place wedding ornaments. On the lid in gold paint were the words, Gulab, 1980. She opened it. It was empty. There was an indented place in the faded satin where a necklace had been and a small rounded mound for bracelets. Jamilah walked to the table where 'her' dowry jewelry had been displayed for the wedding ceremony. She picked these up and returned to the safe and carefully fitted the pieces into the box and closed the lid. Hatred welled up in her.

She could hear groaning and retching from the adjacent room. She stood, tears in her eyes thinking of home, her school and friends. There was a loud groan. She mumbled, "I hope you die. Even the dowry is a lie."

In the safe there was a notebook with a red cover. Some of the pages were water damaged and stuck together, others were wrinkled. She opened the notebook and glanced at the page in front of her and began to read. "James, this is difficult for me! I could not write for three days. I can hardly believe this, but my captor is Sher Khan the Superintendent of Police from Lahore." The words Sher Khan leaped out of the page at her. That was her father's boss before he was killed! She put the book under her arm to take to her room to read. Next to the jewel box was a small folding comb. She picked it up and opened it and ran it through her knotted hair, then put it in her pocked. She locked the safe and put the keys in her pocket and returned to the bedroom and sat on the bed. She was angry. All she could think about was her dowry, how Feroz had deceived her into saying yes and then cheated her of this as well.

She got up and walked to the bedroom and glanced at him where he lay on the bed. His face was a mask of pain. His eyes were closed. She looked at him, now nothing more than a filthy sweat drenched body. She returned to her room pleased he was suffering and began to read the notebook from the beginning. "Story of my Abduction" The word Abduction was unfamiliar to her but she continued to read with interest. "This will be a log of my life here. After my long trip from Lahore I was brought to this place where I have been since." She looked up from her reading when she heard the door to the bathroom slam shut.

Feroz's condition worsened. He tried to wash himself off in the bathroom and dressed in loose pajamas. He called on his cell phone to the police station and requested that a patrol car come immediately to his home. He sat and waited but again was seized with cramps and nausea so severe that he sagged to the floor where he lay dry-heaving. When the police car arrived they pounded on his door, then opened it and shouted if anyone were present. They saw him lying on the floor, shaking and groaning. It was now two in the afternoon.

He smelled terribly of feces, so badly that the two men could hardly bear to lift and carry him to the truck. They stretched him out in the back of the van, turned on the claxon and the blue flashing lights and headed to the Jinnah Hospital which was the closest medical facility.

Jamilah read for an hour, going back to re-read sections. Maria. Her father had never mentioned that name but Sher Khan was her father's boss. She put the notebook down and lay back and slept. She awakened hours later and watched television and then became bored again. Being absolutely alone with no one else present was new to her. Either she had always been with other girls in school or family members were present or in the next room. Girls were not left alone, ever. There was always something to do at home, cooking, child care, house cleaning, shopping, washing clothes, eating, cleaning up and talking. There was always talking. It was quiet now, so quiet that she could hear a dog howl outside. She took a cold bath and dressed in her school uniform, disliking the clothing she had been made to wear for the wedding ceremony. In the kitchen she found uncooked lentils, rice and two bananas. She prepared herself a meal and ate a huge pile of food, watched television again and fell asleep with the air conditioner going full blast.

Later that day a police car pulled up in front of the Deputy Superintendent's house. The sun was intense and the temperature one hundred and sixteen degrees. A bloating dead dog lay in the ditch. They glanced at it, hardly paying attention because they saw dead dogs in the city almost on a daily basis.

She was awakened by knocking on the front door. The same two policemen called out and then entered. Jamilah let out a squeal and closed her bedroom door.

"Who is there?" She stood by the bedroom door.

"Police. Who are you?"

"Jamilah. Why are you here?"

"Come out. We want to talk with you."

Jamilah pulled a scarf around her head, and still dressed in her school uniform stepped out from the bedroom. "What is wrong? Where is Feroz Sahib now?"

"He is in the hospital. What happened here today?" The policemen looked around at the house and noted that it was tidy.

"Nothing happened here. Yesterday he called over the mullah who read some Arabic words and he said that Deputy Feroz Sahib and I were married. Later he got sick. He had stomach cramps and vomited and dirtied himself. He said he had food poisoning."

"Where is the food he ate?" they asked.

"He ate it all," she replied.

"Did you eat it?"

"No. It was not a good time for me, not a time to eat anything." Her face was long, almost in tears.

"Show me the dishes he ate from," asked the lieutenant.

She walked to the kitchen and pointed at the tray and bowls, now washed and neatly stacked in the cupboard.

"Where is the left-over food?"

"There is no left-over food except the food I cooked. There." The pots and pans were still on the stove.

They poured a sample of lentils and rice in a bowl, covered it and were about to leave when the lieutenant asked, "Why are you in your school uniform? Are you his wife or his daughter?"

"His wife was here yesterday, but she must have left. There is a note on the table. I was a school girl yesterday until he ...." She turned away from them, ashamed. "Take me home to my father."

"Who is your father?"

"Mistiri. He is the repair and maintenance man for the Lahore police station. Feroz Sahib is his boss. We live near the railroad station. I want to go home now."

"No. We cannot take you away from here. This is his home and you are under his family's protection now as a widow in his *zennanah*." They turned to leave, samples of the food in their hands. "Shame!. *(Sharam)* You should not dress in a school uniform and you should cover your face before strangers. You are a married woman!" He stepped through the door and turned again. "He died this morning. Lock your door!"

The policemen left as they had come without greeting or ceremony, they got in their truck and drove away. Jamilah watched the truck disappear up the road. She stood and looked around at the house where she was a stranger, yet a widow. A widow! It made no sense to her. There was left-over food on the stove and she had seen tins and boxes in the cupboard. She would prepare food for herself and then think about how to contact her father. He had no phone. She locked the front door.

The kitchen was unpleasant and hot. She found two tins of mixed fruit cocktail in the cupboard and opened these. She ate cold flat bread and then retreated to the bedroom where it was cooler. She lay back on the bed and watched television and fell asleep again.

Mistiri waited until the sun was overhead, the hottest time of the day. He would not be observed. No one walked the streets in the blazing heat. Perspiring profusely he pedaled his bicycle across town to Feroz Hakim's house. He pulled up in the shade of a tree, still sitting on his bicycle seat and watched Feroz's house. The car was still parked behind the protective wall. Why had he not gone to the office as usual? A vulture flew in circles above the house and as he watched as it glided down and landed on the street and hopped toward the ditch. He had not seen it before, but had smelled the putrid stench of rotting flesh, making his gorge rise. He now saw the bloated carcass of a dog and watched as the vulture pulled at the eyes removing them from their sockets. Another vulture slanted down and joined the first which challenged it but then the two worked at the carcass, one at the head the other at the anus. The stench was overwhelming.

He waited, wondering if Feroz would leave the house. No one was around. He was surprised to see two police vehicles drive up and park on the road in front of the house. Six men got out and approached the house. He recognized one, Deputy Inspector Masood-ur-Rasuul from Islamabad who had come to Lahore many times when Sher Khan had been Senior

Superintendent of Police in Lahore. Masood put a handkerchief to his nose when he got out of the car.

The men pounded on the door and waited impatiently. Then they tapped the windows and pounded again, this time with their sticks against the wood. The door opened and Mistiri saw his daughter Jamilah, dressed in her school uniform with a scarf pulled over her head, open the door. She looked terrified. The police moved inside the house as she retreated.

☪

Jamilah retreated to the bedroom and stood behind the door but did not close it as the men entered.

"Who are you?" asked the Deputy Inspector.

"Jamilah," she replied with a quavering voice.

"Where is the Feroz Hakim? We see his car is in the driveway. Is he hiding here?" The Deputy moved toward Jamilah who pushed the door closed. "Look, we are police from Islamabad. Cover yourself and come out. We need to talk to you about your father."

"He is not my father." She called out in a frustrated voice.

"Well, if he is not your father, who are you and why are you here?"

"I don't know why I am here. My father brought me here day before yesterday and there was a mullah and Feroz Hakim and he said words and then they told me I was married to him." She began to cry.

"Jamilah, cover yourself and open the door. We want to talk to you." He turned to the men standing behind him who all stood engrossed with the conversation. "You can begin to search the house. Look everywhere, under beds, in closets, behind pictures on the wall under carpets. You know the routine. Paper files are bulky and if they are here we will find them. We will search the car for tools last." He watched as the men began to search the room. One went to a tin trunk placed near the wall. "Wait! I will look at that myself. Search the other things first." The trunk had a heavy padlock hanging from it which was open.

Jamilah opened the door and stepped out and looked at the floor.

"Did you say that Feroz Hakim married you two days ago?" He sounded incredulous. She wagged her head from side to side.

"Why isn't he here now with you? Where is his first wife?"

316 Harold M. Bergsma

"He became sick and vomited and had diarrhea. His wife left the night he married me. She prepared our food for us and then when I came out later, she had left. The other policemen who were here a couple of hours ago know about it. I told them." She wrapped her hand with the end of her scarf.

"Other policemen? What do you mean?"

"I think they were from Lahore. They came in a truck with blue lights on top." She looked up at his face momentarily and then dropped her eyes respectfully.

"What did they do? What did they come for?" She shook her head. He took out his cell phone, walked to the kitchen and made a call. She could not hear what he said.

He returned with a look of amazement. "Did you know that he died in the hospital?" She turned away from him. "Girl, answer me. Did you know that he is dead?"

She nodded her head and said softly, "The other policemen said he died in the hospital. I did not understand what he meant."

"Allah. You are a widow! Amazing. Amazing! Sit over there. I will try to find out where his other wife has gone. Do you know?" He motioned for her to go to the couch.

"They took the note she had written with them when they left. They did not tell me where she went to. I read the note and she said she would be back in three days and that he could come and get her." She looked up from the couch and saw that the Deputy Inspector was short, bald and had a strange dark mark, a scar on his cheek shaped like a bean.

Masood-ur-Rasuul shook his head and walked into the other bedroom where two men were systematically searching it. "Have you found anything?" They shook their heads. He moved to the tin trunk and took off the lock.

"Sir, there is a safe here and it is locked." The sergeant called out from the small bedroom.

Jamilah got up and walked into her bedroom and sat on the bed near the air conditioner and looked at the television set. She held the safe keys in her balled fist.

They formed a semi-circle around the trunk as the Deputy Inspector opened it. He knew what he would find but wanted to see the expression on the faces of the men with him. He lifted the lid with a flourish. They all leaned forward to look at the rows of cups of the brassieres covered with a thin scarf. There was a strong smell of incense and perfume. Then they looked up at Masood-ur- Rasuul who kept a straight, professional face. They all looked again, bending down to examine the large brassieres.

"Feel along the sides of the trunk all the way to the bottom." He pointed at the sergeant who smiled and stepped forward. He slid his hands along the sides and then pulled out a tampon, which he dropped immediately onto the floor. The other men laughed, looking at the tampon.

The Deputy pulled the lid of the trunk shut. "It really doesn't make any difference. He is dead. But since we are here, let us check out the car and then we can leave. Case solved." He turned toward the bedroom door. "Begum Jamilah we are leaving now. Do you know where he kept the keys to the safe and his car?"

She came to the door and shook her head. "He never showed me anything. Perhaps his wife knows." She looked back at the television set. Her left hand was in her pocket, her fingers wrapped around the safe keys.

The men worked in the blazing sun for half an hour. The boot of the car was pried open and they removed a few objects from it. Mistiri, squatting in the shade across the street, watched as they removed tools. The men left. He walked his bike to the front door and pounded on it.

"Jamilah. Open the door." He put his mouth next to the lock and shouted.

She opened the door and seeing her father began to cry. "Is there anyone else here?" he asked. She shook her head. "Why are the police here? The Islamabad police?"

"I don't know. He is dead. He died in the hospital?"

"Who died?'

"Feroz Hakim. He got sick after the wedding when he ate the food. He was very sick and dirtied himself and the police came and took him to the hospital and then they came back and told me he had died and then the other police came now and they did not know he had died until the short dark man called on his cell phone." She breathed hard, catching her breath. "I want to go home now. It is not good here. He was a bad man, a *badmash* and he ..." She began to cry and sagged to the floor. She looked up at her father. "Why, why did you make me do it?"

Mistiri stood looking around uncertainly. He glanced toward the small bedroom where he had installed the safe six months earlier. He looked at his daughter sitting on the floor. His hand was on the garrote in his pocket, now useless.

"I will take you home. Let us go home so you can be with the family. I don't know what will happen, but you can't stay here alone. Get your things and we will leave. Hurry before anyone else comes." He reached down and lifted her up, still not thinking about her new status as a widow until she looked into his face. "Tomorrow I will return to my job, *inshallah*. He may not have had a chance to tell anyone about me or about the wedding."

"Why did you make me do it?" She cried as she spoke.

"What? Oh." Then it occurred to him. His daughter was a widow. Now he became very agitated. "Hurry. We have to leave. Hurry!" He turned his head to the side, staring at her wondering if....

"Wait. I have to get my clothes and my dowry from the safe and the notebook that Maria wrote." She scurried away, the safe keys jingling in her pocket. She opened the safe and took out the jewelry box and removed the gold bracelets which she put on her wrists. She fastened the gold necklace around her neck and pocketed the small gold bar. She locked the safe again. She took Maria's log from the bedroom and looked around, then turned off the air conditioner and left the house, the safe keys jingling in her pocket.

☪

The caravan, Humvees and Desert Patrol Vehicles moved slowly across the hilly terrain toward the Pakistan border. Soldiers with their gear sat crowded together in the lead vehicles which lurched over the rough road. They tossed empty Coke cans and wrappings from their field rations out the window to the ground below. Major Brian Handfield, of the US Army Reserve, 452 Combat Support Hospital in Bagram, sat with three other medical personnel on one of the seats of the truck, hanging with one hand to the metal cross-supports above him to keep from being thrown around as the vehicle lurched here and there on the uneven path. Ahead of their vehicle was a group of soldiers from the Virginia Army National guard assigned to the 116th Infantry Regiment, part of the overall "Operation Enduring Freedom". They were on a patrol of territory that bordered on Pakistan, but, that during 2004 had experienced few attacks from the Taliban.

"Well, Major, I told you that your last combat medic excursion before going home on rotation was not going to be a smooth one. This road leads toward the border of Pakistan and is seldom used except by the Taliban. We are heading toward a little village called Chaman where some guys are supposed to meet with informants about Taliban holed up near there. Supposedly they had a meeting a while back just before the airfield in Narang was attacked by their guys with shoulder rockets. Right at the Pakistani border our planes bombed a village, actually in Pakistan. You remember, about a year ago. It caused a hell of flak in the Pakistani press. We knocked out a weapons cache there." Lieutenant Bosma talked between mouthfuls of oatmeal cookies. He passed the package around again.

"Will we get to that border town? I would love to say I have been in Pakistan."

"No Major. Sorry. Not on this trip. We could drive on the hills behind it though and you could say you saw Pakistan. There is a look-out post there where we will stop. Just like when I once saw Japan, from the windows of the airport." George Bosma laughed. "Never even got a snap shot."

"Well, this digital camera is a hell of a lot better way to record what I do. Now I can shoot a hundred at a time and unload them on my laptop. So, I hope to hell that Chaman has lots of local color. Cute babes wandering around." The Major poked the Lieutenant in the ribs and they laughed.

"That thing is not X-ray. How in the hell will you tell if they are cute. They are all covered, head to toe in big black or blue bags with holes cut out near the eyes. Heh! You know what I did in Kabul?"

"What?" asked the Major.

"I flirted with one of those bags. Honest to God. I saw this bag moving toward me and God, what a figure was outlined under her the sack. Boobs man! I caught her eyes looking at me and I held her gaze. She did not look away and as I got close to her I could see her eyes were sparkling and young and dark brown. I winked at her and touched my chest over my heart. She bent over laughing and continued down the road. Then about ten paces later I turned around to look at her back, you know, just for the hell of it. To my surprise she turned around too. Now I pretended that I was going to follow her, motioning for her to wait. She let out a small squeal and took off down a tiny alley and disappeared." He was smiling happily at the memory.

"You are really an asshole. You scared the shit out of her, man. Jeez!"

"So, when is the last time you had a soul to soul look in a woman's eyes, Major? It is sort of dry here. Don't touch the girls or you will get your head blown off!" Bosma laughed again and reached for his wallet and pulled out a picture. It was of a blonde girl in a bathing suit standing on a beach. "Joyce. On the Holland, Michigan beach."

Major Handfield stared at the photograph for a long time, so long that George snatched it away. "Easy man. It is really time for you to get back home."

The driver in the Lead Patrol Vehicle called the Major on the phone. "Major, we are on the outskirts of this dump called Chaman. Keep your field glasses ready and tell all the men to be on alert. Maintain you weapons."

Outside, as the line of vehicles passed by, villagers stood back from the road staring at the American trucks, their faces expressionless. As they passed a crowd on a street corner a little boy picked up a rock and threw it at their vehicle which was marked with a large red medical insignia. It clanked against the side of the vehicle.

"Fuck. Damn kid. He could set off a whole bunch of stuff. Keep cool." The Lieutenant stared out the back of the Humvee, then stood and leaned out and peered at the six trucks and patrol vehicles ahead of them. The line of trucks pulled over on what looked like a small football field with large rocks marking the goal posts. The Reserve soldiers climbed out of their trucks and looked around. Most of them lit up a cigarette as they scanned the crowds that gathered. There were no women among the villagers, just children and men of all ages.

The Captain in the patrol vehicle had a phone to his ear and talked to someone, then pointed to what looked like a rock wall behind which many goats were kept. The noise of their bleating could be heard from where they stood. He pointed to a small group of buildings directly beyond the goat corral. The men split their forces and moved toward the building about a block distant. As they passed the goats they looked over the walls to check out whether anyone was in the area. They saw a woman milking goats and glanced away. She had her back to the men, holding a she-goat and milking it with the other hand.

"All clear here!" shouted Bosma. "Just a native woman milking goats."

The woman turned and looked at the men. Maria could not believe that what she saw was real. American soldiers were walking past the goat corral and talking English!

She stood up and began to call out *rokna!*" (Wait!) The men laughed as they walked by and waved at her, draped in a worn and dirty Pashmina shawl. "Sorry babe, not on company time!"

She reverted to English and her tongue was almost tied. "Wait! Help me. I am an American from San Diego. Help me!" She ran toward them shouting. "My name is Maria. I am a prisoner here."

"Lady, did you say you are American?" Bosma called for the men to halt and they spread out around him watching carefully, checking her out for a bomb. "San Diego? What is the name of their football team?"

"I don't remember. Chargers or Padres or the... I don't remember." She began to cry.

"Take it easy lady. Bring her to the lead Patrol Vehicle." Two soldiers moved toward her with their arms held out to help her.

"My baby! I can't leave without my baby." She backed away from them. "Help me get my baby. The old mid-wife is caring for her while I am doing the milking."

"Good Lord! Baby? I don't fucking believe this!"

Major Handfield had returned and took over. "I am a combat medic, a doctor. We will try to get your baby, Lady. What is your name?"

"Maria Bernard. Dr. Bernard's wife. I was kidnapped in Pakistan more than a year ago." She held her palms up in supplication.

"Pakistan?" He stared at the eyes, now tear streaked. He looked at her clothing, at the dirty paisley shawl she had pulled over her head, at the obvious swell of her abdomen in mid-pregnancy. He smelled the strong odor of goat urine. He glanced at her calloused palms and he could not believe that she was not a native. "Okay. Maria? Look me in the face, Maria." She was embarrassed to look directly at a man. "God, I would never have recognized you as an American. Where is your baby kept?"

Maria pulled the Pashmina shawl from her head, the same antique shawl given to her almost two years before by the Senior Superintendent of Police, Sher Khan in Lahore. Her hair was long and uncombed. "Over in those buildings where you guys were heading." She pointed to the compound directly in front of them with a blue wall.

"Shit! This is going to get complicated, Maria, but I promise we will do everything we can to get your baby. We heard there were Taliban in those buildings. Do you think it is true?"

Maria started to laugh weakly. "Taliban. Allah man! That is a name everyone takes on when they hate Americans. It is their word for being a student of the truth. It is full of people that hate Americans. Taliban? Look, let me get the container of goat milk and then I'll go ahead of you and you guys follow me to my home. I will get my Ankhi and then we can leave." Maria tried to pull away.

"The milk? You've got to be kidding. It is not that simple, Maria. Our troops are going in to do a room-to-room search. There may be shooting. We may get shot. Right now insurgents may be looking at us and deciding what to do, holing up, getting ready to blast us." He held her elbow and steered her toward the lead vehicle where two men stood with their weapons.

"Insurgents? What are insurgents? Oh God. Joe! Atiqullah! What will happen to Joe?" Her hand was on her swelling abdomen.

"Who in God's name is Joe Atiqullah?" The doctor looked at her as if she were insane. "Ma'am, what did you say?" He held her elbow again.

In reply Maria shook her head and began to cry, bent over as if in pain. The major put his hand on her shoulder.

A shot rang out from the buildings in front of them leaving a hole in the painted red and white medical insignia of the truck next to where the doctor stood holding her arm. It was answered by hundreds of thundering shots from the small group of reserve soldiers who were now crouched behind boulders. The goats scattered, bleating, knocking over the container of milk that Maria had placed on the ground.

Maria's cries could not be heard above the thundering gun fire as she shouted out, "Ankhi. Ankhi."

"We got the fucker, Major. God, he almost nailed you. A bearded damn cripple at that."

REFERENCES

ONE WAY TO PAKISTAN

and

Oaths of Vengeance

AN ANNOTATED BIBLIOGRAPHY OF USEFUL
NEWS REPORTS, MONOGRAPHS AND BOOKS
ABOUT PAKISTAN

1. "Pakistan-2004 Annual Report, <u>Reporters Without Borders for Press Freedom</u>, Pakistan 3.05.2004. A seven page summary of events in Pakistan in 2004 related to journalist's activities, arrests and convictions.

2. <u>New York Times,</u> April 14th 2004, reports that Kohst airport in Afghanistan was attacked and twenty rockets landed near the airport.

3.. <u>New York Times</u>, Sept. 2004, presents information about Al Qaeda which is reported to be operative along the Pakistan/Afghanistan border and is encouraging insurgents to disrupt up-coming presidential elections in Afghanistan.

4. <u>Clean Air Initiative for Asian Cities</u>, <u>www.nation.com.pk/daily/sep-2004/6/localnews4.php</u>

"Fake 2T oil sold in inner city of Lahore", Oct. 18, 2006. A report by the Global Sustainable Development Network reveals that much oil sold in Lahore is adulterated and of lower quality which leads to environmental pollution.

5. <u>Pakistan Observer,</u> (http:// pakobserver.net/200607/12/news/business02.asp

"Steps to be taken against smuggling lubricants" Jamadi-us-Saani 15, 1427 AH W; reports information about a meeting in Karachi with the Sindh Minister for Industries, Transport and Labor. Adil Siddiqui spoke of special measures to stop smuggling of lubricants from Iran.

6. "DASC keeps MEU ready to strike": www.freepublic.com/focus/news/1143307/posts Submitted by: 22nd MEU, Story Identification# 200452634836, by Capt. Eric Dent.

Discussion of the role of DASC in providing communications to Marines or soldiers on the ground and aircraft as they interface to get to the right place at the right time with the right equipment.

7. Stars and Stripes, July 09, 2004 by Lisa Burgeses. Discussion about troop levels in Afghanistan; 17,900 troops to remain steady for months, the bulk of which are from 25th Infantry Division Hawaii.

8. Jang Group of Newspapers web site. World News, "Vehicles in South Asia spewing toxic fumes" 08-12-2004, indicates nearly 95 percent of the random samples of T2 oil taken in Lahore was adulterated.

9. Pakistan, Violence Against Women in the Name of Honor, Amnesty International, September 1999, 57 pages: discusses Honour Killings in Pakistan. Rape victims held as criminals with life and death penalties, "A man whose honour has been damaged must publicly demonstrate his power to safeguard it by killing those who damaged it and thereby restore it." Page 11.

10. Faith and Freedom.
www.faithfreedom.org/Atticles/AbdulKasem5031p6.htm

Abdul Kasem writes from Sydney Australia about women in Islam. His article depicts the role of women in Islamic societies through Islamic references from a variety of sources from 1784 to the present. He suggests that similar Islamic requirements for women exist today in Saudi Arabia, Sudan, Afghanistan, Pakistan, Iran, Nigeria and Malaysia.

11. El Independiente 3, June 8-21, 1999. "A Report on the 43rd Session of the United Nations Commission on the Status of Women" by Tsung Su. "The Picture out there is not pretty.... the facts and figures of violence against women present an ugly picture." Suggestions are made for meetings to discuss violence, women's workshops for reproductive rights (Nigeria). Sensitivity training modules for judges, law officers etc. This is an important document because it upholds the concept

that, "Women hold up half the sky" from Hillary Rodham Clinton's speech to the delegates.

12. "Vani girls cry for freedom to escape rape as payment for a blood debt", source: www.martinfrost.ws/htmlfiles/vani1html. (3/9/2006) Sympathy expressed for the five young women who as children were pledged as marriage partners to settle a blood feud. The case had been going on since 1991 when a resident of a village murdered his relative on the suspicion of illicit relations. A case study of tragic consequences of Vani.

    Child Marriages; a review of family arranged marriages of a girl, the customary practices of selling girls into 'marriage' in exchange for money and the reaction of the courts.

13. Feminist Daily News Wire, July 29 2002; "Pakistan: Police Response to Crimes Against Women Lacking" "....horrific crimes against women in Pakistan, Punjab province brought to light with the case of Mukhtaran Bibi who was gang-raped as a punishment for her brother.... This report is a precursor to Mukhtaran Bibi's struggle and her publishing a book (2007) about her sorry situation. Subsequent court trials are disturbing reminders of the influence of belief over justice.

14. Canadian Press, Jim Bronskill, March 8, 2006. A synopsis of the heavily edited version of the June report, Afghanistan: Narcotics Profits Integral to Militant Attacks. "The Afghan drug trade was worth $2.8 billion US in 2004, more than doubling in value since 2002..." Profits from Afghan poppy crop are sowing terror seeds.

15. Gulf Times Newspaper, Qatar, Guld and World News-Pakistan/Afghanistan. March 8, 2006

    "Troops launch hunt for clerics behind clashes." A report of searching for clerics accused of instigating the worst fighting near the Afghan border since the start of the "war on terror".

16. (Bloomberg.com: Asia) "Karachi Bomb Attack Kills 4, Including U.S. Diplomat" (Update 1) 3/8/2006

Report of an American diplomat killed in a car bombing, near the U.S. Consulate in Pakistan's southern port city of Karachi, two days before U.S. President George W. Bush visits the country. A history of two previous attacks in 2002 and 2003 were reported.

17. (KansasCity.com) Mar.02, 2006, "Bombing in Pakistan Kills U.S. Diplomat"

"Pakistan has been on the front lines of the war on terrorism. Bush's visit is in part seen as a thank-you to Musharraf for his support. A brief review of terrorist targets in 2002 and 2004.

18. Portsmouth Herald World/National News "Bush: U.S. will nab bin Laden." 3/8/2006

Kabul, Afghanistan report of Bush's visit to meet Karzai and his expression of unwavering confidence that bin Laden will be captured. There are 18,000 troops in Afghanistan, and Bush said that their mission was "to help this new democracy not only survive but to flourish."

19. (www.afghan-web.com) Afghanistan Online: Focus on local efforts to reduce opium cultivation. Nangahar, 10 Feb 2005 (IRIN) Attempts to try tactics to wean Afghans from growing opium poppy. "Last year Afghanistan provided more than 80 percent of the world's illicit opium." Not growing poppies creates a severe economic impact on farmers, and the regional economy. Alternatives are being tried. (Reports have it that since this report in 2006, the poppy crop and opium sales were the highest in history.)

20. Afghanistan: London Conference to Focus on Counter-Narcotics, Kabul, Jan 26, 2006 (IPS) Ezatullah Zawab et al-Pajhwok Afghan News. A report of a conference and UNODC attempts to develop

alternative agricultural livelihoods in just one province. Opium is still 50 percent of Afghanistan's domestic output. Reports exist that the Taliban may have tied up with drug smugglers.

21. (usgovinfo.about.com/cs/waronterror/a/afghanpoppy.htm) Afghanistan's Opium Business Booms During Terror War, from Robert Longley. 3/8/2006 "War on terror conflicting with war on drugs". "As terrorists lose ground, the opium poppy growers win and much of the money from Afghanistan's opium sales goes right back to the terrorists." There is a need to promote and raise public awareness for anti-drug policies.

22. Issues Papers and Extended Responses: Pak42345.E "Structure of the Police Force", www.irb-cisr.gc.ca/en/research/ndp/ref/ , 3/10/2006, A historical overview of the structure of the Pakistan police force since 1947. "Many attempts were made to change the colonial police, but none were implemented until the government enacted the Police Order 2002 in August 2002". A discussion of the roles and functions of Pakistan police hierarchy follows. A 2001 report is quoted, "... policemen commit excesses taking advantage of their uniforms. They have killed people in dubious encounters, many have died of torture in police custody, police investigators have a habit of involving innocent people in heinous crimes to extort money and they get involved with land grabbers and in every other evil that exists in our society. Yet we find only a handful of policemen punished for misuse of authority and unlawful acts committed under legal cover. (24 Jul 2001)

23. Persecution of Ahmadiyas in Islamic Pakistan and Secular India, Kunal Ghosh, in www.mainstreamweekly.com. 11/21/2005, Ghosh reviews the origin of this Islamic sect; "The Ahmadiya believe that all religions of the world including Hinduism are valid religions.... The Ahmadiya protestation that in no sense do they doubt the primary holiness of Prophet Mohammad, this does not impress either the Sunnis or the Shias."... The Ahmadiyas are a minority among India's Muslims. Their persecution by Sunni majority as yet is not as intense as in Pakistan. But the portends are ominous, the trends are disturbing and reflect the events in Pakistan."

24. <u>Religious Intolerance in Pakistan, www.religioustolerance.Org/rt-pakis. htm</u>. (11/21/05) ..."Individuals are now being arrested for blasphemy, and held without bail, while their cases are being investigated. No Christian charged with this crime has ever been granted bail." And "As of mid-2002, only the testimony of a single Muslim is sufficient to prosecute a non-Muslim on blasphemy charges." And "Ayub Masih, a Christian, was convicted of blasphemy and sentenced to death in 1998. He was accused by a neighbor of stating that he supported British writer, Salman Rushdie, author of "The Satanic Verses". Lower courts upheld the conviction." The writer cites a number of instances in which undue force, police violence and legal actions have been taken against minorities in Pakistan.

25. APPENDIX VI, Congressional Human Rights Caucus, U.S House of Representatives, Washington, D.C; 20515, March 1, 1994.

Prime Minister Benazir Bhutto
Office of the Prime Minister
Islamabad, Pakistan

Dear Mrs. Prime Minister: ...."We are writing to express our deep concern about recent events in Pakistan that restrict the right of religious freedom. We are concerned that recent changes made to civil and criminal law undermines the ability of religious minorities in Pakistan to worship freely."

The letter outlines a number of issues relating to Ahmadiya Muslims to practice or preach their faith. It decries "blasphemy" laws and the severe penalties. The report is signed by the members of Congress.

26. Syedwala incident: role of police, by Mirza Sama Ahmad Rabwah, 12 September 2001, source, www.dawn.com/2001/09/12/letted.htm#10 ; The writer reviews an incident in which Ahmadis were endangered by "...maulvis started announcing over the loudspeakers of the village mosque, asking the people to form a procession and commit violence against the Ahmadis." He recounts the mob action and destruction of property that ensued.

27. Wisconsin Project on Nuclear Arms Control, "Pakistan Nuclear Update 2003, The Risk Report, Volume 9 Number 6 (November-December 2003)

"President Bill Clinton imposed economic sanctions against Pakistan as a punishment for its May 1998 nuclear tests. However, by late 1998, he waived most of those sanctions, and President George W. Bush removed the remaining sanctions in September 2001."

..."an American official was quoted as saying that the $3 billion aid package was contingent on Pakistan's continued cooperation in the 'war on terror'".

28. <u>Religious Intolerance in Pakistan, www.religioustolerance.org/rt-pakis.</u>
<u>htm</u>. "Pakistani Blasphemy Law" 11/23/2005

> *"Whoever by words, either spoken or written, or by visible representa-*
> *tion, or by imputation, innuendo, or insinuation, directly or indirectly*
> *defiles the sacred name of the Holy Prophet Mohammed...shall be*
> *punished with death and shall be liable to a fine."*

I particularly enjoyed the last nine words quoted, wondering how the
fine would be paid. Reports of attempting to reform the blaspheme law
are presented, including Benazir Bhutto's unsuccessful attempt to seek
reform.

29. <u>The US Embassy in Pakistan: fortress against terror threats,</u> csmoni-
tor.com/2003

"The sprawling compound in Islamabad is surrounded by thick brick
ramparts, topped with razor wire, and reinforced by steel pillars to keep
a vehicle from smashing through."

"Ambassador Nancy Powell travels through town in an armored car,
with two diplomatic security agents always at her side. When she visits
consulates in Peshawar, Lahore and Karachi, she is trailed by pickup
trucks packed with elite, US-trained Pakistani forces."

The situation for American staff working in Pakistan in 2003 is tense
and staff turnover is high and... "puts a strain on contacts in a country
where personal relationships with local officials are crucial."

Employees also grumble that Pakistan has been a singles-only posting
since Sept.11, meaning partners and children must stay home.

30. <u>Sooner Thought: U.S BOMBS PAKISTAN</u> , www.soonerthought.
com/archives/001861.html 3/10 / 2006. DAMADOLA.Pakistan-
"A U.S. air strike on a suspected Al Qaeda hideout in Pakistan near

the Afghan border that killed at least 17, targeted the network's No.2 man Ayman al-Zawahri, but the suspect wasn't there, Pakistan officials said today."

The report goes on to say that U.S. Predator drones fired as many as 10 missiles at the village in the Bajur tribal region of northwestern Pakistan. DNA tests were being conducted.

31. Christian Science Monitor, June 03, 2003 edition. "The US Embassy in Pakistan: fortress against terror threats" by Gretchen Peters.

"This is now the epicenter of terrorism, says Mr. Evanhoff, who oversees security for the embassy and its consulates here. "It really is. This is the only country I know in the world that has so many groups that are against the US or Western ideals."

32. Asia Times on line, www.atimes.com "South Asia, Assassination 'windfall for Musharraf,' by Syed Saleem Shahzad. Dec.19, 2003.

Review of events related to assassination attempts of Musharraf and security measures to counter these. "As a result, the US changed its priorities, but unlike in the past, Musharraf was dictated to rather than consulted, and Pakistan's strategic interests in Afghanistan and India, as well as Musharraf's political interests at home, were largely ignored."

34. The Detroit News, Wed. January 7, 2004, "Musharraf walks a tightrope in Pakistan." Four assassination attempts since 1999 are reviewed. "Musharraf seems to only have himself to blame for what is the growing vitality of the Islamic militants in Pakistan."

35. South Asia Analysis Group, Paper no.731, 09.07.2003; "Al Qaeda & Taliban Target Hazaras, by B. Raman. "The massacre of 53 members of the Hazara tribe in an imambargah, a Shia place of worship,

at Quetta, the capital of the Baluchistan province of Pakistan, on July 4, 2003, while they were praying by three unidentified gunmen, has come close on the heels of the massacre of 11 Hazaras undergoing police training last month in the same city." The article reviews other violent disturbances.

36. Associated Press (Wire), Fri, 15 Jun 2001, http//www.mapinc.org/medial/27 , by Steven Gutkin, Associated Press Writer, "Former Poppy Growers in Afghanistan Facing Growing Hardship" "The lack of foreign help for desperate former poppy farmers has strained relations between the Taliban and the international aid community. It may also help explain some of the militia's recent mischief, including the destruction of ancient Buddha statues and orders to force Hindus to wear yellow labels on their shirts to distinguish them from Muslims." (The result of the rise of fundamental Islamists is to control all social life and make it conform to Sharia. Labeling non-Muslims with arm bands resembles what happened during WWII when Nazis labeled Jews. hmb)

An interesting analysis of the political interactions of the Taliban 'international community'. Secretary of State Colin Powell mentioned the plight of the poppy farmers and called the poppy ban "a decision by the Taliban we welcome."

37. "Taliban find safe haven in Pakistan's wild west" 31 November, 2001, by Sultan Shahin, www.jammu-kashmir.com/insights/insight20011201a.html.

"Pakistan's tribal areas in the North West Frontier Province (NFP) region hold the key to the eventual success of the United States-led coalition's war against terrorism."

An excellent review of the history of the activity of the Taliban in the NWFP and Pakistan's reaction to their growing influence as well as US interventions. "However, the US's Central Investigation Bureau and Pakistan's Inter-Services Intelligence operations remained hardly a secret after a while as more lethal and sophisticated weapons, among them the US-manufactured shoulder-fired Stinger anti-aircraft missiles, were made available to the mujahdeen." (This group, many of whom may now be part of the Taliban, have access to Stingers. A later US buy back Stinger project was not completely successful.)hmb

38. "Vital intelligence on the Taliban may rest with its prime sponsor-Pakistan's ISI", by Ruth Bedi in New Delhi, 3/9/2006. www.janes. com/security/international-security/news/misc/janes011001-1..

"Pakistan's sinister Inter Services Intelligence (ISI) remains the key to providing accurate information to the US led alliance in its war against Osama bin Laden and his Taliban hosts in Afghanistan. Known as Pakistan's 'secret army' and 'invisible government', its shadow past is linked to political assassinations and the smuggling of narcotics as well as nuclear and missile components."

A critical and in-depth analysis supported from Indian Intelligence information of the role of the ISI as being the 'eyes and ears' of the US-led covert action to seize Bin Laden from the Taliban..." A review of the role of opium cultivation which supported a number of militant efforts in Pakistan and Afghanistan.

"Opium cultivation and heroin production in Pakistan's northern tribal belt and neighboring Afghanistan was a vital offshoot of the ISI-CIA co-operation. It succeeded not only in turning Soviet troops into addicts, but also in boosting heroin sales in Europe and the US through an elaborate web of well-documented deceptions, transport networks, couriers and payoffs. This in turn, offset the cost of the decade-long anti-Soviet 'unholy war' in Afghanistan."

39. Dhimmi Watch:Pakistan: Christians protest against official's injustice, August 17, 2005, www.jihadwatch.org/dhimmiwatch/archives/2005/08/007713print.html

"Lahore: A large gathering of Christians on Tuesday protested against Baghbanura's assistant superintendent of police, ASP- investigation for allegedly supporting a kidnapper. The protestors chanted slogans against the police and appealed to higher authorities for justice. They said that Muhammad Abbas, a resident of Gohawa village, had kidnapped a 14-yer-old Christian girl Asama" Asama's brother had tried to contact higher authorities but he was shot by members of the abductor's family."

The Madagaar Research Report of 2004 shows rising numbers of children and women being kidnapped. In 2004, 2906 abduction cases were reported in national news sources of which many were children. The kidnapper is often known to the victim, that is they are relatives or acquaintances.

40. The Guardian (31.01.2003) Pakistan. "Hard-line region tries to impose Sharia law," by Rory McCarthy. "In the general elections in October- the first since a military coup three years earlier-an alliance of religious parties riding a wave of anti-American sentiment swept to a majority in the parliament of the North West Frontier, next to the Afghan border."

The article reviews the rise of power of the United Action Front which supports Sharia as the supremacy of all law. However, it offers ideological support base for Taliban and Al-Qaeda remnants. It calls for "jihad" the struggle for the glory of Islam.

41. Aljazeera.Net-Flesh traders traumatizing Pakistan, //english.aljazeera. net/NR/exeres/04C101DD 6/23/2005

"The fact that women and children are placed in the same category as arms and drugs is in itself a flagrant violation of their dignity and the rights as human beings," said Nazish Brohi, who also works for Action Aid. Firyal Ali Gohar is equally bitter about the situation. "The landed aristocracy, a corrupt and conniving bureaucracy, and a people essentially mired in anti-women conservative culture all combine to put poor women and children at the mercy of unscrupulous traders," Gohar believes.

42. Hindu-Muslim Conflict and the Partition of India, by Rit Nosotro, Change Over Time essay, from http://www.hyperhistory.net/apwh/essays/cot/t3w30pakistanindia.htm. 10/22/2004.

The writer describes the causes and outcomes of the partition of India to create Pakistan. A concise historical overview of the Kashmir Pakistan-Indian rift. He traces historical reasons for bloodshed that is "centuries old". He reviews Indian history beginning from 1905 until the Partition to the present.

43. (GSD-list) Lahore's brothels dens of AID, Hepatitis C, Daily Times (Pakistan) by Wakid Ali Sayed and Waqar Gillani, 5/8/2002.

"Lahore: Most of the sex workers of the brothel houses of the city, mainly the ones located in Taxali Gate area and its surrounding streets, are suffering from HIV-AIDS and Hepatitis C. This finding was reached during a survey of red-light areas conducted recently by Daily Times." NIH survey provides empirical data of sex workers. It reveals that sex workers are hesitant to have blood tests which would reveal if they were infected, and saying that the tests themselves would infect them. Use of condoms by older sex workers is beginning to occur.

44. Lahore police tops embezzlement of funds: report, Daily Times (Pakistan) Aug 8, 2005. by Shahnawaz Khan.

"Lahore police made the highest embezzlement, around Rs.3 million, in different funds as compared to other Punjab districts, revealed a Home Department audit report for 2001-2002. The report accused the inspector general of police (IGP) Punjab of embezzling Rs 1,193,085 in irregular lapses and Rs 548,876 in regular lapses." The article reviews a number of other cases of embezzlement by police in the Punjab and refers to misappropriations in other districts.

45. <u>Nach Dem 11. SEPTEMBER.</u> "The War in Afghanistan: South
Asian Perspectives, <u>www.boell.de/en/04-thema/1152.html</u> 8/20/05

"The mood here, in Pakistan, is grim, fearful, depressed. This war
is not popular. From the emancipated women's organizations to the
bearded fundamentalists all agree on one thing: it is disgraceful and
wrong for the most powerful nation on earth to mercilessly pound
perhaps the poorest and most oppressed of all peoples with huge
bombs, cruise missiles and artillery." ...until they have destroyed the
last ant...."said the well known journalist Ayaz Amir."

"They distrust the US because of its double standards. The country
that claims to be the world guardian of democracy supported and
sustained the worst dictator that this country has ever known: General
Zia al Haq. The puritanical General destroyed the liberal fabric of
Pakistani society....He destroyed democracy, the arts, education and
curbed women's rights." Americans in Pakistan are no longer highly
respected, rather, are seen to be the extension of Bush's international
policies which are called by many "the big bully." hmb

46. <u>Amnesty International:Pakistan News</u> 8/22/2005. <u>www.amnestyusa.
org/countries/pakistan/news/do</u>

A valuable listing of human rights violations and crimes including
"honour crimes" in Pakistan from Feb. 2002, until May 15, 2005,
with links to references for data or full reports.

47. Police baton-charge Lahore Journalist: Freedom press rallies held,
(Pakistan) <u>Dawn,</u> the Internet Addition, May 4, 2005 Wednesday ,
Rabi-ul-Awwal 24, 1426/

"Lahore/Karachi, May3: A number of journalists were injured when
police baton-charged a procession taken out in Lahore on Tuesday to
mark the International Press Freedom Day. The strong-arm tactics of
the government was widely criticized by the media, political parties
and peace activists who said the incidents had exposed the hollowness

of the government's claims about freedom of the press, tolerance and democracy."

48. <u>Description and Access to Copies of First Information Reports (FIRs)</u>, Country of Origin Research, Canada, 22 July 2004.

"On 22 January 2001, a Rawalpindi–based lawyer provided the following information about FIRs:

Police reports in Pakistan are recorded in the vernacular, in the language of the person lodging the report."

The article reviews the use of FIRs according to reports from Lahore 15, Dec. 2003 and that FIRs can be obtained from the Senior Superintendent of Police as well as from Magistrate's court.

"Laws and practices are two different things. If you have influence or are able to bribe the police you can get anything. If you are poor and marginalized you do not even get an FIR against you... I have found several clients in jail who do not have the FIR or know its contents."

A good source reference for Lahore police matters. hmb

49. Ban on music turns singers, dancers to prostitution, <u>Agence France Press</u>, Feb. 16, 2003, by Mohammad Shehzad.

Personal reports by singers and entertainers are reviewed who because of Islamist-led crackdown on musical performances led them to return to prostitution to support themselves. The MMA, alliance of pro-Taliban Islamic Parties, "... have torched posters of film stars, torn cassettes out of public buses and forced drivers to halt their vehicles for the five daily prayers."

Large areas in major Pakistani cities that are devoted to prostitution continue to thrive while the MMA cracks down on banned movies from India, posters, billboards and pictures of singers, actors and the like. The double standard applies here as it did in other fundamental religious societies which 'torched' offenders for lewdness while leaders utilized available sex services or maintained multiple concubines, or in other societies, four wives and 'hidden marriages' in order to not use up the 'quota' of wives as allowed. Additionally, the ability to divorce by the male remains easy. All that is required is to say, '*I divorce you four times.*'

50. A Traveler's Guide to Pakistan, Hilary Adamson and Isobel Shaw, Asian Study Group, 1981, PanGaphics Ltd. Islamabad.

The historic town of Sukkur is on the lower Indus where there is an island, mausoleums of saints. When I traveled there in 1985 I kicked up something blue in the sand and found two discarded broken blue tiles which I took home to Lahore and had a couple of pieces thinned and wrapped in silver as necklaces. Others were made into trivets. I was told that they dated back some four hundred years. hmb

The city of Karachi, "Karachi, thou shalt be the glory of the east, cried Sir Charles Napier, the first British Governor of Sind, in 1843, according to the authors. It was a place of good eating of blue ocean crabs, seeing turtles come to lay their eggs at night at Sandspit , swimming in the ocean at Hawkes Bay, hiring a *bunder* boat to go out in the harbour and fish for crabs. The authors did just what we did! "Lower your bait to the sea floor. When the crab starts pulling, haul it very slowly to the surface and call the boat boy with his net to land it for you. Meanwhile the crew light their primus stoves, fry up potatoes and onions and boil water. They either boil the crabs or fry them with spices." They were delicious. hmb

51. English-Hindustani Dictionary This crudely covered partial book is a rare jewel. It was written some time before Partition, 1947; some of its pages torn out for a smoke or toilet paper, but in the main, intact. No date, no name of compiler, no publisher. But the richness of the contents supported my writing some sixty years after it was written.

The British author had read the classics and dropped references to these throughout the volume. My thanks. See Urdu and Hindustani proverbs at the beginning of each chapter which were verified from this source. hmb

52. Pakistan Handbook, Isobel Shaw, Moon Publications, 1989.

A wonderful reference book on Pakistan! Her publisher writes his praise so well. "For those of us to whom travel is the favored muse, it's a comfort to know that our diminishing geography still allows a landscape as fabulous as Pakistan's. And for those who would follow that muse and put desire into motion, we are fortunate that Isobel Shaw has gone before us." Traveling through Pakistan, five years before this book was published, and then looking back at it through Isobel's eyes as I read her accounts of places I have been, and I say, *shabash!* Would that I had had the book back then. hmb

53. The Meaning of the Glorious Koran, An Explanatory translation by Mohammed Marmaduke Pikthall, Mentor Book, 1953.

I have made many quotations of the Holy Koran in this novel. All of these translations in English come from this valued book. The holy words in Arabic are on the lips of most of those I met when I lived in India and Pakistan; words that gave comfort about an often uncomfortable life and a hoped-for heavenly future, their great reward for submission and faith. hmb

54. Guide to Lahore, Prof. Masud-ul Hasan, Ferozsons Ltd. Lahore, Pakistan, undated. Price 60 Rs. ($1.00) circa 1970. The writer, a resident of Lahore for 47 years came from India. His knowledge of the city was shared with professorial style, lean prose, often boring but pointed and relevant. As a resident of Lahore, I carried the small book and verified points of interest from another's viewpoint. His viewpoint was to look at past 'saints', their tombs and legacies. I wish he had looked more at the fascinating bazaars, carpet making facilities where children weave artistic wonders, at sinners, at the sex markets,

the places of music and dancing where common folk, weary of a day's sweaty existence, went to forget their own dreary life. Lahore has so many places to eat a fine meal which the professor missed. hmb

55. <u>Lahore Fort</u>, by Muhammad Ishtiaq Khan, undated, published by the Department of Archeology and Museums, Government of Pakistan, Karachi.

What a fort it is! I can see now how it must have been, elephants with howdahs, drummers marching ahead, the Emperor Akbar the Great returning from Kashmir. Now it is in decay, in partial ruins. I am grateful to the author for the quotation of the great Persian poet in the ancient Ghaznavid court at Lahore:

"Thou knowest that I lie in grievous bonds O'Lord! Thou knowest that I am weak and feeble O'Lord! My spirit goes out in longing for Lahur, O'Lord. O'Lord, how I crave for it O'Lord." It must have been magnificent back then. This must have been written in the month of April before the searing heat engulfed all in its sweaty grasp. hmb

56. <u>Pakistan, Places of Interest</u> , Prof. Masu-ul-Hasan. Ferozsons Ltd. Lahore. Undated.

The Professor did not change his style. He had an unusually strong interest in holy places and personalities. His prose is spare to the point of aching brevity. "Here is a militia post." Or "It is a civil station with a small bazaar." Or "It is a market for wool." I was unable to find out what he was a professor of. I feel grateful, however, that of the undated 2000 copies printed in the 1st. Edition, that I own one, number 11! hmb

57. <u>Women Living Under Muslim Laws</u>, "How are penal laws effective in protecting women", by Asma Jahangir, WLUML Dossier 3 June/July 1988, D3-07 pakistan.rtf.

This 14 page document is one of the best I have read about the implications of the Hudood Ordinance on *zina*, what is termed adultery and defines what is considered to be adultery. "Although the Hudood Ordinance was promulgated in 1979, its seems now, 8 years later, men have become more confident of the manner in which they can get away with the sexual exploitation of women-rape and the ways in which they can control the lives of their wives and daughters. Furthermore, men and women who have found that they are unable to make their choice concerning marriage, with the consent of their parents, have eloped and found themselves in jail facing the threat of the death punishment for *zina*." Page 12. The Dossier is well documented and presents a disturbing picture of the lot of women in Pakistan, which in turn reflects on their men folk of course, who are all under the 'burden' of the ordinances. hmb

58. <u>Women and Islam, "The Prophet Preached Equal Rights; Now the Task is to Restore Them,</u> by Benazir Bhutto, Former Prime Minister of Pakistan, <u>Asiaweek , August, 1995</u>

Benazir presents an overview of the status of women in the Koran as independent beings, ones with honor and dignity, entitled to a share of inheritance and not to be forced into an unwanted marriage. "The egalitarian message of Islam and its insistence on the spiritual equality of men and women, however, was eroded as Muslim societies suffered moral and material decline." She calls for the restoration of equal rights for Muslim women who in many countries of the world live in male dominated, male authoritarian, male judges in societies in which women struggle for identity, particularly if they are forced into *purdah* or put behind the four walls, real and social walls like iron, *char divari*, from which they do not escape. At the time this was written there had been three heads of government who were Muslim women! In the history of the United States of American, in this Christian land, to date, Jan. 2007, no American woman has ever held the position of President or Vice-President. In spite of this, the role of women in America is highly egalitarian as compared to most of Muslim world. Their right to vote, to appear singly in public, to own property independently, to make independent decisions about their life and livelihood are indeed the hallmark of women in American and the Western world. hmb

59. "The Role of Literary and Education in Women's Development: Pakistan", by Harold M. Bergsma and Lily Chu, **International Education, 1989.**

Rural women in Pakistan have one of the lowest literacy rates in the world. They represent a large part of Pakistani society, however, because of their isolation brought about by cultural and religious sanctions, participate little in the country's economic and social development. See website www.haroldbergsma.com for a listing of other related works and to read the entire article.

60. Islamic Law and Social Change, A Comparative Study of Institutionalizational Codification of Islamic Family Law in Nation States Egypt and Indonesia, 1950-1995.

Dissertation zur Erlangung der Wurde des Doctors der Philosophie der Universitat Hamburg, by Vogelegt von Joko Mirrvan Muslimin aus Bojonegoro(Indonesia) Hamburg, 2000

A discussion of nikka urfi marriage (pages 224-227) substantiates that this type of marriage is entered into for mainly religious purposes; however, no formal contract is filled out and recorded with the local religious or political authorities. hmb

61. **Islamic Marital Jurisprudence,** Wikipedia the Free Dictionary, **2006**

Nikah in Arabic literally means to have sex, and *nikah mut'ah* is simply to have sex for satisfaction. In this type of marriage there is often a time limit established. hmb

62. Your Islamic Marriage Contract by Hedaya Hartford, Asraf Muneeb, printed at Daral Fikir, Damascus –Syria. (undated)

Section 6 discusses types of contracts and 8 are listed and discussed. hmb

63. The Dancing Girls of Lahore, Fourth Estate Publishers, 2005 by Louise Brown is an important book to pick up. Heera Mandi, the brothel section of Lahore was the subject of six years of research study and portrays a disturbing story of the lives of women there as well as their 'fatherless' children. In spite of the application of *Sharia* to the lives of so many of its citizens, Pakistan retains old vestiges of dancing girls, prostitution and alcohol and drugs for many to seek escape in Lahore, Peshawar and Karachi and numerous other cities. hmb

64. Into the Land of Bones, Alexander the Great in Afghanistan, by Frank L. Holt, University of California Press, 2005.

I was interested in current verification of Alexander's India sojourn, particularly to Taxila and then to Sukkur and the coastal area to the north of Karachi leading to Persia. On a trip to Taxila, (my childhood home) in 1985, my wife Lily Chu and I visited many ruins and a few small villages. One native told us he had unearthed a pot containing some ancient coins from the time of Alexander. We looked at these and then bought them. Holt writes, page 161, "One pitcher (unearthed) held five hundred Greek coins, and another ten thousand *karshapana* coins from Taxila." The dozen coins we obtained had both Greek and ancient Indian writing. Near Sukkur is an island which is featured in this novel. North of it on the Indus, are a barrage and a floating bridge that crosses the river. People there told me that Alexander was the first to build a boat bridge across the Indus. I checked. "...they reached the Indus in early December. As they set about assembling a pontoon bridge, a revolt erupted behind them." Page 100. As one writes, one lives the lives of people in the past, who become imaginary people in the mind of the writer, but how exciting it is to blend all these into a mélange of fiction.

65. **Castor bean Poisoning,** "Ricin: A Deadly Protein", http://www.
ncbi.nih.gov/entrez/query.fegi?cmd=Retrieve&db=PubMeds&lis...
7/9/2007

"The active poison in castor seeds is ricin (RYE-sin), a very deadly
protein called a lectin. Ricin is found in the meal or cake after the oil
has been extracted.... a dose of 0.035 milligram (approximately one
millionth of an ounce) may kill a man, and even small particles in open
sores and in the eyes may prove fatal." The article states that as few
as four ingested seeds can cause death in an adult human. Symptoms
are vomiting, severe abdominal pain, diarrhea and convulsions. Even
horses that accidentally eat the castor beans have died. The oil was
used extensively as a most effective purgative, to which I can assent,
having been made to take it as a child; the dreaded castor oil. One of
the wives in the story poisons her husband in a fit of rage, using ground
up castor beans.

Printed in the United States
110166LV00003B/70/P